ONCE UPON A TIME...

...there was a man named Tim Harper. He was born in Anno Domini 1945, probably dropped dead in 1970, using the same rather dead calendar, and was last seen gallivanting about in the year 47,923 by the Long Count—or maybe 90,000 on what he was used to, having gone AWOL for three thousand years in an invisible flying saucer, accompanied by Niculponoc Onnul Nyjuc, who was the most beautiful girl in the world. Several worlds.

What else? Oh, yes, the flying saucer happened to be a time machine. And the girl was a mind reader.

Books by Mike Shupp
published by Ballantine Books

THE DESTINY MAKERS

Book One:	*With Fate Conspire*
Book Two:	*Morning of Creation**
Book Three:	*Soldier of Another Fortune**
Book Four:	*The Last Reckoning**

*Forthcoming

Mike Shupp

With Fate Conspire

Book One of The Destiny Makers

A Del Rey Book
BALLANTINE BOOKS • NEW YORK

A Del Rey Book
Published by Ballantine Books
 Published in the United States by Ballantine Books, a division of Random House, Inc., New York, and simultaneously in Canada by Random House of Canada Limited, Toronto.

Library of Congress Catalog Card Number: 85-90766

ISBN 0-345-32549-4

Manufactured in the United States of America

First Edition: December 1985

Cover Art by Ralph McQuarrie

For
Tara Noel Shupp
Stephen Bradley Shupp
Emily Carol von Derau

Uncle Mike says "Hello"

The First Compact

To end eternal war, it is agreed by the telepaths and normal men that never again shall telepaths establish a separate state and exercise their dominion over men.

This Compact shall be preserved by the thoughts and actions of both human races and witnessed by the tiMantha lu Duois.

The penalty for violation, in thought or action, shall be death.

The Second Compact

To end the Second Eternal War, the Great Compact is reaffirmed by the Teeps and the Normals. It is also agreed by the Teeps and the Normals that never again shall Teeps employ their abilities in the service of national states and thus exercise their dominion over men.

This Compact shall be preserved by the thoughts and actions of both human races and witnessed by the spirit of the tiMantha lu Duois.

The penalty for violation, in thought or action, shall be death.

Hemmendur's Solution

"We have observed that neither Compact prohibits the employment of the Teeps, in whole or in part, in any role whatsoever, by a single all-encompassing world state. I suggest to you that such a state must ultimately arise. By its nature, it will be everlasting and unopposable.

"I suggest as well that given that inevitability, we attempt ourselves to give birth to that state and shape its growth. If our intentions are worthy, our actions honorable, and our ambitions steadfast, we shall be successful, for we shall gain strong allies.

"Not the least of these will be the Teeps, who are entitled to a role in human affairs and for whom I propose a most sacred responsibility—which is to ensure that men exercise no dominion over men . . ."

Part 1: In the Bubble

Tim Harper—January 2, 1970

CHAPTER ONE

Something smacked hard against his window, but Tim Harper was busy typing and ignored it. The sound was repeated; the window rattled noisily. Harper stretched his left arm awkwardly toward the sash. When the window refused to budge, he stood and pried it upward with both hands, then leaned through the opening. The yellow-painted radiator cover pressed against his thighs, searingly hot but unnoticed.

The evening air was cool and damp. A breeze passed over his face, bound eastward for the ocean. Newly fallen snow covered the ground in front of the deserted dormitory. The streets had not been plowed, and the cars five stories below were white-blanketed hillocks nestled under the tall sycamores that stood as sentinels along Memorial Drive. Beyond the trees was the Charles River, a wide band of black over which hovered the lights of the Boston skyline. Far above, a quarter moon plunged through wisps of cloud, a ship's prow in skyborne whitecaps.

Light over there, dark here, he mused. *How damned appropriate*.

Another snowball splattered bricks to his right, casting a

powdery plume across his face. Harper wiped it mechanically with a flannel-clad arm and looked down at the figures capering on the sidewalk before Baker House. He recognized faces.

"Watch it!" he shouted. "It's the only window I've got."

". . . phone off the hook," he heard. "Elsie's. Want to come?"

"Thanks, but no. I'm typing my thesis and don't want to stop."

"Harper, it's Christmas vacation! Enjoy, enjoy!"

"I'll enjoy finishing," he called back, flat-toned. "I want out of this place."

Silence lasted for a moment. "Tim, don't take it so hard. There are a million girls out there, you know?"

"Yeah," Harper responded sourly. "I know." *I only wanted one of them.*

"You'll get over her," the voice said encouragingly.

"Yeah."

"There are other girls," the voice repeated.

Harper forced a laugh. "And other guys to take them away. Forget it, kids. Bring me back a Special if you want."

"Sure." The freshmen vanished around the side of the building.

Crazy Angelinos, Harper thought. *Bright enough to be MIT students, but those damned twins are going to freeze their hands off if they don't start wearing gloves. Bet they never saw snow till last month.*

Last month—Sharon. Sharon. Had a month gone by already? Yes.

Time passes, chum. He sank back into his chair and stared bleakly at the snapshots taped to the brick wall. An Army nurse standing before a low wall in Bangkok; a stout, graying nun posing self-consciously at a blackboard; a Huey cruising over rice fields; two short-haired men in camouflage fatigues; a blurred image of San Francisco seen from thirty thousand feet on a Pan Am flight. *Two years ago already. Time passes.*

Other girls out there, he remembered. *Nothing unique about Sharon.*

Other girls. Sharon's face smiling. Sharon running a hand through long blond hair, Sharon's laughter, Sharon frowning at a problem set. Sharon half gasping while his tongue and fingers caressed swelling nipples, feather-stroked golden down upon her belly, and tugged at yielding elastic. Sharon being so very sorry, but . . . *You'd like him, too, Tim.* Sharon!

Other girls.

But not many in the market for a crippled vet. His eyes turned to the flag he had pinned on the back of his door. "Or any vet," he explained patiently. "Not around this place, anyhow."

So, don't stay at the Institute, the thought came back. *Enough hours already, once the thesis is in. Take a semester off. Weinberg'll be offering that relativity course again next year, and there's nothing else I'm particularly eager to take, anyhow. Go to California or somewhere else warm and get a part-time job until graduate school starts.*

But doing what? he wondered sourly. *Not a great job market for future physicists. What's in California, anyhow? Picking fruit? Security guard work? Sign painting? Unskilled labor, all of them.*

And they all took two arms.

No family to hole up with. No family, period. And now, not even the glimpses of family life that he had seen through Sharon. *Sharon.*

"Type that thesis, damn it!" he snarled. *I can't let everything fall apart. Come on, guy. Get the lead out. Do something with your life.*

Take an oversized orphan no one ever wanted, send him off to Ohio State, and let him flunk out trying to support himself. Have him join the Army because he can't go back to school and can learn a skill, and because, anyhow, there's a war on, you know?

Put him into the infantry business, keep him at that trade for three years, then pitch him out when he catches a bullet too many—crippled, with only GI Bill money between him and the street.

But give the kid some breaks. Make him bookish, with a lot of smarts, so the teaching nuns give him more than his share of affection, so he makes it through three years of mechanical engineering before the work load flunks him out, so other schools give him a second chance after his discharge. Give him a disability pension along with the GI Bill so he can afford a decent school without working. Let him rediscover that he likes student life.

"Some parts of it, anyhow."

The country had changed while he was off not looking at it.

Drugs and sex, for example. Those bothered him a bit. Sure, he'd smoked some grass in 'Nam, like most grunts. He'd heard of guys on horse. And growing up in an orphanage, spending time in Westmoreland's foreign finishing school, he'd done enough that he had no right to feel prudish. But it was troubling to see the gap widening between the morality he had been taught and what he witnessed nowadays. *Promiscuity.* Didn't anyone fall in love anymore? Didn't anyone stay faithful? And where would it end?

The peace movement bothered him a lot. What would happen to the country if the radicals won? The kids in the movement meant well, and he always smiled tolerantly when Sharon's friends pointed to him as a benighted example of just what they wished to prevent. He could argue with them and get them to agree that the USA shouldn't go down the tubes. They were just being idealistic.

Like Tet and Hue never happened, never proved a thing to them.

It's a rough world; things have to be defended or you lose them. Debating society rules don't work diddly.

He sighed and shook his head. He was never going to get them to understand that, never going to get them to understand him.

"Patriotism" was too strong a term; say instead that the difference was one of philosophy. For Harper, the nation was an actual thing, every bit as solid and just as real as the Selectric typewriter on his desk. And as an entity, it could be changed, it could be harmed, it could be fought for and defended. For Sharon and many of her friends, "the country" was purely an abstraction. The only thing of real significance was the people living in it. The society comprising those people was plastic, infinitely malleable; the nation itself was no more to be defended from harm than the definition of "blue" or the Second Law of Thermodynamics.

Sharon. "Damn it, guy! Get back to typing."

But he could not restart the smooth flow of words from mind to paper. Harper drummed his fingers on the desk, then sighed and switched off the typewriter. He'd return to work when his mood improved.

Soon enough, he told himself, poking aimlessly at the open copy of *Physical Reviews* on the desk. His thesis was going to be good, applying statistical mechanics to the "many-world interpretation of quantum mechanics" invented by Wheeler and Everett to describe how parallel universes might work. Sure, a lot of it was hand waving, but the idea was new enough that originality would count for more than execution.

The theory could not be tested. That made it metaphysics rather than physics, he realized. Not real science at all, and that was a weakness. Still, the thesis committee had approved the topic.

"And it is a B.S. degree." Harper shrugged and went to get a can of beer from the small refrigerator by the door.

"Bores people, though," he admitted as he yanked the tab on the can. Even his thesis adviser preferred to talk about his own research—a so-far fruitless attempt to isolate a fifth isotope of hydrogen—instead of Harper's work. Rueful memory brought Harper back to a House Christmas party where he had expounded multidimensional phase spaces and the evolution of the universe's state vector to a Cliffie who had misplaced her date. *Missed a chance to make a pass there. Oh, well, no loss. Any English major who thinks John Donne was a professional poet . . .*

Ought to learn when to keep quiet, though. Become a professor first. "Then bore the hell out of my students legally."

Did he really want that? Well, research could be interesting, though he suspected his life would be dull, tame. It would not make him rich, though he should live comfortably, which was something. Maybe he *would* find another girl. Maybe Sharon would change her mind.

He sipped beer and looked around his room. A red brick cell, seven feet by fifteen: a "coffin single." He had once been told that officer POWs got cells with twice as much space—if anyone in southeast Asia was paying attention to the Geneva Conventions. He wondered idly how much space a captured sergeant would have rated.

But he was not a sergeant anymore. This would do.

He had a louse-free bed, long enough to sleep in without curling up his legs; a wall-mounted desk top almost as long; a stock of ice-cold beer, a wardrobe filled with clothes not all olive drab or khaki; bookshelves holding a three-term accumulation of texts and a heavy long sword; photographs on the walls of space-suited men on lunar landscapes . . .

"And no incoming. Just too bad you're ugly, chum."

In fact, what he saw in the mirror over his sink was acceptable. His ears might be a little prominent, and perhaps his nose as well, but that surely was not enough to worry about. His face was square, broad-boned, lightly tanned in appearance, with gray eyes harbored under thick, crooked brows. Thin lips gave him a wary expression. A thick white scar on his left temple notched jaggedly into short red-brown hair. Under his flannel shirt, his shoulders were those of a football lineman, and his arms and hands *looked* all right. Someday . . .

Just a little sensory nerve damage, they had told him. The bones had knit quite nicely, and there really had not been any major problems with the motor nerves. Even the scar was a small one, a little souvenir of the war with which to impress his children. The only difficulty was simply that what couldn't be felt couldn't be controlled. And a limb that wasn't exercised would degenerate. Inevitably.

The VA doctors had been very pleased with their work and the speed of his recovery, and the delay in getting the medevac to him had had nothing to do with his injury.

He scowled, remembering. The arm was going to come back, no matter what they told him. Someday.

The light went out. The unobtrusive hum of the refrigerator stopped.

He swore mildly, then set the beer can on the refrigerator and opened his door.

A power failure. The hallway lights were off as well. The corridor was still and gloomy, filled with shadows.

He stepped into a wall.

But there was nothing to be seen. He stepped back from the invisible barrier and reached out gingerly.

A glass wall?

The barrier was warm to the touch; a sticky coating on it resisted the motion of his fingers but left no residue. His class ring shook, vibrating roughly as he pushed against the barrier, and subsiding when he moved his hand away. He pulled the ring off and shoved it into a back pocket, then reached out again.

The barrier was curved about him, he found, and extended from near the ceiling to the floor. Four feet to his left, it was flush to the brick wall of the corridor; on the other side, it bisected a neighbor's door. It seemed airtight.

Did it go through the walls? And the floor? He moved his hand down the tacky surface, estimating. If the curve continued smoothly, the barrier was a sphere with its center located beneath and behind him.

He could not move the barrier, no matter how hard he pushed.

"Hey! Anyone hear me?" His voice was strangely flat, and there was no echo from down the hall. There was no answer.

Vacation. No one here. On your own, guy.

"All right." He returned to his room.

His room was very dark; evidently the moon had moved behind clouds. The skyline across the river was no more than a silhouette, so the power failure was more than local.

He lifted the desk chair by its back, raising it gently so the legs did not scrape against his bed, and returned with it to the barrier, intending to smash the shell open. A pale light could be seen now through the windows on the other side of the hallway. Perhaps someone had started an emergency generator. As he watched, the lighting grew more intense, blue-tinged and garish. An arc light?

The lighting became even brighter, and Harper could see clearly little more than the shapes of the windows. Then it vanished; he was left in blindness interrupted only by slowly fading orange-red afterimages.

He swung the chair halfheartedly against the blackness and was not surprised when the impact did nothing but sting his hands.

Sharon. And now this. Harper dropped the useless chair, which bounced off one leg and fell sideways to the floor. Then he waited for additional afflictions.

After a minute, a faded red glow appeared on his right. It grew brighter, more focused, turning into a tall, distant, burning pillar. The corridor walls reflected miniature images of the glowing column, as if they held up long lines of dusty mirrors. The flames changed color to yellow, to green, to blue, then winked out. He was surrounded by darkness again.

He had not seen the windows opposite him, he suddenly remembered. He should have. And had not a blank wall originally stood in the direction of the flame?

Another burning post appeared before him, brighter than before, nearer. It, too, showed the colors of the rainbow, and he was again surrounded by ghostly images of flame. Then it, too, vanished.

This happened again and again. Harper at last realized that

the reflections he saw came from the steel frame of the building. The dormitory walls had dissolved.

Girders but no crossbeams. What kept him supported in the air?

He turned to look at the wall behind him. It at least was still visible while the flames flashed, still solid. He ran his hands across the rough brick, pressing hard so the surface tore at his fingernails and his nails scraped over mortar. Something still remained.

Red light washed over him and remained constant. He turned slowly.

"Oh, my God," he said weakly. "My God."

If there were a hell, it would look like this. He moved his hands jerkily down the tacky surface of the barrier, leaning against it, half expecting it to break open at any moment and spill him into the inferno.

Hell—or Hiroshima? Before him was just the blood-crimsoned skeleton of a city. Minutes before, a hundred thousand people had lived in Cambridge. And now?

"And only I alone," he whispered.

There was still a wall at his back. His darkened dormitory room remained, as did the arc of flooring upon which he stood. But nothing else was left of the building that had not been enclosed within the barrier.

And no building was left standing wherever he looked. He saw only debris and the scarlet fragments of buildings, hanging fixed and specterlike in the air as if gravity were now abolished.

Where the graduate students' apartment building had been there was now a broken latticework of ruby girders, glowing softly against the ebon sky. A scrap of roofing floated above the fire-scorched earth, anchored in place by a twisting, dangling, flame-lustered beam that did not reach the ground. The gleaming curve here had been Kresge auditorium, this dark circle the chapel, that elfin lambent trellis the women's dormitory. In the distance the Great Dome hovered atop a giant's jackstraws, now at last a burnished orange shell. Harper smiled at that, sadly, affectionately.

War. Cambridge was gone. A fireball had taken its place.

Death. In another instant he would be gone as well.

Good-bye, Sharon. God bless you and keep you.

The air flashed white about him, dazzlingly bright as if a

curtain of lightning bolts had dropped past the barrier. When his sight returned, even the ruins of a city were gone.

Before him was the bowl of a great lake, which stretched almost to the northern horizon. Its dark waters seemed frozen; they sparkled as though emeralds and sapphires were scattered over velvet. Ice-blue lines, diamond bright and thin, were etched across the black-metaled sky. For a few seconds the northern lakeshore gleamed. There was no other movement, no sound.

Death, Harper thought. Was this his death? He still breathed, still felt his weight upon the floor. Was this the afterlife he had rejected, the heaven in which he no longer believed?

Heaven. Hell. Purgatory. "I still don't believe in them. I *still* don't believe."

There was no response to his bravado.

After a long while, Harper sighed quietly and returned to his room. Through his open window he saw a broad turquoise arch. Wide as an outstretched hand, more than sun-bright, it rainbow-spanned the dark sky and slowly shifted up and down. He saw no moon. Before him was a river of indigo, green-flecked in places, which fitted beneath the lake like a snail under its shell. Beyond that, a city skyline reached over the horizon, a silhouette dimly lit as if by fireflies and torches.

Boston had survived, but it was not intact. Where was the John Hancock building? Or the Pru? And were those piles of rubble that spotted the Esplanade?

The distant fires grew brighter. Harper turned his head slowly, looking for signs of life. But there were none, and he finally realized that Boston had become a city of ruins also, another barren landscape heaped with broken matchbox buildings. Boston was dead, and there was nothing to watch for but its decay.

And it did decay. Structures dwindled and vanished, leaving such vacant ugly splotches as might be found on the flanks of a dead beast. Whole rows of buildings disappeared instantaneously as if Titans flayed the corpse. For long periods no blows would fall, and Harper would stare frozen-faced at the scars and wounds that disfigured the city. Then at last the scourging would begin anew.

Only after much time did he see some pattern emerging. A cordon was being drawn about Beacon Hill and the Government Center section of the city. Finally a broad black band extended into the distance, like a strip of crepe laid in mourning across the chest of a corpse. The band widened, pulling erratically to the west and past him, as if unseen hands tugged at the crepe, trying to draw it taut. The band crossed over Massachusetts Avenue, then stopped only when the shattered towers that marked the Boston University campus toppled onto it and vanished. Harper closed his eyes in anguish. That had been *vandalism*.

When he reopened his eyes, hills were visible miles to the south. For some while the destruction halted; then the hills quivered, as if blanketed by vermin. Dorchester and Roxbury were being—removed.

Harper suddenly felt uncomfortably warm. Mechanically he reached out and pushed the window higher.

His action might have been a signal. The forces tearing at the city quickened. Broad passageways thrust into previously untouched portions of the Boston outskirts. The city crumbled as serpentine lines of decay and destruction passed over it and into the invisible distance, leaving behind broken fields of rubble.

Here and there a few buildings survived that savage combing. And far to his left, where Government Center had been, tall cross-shaped towers rose as if to balance what was happening elsewhere. But these were only transparent ghosts of buildings, seeming no more substantial than the plastic models of an architect.

Piers sprang out of the water from the opposite riverbank and pushed toward him, then stopped. A high wall came into being, flowing down from the distant hills to reach to the end of the ground and partially across the river. Rainbow-hued, the wall shielded the docks from his view. A second wall lifted out of the earth, more slowly than the first, just behind and parallel to it. Those might be guard embrasures along their upper surfaces.

Perhaps an hour had passed since Harper had cursed at a power failure.

His phone did not work. He had expected that but had felt duty-bound to try it. Water would not flow into his sink, and that was no surprise either. Harper finished his now-warm beer and leaned out the window.

The form of the city had stabilized, and only minor changes were being made to it. The lights he had once thought were fires were brighter now, but less numerous, frozen blue and yellow flames that consumed nothing and cast no shadows but painted narrow rainbows onto buildings and open streets. Above them the blue-green arc of light fell toward the horizon and returned, each cycle lasting a quarter of a minute.

That was above him. Below—the view was not changing there either.

The barrier *had* gone through the walls. All that remained of the dormitory was the portion wedged into the sphere. When Harper glanced downward, he saw one intact window directly beneath, and under that, part of another window, sliced in half as if by a knife. If what was left of the building seemed an oncoming pumpkin pie to those who might be watching, that cut-off window would be a bite into it.

A very small bite into a very large brick mouthful. Harper wondered if anyone had noticed the invisible jaws closing, if anyone else had been— His eyes closed. "Goddamned good thing the place was near empty," he growled.

He crumpled the beer can in his hand, then flipped it absently out the window. It halted about six feet away, then slid down an arc on an invisible circle, coming to rest with a muted *tink*! beside the sliced-off window. Its red and white label was bright against the inky river.

Harper turned away abruptly and returned to the scrap of hallway.

"If this is a hack, tell me now," he shouted. "I'm not getting stuck for anything I do because of a stupid joke."

There was no answer.

The door to the right was locked, he found, but the barrier had passed through it, leaving a curved edge like a wooden reflection of the rim of the hallway. It would not move when he pressed at it, so he stood to the side and kicked. The curved edge splintered and slowly let itself be forced inward. Then the door fell with a noisy crash.

Shoot it up first, he remembered. *From the outside. Watch all the other exits. A grenade after the door falls in. Go through fast and low and spray rounds into the doorways and ceiling and give your buddies cover.* He was inside before he finished the thought, crouched beside the fallen door, weaponless.

"Idiot!" No one was lying in wait, of course. Harper grimaced with ill-contained embarrassment as he stood.

Calculation replaced chagrin as he looked about. Little was left of the room: part of the floor, one complete wall, portions of two others, some furniture, all enshrouded by darkness. Half a wastebasket sat on the floor, leaning against nothing. Above it floated a curved desk top, which clattered down onto the floor when he tugged at it, knocking over a chair and the wastebasket, spilling papers and empty soft-drink cans.

The wardrobe by the doorway had not been disturbed. Harper tugged a bright blue Kelty packframe from its top, then rummaged through drawers till he found a flashlight. He dropped that into the pack; a set of small screwdrivers went into the back pocket of his jeans. His hand rested next on a pair of hiking boots, but they would be too small, so he left them. His own shoes should be sturdy enough.

He rose and opened the window to watch the cruciform buildings across the Charles throw out forked extensions. On the southern hills, a trio of violet streamers glowed against the black sky, searchlight beams reaching for the heavens. The blue-green ribbon overhead swooped toward them and retreated. Crimson ripples flowed the lengths of azure boulevards. An oval clearing appeared suddenly, a festering wound gaping raw and red: Alston had been there.

Harper dropped the wastebasket out the window. The chair followed. What was left of the desk went next. Then he turned to the bed.

The furniture in the dormitory, like its architect, had been imported from Finland. Blond hardwood, clean-lined, easily dismantled, fiendishly expensive—all much too good for undergraduates, Harper had once heard the house manager say. He whistled tunelessly as he took the bed apart and shoved the pieces one by one out the window.

He left the room momentarily, returning with his sword cradled in his left arm. As he took the hilt into his right hand, blue-green light flashed, reflected from the blade to the walls and ceiling, then vanished as Harper raised the sword. For an instant he was motionless.

Quang Tri city two days to the south or maybe west . . . Troopers of the First Cavalry Division prowling on foot through long grass and scrub timber like overgrown Boy Scouts playing hide and seek with NVA regulars, and Staff Sergeant Timothy Allan Harper playing assistant scoutmaster . . . The point stopping, looking so goddamn surprised and the lieutenant screaming everybody get down, everybody-get-down, everybodyge—glurg! Gunfire and shouting and the down-drifting leaves . . . The medic wasted at trail side . . . firing at moving grass, hoping it isn't— Medic! I can't get Battalion, Harp, and hell, Thomas, we're making us enough racket it probably ain't all that important . . . Sunlight dancing so gracefully on the warped tree trunks, flashing off the falling splinters . . . The warm stones under him that were probably spent rounds . . . Dizziness, darkness, distant voices wondering he's gonna pull through ain't he . . . Yeah, but that arm, he ain't gonna be no lifer no more . . .

January 1970 now, for all of two days. Two years gone by, shy a month. He had not held a weapon for a long time, a very long time. But he had sworn no oath of nonviolence, despite his bullet-shattered forearm. Surrounded by gentle, peaceful people, it had simply seemed proper for him to behave as they did. He had been being polite.

"Polite!" He snapped down the sword, shattering glass and wood.

He displayed no art, no science, no grace. He simply hacked away at the window until it was gone. Harper knew nothing of swordplay, and his weapon was little more than a crudely shaped, forty-pound weight of martensitic stainless steel, a tool for exercising his weak arm. A friend had forged the sword from a bar of 414 alloy as a metallurgy project, then worn it once to a costume party. Too heavy for use as such a masquerade prop, it had been passed on to Harper "so one funny dumbbell would get another." "From a third," Harper had replied, laughing, and laid the would-be Conan's blade atop his bookshelves and left it there.

Now he shook glass from his hair and propped the sword against the wall before turning to the wardrobe. It would be heavy, too heavy for manhandling with one arm. But if he removed the doors, then bashed out the interior partitions . . .

When he left, he carried away the sword and the packframe, leaving behind only the trash on the floor. Back in his room, he dumped his load onto his bed, shoved the flashlight into his back pocket with the screwdrivers, and clambered out the window.

Keeping a death grip on the inside of his window frame, Harper moved his feet cautiously from one projecting triangle of brick to another. When he could descend no farther that way, he held his breath and leaned against the building while shifting his hand to the outside of the sill. Once he had watched another student climb two stories using only those protruding bricks, but that had been an experienced rock hound, in good shape, with the use of both arms.

Also it was just before finals week, Harper remembered. *And Paul was three-quarters drunk.* "Maybe five-quarters."

His left foot reached the top of the bedsprings. Harper inched it along the metal frame until there was room for another shoe, and flattened himself against the wall, letting his weight settle gradually so the pile of broken furniture beneath him would not shift.

He paused to catch his breath, then lowered his right foot and jammed it between the thin metal slats near the edge of the springs, pushing down till it came to a cross-link and moved no farther. He let go of the sill momentarily, and when he did not fall, he brought his hand to a projection just over his head. Then he wedged his left foot into the springs. He repeated this process twice, bringing his knees to the level of the window in the room beneath his.

He pulled his right foot free and kicked at the top of the window until the glass was gone, then shifted his grip and swept his foot sideways to brush shards from the sill. Pressing against the springs, he reached down to unclasp the sash and tug at the lower window.

His hold regained on a projecting brick, he swung his left foot onto the sill, then bent his knees and kicked out cossack-fashion to get his weight onto his legs, cursing briefly as he landed on the flashlight and screwdrivers in his pockets. He squirmed forward until his legs were dangling, then rolled onto his belly, pushed himself away from the springs, and dropped through the window.

Inside, Harper stood a moment breathing deeply. No new changes had been made in the city. The same translucent towers were still rainbow-tinted by colored flames, the same turquoise band overhead swept inexorably across the black sky, and the same violet beams rose from the same hills. The descent had taken only a few minutes—not long enough for major changes to occur.

When he realized he had delayed long enough, he switched on the flashlight and turned abruptly to point its beam at the ceiling.

The logical place to locate the generator of a spherical field was at the center. Once he had reasoned that and determined where the center of the field must be, his course of action had been obvious—as the source of the field was now obvious.

A bomb, Harper thought at first as his flashlight beam darted over the long torpedo shape. But there were differences that made that identification unlikely.

What hovered at the back of the room was a white tube about eight feet long and a foot in diameter at its thickest, narrowing to a three-inch waist midway along the cylinder. Instead of being aerodynamically streamlined, the front of the object was shaped like a crushed box, mounted slightly off center and twisted. Behind this "head" a pair of gauzy wings, seemingly no more substantial than smoke, stuck out perpendicularly from the body to press square-cut tips against the ceiling. The wing material seemed to disappear where the flashlight beam shined directly on it; it came back when he moved the light away.

Harper reconsidered. Not a bomb after all: a gigantic plastic wasp.

Wasps could sting.

Keeping the flashlight beam focused on the object, he moved his left hand along the desk top beside him until his fingers encountered a pencil stub, which he tossed awkwardly under the cylinder.

The pencil hit the floor and rolled. That seemed normal enough.

He felt for a sheet of paper and advanced, holding the paper outstretched and passing it under every inch of the cylinder and its wings.

The paper did not burst into sudden flames. It did not disintegrate along with his hands. It was not pushed to the floor by invisible forces. It remained perfectly intact.

Wadded up, the paper had no effect when he threw it over the cylinder, and nothing happened when he tossed it against the side of the fuselage or at the undersurface of a wing—it simply bounced off and landed on the floor.

Just like something's really there, he decided. *Yeah. That's easier to believe than hallucinations like nobody ever heard of.*

Nor would he doubt that the wasp might yet sting him. But

he felt justified now in taking a closer look. *Not much choice. Be damned if I'm just going along for the ride.*

What else was here? He moved the flashlight beam around the room, taking inventory. A neatly made bed, a desk, an electric clock stopped at 7:28, a wardrobe. A chair was beside the wardrobe, black metal framed with a plastic seat cushion and wood block arms. It should be downstairs in the lounge, he realized with amusement.

He pushed the chair under the wasp shape with a foot, then stepped onto the wooden armrests so that his eyes were even with the center of the tube. He moved the flashlight into his left hand, then tapped on the fuselage cautiously with a screwdriver before resting a hand on it. The white material was cool, glassy, and unyielding. "Anyone believe a porcelain wasp?" he wondered.

He could see no opening, though an impressed line ran the length of the tube. "Bends, I bet," he muttered. "Hmmm . . . writing?"

Irregular groups of red symbols arrayed in three lines were etched near the back of the fuselage. He noticed no similarities at first, but continued inspection showed that each symbol was composed of curved and straight lines that did not overlap. "Ideographs," he guessed aloud. In that case, the groups could be nothing but sentences.

"Warranty void if opened by non-factory-trained personnel," Harper quipped. He dropped onto the floor and pushed the chair sideways with a foot. "Or, 'Made in our version of Japan.'"

He grunted. Just who was "us"? Ignorance was not funny.

"Allen screws," he muttered next. "If someone makes four-side allen wrenches." One of the screwdrivers had a blade narrow enough to fit diagonally into the depressed screw heads he had found, though turning it would be awkward. "Gonna be slow."

The process was slow and awkward, but it worked. First, however, he had to discover that the alien screws loosened only when turned clockwise. His second discovery was that the screws did not come all the way out but were held to the plastic skin by small pliable cones, so the screwdriver simply spun them uselessly once they cleared the lower entry holes. "Local product, after all," Harper commented. "Ah, cute!"

He repeated that remark when he finished the line of screws

and the entire top of the fuselage folded up in accordion pleats and fell backward. "Neat trick to do that without springs."

He swapped the screwdriver and flashlight between his hands to get a closer look at the insides of the machine. "Complicated, aren't we? Hmmm . . ." *More wiring job than plumbing, though. Nothing looking like a motor or generator. Is that a battery? Why all the gauges on it? Damn! I wish I could see through this gunk.*

The machine's casing might be open, but its interior was still inaccessible, filled with a blue translucent substance that looked gelatinous but was actually solid. Perhaps that could be broken through as well. He tapped the flashlight absently against the blue material, then decided against trying; there was nothing here that looked like a control. "Try the front."

Now that he had learned the trick, unfastening the screws that held the squashed box shape to the nose was simple. What was underneath was not.

Untidy mess. "No glove box, no owner's manual, no shop guide, no Triple-A number to call. So where do I start?" He put his hand around a metallic pipe with a D-shaped cross section and tried to twist. It did not move. The end of the pipe was glassy; he tapped it lightly with the screwdriver, then with a fingertip.

"Not a death ray, after all? How disappointing. Camera lens?" Eight of the D tubes protruded in as many directions, silvery afterthoughts glued randomly, it seemed, to the thick wire-wrapped bundle of bronze pipes that made up the nose of the vehicle after its cowling had been removed. Different-sized boxes were fastened in turn to the silvery tubes or hooked loosely onto the wires.

Harper cautiously touched one box and watched it rock back and forth. The supporting wires made tiny squeaking sounds, and he shook his head in disbelief. "Sheesh! Sloppy!"

Jury-rigged, he decided. *Not production stuff in anyone's culture. One of a kind.* "Experimental apparatus?"

He snorted. "I'm going to be real annoyed if this is someone else's thesis project." For a moment, he pictured a worried graduate student with four arms and tentacles explaining to a skeptical alien faculty adviser that an extension of his grant was necessary, then he laid amusement aside and returned to inspecting the machine.

Suppose the D tubes were cameras or other sensing devices. Then the wasp was an exotic reconnaissance drone. "Possible."

He resisted an impulse to make faces at the nearest lens and systematically ran the flashlight beam over the bronzed pipes. On this side, the boxes were all featureless. He moved the chair and himself to check the other side.

A blue-white box the size and shape of a small first aid kit was fastened to a slide on the tip of the bronze piping. Its top was covered with the red ideographs. The surface he touched was flexible and greasy-feeling, like a soft plastic. And it was warm.

"Something working here?" Harper reached to slide the box loose, but stopped as a thought occurred to him. The drone was hanging in the air near the center of the transparent sphere around him, and that was as he expected. But where was the actual center?

"Real close to the nose of this thing," he said slowly. Perhaps moving the box would be a mistake. Could it be opened where it was?

He ran his hand around the edges until he found a small raised dot and pressed that. The lid opened slightly, bending about a grooved line at its base. Harper pulled it parallel to the floor; it would move no farther, and he used it as a ledge to hold the flashlight.

Maybe it is *a first aid kit*, he thought momentarily. That could be a box of Band-Aids on the left; the flat container at the bottom would hold a tourniquet; the thing on the right could be a roll of adhesive tape; and those would be Q-tips resting underneath.

A closer look showed a tiny lever on the tourniquet box, held at the left end of a narrow slot by a blue spring. Wire was coiled around the tape roll. The cotton swabs were leads with something like alligator clips on them, connecting the Band-Aid box, which had to be a battery, to the other devices.

Harper touched the lever delicately. Nothing happened; the spring was stronger than it looked. He pressed harder, moving the lever tip half an inch.

The room was brighter. Harper glanced at the window and saw that the blue-green band sweeping the sky had become painfully intense. It might be moving at a slower pace. It might be narrower.

He closed his eyes against the glare and lifted his hand from the lever, counting seconds until a minute had passed. When he reopened them, the turquoise band had gone back to its previous brightness; the lever was once more at the left end of the slot.

"Interesting." He put his forefinger inside the roll of wire and flicked. Markings appeared on the interior surface, which moved about an eighth of a turn. The exterior remained in place. Again, nothing seemed changed. Harper dropped off the chair and went to the window.

Nothing? The view of the city across the river was the same; the shifting band in the sky was no different. But the pile of broken furniture beneath him was smaller. When he looked to the side, he saw that the brick circle he moved within had shrunk as well. The top portion of his own room was missing now.

He was swallowing. Annoyed, he deliberately clenched his jaw to make himself stop.

After a moment he changed his mind and began swallowing intentionally; the pressure against his eardrums lessened.

"Interesting." He went back to the chair and resumed inspecting the pipes. He avoided looking into the still-open first aid kit.

Next he found a row of six thin knobs with split ends, like those used for making fine adjustments on television sets, under a row of dials with sliding indicators. The knobs seemed frozen in place; there was a trick to them as well. They would not move in or out, and it was necessary to pull on them with some force before they could be turned. Only then would the knobs unlock and the sliding strips in the dials above move from their central positions.

He gave the first knob a small twist, and when nothing happened at once, he turned it farther. Then he noticed that he was leaning sideways.

"Oops." The turquoise band visible through the window that moment did not look right. It had tilted. The tilt was increasing.

Harper hastily moved the knob back to its original position. That stopped the sideways motion, but it did not make the room level. To do that, he had to overcorrect with the knob, fiddling with it until the slide indicator came back to the middle of the dial. So the same knob controlled both the flight angle of the drone and the rate at which the angle changed. "Cute. Very cute."

Three controls for roll, pitch, and yaw. And the other three? "Up and down, sideways, backward and forward," he guessed. That would be easy to test. But it made sense only if the probe was a flight vehicle. "Doesn't everyone believe in antigravity?" he asked dryly.

He picked a reference, a dark green hourglass-shaped flame in the far distance. Could he make that move?

Yes, but only slowly, he discovered eventually.

And by then he was discovering his own exhaustion. It must be after midnight, he realized. Enough time had passed that another five or six hours would probably not change his situation appreciably, so he might as well get some sleep. Perhaps when he woke, this bad dream would end.

"To hell with that," he said sourly, and kicked hard at the radiator, like Johnson refuting Bishop Berkeley. The radiator was something real. The room was real. His hands pressing down on the wooden windowsill, the gritty dust and the shards of glass—those were real. Even the moulting wasp shape hanging behind him in the darkness was real. What he could hold and touch he would continue to believe.

Spurning speculation as a Puritan would pleasure, he wrapped himself in bedcovers, arranging the pillow so he could view the window. "Tomorrow," he vowed. "Just ride this out and I'll do something tomorrow."

A blur of motion caught his eye. Across the indigo river, the fires that limned the silhouette of Boston and threw rainbows across its buildings winked out. It took only a few minutes, and the city was again darkened, night-wrapped.

There were two rather than three violet beams in the distance. Then only one. Then none.

Here and there faint blue lines glimmered momentarily, as if a tally on a vast blackboard were being endlessly erased and recounted by an unseen giant. There were fewer marks at each appearance.

At last four tall parallel lines bent at the middle, their lower sections remaining perpendicular to the ground while their tops moved in a majestic bow. Crossbars connected the tops of the lines for an instant, as on a sketch of a building. Then all the blue lines vanished.

Harper finally admitted to himself what he was seeing.

Slowly, silently, invisibly, the city fell.

CHAPTER TWO

He was awake. On his back. Lying on someone else's bed, not his own. Still dark—he had not been asleep long. Silence was about.

This wasn't 'Nam.

Harper moved then, arching his back and stretching cat-fashion before throwing himself up into a sitting position. His clothes, except for shoes, were still on under the tangled blankets. Had someone put him to bed?

Four hours of sleep, he estimated, monitoring the stiffness left in his body and the fuzziness inside his mouth. *Bearable if a good breakfast comes along*.

"Should have gone to Elsie's," he muttered. Then he remembered. "No more Elsie's. No more—hell! Hell, hell, hell, hell."

He stood stiffly and went to the window.

He had indeed moved while he slept on the borrowed bed. There was no river under him now but instead a featureless plain, black like pitch or obsidian. The hills to the south were black as well, and it was difficult at first to distinguish their shapes from the dark sky. But the texture of the ground seemed softer; occasionally light sparkled from it, reflections of the ceaselessly moving turquoise band above him.

He had seen enough. He picked up the flashlight he had left on the desk and went to the wasp form at the back of the room.

"Good morning and soon good-bye," he said somberly. He stepped onto the chair arms and reached for the drone's controls. "I hope."

A vagrant thought struck. "Ill winds and all that." He had not had a memory of Sharon for some minutes.

He twisted knobs. The bottom of the sphere had been about forty feet above the ground, and he had reduced the radius about five feet more . . . at roughly an inch per second . . . "Touchdown in nine minutes."

He counted seconds, then reduced the rate of descent. When the body of the wasp itself began to move downward, he restored the controls to neutral. Now he should be on the ground, logic told him, even though his eyes still told him that the black surface was still far below. Harper shrugged. "Close enough."

He reached to open the "first aid kit," then held his breath while he twirled the dial inside the roll of wire.

Suddenly he felt *hot*. His clothing pressed against him, making him conscious of every irregular fold and pleat. He might have been surrounded by water. He exhaled without thinking, then pursed his lips to shut off the air that rushed into his lungs. Annoyance showed on his face.

The barrier had come well within the room. The bottom half of the front wall was gone, along with most of the window. The headboard and pillow on the bed had vanished; what was left of the mattress had slid partway down the sloping springs and was pressed limply against the seemingly empty air. Beyond the circular lip marking the edge of the floor, a disordered heap of lumber and bricks rose slowly as the building settled.

Blank-faced, Harper turned the dial till the barrier no longer pressed against the structure. A muted creaking sounded over his head. He felt himself dropping, then the ceiling touched the wasp wings once more and the motion stopped. Unimpeded, the mattress flopped forward, dragging the bedsprings, then leaving them propped against the floor like a makeshift ladder. Bits of cotton stuffing littered the bricks.

Exhaling minutely, he pushed gingerly on the plastic box until it slid past the end of the bronze pipes and plumped into his left hand. It was heavy, about five pounds, and he brought the hand down quickly.

A harsh grinding *cr-rack*! sounded on his right, followed by a rustling noise. Harper ran the flashlight beam over the wall to find the source. A network of cracks was appearing in the bricks at the far end. Dark gaps showed where mortar fell. Powdered brick, like red sand, trickled onto the desk top. Chinks opened and grew wider as he watched.

"Time to skedaddle." Harper ducked under the wasp and pulled the back door open to inspect the view.

No more than six inches of the outer hallway was left at this level. The ground was dark, an asphaltlike surface littered with blackened shards of rubble, perhaps a three-foot drop from where he stood. Thin pasteled lines were inscribed across the ebon sky.

The building cracked thunderously, like a rotting log. The floor shuddered beneath him. Bricks skidded over the sloping floor. Harper moved the dial in the wire roll till the air was warm and dense about him once more, then twirled the dial back to its original position. That knocked off another chunk of the building, including the back wall.

"There will be a pop quiz Monday dealing with cantilever structures," he said gravely. "And more lecture demonstrations."

He stepped off the edge. Into darkness.

It was a drop of a foot, not a yard, and he stepped onto grass. Wet, slippery grass—he wound up on his face and knees, then scrambled to retrieve the plastic box he had dropped.

Time to take stock, he thought. *I don't like the stock. Sell it*. The front of his flannel shirt was wet; the knees of his jeans were grass-stained. Mud was on his hands. "And I just did a belly-whopper out of this damn abstract sculpture. Hope it pleases an audience."

No audience was visible. *Not that that proves anything*, he admitted. *Maybe I'm on* Candid Camera. *Or a lab rat in someone's maze. Could be all sorts of people watching*.

Most of his more exotic speculation had collapsed when he hit the ground. It was perfectly normal ground, after all, brown-black soil and ordinary grass that just happened to need mowing. It was not the big parking lot he had been expecting.

If the ground looked odd outside the bubble and normal

inside, he should assume that the entire world had stayed normal. It only looked different because of the sphere around him. *Could be buildings around me, could be a maze, with cheese in the middle.*

Good thing the box didn't bounce, he told himself. *If it had cut me in half, I'd probably feel even sillier.*

And if I ever get my hands on whoever is responsible for this, they'll be sorry.

With that promise, Harper walked away.

A dozen paces brought him into winter—crisp white snow made blue by the colored band of light above him. The snow grew deeper as he advanced, pouring into the tops of his shoes like loose sand. Harper cupped snow into his hands and licked at it to ease his thirst. His footsteps whispered at him.

Then the snow was gone. The ground beneath him was dry, then sere. Withered grass revived as he walked through it, growing higher and brighter, swishing impatiently at his legs. When it was knee high, he paused to shake snow from his shoes. Tiny drops of water sparkled on his socks and shoelaces, and dampness made his pants legs dark. Harper kicked at the grass. It seemed normal enough. He heard nothing; evidently no animal life was nearby to be disturbed. He shrugged philosophically and continued toward the river.

He marched into snow. And short-lived fog. Clinging mud. Snow. Fire for a few perilous strides. More mud. Snow. Winter night—summer night—he paced through the brief seasons without hesitation and without haste.

He had lost count of the cycles when he came to the bank of the Charles. There was a sharp drop here, not the gentle slope he associated with the Esplanade. He could see no water in the darkness, so he stepped cautiously, threading over slick jumbled rocks and clumps of damp weeds. *Where are the beer cans?* he wondered. *And all the whitefish?*

Then the water was about him, a dark coating that rose and subsided rhythmically on the shell surrounding him. The current did not threaten to sweep him away, and he moved ahead until the shell was covered. Ooze sucked greedily at his feet.

He waited a short while. Nothing happened, and he stepped back until he could again see the black sky. A watermelon-sized boulder pressed against the shell; it rolled about with tiny twitching motions, like some sluggish but inquisitive animal, till it was inside.

Harper raised an eyebrow. It would take a torrent to shove around a rock that size, not the sluggish Charles. Even a flood would not move such a rock on the level that way, and he had seen no signs of great currents as he had clambered down the bank. "*Nothing* speeds up a river by a factor of thousands."

Nothing? He stood frozen on the edge of the riverbed and stared at the turquoise banner in the sky. The sun?

"Running out of other impossible things to believe," he said slowly. "Even without having breakfast." He poked a finger at the plastic box inside his shirt, then nodded abruptly. "Find the dorm."

He could not find footsteps to retrace. That made sense. How much time had gone by? It had seemed no more than half an hour.

His pace lengthened. Soon he was almost running. As he raced through the hurried seasons, he tracked the mud of spring into the dust of autumn and splattered the summer grasses with dripping snow before plunging into each new winter. Over his head the sun-bright turquoise ribbon swung lazily across the starless night, mocking his haste.

God! How much time had gone by?

A brick. He had found a brick. Well, by now he deserved to find something. Harper kicked the brick from the frozen ground and bent to examine it. A trickle of snow ran down the side of the small cavity he had created.

A great deal of snow was about him now. Was it simply imagination, or had the periods of "winter" actually lengthened? It was still warm inside the shell, but Harper shivered nevertheless.

The corners of the brick were rounded, weather-worn. Harper rubbed his thumb along one side, dislodging ice and earth. The brick was oversized, rough-textured, off-colored. "One of Alvar's Finnish bricks, all right."

How long would it take to wear down a brick? "Decades," he said, guessing. "Centuries." There was a harsh note to his voice, as if that too had been lying unattended for long years. "Where's the rest?"

He walked about methodically, circling the brick until he reached a small hill, so slight that at first he thought it only a large drift of snow. Then his eye was caught by a gleam of white, too regular to be a patch of snow, too large to be a pebble. He approached warily, trying to ignore a feeling of recognition.

A corner of a small refrigerator. Harper identified it somberly.

The paint on the refrigerator was peeling and scratched. He kicked at a hand-sized expanse of bare metal, putting a small dent in it and scuffing off flakes of rust, but his foot did not go through. He shrugged.

The top few inches of the cooling coils were visible, still black-painted and sturdy, though the rubber and much of the supporting grid had corroded. Harper grimaced fastidiously, then dug into the cool earth with both hands.

He made no effort to get into the refrigerator. There could be nothing of value left in it. But eventually he got the warped bank of coils pulled free and out of the ground. Now he had a tool.

Hours later the hilltop was cratered with large and small holes. Harper stacked bricks to make a seat, heedless of the damp earth that clung to them. "Definitely time to take five."

He wiped sweat from his brow with a grimy forearm, his nose wrinkling at the soap-tinged aroma of clay, then looked over his tiny domain with satisfaction. His torso and bare feet gleamed in the shifting blue-green light. Stakes held his shoes and socks and his snow-washed shirt. "Should have had a gopher for school animal," he muttered. "Not that goddamn beaver."

But he had been lucky. The room's contents had not been shaken about too badly. "'Course, there's damn all left in decent shape."

The blue "first aid kit" was within easy reach, nestled between a soil-stained packframe and a corrosion-pitted broadsword. Inside the pack were the books that were salvageable: volume one of Courant and Hilbert, Morse's *Thermal Physics*, both volumes of the *Norton Anthology of English Literature*, and some poetry. Earth, rain, and insects had ruined the others.

He bent and rebent a section of the refrigerator cooling coil until he had broken off a six-inch length, then set the plastic box on his knees and opened its lid. The end of the piping fitted snugly over the matchlike lever on the "tourniquet box."

Harper barely hesitated before pulling the makeshift handle.

The turquoise band in the sky narrowed and froze into one

position. It was arc-light bright for an instant, and then it vanished. The other narrow lines across the heavens and the distant sparkles on the hillsides were gone as well. He saw nothing.

He closed his eyes tightly. Colored splotches and snowflake forms moved behind his eyelids, reassuring him; he had not gone blind.

He heard a click and opened his eyes to see faint violet clouds gathering over the dark eastern horizon. The clouds thickened, growing denser, moving toward him rapidly. They turned to blue, then yellow, unmasking a pale green disk. The black sky was suddenly blue; the disk became a burning white-yellow ball over a bank of red-tinted clouds.

Sunrise.

A warm breeze was in his face, bringing with it the smell of the sea and the distant sound of breakers. Dew beaded the tall blades of grass. A small stand of scrub timber was on his right, and beyond, an evergreen forest rose to the tops of the southern hills. Birds twittered nearby, and a small furry animal poked its head above the grass to peer at him unwinkingly. There was no sign of Man.

Harper breathed out stale air and released the control lever. The crude handle remained upright. He took a handful of soil and squeezed, making a clod, which he threw downwind. The dirt arced through the air, falling to the ground somewhere in the mid-distance.

The barrier was gone.

He nodded with satisfaction and nudged the lever. The clouds dwindled, turning from rose to yellow. The sky blackened; the sun was green once more. Then the world regained its proper hues. But the day was definitely older.

He could not go back.

He could go on.

"Go on," he said aloud. Staying here would be only a triumph for cowardice.

He smiled, his memory bringing back lines of verse:

> If to the fleeting moment I should say
> "Stay now, so fair thou art, remain!"
> Then bind me with your fatal chain.
> For I will perish in that day.

"Mephistopheles? The bet's on," he finished softly. "Sharon—good-bye, Sharon." He pushed the tourniquet box lever to the far left. The dawn vanished.

He came to a road at last. It was little more than a simple gravel-strewn dirt path sunk a foot into the ground, but it seemed headed toward the hills, as he was, so he decided to follow it.

"If nothing else, the footing will be better," he growled. The turquoise band in the sky was not bright enough to show detail on the ground outside the shell, and he was saving the flashlight batteries for an emergency. During the last hour he had walked continuously through snow, all in darkness; slips had left him with a torn sleeve and convinced him there was far more ice than dirt underneath to step on. Fortunately, though his feet were cold, the temperature within the shell remained warm; he had not decided whether this was a by-product of the time engine or simply body heat that could not be radiated away.

Reasonably level for a dirt road, he noticed. *No ruts. Not getting much traffic these days? Where did all the people go?* He stepped down and scuffed at the gravel, the packframe swinging loosely across his back. The gravel did not move.

He pulled the sword from his belt, being careful not to slice more notches into the leather, then pried at the ground with the point until a handful of pebbles had come free. The surface under the gravel was white, though tinged pale blue by the turquoise sun-band. Harper sank to one knee and probed with a finger.

Ice. Who would build a road on ice? "Someone expecting the ice to be around for a while, that's who," he commented. "You may not like this, chum."

He stuck the sword back through his belt and continued. Soon he was on asphalt. *But why bright red asphalt?* he wondered. *For visibility?*

Then he was on a dark green material, smooth as glass but not slippery. Striking at that with the sword put an ache into his forearm and further dulled the edge of the weapon; it did not mark the road.

The snow at the side grew higher till it towered over him. "What comes first?" he asked himself. "Tunnel or avalanche?"

Neither, it developed, for the road soon sloped upward.

Sparkles in the air vanished and reappeared as the blue-green ribbon swung through the darkness. He was in the hills.

The roadbed grew even with the snow. Harper took the blue plastic box from his pack and set the controls to neutral.

"Damn!" The pavement really was green plastic. "Yellow brick would've been better."

And that was really snow. He cursed again, and his breath might have been steam. The air was cold, dry, and very clear. The snow was cotton-white and powdery. The sky was robin's-egg blue, totally cloudless. "Christmas card-ish. But no trees, no bushes, no grass—nothing."

Here and there winds had swept the snow away, revealing blue-white patches of ice. Far behind him, a broad trough ran toward the unseen sea. The Charles, he decided; the river was apt to freeze over in winter.

"Just too damned bad this is probably summer," he muttered. "You do *not* like this, chum."

The road had not brought him to a town or even to scattered houses. "Not even a few lousy phone poles. Boy, am I in the boonies!"

His fingers were cold and stiff. His ears felt as if vises were being tightened upon them, and his face was becoming numb and thick-feeling. He reset the controls in the first aid kit and continued walking into the hills.

He was hungry. His feet were wet, and he could tell that a bumper crop of blisters was germinating on them. His hips were sore, and the constant slapping of the pack at his back was annoying. He could use a bath, a shave, clean clothing. "And hot and cold running blondes. Oh, well."

He felt dissatisified, troubled by an obscure sense of betrayal. Suddenly he realized why. This was dull, tedious, uncomfortable—boring, in fact. Time travel! "Where's the glamour and adventure, damn it?"

Then he laughed. What else was an adventure but a miserable experience someone else had survived? And what had happened to that hard-bitten noncom he remembered who had no space in him for illusions?

Besides, if I had the two blondes, would they fit in the pack?

The road turned to the right, leading past overhanging boulders and black soil, and descended to another turn on the far side of a small valley. A slide had left scattered rocks but no soil on the green pavement. A dark curtain of spangled material billowed beside him, keeping step with his paces—the rock wall that had been carved away to lay the bed for the plastic road. Perhaps a mile away, an object gleamed quicksilver under the shifting turquoise light. A building.

The building should not have been visible.

He was not seeing normal light now, he had come to understand. If half an hour passed for him while clocks outside measured an hour, the frequency of the light entering the field would appear doubled to him, so the apparent wavelength would be halved. What was red would seem blue, what was blue already would be into the ultraviolet from his viewpoint—and thus invisible.

He was moving through time much faster than that. The blue band that was the sun, swaying across the sky—each slow to-and-from cycle must be a year. Call it fifteen seconds of his time: so he had sped up not by a factor of two but by roughly two million. Normal light wavelengths were about five thousand angstroms long. Multiplied by two million: a meter. He was seeing radio waves.

Radio waves—and television stations. The fireball he had seen yesterday—yesterday? Six thousand years ago—was probably channel 12.

He had not abandoned his country to a nuclear war. Harper knew relief.

Radio waves. A wavelength of a meter meant resolution of about a meter; it was no surprise, then, that what he could see of the outside world had little detail. And there were no natural sources of radio waves, unless one counted the stars and perhaps some planets. So the sky was black, except for the turquoise sun-band and the thin bright lines that must have been quasars.

Would there be scattering? No. Light photons could be shaken about by dust and air molecules, but the wavelengths and particles were of comparable size. Rayleigh scattering effects dropped off quickly for larger wavelengths; why else was the sky blue? Thomson scattering could bounce larger-wavelength photons around, but that would require a sizable number of free electrons with space to roam. Which meant metal, or large ore-bearing rocks. So he walked in a darkness broken only by the radio "light" scattered from the chance concentrations of metal he approached.

Metal? When he switched the time engine off and viewed

the building before him in normal light, it looked like a concrete Quonset hut.

But Quonset huts were not made of concrete. They were not a hundred feet tall. They were not deliberately half buried in mountainsides under unstable overhangs ready to finish the process at any moment. They were not supposed to have great irregular holes in their sides, pierced by green plastic roads.

This one did.

Up close, Harper whistled shrilly. The walls were reinforced concrete, four feet thick, and all along them ran pockmarks and deep gouges. Perhaps the damage had been done by landslides. *But the smart money would be on sledgehammers and blasting powder.*

Certainly shaped charges had opened the gap in which he was standing.

Explosives had been used to open up the walls, but the blasting had done nothing to the foot-and-a-half-thick metal plate inside those walls. Someone had very neatly carved a doorway in the metal eight feet high and twelve feet wide. A scrap of the plate material lay on the shattered concrete at his feet; Harper picked it up.

Heavy, it made his fingers itch as if he were handling very heavy fiberglass, and its surface had a fuzzy appearance. He moved the fuzz along the blade of his sword; where the weapon was touched, it took on a polished look, rust-free. When Harper tapped the scrap against the concrete, metal dust fell from it, gleaming in late afternoon sunlight.

"Bet it made jim-dandy razor blades," he said. He dropped the metal scrap onto the ground beyond the side of the elevated roadbed and then wiped his fingers carefully on his flannel shirt. Perfect long crystals of metal would have three to ten times the strength of conventional metals. There was a great future for them in metallurgy, he had once been told, if someone could discover how to produce them cheaply. And a great future for the discoverer.

"A great future," he repeated. How many hundreds—thousands—of years had men tried to breach the walls of this building? What kind of weaponry had done the job? And what was in the place, anyhow?

Rather, what had been there? Nothing valuable would be left; casual looting would not have justified the effort needed to break into the almost impregnable structure. The brute-force excavation of the building alone would have required a major work crew. A lot of workers, a low level of technology. "Slave labor. Had to be." Harper grimaced, then cursed.

He walked through the opening and dropped three feet from the end of the road to the floor. High above him, dim red-yellow lights came on. Harper ducked under the end of the plastic roadway. A metallic rasp sounded from a nearby speaker, followed by plaintive mumbles, then silence.

When two minutes passed without further sound, he re-emerged, whacking dust-grimed hands against his jeans, leaving thick gray streaks on them.

No one else alive was in the building. He was surrounded by coffin shapes distributed uniformly over the warehouselike interior in stacks that rose to the top of the Quonset structure wherever he looked. Layers of catwalks were arrayed about them, and there were movable ladders on forkliftlike vehicles so that all the coffins could be accessed.

Despite the sophistication of the handling equipment, some of the coffins had been dropped. One lay upside down thirty feet from him, half hidden behind one of the tall stacks, partially covered and partially supported by drifts of frozen dust, wedged in place by its hinged lid. There might have been room for a midget or a small child to crawl underneath. Or for bones to fall out.

There were no bones. The casket was empty. It was made of lead, and there was neither name nor loving inscription engraved on it. Instead, large circular trefoils, which Harper recognized instantly, had been painted on its tops and sides. They were black in the reddish light. Outside, under sunlight, he knew, they would be a pale violet.

A metal plaque had been welded to one end of the casket. He needed the flashlight to read the nine-digit lot number and the date: February 2037. There was the name of a power company of which he had never heard. The bottom two lines read "Permanent Waste Repository—United States Nuclear Regulatory Commission."

February 2037. Sixty-seven years plus a month. Sharon would have been eighty-eight then, just about eighty-nine. *Old. Or dead.* Harper gnawed his lip.

"All right. So what happened to the AEC?" He was not worried by the implications of the plaque; nothing would be left now but the longer half-lifed isotopes, so the radiation he might absorb would be at background levels. *If anything hot is left in this atomic piggy bank.*

There wasn't much of anything left, not even cobwebs. His casual searching turned up drifts of frozen soil, two really impressive icicles affixed to some scaffolding, a headless skeleton beneath a shattered coffin lid—and a stairwell leading down to a red-painted door.

The door was locked. Cold, with the feel of iron, it rang hollowly when he tapped on it. When a kick at the handle failed to make it budge, Harper shrugged. He probed with his sword at the dirt covering the bottom of the door, then dug till the sill was exposed, revealing a crack between the door and its frame. "Good. Unless this is more superdooper alloy."

Using a chunk of casket material, he hammered on the pommel of his sword to wedge the point into the gap, then heaved upward to dimple the bottom edge of the door. "Convention of blacksmiths," he muttered.

He tugged up on the sword hilt once more. The door was bowed inward along its length, and Harper slammed his shoulder hard into it, then again, dislodging the tongue of the lock. The door came open reluctantly, a corner of the warped bottom edge scraping noisily on concrete. The hinges did not creak, he noticed. "If I ever get back, remind me to sell 3-in-1 Oil short."

The corridor behind the door was dust-free. When he entered, red-yellow fluorescent tubes flickered on. "Handy for photographers."

The ceiling was low, and there were no windows. "Also great for claustrophobes." Doorless rooms lined one side of the corridor. All were empty; there were no marks on the linoleum floors to show where furniture had rested. When he stepped into each room, more red-yellow ceiling lights switched on and the corridor darkened. "Wonder what it was like to work here. No way; I'd have gone batty."

An open-air shower was at one end of the corridor. Otherwise, he found no sign of cooking facilities, no lavatories. "No way to go at all," he commented. "Ah, the superhuman servants of the atom!"

A metal door at the end of the corridor opened onto an empty loading dock. An open freight elevator gaped at the far end of the dock, next to another doorway. *Space for a dozen semis*, Harper noticed. *If that's what they used*. He walked off the platform, dropping four feet to the floor, and crossed to a glass-walled booth between two tall corrugated metal doors at the back.

A narrow console bolted to a wall held outsized buttons and an empty phone jack. Nothing happened when he pushed the buttons.

"Maybe a good thing," he admitted. This part of the building was still buried; it was just as well to keep all that rock and dirt outside. He drummed his fingers on the console, then left the booth abruptly.

A metal ladder brought him back up to the platform. There was nothing out of the ordinary about the freight elevator, but his subconscious noted something unusual about the dock, and he turned in the doorway for a final look, trying to detect it. "Ah, no oil spills. Neat, weren't they?"

The next room he entered was a large one with metal benches bolted in place. "A shop, by God!" It was stripped of machinery, but cardboard boxes rested under a bench. He cursed the poor lighting and began searching for some tools.

He was not well paid for his labor. The boxes disintegrated when he touched them, leaving scraps and rags that also fell to dust. Harper scuffed debris aside with his foot, finding only a pair of pliers and a ball peen hammer head, both deeply encrusted with rust. "Better'n nothing."

He smiled ruefully and slammed the tools together to dislodge thick flakes of rusted metal; then he opened the blue plastic control box and unclipped the leads to the tourniquet box. With a metal flake held by the pliers, he delicately scraped at the ends of the slot in which the control lever moved. The material resisted at first but crinkled as he pressed harder. Using the pliers, he twisted and pulled the plastic, then reconnected the battery.

"Now try." If the lever could move farther, the rate at which he could travel through time might increase. "Maybe I'll get someplace interesting soon now."

Someplace interesting—Sharon! Sharon. Harper bit his lip, remembering. "Come on, guy."

He pushed the lever to the far left and was in total darkness.

"So far, so good." He felt for the tape roll and expanded the field to encompass the shop area. The ceiling lights came back on. "So far, so better." He shoved his sword back into his belt and left.

He would go south, he decided. "Find something warm." He took the steps leading up to the repository two at a time, whistling the "Colonel Bogie March."

The whistle died.

The hole in the side of the building was stopped again. The stub of green roadway was no longer visible: In its place was a pile of ice and rock and dirt. A tier of lead boxes had been forced aside; the scaffolding leaned drunkenly against steadier companions, and jumbled coffin shapes filled the nearby aisles.

"Trapped."

Chapter Three

Getting softer, *Harper noted dully.* Surface must be close. *Or is it just another soft pocket?* He leaned forward again on the outstretched sword and levered it counterclockwise. Dirt and pebbles cascaded down, rolling toward his knees. Moisture was on his wrist; he licked it absently, not noticing the grit it left on his tongue.

A drop of cold mud splashed on his forehead, recalling him from reveries in which caged men were given as wedding presents to blond women who refused to recognize them.

Another drop reminded him of his present location. A third splashed on the back of his neck while he shook his head.

A fourth splattered his hair as he struggled to his feet.

Rescue? Harper waved his arms till he found the pack on an earthen shelf. Was this the emergency that would justify running down the flashlight?

Water was seeping through a blackish splotch in the brown dirt roof, beads collecting dirt and color as they rolled along the surface. At intervals, drops merged at the underside of a protruding pebble, quivered as if with anticipation, and finally released their hold.

Rain, he concluded. Heavy rain had saturated the ground—which meant that he was close to the surface.

He might escape. Today. After three days.

Today! Harper pushed himself upright, then groped until his fingers closed over the hilt of the sword. He shoved upward with both hands, probing the roof. When he met resistance, he jammed the point firmly into the ceiling of the shaft.

Metal scraped over rock; the hilt twisted in his hands. He levered the weapon to and fro, creating sucking sounds, then swung his arms to dislodge the wet earth. A tiny Niagara of dirt and gravel cascaded past him, rattling to a standstill in the depths. Ice water ran down the blade and trickled over his wrist.

"Good size rock," he muttered. "Need leverage." He felt for a handhold and pulled himself upward to place a foot on the shelf, then braced the other foot against the opposite wall. He shoved the sword upward again, prying with it until the trickle of water became faster, then, suddenly, much faster. He thumped backward against the wall of the shaft and braced himself.

He was just in time.

The earth about him lurched violently. The boulder was gone, bouncing down the walls of the shaft. He was drenched by falling water. Harper gasped in the sudden cold, fighting the instinct to release his grip, somehow managing to endure the pelting of gravel that followed.

He kept his face upward even after the torrent stopped. There was a faint blue-violet cast to the darkness, spreading as he watched.

The opening above took shape slowly at first, growing larger after he contracted the field again. A chimney formed miraculously about him as Harper gazed in awe.

The walls were unstable, water-saturated mud interspersed with rocks and gravel. But he could find large stones to step on, and handholds. Harper found strength to bind his equipment to him, then half crawled, half pulled his way upward.

The ground he collapsed on was ooze. He stretched out regardless, cradling his head on his shoulder, and let the earth embrace him.

Lazarus, he thought when sensation yielded to words. *Jonah*. "'Virtue also says: We are not yet friends enough,'" he quoted wryly.

There was victory in a grin. Harper struggled to his feet, the smile still on his face, and stepped forward without destination.

The ground remained soft, puddle-scaped and without grass. A sprinkling of stones promised solid footing but sank under his weight. He gave up after a few paces and simply accepted the mud, letting it slop over the bottom of his jeans and into his shoes, caring only that he moved, that the seashore trail of footprints he left behind was straight and even.

A blue band had replaced the turquoise ribbon in the black sky, no wider but swinging back and forth more rapidly. In the dimmer light, the world outside the shell seemed far removed, strangely tenuous. But for the mud, he might have been walking on a table top. *Some mist and a five-foot fall to a black carpet—always just one step off. It ain't so, guy, so stop dawdling.*

Instinct slowed him nonetheless. At his feet and some distance away, specks of light danced to accompany his steps.

Inside the barrier, objects cast purple-tinged shadows that darted about annoyingly as the blue band moved.

He was on rock suddenly—not gravel or even large boulders but what proved to be a great slab of sandstone, smoothed out like a bedsheet and dappled with splotches of dust and snow. Bedrock, he realized, the solid earth that undergirds the thin skin of the planet. Stones, dirt, plants—the ground itself had been pushed aside. Finger-deep grooves and scattered depressions showed how the rock had resisted as ice and stone scoured it.

One path was as good as any other. Harper followed the striations toward the south for more than an hour and continued in that direction when the sandstone gave way to granite. The terrain was rougher there, a succession of sinuous upcroppings. Boulders and fragments of rocks lay beneath overhangs.

Summer heat sometimes warmed his hands as he scrambled over the talus; just as frequently, snow and patches of ice stripped the heat away. Fog was about him much of the time. Once he was pelted by a flurry of hailstones. Once his hand fell on bird droppings.

A cliff was before him at last. Harper stepped back hastily from the edge, then followed it eastward, searching for a trustworthy slope.

He descended to dirt, then mud. The mud stayed rain-slicked, untouched by climate. A lake, Harper realized, its waters kept away by the field around him.

My lake. The one that is filling up the repository. This is what I escaped from. "I dub thee Lake Me."

Ghost images of gravel and dirt stretched to join a long hill that ran along one side of the ice-broadened valley, like a tongue in a serpent's cheek. It sloped toward the southeast, where he estimated the ocean lay.

He turned for a last look at the hills around him. They had not changed greatly, as well as he could tell from their specter images. Perhaps they had become rounder, softer in places.

To the west and north there was a mass he had not seen before. Short, fat rainbows sparkled in the air before the mountain, flashing in synchronization with the movement of the blue sun band above him. As he watched, the mountain shape diminished; the rainbows became longer and narrower, fainter.

Harper sought for a quip.

None came.

The glacier continued to retreat.

Farther to the south Harper crossed a long row of barren hills. In a day they passed out of sight.

When he was tired, he slept. He woke and went on.

Then snow was around him once more, even within the shell, and he was wearily trudging up a shallow incline that never ended. From time to time, his path was interrupted by white-shrouded ditches and once by a long thin valley, suddenly carved as if by a knife before him in the blackness, treacherously steep and slick-sided. Snow poured into these chasms as he skirted their edges, damp at first, then firmly packed and thick-crusted.

Glacier, he realized at last. The ice had returned.

"Hell." Exhaustion rather than anger sounded in his voice; hunger and fatigue made him tremble as he raised his eyes to the blue ribbon swinging across the dark sky. "I didn't need this, you know."

The ribbon moved to and fro without concern; the purple shadows continued to dance like mischievous children around his blue-rimmed shoes. "All right," he said sourly. "Don't help." *I don't need you, anyhow.*

True ground would be far beneath him, he remembered. The weight of the ice forced soil and rock downward, distorting the very shape of the earth even as he marched skyward across the unmelting snows. After the ice retreated, the earth would rebound. And he could stay in place on the surface and ride the melting ice back to the ground. If it did not melt too rapidly, he should be safe enough.

No. He could not stay in one place. The snows were still falling about him, and if he stopped for long he would be buried. The entire glacier was itself a fluid, moving "downhill" toward the equator—the ice would carry him to the sea. He had to go back or risk being dumped into the Atlantic.

"Oh, hell," he said tiredly, then sighed. *No other choice, chum. Now get back from the edge and trace the crevass to the end and beyond a bit. Careful now.* "Never wanted Virtue for a friend, anyhow."

No other choice.

He was on a rocky plain scraped clean of soil by the departed ice. Soon there was dust upon the surface, alternating with layers of snow, and the rocks crumbled about him. The dust turned to dry-baked earth, then to normal dirt anchored by lichens and clumps of dark, thick-bladed grass. Shrubs thrust up about him; the grass was fine-textured and springy under his feet. Harper suddenly knew that he was walking on what had once been sea bottom.

Shrubs grew up before him, and he moved among young birch trees. Spruce and firs waited for him in ragged lines, becoming taller and more closely spaced as he moved among them. The underbrush became thicker. The soil was dark and damp, with a soapy feeling. The trees he passed were tall and thick-trunked. All the while the blue sun band remained visible; would the forest let the skies be seen in normal light?

A scorched clearing . . . more grass . . . an ice-rimmed stream . . . a stand of pine mixed with occasional hardwoods. He walked over tall grass, along furrows of upturned black-brown soil, through widely spaced rows of tall golden stalks—not corn—that gave way to low-cropped green stubble and twine-wrapped bundles of water-sodden shocks, and along a split-rail fence.

The yellow fence rails became weatherbeaten and gray, then were replaced by newer planks, which were themselves replaced by a low stone wall. Harper smiled at that despite his fatigue.

Whatever they might plant, New England farmers continued to harvest bumper crops of rock.

The stones had a midmorning warmth when he touched them, and he was ready for a rest. *Taking five too often*, he mused as he shrugged off the pack. *Nice to be trim again, but—hell! I'm good for a few more days*. With his wadded-up shirt, he wiped sweat from his face and ribs, then took a seat. What was happening in the world? He shook his head slowly, watching the blue band in the sky and calculating.

A seven- or eight-second "year" meant five centuries for each of his hours. Outside the field, in ten minutes a person could be born and die of old age.

Did they see him? he suddenly wondered. Did the outsiders think him a ghost? Did he seem some strangely frozen near statue?

No. If he could be seen, he would have seen signs of it. Some effort would have been made to communicate with him. He would be blundering into scientific instruments, crowds of tourists, or altars bearing beautiful sacrificial virgins with long silky hair and heaving alabaster breasts. "Or all three. Nah—that's silly, guy. Never were any pretty virgins in this part of the state."

Even Sharon. "Let it rest, guy."

He swung his legs over the fence. He was in an apple orchard.

Not winesaps, he decided after a few bites. *And sure not Red Delicious*. "Great American Wormy, that's more like it. If this is Eden, I'm going to take a rain check on Eve."

But they were the first food he had found in five days. With only minor feelings of guilt, he knocked down more apples with his sword and ate his fill. Then he stuffed his pack with fruit and left the orchard.

Eventually he came to a dirt trail lying east and west. He shrugged and went west. After a few miles the trail widened, and he was on a dirt road that rose until he was walking along the top of an embankment. The roadway seemed to be mounting steadily, although he noticed no slope. Perhaps the ground on the sides was dropping away.

Cobblestones appeared under his feet. A mile later he came to a T-shaped intersection with a narrow access road coming up the northern slope of the embankment. Soon after that, he found a pile of clear plastic sacks, some stuffed with earth. "Sandbags, sort of."

On his right were dirt and grass; on the left, a green-painted concrete stucco facing that plunged downward steeply. He was walking on concrete as well, of the same color. Esthetics? Camouflage?

The road surface clearly was sloping up. The dark forms of hills were before him, blue-sparkled by the shifting band in the black sky. A parapet appeared at his left, dark stones roughly dressed and cemented together to breast height. It was crenelated; there were thin vertical slots in the thick walls, and metal-covered wooden hatches were bolted to the floors of the projecting merlons. "So much for the idea that this was some kind of dike."

Then he was in the hills. The broad paved road was winding to the left. The wall on that side was built of brick, yellow hand-sized blocks covered with glass. The builders had not used mortar. Above him, on the hill at his right, perhaps a hundred yards away, a dark blue line paralleled his path. Another road? And what defenses would be mounted on it? Greek fire? Disintegrator rays?

The road swung left again to detour around low unornamented buildings with dark stucco exteriors: stables and barracks. The hay in the horse stalls was fresh and smelled of spices. The straw on the earthen floor was clean. The pegs on the walls held no pieces of harness, and the water troughs in the empty corral were dry. The barracks were also deserted and unfurnished, but the interior walls were newly whitewashed. "Bluewashed, actually," Harper noted wryly. "But it's the thought that counts."

An alcove held a pair of oil lamps and a limestone block with figures carved in high relief. A man wearing a skirt, Harper noticed. A woman in trousers carrying a scythe. A pair of teddy bears floated in the background. "Or else ugly angels."

A deserted room that could have been an office was graced by a painting of an annoyed middle-aged man in a black uniform. The portrait hung askew, and there were three holes in it. The bullets were still in the wall.

When he returned to the road, he found the concrete surface gone. Instead, what looked like a dirt lane was mirror shiny and flat and very hard. "Esthetically pleasing," he commented.

"Depressing to think it probably came about purely as a cost-cutting measure."

He was soon at the crest of a hill. Patterns had been placed in the dirt road now—circles and swords in meaningless combinations. The wall to his left was only waist high and had been made from the same hard earth. North of him the black silhouettes of another line of hills were crisscrossed with fine blue lines. "Roads. Or a nasty case of varicose veins."

A road network like that implied a city. Did he wish to go that way? He stopped to lean against the hardened earth rampart at the side of the road and thought about that. *Don't want to trap someone inside this field*. He chuckled grimly. "Not even silky-haired virgins with heaving alabaster breasts."

But so far the field had not caught anyone else, and he suspected there was some good reason for that, which he had not figured out yet.

There was a shimmering in the air to his left. He could stand some distraction, he decided, and went to investigate.

"Another orchard? Ah, Japanese gardens." None of the trees were more than his own height; few were shorter than his chest. But they were trees, not bushes, with spindly trunks and incongruously thick, stubby branches jutting out perpendicularly. Harper was reminded of tiny paper umbrellas. The branches were decked with waxy green leaves and hive-shaped clumps of red-purple berries dangling from short stalks. "Bonsai strawberry trees."

Berries would be a nice change from the too-tart apples. Harper pulled a berry from a nearby branch, wiped it from habit on his flannel-clad arm, and dropped it into his mouth.

That act almost cost him some teeth. He gagged, coughed up bits of pulp, and spat them out. "Yeech!"

The berry had had a slimy, bitter taste, and it had been rock-hard. "People eat these? I don't believe it."

But someone must love them. There were no berries on the ground, which suggested that the crop was carefully harvested. Why?

Harper took another berry and scraped at the seeds with a fingernail. The purplish skin rubbed off easily. He placed one of the shiny kernels in his mouth and bit down; then he removed it for examination. His teeth had left no impression. "Like chewing on bird shot."

Sparks attracted his eye. There was suddenly a fire in the

distance: Someone had discovered radio. "Two someones . . . three. Next week, singing commercials."

The grove shielded him from a clear view, but the radio sources he saw were becoming uncomfortably bright, and new ones were appearing close to him. "Be running like hell now if I had gotten into town," he commented. He flipped the metallic seed away and went back to the road.

"Oh, migod!"

There was a city. It writhed and contorted itself before him like a thing alive. It was golden, scarlet, azure, platinum, aquamarine. It hung suspended between dark ground and darker sky, and a thousand searchlight beams might have played upon it. And it *danced*.

Firestormed Dresden would have burned like that. Or hell.

Harper shook his head angrily. He had seen Quang Tri, heard of Hue. Destruction was not here, only glory. This city was a unit, intact and growing. Colors swirled around its axis, coalesced, then separated again. Limbs reached out in unison to embrace nearby hills. A slow rhythmic pulsing ring of lights surrounded the core of the city, and an auroral curtain glowed in the far distance above the hills. Sparks jetted into the air.

The city threw itself at him.

The flames were out. The dance was done. There were white-walled buildings about him. A gigantic marble cube sat kitty-corner on the flattened top of a nearby hill. Tiny trees with purple berries were planted along the roadside. A white-yellow sun disk glowed intensely, fixed motionlessly to a cloudless blue sky. Somewhere birds sang. Brightly colored flowers, which seemed to be half rose and half tulip, were at his feet, and the short grass was damp from a recent rain. The air was cool and very fresh, with a faint tang of salt water. A trio of black dots rose lazily from a tall building in the mid distance.

He had arrived. Somewhere. Somewhen.

Harper pulled the plastic control box from his pack. The control lever on the tourniquet box was still at the far left end of its slot.

"Out of juice?" He poked gingerly at the lever. It moved easily, but nothing else changed. "End of the line, fellow."

"Run out of time." That was supposed to be a figure of speech. "Guess it isn't."

The three black dots were closer now, much larger, oblong. Protuberances became visible as the shapes moved toward him.

Men. They rode machines that might have been motorcycles with wheels replaced by landing skids. They wore powder-blue uniforms, and dark rods in holsters at their sides. The man in the lead pointed at him; another nodded.

"Looks like the cops," Harper said shakily. He closed the plastic box and fitted it inside his ragged shirt. He made no other motion.

Black cowlings covered the legs and feet of the machine riders. Stubby vanes mounted horizontally moved up and down as the men circled thirty feet above him. *Control flaps?* Harper speculated. The vanes were actually staying parallel to the ground, he noticed, while the machines and their riders banked and turned. *Neat trick.*

He was not surprised to see no similarity between these craft and the drone that had trapped him days before.

The men gestured to one another with their hands, then their machines dropped straight down, slowing just as they reached the roadbed. "Oh, hell," Harper muttered, recognizing the style. "Oh, shit. Ranger types."

The machines had made a faint buzzing sound while in the air; otherwise, there had been no sound yet except for his own voice. Now a uniformed man came running at him with something like gauze in his hand.

Harper stepped back and to the side and pulled his sword free. "Say please," he growled.

The man looked dismayed. He was a rather ordinary-looking man. His skin had a faint olive cast, and his hair was black. He was perhaps just over six feet tall and in his mid-twenties. A small green rectangle was at the center of his forehead. He said something and held out the gauze in both hands.

"No speaka da Inglis." Harper noted with some amusement that he was enjoying himself now.

The man spoke again, this time managing to express urgency despite the totally foreign language. He held the gauze over his head and patted it in place, then removed it and held it out toward Harper.

"Thanks, but I'd worry about cooties," the redhead explained.

The remark was ignored. The man was not looking at him. He was staring at the sword. When Harper waved the blade across his front, the man's eyes remained focused on the weapon as if hypnotized.

"Mongoose, meet cobra," Harper muttered. *What's with you, fellow?*

Another voice spoke. It was loud, intended to get his attention, not to communicate. The other men were at his sides, pointing bulky brown rods with silver tips toward him.

"I hear the voice of reason," Harper said dryly. "I even see it." He lowered the sword slowly, thrust it back into his belt, then raised his hands into the air, using the right one to keep his left erect. Only one of his captors had the green forehead badge; he wondered what that meant. And all three of the soldiers were sneaking glances at his sword.

The green-badged man stepped forward and pushed the gauze over Harper's head, tugging at it till it settled through his hair onto the scalp. The weight was small, and it did not seem to be doing anything, so Harper decided to tolerate it. Then he winced as a needle jabbed his right temple. But the pain was soon gone.

The soldiers appeared more relaxed, he noticed. They had expected his start. *Wish I had been able to disappoint them. But . . . spilt milk.*

The badged man had smelled of spices, but not offensively, and Harper wondered now whether the aroma was natural or a cosmetic. He smelled like a dead horse himself, he realized, and gave the soldiers credit for not showing the distaste they must feel.

A unbadged soldier approached, both hands out, saying nothing.

Harper guessed at his intentions and nodded.

The soldier drew back.

Weapons were pointed at him once more. His arms were jerked down and held behind him while the second soldier pulled the sword from his belt. Someone tapped at his whiskers, gently, then more vigorously. He heard a nervous laugh.

A cool circlet of rope was forced over his wrists. The rope contracted, molding itself to his skin and becoming warmer. He tried but was unable to create any slack.

So he was a prisoner now. Sharon would never know what had become of him.

A man lacking the forehead badge took his shoulder and pointed him up the embankment toward one of the flying motorcycles. He said something that sounded to Harper like a long string of vowels rather than distinct words, and when Harper did not move, he gave the redhead a gentle shove. He looked apologetic.

Harper turned to face him. "I'll go peacefully. Just remember, though, regular feedings and I don't have to give you more than name, rank, and serial number. Oh, yes, one thing more: I'm entitled to a cell with at least two hundred square feet of space."

Part 2: A Yank at Ragnarok

Timt ha'Ruppir—47,929 L.C.

Chapter Four

Stone bars do not a prison make, nor iron bars a cage. *And* what were the lines to follow? "Cage . . . age, beige, dage, fage, gauge—" Harper shoved a palm against a bright green triangular door. "—hage, iage, jage." The door still wasn't moving. The chicken wire that covered the walls and ceiling could be torn down, but that would only produce a visit from taciturn soldiers who would keep him under guard while a repairman fixed and remounted the mesh. The excitement wasn't worth the effort anymore.

"—page, quage, rage, sage—" The narrow windows didn't slide up, down, to the right, or to the left. They couldn't be pushed out or pulled in. A corner of a tall building could be seen on the left, white and featureless. An empty parking lot apparently surrounded its base. Brown- and gold-leafed trees stood on hillsides.

"—yage, zage. Hell! What is that rhyme?"

The floor was amber-colored wood, clean but cold, sealed with something like a thick varnish. The walls were of white plaster coated with the same material. The ceiling looked the same. The room appeared airtight, but ventilation ducts must have been hidden someplace, for the air was fresh and scented with autumn smells.

"Age, beige, dage, fage. Phooey!" An open doorway was an entrance to what was obviously a bathroom, with a urinal, stool, and shallow sink. Liquid soap trickled from one of three faucets when he pressed the handle. Vents for hot air took the place of towels. There was no tub, but he had a telephone-booth-sized shower lined with white tile. No mirror.

His room had a pair of fleecy throw rugs and a small table on a pedestal, but no closets, no shelves, no television or radio gear, no books or magazines, no paintings or pictures on the wall. *Sterile. Not a place for living in. A cell or a holding pen, no more. A prison made without iron bars, all right.*

Harper went back to a seat on a cubic yard of black plastic. The block collapsed slowly under him, forming an overstuffed armchair. None of the starkly functional furniture in the room could be moved, he had found, but from the chair his bare feet reached the bed, stark pink and white on a crinkled gray blanket. The bed was without sheets, the mattress covered by a tan material that resembled the blanket. *Plastic. Every damned thing's plastic. This is the future, for sure.*

The squeaky-clean future. The windows were untouched by dust. The wooden floor showed neither dirt nor scuff marks. He had noticed no beards or moustaches among his jailers. His own face was smooth now, he had noticed after waking, and no stubble had reappeared in the past eight to ten hours. He had been stripped and bathed and probably massaged during his sleep, to judge from the pleasant ache in his muscles.

He had not been fed, but for some reason hunger remained at bay. Metal mesh still rested on his hair; his captors sent people in to check that, too, whenever he tried to move it.

Two holding pens and a Hanoi Hilton. Some future.

At least I get running water and four hundred feet. But big damned deal! He pulled the bathrobe they had given him over his knees and thought longingly of freedom and socks.

The triangular door split from top to bottom, the halves pivoting about the apex to slip into side recesses. A man walked in, a gun in his hand, and took a stance by the doorway. Such an occurrence had ceased to be a novelty, and Harper ignored him.

The first stars of night could be seen through the windows,

and the ceiling of the cell was glowing brightly, but he had not seen other lights. Why was the city so dark?

A second man entered, with a covered tray in his hands. Like the first, he wore a brown coverall with red stitched emblems on one shoulder. Guarded by the gunman, he put the tray on a small table near the black cube chair and half bowed to Harper before withdrawing. A glint of metal was in his hair.

Supper. Say something polite. "Are you a Morlock or an Eloi, pal?"

An Eloi evidently. The young man seemed intimidated. He mumbled something, bowed again more deeply, and backed out of the room. The only phrase Harper heard clearly sounded like "for ants."

"I hope not." Harper lifted the cover.

Steam rose from the food, though the tray was not hot. Eating utensils lay in a recess: a three-tined glass fork and an elongated spoon with one sharp straight side. Supper was golden mush, green noodles without sauce, light blue mashed potatoes with butter, something rolled in a cabbage leaf, and broth in a camper's collapsible cup. "Beats rice."

The green noodles were semicooked and had a vegetable taste. The blue potatoes were flake-textured, with a vaguely chickenlike flavor. The cabbage leaf concealed an underdone egg roll. The broth was highly spiced, with chunks of beef at the bottom. The mush was mush.

None of the flavors was familiar, and Harper realized anew that he had left his own world. Excitement bubbled within him at each bite, held in check only by a desire to appear imperturbable. He ate slowly, determined to enjoy the strangeness, but finished all too soon.

Now get out and see this world. "No seconds?"

The gunman remained silent. Beside him, the doorway was open.

Harper pushed the empty tray aside and stood up. "Let's tell stories then. You want to go first? No? Okay. Once upon a time, there was a traveling salesman. And he was out in the country, and it was night. And he came to this farmhouse and asked the farmer if he could spend the night. And the farmer said, 'Well, I don't have a place to put you. So you'll have to share a bed with my daughter.' And the salesman said—"

The gunman growled and stepped between Harper and the triangular door. He waved the pistol chidingly.

The redhead retreated. "Not amused, eh? You know, medical studies have shown that not having a sense of humor can take years off your life." *And if I can do anything about it . . .*

Two more men entered the room, bringing an aroma of cinnamon and after-shave lotion. The first was medium-tall, about forty to Harper's eyes, with sandy hair. He wore an evening jacket over gray beltless trousers and a white buttonless shirt. A green rectangle had been stuck to his forehead. Harper could not evaluate his expression.

The second man was smaller, slimmer, about fifty, his shaggy brown hair lightly touched by gray. He wore what seemed to be pajamas over evening slippers. Traces of lace ran down his front. Gold insignia sat on his collar, a stylized X and a rolling pin, from Harper's vantage at the window. A half smile rested between creases on his thin face. He had the eyes of a pacification adviser devaluing a body count.

The sandy-haired man spoke first, then the one in pajamas. The gunman shook his head, but moved to pick up the tray with his free hand and left the room.

It was completely dark outside now. The interior of the room was half mirrored on the blackened windows, but the outlines of buildings and hills were clear when he looked outward. Stars were sprinkled in the heavens; he recognized none of the constellations. No building lights or streetlights could be seen. *Polarized glass*, Harper guessed, *with opposite polarization in the room lights so nothing goes through. Neat trick, but why bother?* He focused on the reflection, and watched himself being watched.

"I'll bet *you're* a Morlock," he said politely, glancing toward the older man. "Any chance of getting my pants back?"

That brought him a smile and a nod. Then he was ignored while the two men traded bird-song trills and Teutonic barks. At last, the older man said something with a ritualistic sound and traced an X in the air with his right hand. After a final smile at Harper he turned and walked out. The cinnamon scent left with him.

The gunman reentered, carrying what seemed to be attaché cases in both hands. He dropped them on the bed and smoothed the covers, then left. The two halves of the door slid together.

"Christians still zero, lions two," Harper commented. "If you're staying for a while, do you know any traveling salesman stories?"

Evidently not. The man pointed at him, then at the cube chair, repeating the gestures till Harper took the hint and was seated. Next he scratched at his temples with both hands. That the gesture meant nothing to Harper must have shown on his face: the man grimaced briefly, then reached to stroke the band around Harper's hairline, releasing the grip of the metal mesh on his head and pulling it free.

Mesh in hand like a dirty dishrag, the man stood frowning at Harper while the redhead fingered the small puncture marks behind the top of his ears. After speaking nonsense syllables, he turned and removed equipment from one of the attaché cases—something that resembled a hand-held magnifying glass, and a small flashlight, which he shook to make operational. More gestures told Harper to track a moving finger with his eyes, then to focus on the wall while the flashlight shined into his pupils and the man bent over him with the magnifier.

"Twenty/twenty in the left and twenty/fifteen in the right," Harper assured him. "Do you still use charts with big E's?"

The doctor tapped the redhead's lips sharply to bring silence, then closed his eyes while he ran his fingers through Harper's hair. The scar on Harper's temple came in for particular attention. Discarding his examination equipment, the doctor removed a glossy white tile from an interior coat pocket and scratched stenographic symbols on it with a thimble. A tap on one corner freed a leaf of transparent film, which stiffened and became opaque after he pulled it from the tile.

Harper could not resist. He held out both hands till these toys were put into them.

Embarrassment followed as the doctor watched solemnly, rubbing a wrist in a time-killing gesture. The tile was slick-surfaced but rested comfortably in Harper's left palm; the thimble, of greasy plastic, fitted easily onto his index finger, and the purpose of the tiny spur at the tip was obvious. But with what words should a traveler from the past greet the future?

"We came in peace for all mankind," he printed at last, using block letters. Then, as the technique became familiar, he added in script: "Armstrong, Aldrin, Collins, 20 July 1969." He started to hand the pad back, then reclaimed it quickly. Honesty required something more.

"I am Eagle!" the added line read. "Yuri Gagarin, 12 April 1961, Vostok I."

"The best of my culture," Harper said somberly, wishing

the older man could understand. "Whatever you may have done in space, we were the first." He smiled at himself, and returned the pad to the doctor. "See, I'm literate."

The doctor nodded gravely as he pulled the sheet free, stored the note away, and handed him a small red rubber ball.

Harper bounced it on the floor. "How about a yo-yo?"

The doctor took the ball back, clasped Harper's right hand, and returned the ball to his left hand. He mimicked bouncing motions, then frowned as Harper awkwardly cupped his fingers about the ball.

Harper frowned as well, planning, then flipped his wrist over and pushed the hand down. Thrown that way, the ball bounced high enough for him to catch it on his palm as it descended. He held it toward the doctor. "Found me out."

The doctor ignored this. He twisted his arm about, repeating the gestures till Harper copied him, then made additional notes on his pad. His next action was to push up the bathrobe sleeves on both arms and examine the redhead's wrists and elbows. He seemed less surprised by the bullet hole than by the surgical incision and the healed suture lines.

"Regulation catgut," Harper assured him as he pushed gently at the scars. "Used to know the cat."

The other man ignored his words as he added to his notes. Harper shrugged and returned to bouncing the ball.

The doctor tapped him on the shoulder finally to turn his attention to the table. What looked like a telephone book lay beside a low hooded gooseneck lamp. Clamps on each of these held a blue ovoid, which the doctor removed, shook, and replaced.

"Robin's egg," Harper told him. "Yellow pages. Tensor light."

Ignoring him, the doctor positioned the lamp carefully, then opened the book on the table and held the first leaf so that light passed through it. It stayed there when he took his fingers away.

"Off-gray pages," Harper commented. "Ever get tired of plastic?"

"Plrinch," the doctor said clearly. "Plrinch."

A red ball hung between Harper and the illuminated page.

"Hologram," he answered, and waved a hand through the image. "Old stuff, in principle."

"Plrinch," the doctor repeated, pointing to the real ball.

"Pl-rinch," Harper agreed. "But it's still plastic."

The doctor nodded. He poked the corner of the phone book. "Plrinch," a woman's voice said. Two red balls were showing in the air now. "Plrinched." Two blue balls. "Plrinched."

"I feel that way, too," Harper admitted. "Weena, I presume? When do I meet her, Doc?"

"Plrinch." One ball. "Plrinched." Two balls. "Plrinch-ed." Three balls, then four, then two of different sizes and colors. Then one ball again. "Plrinch," the book concluded with evident satisfaction.

"Soprano," Harper said. "Schoolteacher's voice. First grade. Recess time. I really do want my pants." He made dressing gestures. "Pants. Socks."

The doctor sighed and pressed the book again. "Plrinch," it said cheerfully. "Plrinch."

"Plrinch," Harper echoed. "A plrinch of a fellow. Peter, pass the plrinching potatoes, please. I'd like to get plrinched."

The doctor turned the page down, raised another sheet from the book. A new image formed. "Sludag," the book said. It was a very thick book.

"Toy boat," Harper responded. "I want my clothes."

"Sludag."

Harper made dressing gestures again, studiously ignoring the holograms. "My clothes."

"Sludaged," the soprano voice confided. "Sludag-ged."

"Sit-down strike." Harper drew a finger across his lips, mimed lockjaw ostentatiously.

They brought him a tailor.

Days passed. Or, as locally phrased, the sun killed itself often.

The locals were Algherans, Harper had discovered. One at a time, they were "Alghera," with a *jz* sound; when they were several, they were "Alghered," with a hard g. The surrounding city was also Alghera, or perhaps Fohima Alghera. F'a might be a contraction for Fohima, but it required a half-tongue click that was not part of the original word and was not easily mastered.

There were other names to learn: a name for a room, a name for the small apartment to which he was moved, a name for the miniature castle that contained the apartment, a name for the castle courtyard, names for some of the castle staff, for the breeches and shoes and tunics he was given, for the Velcro-like flaps and sticky seals used to fasten clothing.

The names were not always sensible ones; the mesh cap he had to wear when he left his apartment had one that apparently translated as "people warily watching unsuspecting person." This meant little till inspiration made Harper mime duck hunting. The rapid agreement this produced provided him with another translation: "ambush." He soon learned that the Algherans had distinct names for four different types of ambushes, and settled on "person-blind."

There were no names for beards or moustaches. But his own facial hair did not grow back, so perhaps such words were not needed.

And there was no name for "time machine." He suspected he was not apt to see that return, either. Certainly, whenever he tried to ask about the device the Algherans had taken from him, he provoked only bland stares.

They also wouldn't teach him a word for "theft."

The doctor's name was Niculponoc Swelminor ha'Nyjuc, shortened to Sweln. He was a specialist in learning disabilities, Harper had inferred, not actually a medical doctor, though he did seem knowledgeable about head injuries.

The hard-eyed elder man was Birlin Borictar ha'Dicovys. He seemed to be a government employee of some type, but a constant stream of young men and women visited him in the evenings. Harper glimpsed his living quarters once, finding them no more luxurious than his own, but with shelves lined with holographic books. The gunman, disarmed since the first day, was Garl ha'Dicovys. The nervous valet was Klard ha'Dicovys. None of them were related.

Borct had a wife—more exactly a "hearth-mate" or "fire-sharer." She lived in the countryside, and there were no children. She was a Mrs. Birlin rather than a Mrs. ha'Dicovys, Harper learned after the laughter stopped. Dicovys was a *Sept*, or clan, made up entirely of women. Children, single men such as Garl and Klard, and men who married women in the Sept took the Sept name with the *ha* prefix. There was also a *tra'Dicovys*, a man elected by all the married men to lead the Sept.

Nyjuc was a Sept, too. Sweln had two daughters, Onnul and Cyomit.

His wife had "risen." He would say no more.

Harper finally pushed Klard for an explanation. The hemming and hawing this produced did not have precise English equivalents, but basically it was "like, well, you know, how it is, when you aren't—when things up and stop on you, you see, so you aren't, uh, well, really able, to, uh, at the end, you know? Then you rise up to Cimon. And Nicole, too, you know?" Expressed that way, Harper decided he knew.

His own name they transliterated at first as "Timithial Lin ha'Ruppir." When he was more knowledgeable, he tried to correct this to Harper Timothy-Allan, but Sweln and Borct would not agree to a two-word name. "Harper Timothy ha'Orphanage" outraged them, after he made the mistake of explaining the last word, and "Harper Timothy ha'Veteran's-Administration was rejected even before he could provide a translation. He became Harper Timithiallin ha'Ruppir, and learned to tolerate "Timt" as a nickname.

The language was not Algheran. The language was simply "Language" or "Speaking" or "Speech."

There were other languages. *Lopritl*, or Lopritian, was spoken by those who were *Loprited*. Loprit was somewhere in the west, or had been in the west—it didn't seem to exist anymore, though Lopritians still did. Digging for an analogy, Harper had remembered Rome, which had continued to exist long after the existence of the Roman Empire. But he suspected that the comparison had flaws.

Another language was "Common." It was named as an example. No one he met spoke Common.

There was not a language called "Personal." Some people *used* such a language, Sweln explained one evening, but they did not *speak* it.

The distinction was minuscule in Harper's eyes, but perhaps the flaw was in his understanding. "All persons, they use Personal?" he inquired haltingly.

"All persons use Personal. All people *not* use Personal," he was told. The doctor's face suggested his question had been silly.

Harper drummed on the table top and frowned at the window beyond the doctor. The sun was setting, the short cold day at an end. Supper had included meat in a highly spiced white sauce, and the taste was still in his mouth. If he were at the window now, he might see a handful of people walking through the nearby park, workers going home to their meals, perhaps, though most of them were women. *I'm never going to understand these people.*

In the courtyard at midday, Harper had been raking leaves into a bonfire. There had been voices on the other side of the wall while the leaves burned, speaking the language three times as fast as he could, with one word in ten making sense. If he had had space enough to get up to speed, and the use of two hands, he might have scrambled halfway up the stone facing and found a grip and—

"More words," Borct had told him kindly, coming on him in the courtyard, reading his expression and placing a hand on his shoulder. "More words, young friend. We Algherans can give many things, but we are not comfortable with strangers. You learn more words, and you soon touch many people. By Cimon and Nicole, I say this. Many people, soon." And that had been a promise, he understood.

Keep trying, chum. "Like this?" he asked. He scratched his head several times, cleared his throat, drummed the table top again, and rubbed his palms together. "Not words speech?"

"No." The doctor was curt. "That is not it."

"Finger speech?" Harper suggested. "Hand talk? For they people without ear using? With ears needing repair?"

Sweln nodded, which meant no. He rose from his chair to mount a page in one of the hologram primers, turned the reading light to show a battle scene, and searched over the image carefully till he found a man with twisted palms and splayed fingers on a small hill. "This," he said, jabbing the man with a narrow finger. "You mean this."

"Stingla muor," the book said in a baritone voice.

"Steenglah more," Harper repeated dutifully, not certain as to whether that meant "battle" or "unleashed hell" or "greeting a mother-in-law."

"Stingla muor sfallzty talk," the doctor said disdainfully, closing the book. "There's your 'finger speech.'"

On a "stingla muor" one stole the use of speech, Harper translated. Or one used shameful makeshift substitutes for speech. Ah—improvised hand gestures were used in combat when voice wouldn't carry.

But what was "Personal"? He repeated the original question.

"No people use Personal," Sweln repeated. "Only persons use Personal."

Harper drummed the table top again. "Speak to me Personal," he demanded at last. When Sweln only stared, he asked once more.

"I have, child," the man said softly. "I use Personal on you, but you do not use Personal and do not know it."

Light came. "You are a person."

The doctor shook his head—a yes.

"Me a person."

That got a nod. "No."

He had erred somehow. The term he had translated as "person" did not mean that. It meant a class of person, such as "citizen" or "music lover." Or "ruler."

"Borct is a person," he guessed. "Klard?"

"No, Timt. Not you, not Borct, not Klard, not Garl."

Scratch one bright idea.

"No words speech," the doctor said helpfully. "Inside head only."

Harper swallowed. The ideas that were suggested hit hard.

But suspicion had to be checked against reality. "Tell me what in my inside head I hold."

"Sludag," Sweln said calmly. He tapped the base of the lamp, switching it off. "A red boat with a white sail. Green water is around. Now blue. Now the boat tips and sinks, leaving just the water. Are you comfortable?"

"Not hardly," Harper said in English, staring at the monster. "Oh, migod. Telepathy. Be damned." He turned to stare at an unresponding wall, breathing heavily as half-formed hopes and anticipations collapsed.

Person meant "telepath." Now the other man's careful nuances made sense. Scraps of incomprehensible disjointed conversations between the doctor and others came back to him. A thousand petty mysteries perished. *Telepathy. I'll be pretty small potatoes here. No way to compete with that. All this time learning words—how futile. God!* "More'n a toy boat's sunk," he muttered ruefully.

"Swallow," the doctor insisted, handing him a green capsule. "You're pale." Another hand went to Harper's forehead, then to his wrist. A babble of still-alien words followed, then: "You must rest! Now! Do you feel body-broken?" Genuine concern showed on his face, and Harper let himself be half carried, half pushed into his bedroom.

Once there, however, good sense returned to him. Sweln ha'Nyjuc was four inches shorter and fifty pounds lighter—

almost a third of the man-weight that was the local unit of mass. The smaller man had no business carting him about.

"Sit," he snarled, waving the doctor to a collapsing cube in the corner. He concentrated, stilling the sounds of his heartbeats and breath, then took his own pulse by a clock on the fireplace mantel. *Twenty-six, multiply by four, then remember an Algheran minute has almost ninety-seconds. Well within bounds.* "I'm good," he said calmly.

"Please, lie down." The doctor was seated but not assuaged.

Not exactly an ogre's behavior, Harper reflected. He stretched out on the bed to satisfy the man. "You see inside me, you know I'm good."

Sweln nodded rapidly. "Hard. It's not comfortable inside your head. Hard parts same as people. Soft things different. Shapes are strangers."

The brain circuitry was the same, Harper translated, but the thoughts were different. The concepts that underlay his thoughts were strange. "You see more good tomorrow? And the tomorrow of tomorrow?"

"Yes. But still not easy then. And not when the"—garble—"is on."

Spied on, Harper thought icily. *A prison where even thoughts are not private. They kept this secret from me.*

"I speak?" The doctor sounded apologetic.

He should be. "Go ahead." Harper did not look for words in Speech.

"You are not comfortable with me."

"I am not comfortable. Cimon and Nicole! I am not comfortable." That was blasphemy of some sort; he hoped it would convey the message.

"Do you very not like all persons?"

That sums it up nicely. Unfortunately, he had not the vocabulary to be ironic. Another thought hit him while he was searching for words.

"Your children. Onnul. Cyomit. Are they persons?"

"Yes. Onnul, since before—seven years now. Cyomit, soon."

"The green on your forehead. That shows you are a person?"

"Yes. All persons in Alghera have the"—the last word was unfamiliar.

So all the telepaths were tagged. That brought another question. "You are a person. Borct is not a person. Who is—bigger?

Higher?" Idiom escaped him; he waved to show that he reached for words.

"The ha'Dicovys." The doctor seemed surprised by the question.

"You and Garl. Who is bigger?"

That took thought. Sweln rubbed his wrist as if to uncover answers. "Bigger, smaller, same," he said finally, and snapped his fingers.

Harper leaned outward. "People down here," he said, waving his hand at the floor, then up. "Persons up here. Yes or no?"

"No. No. No." The doctor was emphatic about that and seemed to Harper to be almost terrified. "Persons not bigger than people. Nowhere are persons bigger than people. Persons comfortable, do not want bigger. Do not say they are. Not say Borct, I say persons bigger. No! They not." He was leaning forward, shaking, babbling. "No no no no," he kept repeating. "Not bigger, no no." That much Harper recognized. That much, and the children's names.

This was panic.

The big redhead swallowed hard, fighting back the dry heaves, the horrible familiarity. He scrambled to his feet to pat an old man on the shoulder, to say what could be said, to do all that could be done. "Okay, Papa-san. No biggie. Okay, man, no problem, no problem. It'll be all right, all right."

Maybe it didn't matter that the words couldn't be understood.

Maybe it didn't matter that he knew he had to be lying.

God. Oh, God, the future wasn't supposed to be this way.

CHAPTER FIVE

He probably wasn't supposed to hear the muted snuffling sound.

But he did. Harper weighed options, decided that responsibility counted for more than politeness, and pushed aside the juvenile history text he had been leafing through. Away from the light of his desk lamp, pictures and script faded instantly. The pages were only gray film.

Like mud. Wasn't any clearer when the light was on it, either. He sighed, accompanying another subdued whimper. *Over my head. I don't have enough words yet.*

But was he going to understand the Algherans even when he had an adequate vocabulary?

He fished for sandals and slipped his feet into them. *Probably not.*

The social setup was too different. Intellectually, he could grasp that a Sept functioned as both family and corporation and that schools and a criminal justice system did not have to be run by the central government. He could even see sense in the Algherans' separation of political power, vested in a democratically elected Muster and prime ministerial Warder, and economic power, which resided with the Septs and guilds. That did not give the almost intuitive understanding of the system that a citizen would take for granted.

Septs operated under customs, he had been told. He gave that a few seconds of thought as he scratched the itching spots on his swollen left arm and reached for a floppy-sleeved overshirt.

An Association had formal bylaws and no honorifics but otherwise seemed the same. A third of the people were in Septs, and most of the rest were in Associations, he had been told. Was that difference sufficient to explain the higher social standing of Sept members? It seemed unlikely. Why were there secret Associations?

Why was it so hard to converse with telepaths, so hard to get them to express opinions? What had caused Sweln ha'Nyjuc's panic two months ago? Why didn't the telepaths play a bigger role in government? He still could not answer those questions.

Why are we all wearing metal caps to keep our minds from being read?

And what are they doing with my time machine?

Speculation was useless, he admitted as he slipped his arms into the shirt-sleeves. At least Borct agreed that the machine existed, which was an improvement over his past behavior. And Harper's sword had been returned inside an expensive-looking scabbard, which indicated some trust in him. Maybe he would get answers to his questions before Cimon closed up shop.

Only thing real clear is that Algherans seem to like moving around.

He glanced at the clock that hung on the wall above the sword. Three watches down from the lights, and the hand in the upper half: almost four watches then, with one to go. Say daylight came at seven A.M.—then it was almost two in the morning. *Two A.M.*, he repeated mentally. That seemed the alien time measurement now. *December, maybe*. That seemed alien also.

Any rate, they keep moving me. But a house beats a room in a Sept lodge or one of those communal dormitories. Not bad here, a-tall. In this room, the floor had been carpeted with long soft fur; the rest of the house had wood floors and throw rugs.

And the medical stuff beats the VA. He ran his left thumb

down the center of his chest to seal the shirt, then flexed the fingers on that hand, marveling at the dexterity the Algherans had given back to him. *Except there's nothing to do for an itch except scratch.*

Algheran house-wear was little better than pajamas for holding warmth, so he slipped a short cape over his head, grunting slightly as his hands groped for the interior pockets and pulled the garment about him.

Batman, he told himself as the doorway dilated. *Yeah, two-tenths of a year ago I was a mild-mannered student, and now—I've gone batty.*

The radiant heating that made the bedrooms habitable was turned off at night in other rooms. The air was cold, dry, touched but not tainted by spice scents. The sounds he made vanished into the darkness.

He turned the rheostats outside his door until there was a glimmer of light in the front living room—it was considered good manners to let the world know when you were awake—then brought full illumination to the back living room. Only a tracing of rime showed on the windows between front and back rooms, but his breath was white. Summer furniture hooded for the winter could be seen dimly, like a child's hobgoblins lurking below the surface of a mirror. *Must be under ten degrees in there. Should have asked for central heat with my two hundred squares.*

A clown's face was buried in the high opposite wall: shuttered ventilation-duct eyes in a white stucco wall, a protruding storage cabinet above a brick-fireplace mouth and concrete-slab tongue. Coincidence, imagination, or a builder's joke? The latter, he suspected; Algheran notions of art seemed pretty primitive.

The empty fireplace gaped accusingly. The weather wasn't cold enough yet for the fireplace to be used, he had been told. Wood was a scarce resource, fire an unnecessary luxury.

I'd trade twenty of these physical fitness nuts for one good Franklin stove. He scratched again, then rapped lightly on an interior door. "Cyomit?"

"Y-y—yes?" In Speech, the stutter sounded like a sneeze.

"You want to come out? Let your sister sleep."

There was a pause in the sniffles, then a creaking sound as weight was lifted from one of the crinkly Algheran mattresses. "All right." The tone was mournful.

The door opened on one side just enough to let a small girl slide through, then lowered to shut off the darkened bedroom.

"Good morning, little person," Harper said politely. He had learned another word for "person" and had confused the two; the other word was a contraction of the Algheran phrase meaning "telepath." *Teep* would do as a translation. That the longer term remained in the language eased interpretation: *Negro—nigger. Jew—yid. Telepath—Teep.*

He forced a smile. "How are you, little telepath?"

Cyomit squeezed her eyes against the light. She was barefooted, in blue pajamas. Her hair was dark and disheveled. A tiny hand tried to wipe up a line of moisture that ran across her left cheek. "I'm sorry I woke you up, ha'Ruppir." The voice was small also, apologetic, aimed at the floor.

Harper grunted. "You are—" And what was the Speech for "*absolved*"? Come to think of it, were there terms in the language at all for "guilty" or "innocent"? He hadn't come across them yet.

Try again. "Not you, kid. My arm was itching; I wasn't sleeping anyhow." *You're going to get your death of cold, little girl, no matter what everyone tells me. Kids!* "How is the head?"

"Hurts." Cyomit's voice came through almost as a whimper. "As if it's big, then small, then big. I feel squeezed inside my head. It doesn't stop. I can't sleep. And I'm so tired."

Headache. And they don't have aspirin. Operate without anesthetics and regenerate dead nerves, but they don't have aspirin. And what can I tell them? Just refine some handy acetylsalicylic acid, people. It's in a certain kind of tree bark, and sorry I don't know which kind, because I never thought it was important. Sure.

I feel useless. And with Sweln gone . . .

"Let's see." Cyomit's forehead was cool to the touch, which was standard among these people. *No fever, at least.* "I can put little ice on your head. That much help it is not, but it will, uh, turn your thoughts sideways. You want me to do?"

Cyomit sniffled again and shook her head.

Permission, he remembered. His arm went out and pulled her into the shelter of the cloak. "Let us hit the kitchen."

Like a daughter of my own. A first grader, he thought wryly as he steered the girl before him. *Fourteen years old, acting six right now. Well, she looks about six. Cold weather—they must all mature late.*

Cyomit mumbled to herself, bumping against his leg.

"Hmmm," Harper said back. A murmur was the same in both English and Speech, and equally useful at such moments. He patted the child on the shoulder, feeling unreasonably content.

"You get sleep tonight, sleep late," he suggested.

Cyomit nodded slowly. "School. My tutor won't know."

"One day. He will live with it. He understand, no?"

"She!" The correction was emphatic. "She won't understand. She is from Dicovys, not Nyjuc, and—"

"Thought that—never mind. You change schools?"

Cyomit mumbled. The answer seemed to be yes.

Another mystery. He had been told that general education was the responsibility of the Septs and Associations. Harper mumbled back.

"Let us see." He turned on the kitchen lights and inventoried cabinets mentally. *Plenty of food, and no apples. Fine.* Stove, counter tops, dinner table and six wooden stools, sink—the kitchen even looked like a kitchen, and that was cause for good feeling as well. "Take church seat, kid."

The kitchen window was spring-loaded, with a simple latch to fasten it. Harper opened it with his left hand, willingly accepting some pain in the elbow for the pleasure of exercise. Ledges inside the window box held perishables and a shallow ice tray. The outer window was white crystal, winter-swollen so it could not be raised, so cold that he felt the warmth flowing out of his fingertips. *Damn, man. You saw two ice ages already. Why'd you end up stopping in a third one?*

It was not yet an ice age, of course. Several thousand years would pass before this land was glacier-covered. But they had assured him that the time would come. *Fifty million people on the whole planet now. Just enough land and resources to support them in middling comfort.*

At the peak of the Great Winter, there could be no more than ten million.

Harper twisted the ice tray mechanically, dropping a slab into a sheet of cellophanelike wrap, then refilled the tray from a sink tap. *Domestic, aren't we? Well, why make extra work for Onnul?*

Additional inspiration struck as he replaced the tray. He

took a container of milk from the window box, stirred with a knife to break up the top layer of coagulated butterfat, then filled a small pan. The pan was metal, fabulously expensive, and lined with the ubiquitous gray plastic. The stove top was clear glass, supported on unmarked canisters. Harper pressed a button at random, then placed the pan above a red flashing canister. The flashing ended, but the red glow continued. Nothing else indicated that the stove was in operation. *One lousy Franklin stove.*

One oil well, while I'm at it. One nuclear power plant.

Those didn't exist either. The Algherans made do with firewood and sunshine. Harper remembered the looted nuclear waste repository and grimaced. The human race had lived on scraps for a long, long time.

A low-energy society was metal-poor because refining ore is energy-intensive. By rights, such a society would have a low level of technology. That the Algherans had reached industrialization seemed a miracle.

"Here." He put the ice against Cyomit's forehead, waited till hesitant fingers rose to hold it in place, then stood behind the girl and rubbed her neck and shoulders.

Puberty was far away for Cyomit. Her skin was clear, almost transparent, free of the touch of acne that still lingered on her sister. Her bones were birdlike, close to the skin. *Scrawny*, he thought. But brutal honesty could be tempered by affection. *Tiny little girl. So small and fragile.*

"Am not," Cyomit protested. "I'm going to be bigger."

Harper chuckled. A cartoon Harper appeared in his mind, staring awestruck at a Cyomit grown thirty feet tall. "Like that?"

"Like that." Mollified, Cyomit rubbed the ice across her face.

Tiny and fragile, the man thought again, making the girl stand as a metaphor for the entire human race. *So many of us in my time, with so many hopes. Thick as fleas on a sick dog, with about as many real worries. Now there's so few people, they could be wiped out by a couple of disasters. They don't rule the world anymore, and no one remembers hope. I came expecting to envy these people. And instead . . .* Feeling without words filled him: pity for the race of men, for the child under his hands. *Where did it all go wrong?*

"I say it firm to you, you can slice school day, yes?"

She considered that. "Yes, but Onnul—"

"All settled. I say it firm, stay home. Tell tutor, shout at me."

"Can't. She isn't to know of you. That's why the ha'Dicovys—I can't talk about it."

"Good," Harper growled. "Tell tutor, all ha'Dicovys, for his reasons." A smile followed. "Sure Borct think of some good answer. Always does when I have unhappy-making question. Good for him, keeping in practice."

"Hurts," Cyomit protested, jerking her head. "Too hard."

"I know." Harper dropped his hands glumly.

The pan on the stove was hissing. He poured hot milk into gray plastic mugs, rubbed the lip of the pan, then pulled loose a gossamer film, which he wadded up and dumped through a hole in the wall. The light inside the stove had vanished when he had lifted the pan. It did not return when he replaced the pan. The stove top remained cold.

"Drink up, kid." He handed Cyomit one of the mugs and sipped from the other. *Awful stuff, like spoiled eggnog. And I think they add rotten grass to flavor it. Is the milk always like this? Is it the grass your cattle graze on? Does the milk come from cows?*

Cyomit did not answer. Evidently her embryonic telepathic powers had switched off for the moment. She was drinking the milk, however; a demure white moustache rimmed her upper lip.

Of course, they wouldn't call it a moustache. He could not be sure whether she expected the milk to affect her or was simply obeying orders. The latter, he suspected, taking a seat and smiling at her.

Penny for your thoughts. That was in English, a private irony he could not hope to translate. *What's it like?* passed through his mind next. *What is seeing into another person's head like?* But that also had to be rejected. Subtle questions about telepathy were ignored, he had discovered; direct inquiries provoked embarrassment and apologetic refusals to answer.

Sex and romance were also taboo subjects, he suspected. Of course, he had not yet read any Algheran literature, nor did he have the necessary background to appreciate the symbols this culture might use in its art. But he had not seen many displays of spontaneous affection among the people he had observed; he had not heard much talk of boyfriends from either

Onnul or Cyomit; the casual references to women he had heard from Klard and Garl had been few.

"Season-taken" was apparently a local euphemism for love, as if to imply that all passions must perish. The term had connotations that were ribald and slightly disreputable; any piece of folly or stupidity was apt to be attributed to the one responsible being season-taken.

Still, these people do form families and cling together. And Sweln has never remarried, which implies a lot of loyalty. The fact that they don't speak of something is no proof that it does not exist.

"Bad thoughts about your dad being missing?" he asked. Surely that could be asked without causing distress.

Cyomit nodded, finishing off her milk. "Onnul talked to him earlier, and I listened in on part. He's fine. And I'm used to him being gone, ha'Ruppir, really, so I don't worry."

"Oh." Harper nodded gravely. "You have pretty special dad, do you know? When they cut my arm open—or am I usual patient and boring you?"

"It's all right, ha'Ruppir. You can tell me if you want."

Put that way, he didn't want. Harper chuckled grimly and forced himself to ignore psychosomatic twinges in his swollen arm. "I think it old story to you, even if not me. But in my time, we put people to sleeping before they were cut into. We didn't have anyone keeping them from pain."

"Different then," Cyomit agreed. "I'm ready for bed now." She stood abruptly. "Thank you for looking after me, ha'Ruppir. I'm sorry I intruded in your house."

Harper blinked. "Your house, kid, is it not?" He took the mugs and replaced them in cabinets after pitching the wads of plastic inner layer. "I am the intruder." *Damn, it's cold!* he thought. *Even with this silly cape on, I'm nearly frozen.*

"Oh, no, they moved us." Cyomit looked around gravely. "We were in a Nyjuc kennel before. We'll go back to it someday, but this is much nicer. Onnul says it's because—we owe it to you."

Harper leaned backward on a counter top and grunted. Borct had not lied to him, he reflected, but words had definitely been used that had misled him. Perhaps that was an accident. Probably it did not matter, but this should be cleared up. "You don't owe me anything," he explained. "Things go another way. Borct and your dad made thoughts that I should live with family for some time, is better way of learning Speech and others. I thought—"

"No, it wasn't Daddy. This is political, and he couldn't decide such a thing. He wanted to keep us away from things like you. So it had to be the ha'Dicovys. Like my school." Cyomit was supremely matter-of-fact. "Good night, ha'Ruppir."

More mysteries, Harper realized unhappily. "Tell your sister she is wrong." *And she should have known that was wrong. The time we've spent together . . . Why?* But there were reasons for inattention, he understood suddenly, feeling unhappier.

Cyomit nodded and looked at him with concern. "Onnul doesn't have a future hearth-sharer, ha'Ruppir. She hasn't decided on a man yet."

He grinned wryly. "That is relief."

"I know. Good night." Cyomit moved toward the doorway.

The grin and embarrassment stayed on his face, then faded as he remembered one more mystery. "Cyomit, before you go. The history book I was reading. I looked at the back, and I gather Alghera got into some kind of war about six or seven years ago. Who won, and when did it end?"

The little girl looked at him as if for the first time. "It hasn't ended. Good night, ha'Ruppir."

CHAPTER SIX

Another morning.

"The Alliance reports to the Algheran people!" the manikin on the desk top announced. "Killed in the fighting at Hendanner's Pass yesterday were twelve members of the Forest Guard: Bendar Chilschur ha'Cuhyon, Bendar Dselturim ha'Cuhyon . . ."

The names meant nothing. Harper leaned over, scowling, as the tiny man shimmered, then vanished. The voice continued.

A mountainside lay before him now, a yard-high miniature beautifully modeled with tiny treetops protruding from impossibly white snow, carefully drawn brown and black lines that were roads, and precisely scaled frozen lakes. A perfect Christmas gift for a child with a model railroad. Or was this February?

Men smaller than ants trudged across a handkerchieflike expanse of snow, desperately racing toward a row of half-inch trees. A black marble and other man-ants waited for them in one of the handkerchief's folds.

The announcer was still at last. The scene was soundless. The curses and gasping breaths of running men were only in Harper's memory.

One of the walking ants stopped moving, fell over, and lay on his side, without drama. After a pause, the remaining ants in his file continued.

A dragonfly fuselage darted high above the black marble, dropping abruptly as it entered the anti-induction field, then recovering as momentum carried it out of range. On each pass a dozen specks plummeted toward the ground.

"Casualties among your 7th Falltroop were reported as minor," the announcer's voice told Harper. "Seven killed, fifteen wounded. Dead are—"

"Timt! Breakfast! And Tolipim's here." The voice was Onnul's.

Fingernail-sized parachutes appeared above the falling specks. Centimeter-wide pits opened on the slopes. The handkerchief shook, toppling ant forms about.

"Timt!"

Harper sighed and tapped the button on the side of his desk. The announcer's voice vanished. His desk top was only a desk top.

"Coming," he answered.

The future wasn't supposed to be this way.

Tolipim ha'Ruijac was satisfied with the present. When Harper arrived in the kitchen after restocking the living room fire, he was scarfing down the last of a piece of sweetbread and reaching for another with the cheerful abandon of a short man who never hopes to see the downside of one and a quarter manweights again. With the unfilled portion of his mouth he was busily explaining to Onnul his prospects for promotion in the coming year. Plagues, homicides, and joyously awaited senility among the senior faculty were soon to do wonders for his career, it appeared. His eyes were occupied with Cyomit's homework. He was still in his parka, so the visit was to be a brief one.

A normal morning, Harper decided from the doorway. Algheran soldiers fought against an Alliance breakthrough a hundred miles to the west, and the newscasts came from the enemy, but domestic life continued. *A fool's paradise*, he judged unhappily. *No protests as far as I can tell, no demonstrations. No way they can win this war, but*— He frowned in lieu of a sigh, then overcame his hesitation and entered the room. *Count your blessings, chum.*

Sweln was absent, but that was an ordinary occurrence lately.

Even while browning and buttering sweetbread on the stove, Onnul was her Scandinavian chorus girl self, not a long blond hair out of place, impeccably dressed in blue and gold as if prepared to go to work. The green plaque on her forehead might have been placed there as jewelry. Cyomit's dark hair was already threatening to escape from its loosely braided ponytail, and there was orange-colored jam on one cheek. Except for the hair, she might have been a little boy dressed for school in blue slacks and sweater, but she was—what? Fourteen now? Fifteen? He had the impression her birthday had gone by a few ten-day periods ago, but no one had drawn attention to it.

Over the headaches now, he thought gratefully. She had become a full-time telepath, and he had been there during the transformation. He felt as much a proud father as Sweln.

The too-large plaque on Cyomit's narrow forehead reduced the pleasure, however, and the silver mesh that lay on her book bag brought guilt. *Poor damned kid. A God-given gift and she gets branded for it and then isn't allowed to use it outside the house. My fault.*

"Add X squared over two outside the integral, subtract integral XdX," Tolp was explaining. He was smiling—that was the normal expression on his young-old face. Silver wire showed in his own hair. "Simplify. Now we've got a cubic in X. Which factors. A quadratic, multiplied by, yes, a linear expression, which is the derivative of the quadratic. So evaluating the integral is simple. Then we add this thing and—you see?" He waved eagerly at the writing block with a piece of bread, threatening to smear it with butter and jam.

What was his function? Harper wondered, not for the first time. A teacher, according to Tolp. A colleague of Borct's, Sweln had told him. And Borct was a functionary of the Institute for the Study of Land Reclamation Issues, an adviser to the government. Why did Tolp come around each morning? Not to spy, surely. Not to impress Onnul. Not to check Cyomit's homework.

"But why?" Cyomit asked herself as she pulled the paper away from danger. "Teacher says—"

"Because term by term is so ugly, so meaningless. And often less significant in a physical sense. So when you recognize a simple pattern—a simple beautiful pattern—here, give me the block, please. Let me show you some examples."

"Good morning, Timt." Onnul's voice, halfway between

alto and soprano, hovered somewhere between warmth and amusement.

He forced a smile, contrasting her appearance with his own rumpled pajamas and uncombed hair. *Ah, well, I'd look like a slept-in bed next to her no matter how I dressed. But I should make a better effort.* "Morning, peoples. Onnul, how's your dad?"

"Not back yet. That accident case at—Cyomit, where was it?"

"Whitelost Fields. North of Port Homefree." Cyomit slurped fruit juice. "They had to get 'nother surgeon 'cause the first was drunk all the time and the settlement chief hadn't reported it and Daddy said—"

"That's enough, dear," Onnul interrupted. "How are things with the barbarians today, Timt?"

Harper grunted. "Well enough." *Newfoundland*, he translated. The capital was cold enough. That far north, Sweln ha'Nyjuc must have been surrounded by masochists.

For a frozen second, he traded glances with Tolp, as if each man were daring the other to notice the silent conversation of Onnul and Cyomit. *Only two telepaths here, and we all know what's being said.*

Hell of a way to run a civilization.

"I think the barbarian is ready to sack the city and carry off all the beautiful women," he said lightly. "Are you two packed yet?"

Onnul smiled. "I need to do some shopping first. And Cyomit really must attend school today."

"I'll go away with Timt! I'll have my own room then and —Can I have some time to pack? And can I take my—" One party to the reprimand had not taken it to heart.

"Cyomit!" Onnul looked and sounded scandalized. "I won't have this."

Harper swooped down on the smaller girl and raised her till her head bumped the ceiling. "Your very own room," he promised, jostling Cyomit up and down. "And a sexy set of pajamas. Two sets. And all the sin and depravity your little heart desires. And your big sister will be so jealous, she'll never speak to—"

Cyomit squealed with glee.

"I will not be jealous," the big sister insisted.

"Onnul will be jealous. Onnul will be jealous," Cyomit chanted. "Onnul will be jealous."

"I will *not*! Tolp, will you take the child to school? Timt! Put her down."

"Onnul is jealous. Onnul is jealous." Cyomit wriggled happily.

Harper chuckled and lowered her to the floor, letting go reluctantly. "Maybe today you should go to school. We'll run away and make your sister mad tomorrow. *I got to have kids of my own someday.*

"Promise?"

"Well. One of these days. We don't want Onnul to be too mad."

"That's because you really want *her*, not me. But—"

"Cyomit!"

"Yes, Onnul. I'll go to school. But Tolp says my homework is all wrong and I have to change *everything*, so if my tutor—"

"Cyomit!"

"Yes, Onnul. Come on, Tolp." Cyomit briskly slipped papers back into her school bag and scurried around to Harper and her sister for parting hugs. "Can we have rabbit for supper, Onnul? Come on, Tolp."

Tolp stopped in the doorway, resisting small girl tugs from the antechamber. "You'll be here early afternoon, Timt? Been playing with your gizmo, got something to show you. Cimon guard."

"The child," Onnul said severely. "I'm sorry, Timt."

Harper poured more cider. "The child is a nice kid. Don't worry."

"May I?" Onnul pushed back hair with one hand and held a cup out with the other. "She shouldn't—"

"Shouldn't be a little girl acting like a little girl? Hmmm?"

"But in front of—"

Harper sighed. *I doubt that Tolp was upset.* "Children should be strangled at birth. All of them, without exception, and kept that way till they turn eighteen. Normal and Teep alike."

"That's rather drastic." Onnul sipped cider demurely.

"That's us barbarians. Simple solutions for simple problems."

"Well, I'm sorry about it."

Harper sighed again. *You and me both, babe. Change the topic.*

"You were up late last night. Your arm was hurting."

Hard to keep a secret from a Teep, isn't it? Harper flexed his left arm and stared at the elbow. "Some itching still."

"Timt, this isn't normal! Talk to Dad when—"

"I'm just a little sensitive to pain, that's all."

"But you shouldn't have to suffer!"

"It's just an itch, Onnul. And just now and then. A cheap price for a working arm."

"Well, have Dad look at you. He'll be back tomorrow."

Harper scowled. "He's due some rest. I'll get by."

"Don't be silly. He'll be happy to. And we owe—"

"You owe me nothing. Thank Borct if you think this is so great."

"Borct! That man is—"

"A schemer. A politician. An empire builder. Yeah. I get hints."

"I wish." Onnul sighed. "I just wish."

"Lots of things to wish. Oh, well. You were shopping today?"

"It's a meat day. I have to shop."

"No quarrel." *Where does the money come from?* he wondered. *Not from Sweln's pay, is it?* "You want to check my homework this evening? Or shall I ask Cyomit to do it?"

Onnul frowned. "I hate homework. What is it?"

Harper grinned lopsidedly. "Arithmetic with fractions. A few more days and I'll be up to fourth-grade arithmetic. Isn't that exciting?"

"Very. If you say so." Onnul gathered plates, stripped off the outer layers and threw the breakfast waste down the trash chute. The clean dishes went back to the cabinets. "You're a ward of the Institute. Didn't you know? We all are, while you're here, or until—" Spoons and forks went into the sonic sterilizer. Sweetbread and jam went into their containers. Arctic cold probed as she thrust the cider jar into the window box; the cold retreated but left the smell of winter behind. "If it were . . . essential . . . you could sell your sword, couldn't you?"

The big man raised an eyebrow. Be a mercenary? "Go Blankshield? I thought this was the final war." In another world, he remembered, there had been antidraft demonstrations with signs reading "Girls say YES to Men who say NO."

"Sell the sword," Onnul repeated, pushing bread crumbs

into the sink and flushing them away. "It's almost pure iron. You could live in comfort many years. Lewd thoughts are not good for you, Tim'thy." The breakfast cleanup was done. Onnul vanished into the antechamber.

Well, if I'm rich, you could run away with me. We could demonstrate the error of my ways, and I'd promise not to ask for help with homework.

"I don't think that would be practical." Onnul's voice was soon followed by Onnul, bulky in a parka, with silver glinting in her golden hair. "I hate this thing," she said, worrying the Teepblind into place. "It messes up my hair so. Run away with Cyomit, Timt. She thinks helping you do homework is funny."

"It *is* funny," Harper admitted. "But she's too young to really enjoy improper fractions."

Onnul smiled, then kissed him on the forehead. "Don't do anything sinful without me. Cimon guard."

Cold air entered from the antechamber. Wind made blustering sounds. A door slammed. Then he was alone.

"A home away from home," he muttered at the empty kitchen. "Eighty thousand years, ninety thousand, and I walk into a Cimon-taken sitcom."

The last word was in English. There was no Algheran equivalent.

"Sell the sword," he muttered. "Or shave it down. Might have to."

Algheran charity was not likely to last much longer.

"Need a job." He grimaced. "What a rotten future."

A chime sounded. The day was one day tenth old, and he had a full watch—two day tenths—to go before afternoon. There was time to work on improper fractions. Time to—

Not a whole lot of time.

The war was not going well.

"'For I dipped into the future,'" he said sarcastically.

"Far as human eye could see,
Saw the Vision of the world, and all the wonder that would be."
Saw our damned descendants struggle, divided both by race and creed;
Sensed the fear that glaciation made normal men a lesser breed.
Walked straight into unholy mess, when proud defiance was hurled,
At the Parliament of Man, the Federation of the world.

Where the common sense of most means waiting for disasters
Inflicted by the vicious earth, lumbered by Teep-served masters.

"Oh, well." *No sense blaming it all on Tennyson.*

Irony held no cures for the situation. More learning, perhaps.

"'Knowledge comes but wisdom lingers.'" What had the Algherans taught him, and what part was true?

Folklore, just about all of it. Twelve hundred years ago the world had been populated entirely by barely literate nomads. A long stretch of bad weather had forced tighter organization on some peoples and had given rise to knowledge-preserving bodies such as Alghera's Institute. A fixed abode for a handful of wise men had become a town, then a city, then the capital of a nation. Other cultures organized in self-defense. Civilization was born.

Had the Algherans been first, as they claimed?

They might have been, he conceded. "First of the Fifth Era."

There had been previous eras, previous times when men built cities. There was evidence for that, archaeological and theological.

To end eternal war, it is agreed by the telepaths and normal men that never again shall telepaths establish a separate state and exercise their dominion over men. This Compact shall be preserved by the thoughts and actions of both human races and witnessed by the tiMantha lu Duois. The penalty for violation, in thought or action, shall be death.

To the end the Second Eternal War, the Great Compact is reaffirmed by the Teeps and the Normals. It is also agreed by the Teeps and the Normals that never again shall Teeps employ their abilities in the service of national states and thus exercise their dominion over men. This Compact shall be preserved by the thoughts and actions of both human races and witnessed by the spirit of the tiMantha lu Duois. The penalty for violation, in thought or action, shall be death.

And how much of that was history and how much religion? Harper frowned and closed the book he had read from. It was not a question he could phrase yet in Speech, which perhaps gave him his answer. There was a worldwide religion, centered on a couple named Cimon and Nicole who had sacrificed themselves long ago, and supplemented by supernatural beings called either the tiMantha lu Duois or the Friends of Man.

But *The Chronicles* was less a religious text than a farrago of military history and personal reminiscences. It did not suggest that Cimon weighed the souls of those who died and assigned them to everlasting bliss or tedium or that kindly Nicole shielded the deserving from peril with her cloak of good luck. It did not mention the tiMantha lu Duois, except in the text of the two Compacts, and those were quoted only on the last page. It was an account not of victory but of struggle.

Folklore provided the context.

All human history, it seemed, had been dominated by ice ages and a recessive gene. The glaciers brought each incarnation of civilization into being, then ended it; the gene bestowed slightly greater fertility and made one person in fifty a telepath.

Long ago, a great wintry period had forced men to unite in cities. That Second Era had been dominated by telepaths—the "Skyborne of Kh'taal Minzaer." Powerful, arrogant, they had provoked a futile revolt by the nontelepath Cimon, then crushed it with such cruelty that rebellion flamed.

Twelve thousand years passed before the Friends of Man arrived to assist the Normals. Only then did the Eternal War end, with the defeat of the telepaths and the signing of the Great Compact, in which the telepaths agreed to never again rule over men.

An Era followed in which Normals ruled. But the ice returned, and in the fighting for resources and living space that resulted, the brief Third Era was destroyed. Legend held that telepaths had served as gray eminences or kingmakers in many of the belligerent states.

Many millennia later, a glacial period once more forced organization upon men. Normals, fearing a small state founded by telepaths, united against it in war. There were no tiMantha lu Duois to help this time, but after thousands of years, superior numbers won out. The telepaths agreed to the signing of another Compact.

The Normal triumph was short-lived. Ice crushed the Fourth Era.

Folklore, Harper reminded himself.

What had happened next was recorded history.

Civilization had been reborn in the Fifth Era as a response

to a gradual reduction of the growing season and a contraction of croplands in the region Harper still identified as Canada. Nations shifted southward as the glaciers grew. It was recognized that population would have to be curtailed before the depths of the ice age occurred; it was foreseen that coordination and organization would be needed to ride out the disaster.

But there was hope. Teeps and Normals had not come into conflict in this age. Civil war between the two races of man was not inevitable. Neither barbarism nor tyranny would fasten on humanity again.

It had been year 47,579 by the Long Count calendar when Jablin Hemmendur first appeared in formal robes to address the Compolity of Chelmmys. He was not a young man but an experienced legislator who had become premier less by design than by longevity, and his remarks were not expected to be memorable, nor to provoke interest far beyond the confines of the inconspicuous Sicilian state.

The day had been clear, chroniclers agreed, and the air brisk. The applause that met Hemmendur was perfunctory, the response to his address equally brief. But it had been a long speech, with little to draw attention to what he termed the Solution.

What was remembered now was that 542 years after the founding of Fohima Alghera and slightly over 350 years ago, Hemmendur had said:

> *We have observed that neither Compact prohibits the employment of the Teeps, in whole or in part, in any role whatsoever, by a single all-encompassing world state. I suggest to you that such a state must ultimately arise. By its nature, it will be everlasting and unopposable.*
>
> *I suggest as well that given that inevitability, we attempt ourselves to give birth to that state and shape its growth. If our intentions are worthy, our actions honorable, and our ambitions steadfast, we shall be successful, for we shall gain strong allies.*
>
> *Not the least of these will be the Teeps, who are entitled to a role in human affairs and for whom I propose a most sacred responsibility—which is to ensure that men exercise no dominion over men . . .*

Three-and-a-half centuries later, only one nation had not joined the Alliance of Mankind. Hemmendur's all-encompassing state was not yet a reality. But if it were not established, the Alliance only qualified as a large national state, and by the terms of the Second Compact all those who worked for it, whether Normal or Teep, should have been executed.

"Helluva incentive."

Six years and a bit is not bad, but the Algherans aren't going to keep it going much more. Fifty men a day killed on average, from a population of a million. No, not much longer.

When it ended— He slumped onto a couch, letting it re-form beneath him.

Well, the Chelmmies were likely to be soft on Teeps, and he had three of them living with him. It would probably take a while before they got around to hanging him.

Unless they needed him to run the time machine, of course.

No one would ever revolt if Hemmendur's state had time travel.

There were worse things than being sequestered as a military secret. There were greater evils than asking a Teep child not to speak of secrets to other telepaths.

"I goofed," he admitted. *Should have found some comfortable low-tech society, settled in, and smashed the machine to pieces.*

Maybe it was not too late. Perhaps he could ask Borct to return the time machine, and go away with it. Leave Alghera, leave Cyomit, and—leave Onnul.

No. The damned thing had been built. There might be other time travelers around. Hiding away while less responsible people might be playing with such a thing was reprehensible. *Tiger by the tail, chum. Someone else's tiger, your tail.* "Hell!"

And Cyomit was right. He really wanted the big sister.

Chapter Seven

The thud of a flying motorcycle touching onto the landing platform. A creaking door. Footsteps in the antechamber.

Tolp.

Harper met him at the inner door and mimed shivers at the chill that had entered the antechamber.

"Another year tenth, you'll probably discover it can get cold around here," Tolp said blandly. "You aren't dressed."

"I was studying."

"Good. But you need a change." Tolp pushed past him and dipped to a knee in the living room to view Harper's reading matter. "How dull." Appropriating the house as if it were his own, he rummaged through the closets, selecting clothes. "Wear this. And this. Cover up with this; leave the cloak because it won't fit. Don't forget the Teepblind."

"Won't fit *what*?" Harper asked. But Tolp refused to say.

I'm being bullied, Harper thought with amusement. *This chubby little twerp is giving me orders, and I'm letting him get away with it.*

But a respite from inactivity was welcome. He stuffed himself into the clothing Tolp had selected—pants, shirt, knee-length overshirt, crinkly white coveralls, boots—then endured the pinprick from the mesh skullcap and Tolp's careful inspection without complaint.

When he slid shut the latch on the outer door and followed Tolp's footsteps in the snow up the short stairway to the landing platform, he almost didn't notice the winter cold.

Eight feet of wheelless Harley-Davidson stood in six inches of snow, blue-tinted as if camouflaged. It was not the vehicle Harper would have associated with the smaller man. Most Algherans walked or used miniature flying station wagons for transportation. Onnul's levcraft was red with brown trim, seemingly much used and temperamental. He had not yet discovered whether this society featured annual model changes and used levcraft salesmen. *Probably not. No late-night movies. No movies period.*

"Put these on." Tolp waved gloves at him. They looked like thin off-white cotton and matched the parka he had been given in the antechamber. Harper pulled them on, squeezing his wrists to seal the gloves to his sleeves, but left the parka hood down. The smaller man did the same, then motioned him toward the front seat on the levcycle. "Grab the handlebars near the center; don't let go. Keep your feet on the lift plate. And don't move without reason." He mounted behind Harper, his knees fastened around the big man's hips. "Height bother you? Close your eyes if you want."

A gnat's humming came into existence, then vanished. Harper braced himself on the glass handles as the levcycle pitched forward, then to the left. Snow spilled over the top of the lift plate, cascaded sideways. The seat cushion shuddered. Reflex threw his leg out to stop the fall.

His toe touched only the top of the snow. The smooth wall of the house appeared to shake for an instant, then was steady. The timbers that underlay the roof were at eye level, so close he could reach out and touch them. They retreated and twisted away from him. The levcycle was over the edge of the platform, dipping earthward, then gliding straight ahead like a boat entering a lake. "Ever been on one of these before?" Tolp asked.

"Yeah." Cold air blew in Harper's face and ran like liquid past the side of his head. Seashell murmurs of wind filled his ears. Squinting against sunlight reflected from white snow, he speculated on whether Tolp would clear an approaching tree.

Three times in one night with my hands tied behind me. "When I first got here."

Tolp muttered something. Branches denuded by winter passed just beneath. The levcycle increased speed as its nose dropped, and Harper slid his feet along the plate cautiously to brace himself. *Why don't they put foot pegs onto these things?*

More snow. A haphazard line of blue spruce. Tolp's gloved hands twisted the handlebars, making minute adjustments. "Ha'Ruppir! You ever do any fighting?"

My share. "Some."

"Good! Anything like this where you came from?"

I came from right here. Didn't they tell you? The levcycle had no lights, he noticed suddenly. *What do they do at night?* "Nothing quite like this. We had—"

Dollhouses and moving toy people slid backward as if the wind blew them. The ground dropped abruptly. A wide treeless plain was visible. The frozen Charles River. *The Ice Daughter*, Harper remembered. *Mommy and Daddy must be glaciers*.

"Thought so. Horses, eh?"

Harper sighed and closed his eyes. *Able Company, First of the Eighth Cavalry, First Brigade, First Cavalry Division*, he remembered. Tall grass bobbing under hovering choppers, the Airmobile *whomph-whomph-whomph* of rotating blades, the metal and cotton taste of fear . . . Were those his own memories, or did they belong only to the man he once had been? "We flew also, Tolp," he tried to explain. "*Chinooks*. *Hueys*. Stuff like that. I've seen horses."

"But you had—" Tolp groped for words. "Killing sticks. Things for hurting people at a distance?" He seemed insistent. "Sweln ha'Nyjuc said—"

"Weapons," Harper agreed. "Rifles, pistols, machine guns, mines, bombs, mortars, artillery, tear gas, defoliants, warships, armored fighting vehicles, *napalm*, *punji* traps, kids with grenades. Nerve gas, *atomics*, biological and chemical weapons. We were all completely civilized, Tolp."

"Your own country? Or mercenary?"

Harper sighed. "Part of both. Let it go, Tolp."

"Did you—"

"Six I remember. Seven." *Other times* . . . "Who remembers?"

"I wondered which weapons."

M-16. *BAR*. *BAR*. *M-16*. *Bayonet*. *Knife*. *M-16*. "Rifle."

Harper's eyes finally reopened, and he was aware of weight pressing against his back, warm breath on his ear. "You like this view?" Tolp asked. "Just wait."

Harper shrugged, but the gesture had no meaning in Alghera. "Sure thing."

"Hang on."

His weight doubled.

"Fohima Alghera." Tolp's voice was subdued. Loudness would have been an imposition.

Only a town, Harper told himself, almost with disappointment. A New England hamlet blown up to fill a hundred square miles, but still a small town. *It's the lack of roads*, he realized. *They let the snow cover them up. Transmission lines, railroad lines, factory smokestacks, traffic jams—all the things that spell city to me are missing.*

The wind had ceased, and tiny ordinary sounds could be heard again: Tolp shifting minutely behind him, fabric creaking as Harper turned his body to inspect the view.

Alghera lay a mile below: the largest city in the world.

Hills, woods, and white-disguised river, arcs of shadow that must be the snow-covered fortified line he once had walked. Those were the boundaries. Within, the white cube of the great Temple was easily identified. Working from that, he could locate the park and scattered buildings that were the Institute, then Resolution Stronghold, where he had first met Borct ha'Dicovys and Sweln ha'Nyjuc.

Castles of other Septs were placed at random on the living map below. A narrow bay, rimmed on one side by dockyards made elegant by distance, grew out of the winding Ice Daughter and stretched eastward to the receding sea. Thermal-gradient power generators were arrayed in widely spaced dotted lines inside the bay. Only tugs and other small vehicles were in the docks. Terraces lay parallel to the river, dotted by trees and half-hidden houses. One of those was his; Harper stretched to see if he could identify it. Could he see Onnul from this altitude?

"Easy." A hand patted his shoulder. "A long fall."

Harper froze, then cautiously settled back on the seat. "True enough. Ha'Ruijac, did you ever hear tell of parachutes?"

Tolp laughed shortly. "Only for the Falltroop, boy. Never wore them in the Eagle Slayers."

Air Force, Harper translated. "Back when I was in a uniform, I *liked* being on the ground."

Tolp laughed again. "I've been watching. That'll change. Think we have a use for you, Timt." He slapped handles. The levcycle dived.

"Harper Timithial ha'Ruppir, Selvon Banifnim ha'Hujsuon, Dicton Trelsillar ha'Dicovys, Garl ha'Dicovys you know, Chinnac Borictar ha'Ruijac." Tolp made brisk introductions. "What do you think, Timt?"

No one here but us nobility, Harper thought cynically. He looked about.

A garage. That was his first reaction, but it was probably incorrect. Still, the floor was concrete, the levcycle was parked in the corner by cardboard boxes, a tear-shaped yellow van sat on skids in the center, and workbenches were bolted to unfinished beams. Tall racks of what might have been electronics equipment stood nearby. Chicken wire was stapled to the tar-paper-lined walls and dangled over the doorway and a garage-sized fold-up door in the exterior wall. A window gave a view of the Institute's park-ground campus and arctic quantities of snow far below. *No heat, good lighting, only stools to sit on.*

"A bit bare." He was conscious of stares, of aristocrats scorning a commoner. "Looking for roommates?"

Tolp smiled. Others did not. They all wore Teepblinds.

"Herem ha'Cuhyon," Tolp explained. "This was once his workroom."

Harper waited.

"A faculty member. The machine that brought you to us left from this room."

Surprise met doubt in Harper's mind. "When do I meet him?"

"Never." That was the blond man, stocky and short, young: Ban-something ha'Hujsuon.

"He died, Timt," Garl added. "Two centuries ago, Borct says."

Harper let an eyebrow rise. "How do you know, then?"

"Writing in the box," Tolp said. "We took it apart, found scribbles that looked familiar, and compared them. No doubt about it."

"Hmmm. Good—" *Damn it, don't they have a word for*

"detective"? "Very clever of you to notice. When did you figure it out?"

Tolp snapped his fingers. "The tra'Ruijac gets the credit, not me. Sict studied under Herem and found him difficult to forget. A good gadget maker, but—the ha'Cuhyon's mind leaked ideas as if with diarrhea. He smeared his hands on all of them and built nothing that lasted. You—" He snapped his fingers again. "No accounts that made sense till now, no calculations, no explanations. Just his kind of project."

Disapproving, isn't he? Harper noted. His eyes passed in review over the room again. "So I was constructed by a mad faculty member. When did you figure it all out?"

Tolp nodded. "Not angry so much as—" He patted his head.

Harper smiled to show his teeth and waited.

"Excuse me." Tolp turned away and made gestures as if checking his knuckles for arthritis. The other men responded in the same fashion, now and then throwing uncertain glances toward the redhead.

Stingla muor, Harper recognized. *Be damned. I'd half thought Sweln was making up that combat speech stuff. Except—* He dropped onto a stool and inspected the men who stared at him.

No way. Garl ha'Dicovys could hold a pistol, and now that he knew to look for it, he could see a military officer buried under Tolp's paunch, but the other three men were not veterans. *Boy Scouts planning a panty raid*, he judged cruelly, watching the increasingly vehement gestures. *They want to be naughty and don't know how. So what is this about?*

"Trill will take you home." Tolp's side of the conference had ended. He pointed at a slim embarrassed brunet who was clearly the youngest man present. "I imagine I'll see you in the morning."

Harper nodded, appraising Tolp's tight lips and squint. "Got outvoted, didn't you?"

"Yes." Tolp shook his head irritably. "Cimon-taken glory hounds."

The redhead nodded once more, measuring himself against the too steady gazes and impatient looks of the others. "Well, we can spare the kid. But you need to argue some more. You're about to do something stupid, and you'd better take me along."

In my day, we had car windows that rolled down, Harper remembered.

This probably was not the time to make the remark.

In my time, we also had garage door openers.

He wouldn't say that, either. He kept his jaw clinched and his hands on Garl ha'Dicovys while the smaller man leaned out the open van door and slapped at a black patch on the side of the building. Ten stories below, bushes made ice cream cone mounds in the snow by sand-covered sidewalks. *And we didn't put cloth loops in uniforms to simplify carrying bodies.*

Tolp muttered something from the front seat, words that none of the Niculponocs had used. A T-shaped steering handle was in his hands. Bann ha'Hujsuon, sitting by the left door, giggled nervously as wind currents rocked the vehicle. Borct ha'Ruijac, sitting between them, stared ahead impassively, pretending not to notice his Septmate's difficulties.

"Got it," Garl announced. He dropped a hand from the roof of the vehicle to the back of Tolp's seat and let Harper pull him back into the van. The laboratory's "garage door" slipped into place with a soft clink. Garl slid his door forward, slammed it shut with a satisfied expression, then tossed his head back to lower the hood on his cream-colored military parka, and stripped off his gloves.

Shaking tension out of his fingers, Harper looked for reassurance at the rifles stashed in the rear. "You people *do* realize we have to do this again in about ten seconds?"

"What?" Garl asked foolishly. "Ten seconds? But—"

Tolp was faster on the uptake. He used more of the words Harper had not learned from Onnul and Cyomit.

"Ready?" Bann asked. He pushed switches on the box in his lap, then twisted knobs slowly. The sun drifted eastward.

"We made some improvements," Bann ha'Hujsuon explained earnestly to Harper. He proceeded to elaborate.

Ghost fluid was the local name for an electric current, Harper had discovered in his reading. It went along with the fact that the heated uniform Tolp had given him had embedded wire "pipelines" and a clip-on "reservoir" that served as a battery. *Ghost fluid sink* probably meant "capacitor," then, and a *dam* would be a "resistor." *Waves* were oscillations. So what did they call an inductance? *"Funnel," I suspect. What do they call integrated circuits? Ice?*

"You traded speed for visibility, right? You reverse the current direction to travel backward in time? And you found a way to travel slower than time by jiggering up the plumbing?"

"Basically, yes." Bann seemed disappointed to have his lecture interrupted. "Average speed, anyhow. Peak displacement velocity—"

First-year grad, Harper thought with amusement. *Ninety thousand years, and I fall into the clutches of college students.* "I understand. Sinusoidal rather than direct currents, and—trading up for down—I don't have the words yet. We called it 'polarity.' Forgive me; I have a question: How far forward have you gone?"

The smaller man stared at him.

"Tell him," Tolp barked. "Maybe he has some ideas."

"This is it," Bann admitted. "Today. Now. This is as far in the future as the machine will get us."

"We're *frozen* to this particular instant?" Harper looked out the window at moving clouds. "Doesn't look it."

Bann simulated toothache to advertise thought. "No. It's—Cimon!" He manipulated the box in his lap. The world was suddenly darker as twilight gloomed, with grays and purples visible everywhere. Incongruously, the sun remained a white-yellow disk. "We are moving back in time at the rate of two seconds external for each one internal. Now each light wave we see is actually vibrating at—"

"What we see is blue-shifted," Harper agreed quickly.

"Uh, yes, that's a way of expressing it. You understand that when we go forward—"

"Same thing happens."

"Yes! You're familiar with ghost-and-levitation fluid theory already?" The Algheran sounded disappointed.

"We called it 'electromagnetic' theory."

Bann frowned unhappily, then pushed at the instruments on his lap. "Well, now we're moving forward. Watch!"

He raised his hands into the air. For several seconds nothing of significance happened, then the normal colors of the world were restored. "There is a point in time where a time machine can move forward no faster than you or I alone—one second passes in one second. That point moves forward at the same rate. It's where we are right now, and we can't get past it. We can't get into *our* future."

"Hmmm," Harper said deliberately. So he had not run down

his batteries when he had arrived at Alghera. He had stopped at the time he did because that was as far as he could go.

The front of a wave, he thought. *The universe rushes forward in time, like water racing through a dry creek bed. The front of the water is the actual present. History is the water flowing behind the head, and a time traveler is a guy on a boat who can move faster than the water backward or forward but can't get ahead of it to the unrealized future.*

Which implies some time scale existing outside the universe. And there's no theory for that I can remember.

Bann's conclusions needed review, he decided. If true, they would inspire a great deal of speculation and theory making. But Bann was probably not a good audience for such speculations. Nor was this a good opportunity for theoretical physics.

"Hmmm," he said again. "One more question: Why do you use the phrase 'ghost fluid'?"

Eastern Massachusetts was passing underneath at two hundred miles an hour, he estimated. He recognized no landmarks, but Sharon was down there somewhere, just a few hundred feet away. A few feet, a few years. *So's Big Red One, there at Fort Devons, and if I had a choice now . . .*

The blond Algheran blinked. "It is a ghost fluid," he insisted. "No mass, no volume. We can measure a flow of some sort, but no one is sure whether it actually exists in its own right or if it is an artifact—an illusionary force produced when real matter is arranged in special patterns. Maybe someday—but it's not known."

"It's not?"

"Why?" Bann looked at him strangely.

"Ghost fluid is the motion of certain very small particles," Harper said carefully. "Each has a mass of about ten to the minus thirty-two man-weights. They all have the same value of charge, so when you measure a large current flow, you're seeing many of these particles going by."

"What size are those particles?" Borct ha'Ruijac had a nasal voice, harsh. He did not turn his head to ask.

Harper frowned, converting units. "There's a formula that gives a value of about ten to the minus fifteen man-heights for a diameter. Of course, the particles are rather fuzzy. In some sense, an *electron*—a charge carrier—doesn't have a real size; it just is denser in some locations than others."

"Can't you do better than that?" The younger ha'Ruijac

shrugged off Tolp's restraining hand, turned, and glared. "Show us exactly."

Two point eight one seven nine four, Harper remembered, meeting the stare. "Give me a writing block, and I'll work it out to four places. Will that satisfy you?"

The boy's sneer increased. "You said fifteen places, and now you say four places. Which is it?" He added another word that was probably just as well out of Harper's vocabulary.

The redhead frowned, meeting only wary looks from the others in the vehicle. "A nineteen-place number, if that's the way you define things. But I'll have to use my notation first. We used powers of ten for small fractions, and I'm still learning how to put things into halves and quarters. It'll be, uh, somewhere around two to the minus sixty-second when I'm through. For the last term, I mean. And it will still be an approximation." He smiled pleasantly. "Will that satisfy you?"

The last could not be heard. Tolp was laughing.

Borct ha'Ruijac cursed. "You need teaching to respect your betters, dirt face. If you weren't Septless, I'd take you into a fighting square."

Harper blinked. "For what?"

"To improve your Teep-loving manners!"

"Borct! Enough!" Tolp cuffed the younger ha'Ruijac. "He's under Dicovys protection, he's a guest of Alghera, and if you insist on a duel, you'll meet me first."

"You wouldn't!"

"Try me, Septling, and you'll have another mouth to issue ill-timed challenges with."

"Sict—"

Tolp snorted. "The tra'Ruijac is not going to miss you. Now shut up and save your anger for real enemies."

Borct would not meet Tolp's eyes. He spat out another expletive and turned away, muttering something about know-it-all barbarians.

Harper turned to Garl ha'Dicovys. "What's this about?"

Garl snapped his fingers. "I'm not a faculty member or a schoolboy, Timt, so I don't know."

No help there, Harper thought grimly. And what was Garl doing among this group of lunatics? He turned to Bann and repeated his question. It earned a grin, which faded abruptly. "A nineteen-place fraction is a meaningless one," the blond Algheran said. "No measurement can be so precise. And a sixty-two-place fraction— You seemed so serious, we didn't understand your joke till—"

"I did not make a joke."

"But—" Bann swallowed, squirmed, reddened.

"Cimon and Nicole! *Planck's constant* was measured out to . . . a hundred and ten places in your terms. More. Long ago. You must have—"

"What is—" Bann broke off at the alien phrase.

"Planck's constant," Harper repeated, looking at Bann and then at the now-silent Tolp. "You'd have another name. It's the value of a parameter needed to discuss things that happen at—I don't have the word—very small levels. At the level where—you cut things up and they stay the same, except they're smaller. But if you could keep cutting, thousands of times, you get down to building blocks that aren't the same. What are the words?"

Tolp looked at him with pity. "There are no words. There is no reason for words, Timt. Substance is substance, and if you divide—"

Harper did not hear the end. *No quantum mechanics*, a voice was shouting at him. He sank back on his seat, pressing himself as far away from the others as he could. *No quantum mechanics. No molecules, no atoms. They've lost most of physics, most of science.*

But—levitation, mathematics, holography, radio. Materials we never dreamed of. Nerve regeneration. New species of plants. Impossible batteries. Telepathy. Time travel. "How do you do it, Tolp?" he asked softly, fearing that he might hurt the man's feelings. He waved a hand to encompass the world. "What do you faculty members use to explain how things happen?"

"We experiment. We think. We guess and try things." Tolp snapped his fingers. "When the Plates are unclear, we discuss things among ourselves. When—"

"The Plates?"

"The Plates. The records from the Fourth Era. The ones that gave us *The Chronicles* and told us how to begin making things. You read of them, didn't you?"

A time capsule. What they knew had been taken from other people.

Their science was a cargo cult.

Harper shook his head slowly, then remembered that it would not be understood. *I'd be a lot happier killing for you people if you hadn't told me that*, he wanted to say. But barbarians wouldn't realize that their thievery was wrong.

"I think someone had better show me how to operate these things," he said instead, reaching back for one of the alien rifles. "Like how do I reload it?"

He paid close attention to the lecture that followed. He did not want to ask questions. Unnecessary words would have broken him in half.

Tolp brought the vehicle in low, sweeping up and down the twilight-covered hills with the rhythm of the earth. Bann's motions mimicked those of the pilot, turning controls that swept them between the present winter and a past summer.

Harper stared out his window grimly, hands tight on the shotgun shape clamped between his knees. He had not witnessed the testing Bann had described and lacked the student's assurance that time travelers could not be detected. *Energy flows*, he reasoned. *If radio signals can be seen as light by time travelers, then the light from within the vehicle must be radiated outward as radio signals. Nothing's totally immeasurable.*

Still, as long as we aren't expected.

Garl ha'Dicovys cleared his throat, but he was not expressing alarm. He scanned the snow-clad slopes with patient eyes, an assassin waiting for skiers. Tree foliage returned to tantalize; Garl relaxed and rubbed his right shoulder. A private smile fluttered over his face.

What's in his mind? Harper wondered. It was not the least of the miracles he had met that people existed who could answer that question.

If our Teepblinds slip . . . He swept a hand over his hair, feeling the cold mesh on his scalp, the plastic band that wrapped his head.

"Too far back," Tolp grumbled. "Give me some snow."

Bann mumbled in response as he did things with both hands.

Trees shimmered, their summer greenery whisked away as suddenly as Cinderella's gown to reveal bare outstretched limbs. A half-moon ruled the night sky. Bann exhaled. Daylight followed. A sun jerked into place between streaks of gray cloud. "Twice normal rate," he reported.

Tolp grunted and pushed up on the steering bar handles. The hillside features dwindled rapidly, then grew hazy. Scraps of cloud drifted toward the levcraft, grew steadily, slowly receded, then were still. Tolp pulled the bar back, twisted until a click sounded, and released it.

A minute passed in silence while he rubbed his chin with thumb and forefinger. Harper had time to stare at the gun in his hands, decide it was of little interest, and inspect the valueless land below.

"Run us up to the present," Tolp ordered. "Back a day next. Then a ten-day period back, quickly. No, twenty days."

Bann shook his head and touched switches. "Ready."

The clouds were gone. Harper blinked in sudden sunlight, then again when he saw the acne-pitted, dead white face of the earth. Smoke still corkscrewed up from blackened tree-stump stubble.

Then a line of dots moved through trees slowly, wriggling like an insect pinned to a dissecting board. Men. A half company, Harper estimated, not yet arrayed in skirmish line. Algheran soldiers.

The dots vanished. Otherwise the hill seemed the same.

Tolp cursed. It was just a word, without emotion. He slapped the steering bar into place with one precise, abrupt gesture. The land grew nearer, then slipped into hiding behind the levcraft.

They stopped over a narrow ravine, a gully no different from any other. Trees wavered on the verge. Leaves and fallen branches littered the ground. Bushes crowded for space in a line at the bottom of the trough. Here and there clumps of brown grass and dead waist-high stalks showed above the snow.

Tolp turned his head slowly, carefully. His lips moved soundlessly. The vehicle bobbed, slid down the slope, then hovered briefly over a flat spot. A rasping sound filled the cabin for a moment; the levcraft swung sideways, then straightened out. Harper glimpsed a boulder from which snow had been scraped. He remembered other landscapes that had swung up and swerved to the sides as pilots looked for places to hover. *Least there's no ground-fire.*

The levcraft dropped suddenly, then thumped to a stop.

Harper swallowed for no good reason and sensed others did the same.

"Are you all prepared?" Metal rasped in Tolp's voice.

"I'm not," Harper wanted to joke, but while he was debating it, Tolp asked him to hand up a pair of the guns, and the moment for humor passed. Then there were more instructions to listen to, which were simple enough and passed through his thoughts without leaving any trace, and Harper was getting out of the levcraft and wondering as his feet touched the ground whether he could be said to have traveled a long way or a short way in the last few months. The door snapped shut, and he still was undecided.

Snow scrunched under his boots. Harper pulled the parka hood up and clumsily tightened the chin straps. He waited.

A rifle barrel scraping against the side of the van, a creaking sound as someone shifted weight. No wind, no birds, no engine sounds. His heart beating when he held his breath and concentrated on listening.

To kill silence, he kicked at a mound of snow, feeling just a touch of resistance as his foot went through the confectionery sugar crust. Flying powder made glittering rays in the setting sun and disappeared in night before hitting the ground.

"Easy," Tolp said to someone. He and Garl stood on the far side of the vehicle. Bann remained in the van, holding the time engine controls.

The levcraft was a ridiculous sight to find in the middle of a woods, Harper realized. It wasn't going to offer useful protection since it was mostly plastic and wouldn't be able to fly inside the ChelmForce anti-induction field. It was a vehicle for cities and civilization, completely out of place here, and the ugly, distracting egg-yolk color made it a natural target or a background for targets. Better if it just went away for a while. He turned around with sunrise to see if the others would agree with him.

But Garl had the funny preoccupied look of a man trying to remember a long-ago girl friend's last name, and Harper didn't want to disturb him. He had some reason also for not talking much to the slim man on his left, and Bann was being hypnotized by the PBX gear on his lap. That left Tolp, and he was staring past him as if to greet someone else.

"Easy," Tolp said from the side of his mouth, and night came again.

A little sullen because he had no one to talk to, Harper rubbed a hand down the glassy barrel of his weapon, remembering that it killed without producing visible wounds. There wouldn't be any recoil, he had been told. It didn't need reloading. One pointed it and pulled the trigger after unblocking the trigger guard with a little finger.

The directions seemed easy enough to follow, but he practiced just in case while clouds stacked themselves across the sky and the sun tried unsuccessfully to break through a couple of times.

He was not cold inside the heated uniform, though his cheeks felt a little puffy, but Tolp had been right—there was no room for a cape under the parka, no matter how much he had half enjoyed feeling like Superman. He swung his arms back and forth just to keep the blood moving and made sure no one noticed when jerking his left elbow gave him an old man's pains. It was weird to find himself thinking of aging. It was weird just to realize the weirdness: He was only twenty-six, after all, and the sun was high.

A team of horses turned up the ravine at the far end, looking for all the world like the Clydesdales in the Budweiser ads, except that they were moving at maybe two hundred miles an hour, and he just could see the bodies, not the furiously churning legs, in the waning daylight. *Chelmmies*.

When morning came, more horses were milling about silently, and men in dark brown uniforms danced like marionettes and ran around the ravine in silly Marx Brothers steps. A huge black egg, three times as high as a man, sat waiting in the flat spot in which Tolp had decided not to land. Circus wagons had been parked just behind it. Brown-clad men galloped in and out of them.

Army types obviously. He had been in the Army himself once; just look at him now, only twenty-six and already with old-man pains. He never should have volunteered. Fighting was a damned scary thing to do.

He couldn't remember what "scary" was, but sensible people stayed away from it. He remembered that all too well.

"Not yet, Garl," someone said. "On my signal, Bann."

Fear was in that voice, he realized with satisfaction. Hidden, very well hidden, but he knew enough to hear it. He smiled to himself.

The others raised their weapons. A bit clumsily, he did the same to avoid being left out. Fortunately, it was dark and no one noticed his awkwardness.

Mrs. Harper's little boy should have had more sense than to go soldiering.

But there really hadn't been a Mrs. Harper, had there? Not one that he recalled, anyhow. Not a Mrs. Harper, not a Mr. Harper.

And the older sister he still remembered now and then—what was her name?—hadn't existed either except as a figment of his imagination, someone to be company when he needed company, when no one in the orphanage would do and he didn't know anyone else well enough to have for a friend because he was in an orphanage, and when he fell facedown in the snow and didn't move again there wasn't going to be anyone to notice, anyone to care, and they'd all be sorry someday. Just thinking about it made his limbs thick and clumsy and ugly, and he probably looked like an idiot nodding at the fat man behind the van and saying "I'm ready" just as if he really were, when actually he was—

—scared. The stupid Algherans hadn't told him the word for "scared" even though it was important and he really did need to know it: How could they expect him to be scared when they didn't give him the word for it? Tim Harper wasn't being cried for, wasn't being cared for, and he was going to cry for the mother when there was time enough, and maybe his older sister would, too. And maybe the gooks out there—

—but there was nothing gooklike, really, about the amber-faced man flying across the ravine, so close he could be touched, not till he stopped and started to speak in a guttural, surprised voice.

He wasn't a gook so Harper shot him.

It got noisy then.

Military camp noisy, he judged critically. Voices coming from men waiting to get orders, and from men giving orders, and from men who were obeying orders and trying to hide from more orders, interrupted by complaints from horses who just wanted to know what was going on, by stadium-filling roars from artillery explosions, by distant muffled falling pillow sounds that might have been an avalanche, by nearby cracks of pocket thunderbolts.

Something whined inside the wooden rifle stock pressed against his cheek, then slowed to a soft *whirr*ing sound, to a kitten's purr, more vibration than sound, actually. He pushed the trigger lock aside with a pinky and shifted his hand back where it should be, then waited for the important sound to stop.

The man he had shot was half sitting, half standing on one

leg with the other stretched before him, as if he were about to climb out of an easy chair to wave a newspaper before him and scream about some petty, infuriating news item. *Maybe we can chat when I'm not so busy, pal.*

The *whirr* stopped. Harper was looking through sights at the green lozenge on a man's head fifty feet away, which wasn't the nearest target but definitely the most convenient one, so he aimed at it, squeezed the trigger, ignored the resulting thunderclap, and went back to listening to his rifle stock. About a dozen of the brown-dressed men were on a ledge arrangement at the far end of the gully, with just their heads over the top.

Not bad. Not as loud as a real gun, and no recoil.

The green-touched man let his mouth drop just a bit, as if he were about to say something, but he didn't, only jerked a bit as his knees seemed to melt under him.

Dead 'un. Harper looked at his next targets, while the old one slapped hands together in a parody of prayer, then threw them sideways so they wouldn't be in the way while he—it—bent at the waist and fell face forward on a convenient boulder.

A man holding a horse about the muzzle slipped and fell; he was kicked by the horse but did not react.

Thunder. A man turned sideways on the hillside ledge, pushed himself into space, and splashed snow. A dark stick tumbled down the slope after him.

Am I supposed to be counting these for Tolp?

Someone guffawed coarsely. Harper moved his head and saw a running horse smack headlong into one of the circus wagons. The wagon rocked, and the horse ended up sprawled halfway underneath the chassis, screaming.

No need to be cruel, damn it. Harper put his next shot through the animal's neck. Bone and blood splashed on the wagon as reflex smashed the horse's skull against it. *Wasted shot.*

He was not sure, but the shouting seemed louder; perhaps there was just more of it, some coming from outside the ravine. Harper took his cheek away from his rifle stock—the kitten purr hadn't come yet—and threw a look about.

Tolp had a silly death's-head grin on his face that a younger Harper once had thought meant pleasure but knew now was only a by-product of concentration. Bann ha'Hujsuon was still safe in the levcraft, staring at his dials, statue-rigid, stinking of tension. Harper decided that he liked Bann.

The boy at his side was moving his arms up and down as if rocking a baby rather than a rifle or beating time sideways for an orchestra. Doing that seemed to be a big thing with him, probably more than pulling a trigger was.

The ravine shook. A giant invisible something squeezed him, boxed his ears simultaneously, and dropped him without interest. A fountain of earth spurted from the end of the gully, a black bedsheet, a curtain spreading outward. Men were slipping down the sides of the ravine, some fighting it, some rolling limply.

Incoming. Our incoming. Harper scrambled onto his knees and fell forward to grab his rifle. It was always good to be self-possessed at moments like these.

It took all kinds to make a world, though. Mrs. Harper, as an example, hadn't raised—*squeeze the trigger, watch a man with his back turned get stiff suddenly and throw a rifle into the sky*—her little boy to be no soldier. Yessiree, she—*whirr*!—hadn't.

He rolled sideways and sat up so he could view the debris-pitted side of the levcraft. Swallowing didn't help the pain in his ears.

He saw a horse running free, knocking brown-uniformed men aside as it left the ravine. He could hope it found better masters. He picked up a handful of snow and winced as he rubbed it above his right knee. There was blood, but the gash was smaller than he had feared and more numb than painful.

A little piece of incoming mail, a rock fragment, a Dear John letter from Alghera. "Aargh!" There, getting to his knees hadn't been that tough and—

"Garl," he called as reasonably as possible, "what in Cimon's name do you think you're doing?"

He didn't get an answer even when he used Speech to ask.

Maybe Garl wasn't hearing him. But there was so little sound that it should have been easy to carry on conversations. Harper fell sideways, prompted by nothing, and watched shovelfuls of snow and earth gouge themselves from the ground.

Rocks smashed into his belly; tears blinded him as his chin struck the ground. Harper shook his face clear of snow and got his cheek back against the butt of his rifle. "Garl!"

Garl ha'Dicovys stepped forward without pause, just a dozen

paces away, a serene expression on his face. He was firing from the hip. Harper could see his trigger finger contracting, becoming white with tension, pulling back, slipping forward, turning white, pulling.

He probably got a shot off with each rapid step.

It really was a shame these weapons took five seconds to recharge.

Then Garl was down, and all the answers to his private mysteries would never be expressed. Harper shot the man who had shot the Algheran, decided that anyone as brave as Garl deserved remembrance, rolled uselessly away from the rifle barrel pointed too steadily in his direction, remembered remembering a man who had remembered blond women, listened without success for a whine inside a damned hot rifle stock, and—

—didn't have any more targets.

Dead horse flesh was scattered over the walls of the ravine, raw and red on white and splotches of brown-black soil. Dog food for unchoosy dogs. Some of it was mixed up with scraps of white and brown cloth, half buried under little piles of dirt. Slivers of glass, knife-sharp and diamond-hard, were strewn throughout the ravine. Even with the cold, everything was starting to stink. Add a jungle taint, and he might recognize the smell.

Nothing moved in front of him. Nothing was alive.

The giant black egg had taken a Humpty-Dumpty fall. Egg stuff was not visible inside the fractured shell. *The yolk is on us. The yoke.*

The idiot beside him was still juggling his rifle and dancing up and down. Harper lurched to his feet, stepped sideways, reached to grab the barrel, and jerked the weapon from his hands. "Fun's over."

They couldn't find Garl's body when they looked for it; they didn't find it even when they went back through the same part of history.

They dumped the cherry off, and then one thing led to another.

When morning came, Harper was telling Bann about how the little whore with the forehead plaque had scraped up his back and assuring Tolp that the bar was just fine. Drunk, Tolp insisted on telling the Septless bartender that he was a Ruijac and not to be trifled with, and he Cimon-well would have the holovision on for the news—so they got it.

It was the wrong damned day. Off by one.

The miniature Chelmmy announcer sneered at them from the counter top. "The Alliance reports to the Algheran people!" he shouted. "Killed at the fighting in Hendanner's Pass yesterday were thirteen members of the Forest Guard: Trelsmir Garrilun ha'Dicovys, Bendar Chilschur ha'Cuhyon, Bendar Dselturim ha'Cuhyon . . ."

CHAPTER EIGHT

"*Cimon guard us, Nicole guide us.*"

The final words of the prayer hung in the air for only a moment, then the social hubbub, which had been subdued rather than vanquished for the last day tenth, began anew. The Joseph's-coat form of the crowd stirred, flowing kaleidoscopically beyond the white cloth of the platform. Voices rose. The ceremony was over.

The black-robed man smiled wryly at his compatriots as the microphone and loudspeakers were switched off, then turned to Tim Harper. The golden sword and scythe of a believing priest was bright upon his left shoulder; stitched in red beneath the insignia was the mace of a Sept Master. "Time I was getting back to work, I think. It's your show now, Timithial. But before I go—"

His hands went out in formal benediction. Controlling stage fright, Harper clasped hands with the tra'Dicovys, interlacing fingers and pressing palms together above their heads.

"Thank you, sir."

"Thank you, Timithial," the tra'Dicovys said comfortably. His head bobbed toward the men and women milling around below the platform, and Harper saw mesh resting in the sandy hair. "Not the oldest Sept in Alghera or even the most important one, despite what we tell the outside world. But it's not a bad bunch of people. I'm glad we could find space for you, son."

Harper swallowed. "Thank you, sir," he repeated again. It was difficult to realize that a man so important had made time to be here, difficult to realize the heights to which he had suddenly risen. "It's a great honor, sir. It's—" Panic conquered. "What do I do now?"

The tra'Dicovys smiled again, showing barely restrained laughter. "Be yourself. Don't trip going down the stairs. Be polite to everyone, but don't make any promises—every mother of an unattached daughter will want you to meet her child. They're all very beautiful, of course, and all very accomplished, if not the equal of my wife, and we all want to keep you in the Sept, but it's a little early for such commitments. Don't get *too* drunk. Just enjoy things."

A buxom woman in black velvet swept forward, taking Harper's hands, then folding him in a maternal embrace. "The old fool. He can say that," she explained cheerfully, "because we haven't a daughter of our own. If we did, he'd be in line with her, too, I promise you. Welcome, Timithial ha'Dicovys." She smiled at him fondly, then kissed him soundly. The experience was overwhelming, warm, and pointed. Harper noticed two points.

The tra'Dicovys rescued him, putting an arm around the woman's waist and detaching her before he had decided on a response. She hugged the older man with equal enthusiasm.

"A good thing I have a country to run," he told Harper calmly. "I certainly never figured out how to get control of my household."

"Now dear," the woman said.

"Now dear," the Warder of Alghera agreed. "Let's go down these stairs and away and let the Ironwearer enjoy *his* orgy."

They both smiled at Harper and did just that.

Harper Timithial ha'Dicovys, Ironwearer and Unit Master of the Forest Guard. "Harper Timithial ha'Dicovys." He whispered his new name to himself, enjoying the sound of it, enjoying the feel of the new green and black uniform he had been given before the ceremony. Unit Master. That was halfway between captain and major, wasn't it? Ironwearer was a title of some kind, or an honor, like a medal had been in his era, a reward for the battles he and Tolp had attempted to alter. And the Forest Guard was something like the Rangers. "Nice promo, Sergeant Harper." He slapped the hilt of the sword that had come with the uniform, enjoying the fine anachronistic sensation that accompanied the gesture. *Not an orphan anymore.*

Springtime, day 1 of the new year. A time for new beginnings, well begun. Only Onnul remained to be impressed, and that could be only a matter of time. He smiled at the tall, strong supporting walls of Resolution Stronghold, hitched the sword back on its belt to avoid entanglement, then dropped and pushed himself from the platform.

Members of his new family pressed forward. "Thank you," he settled for saying. "Thank you." He kept moving. The line for mulled cider was longer than the spring wine line, he had noted from the platform. *Spring wine first, deal with the mob later. Not an orphan.*

Of course, he finally met Borct, who was suffering gallantly the presence of a slim, youthful-appearing but facially worn blond woman.

"My wife," he said curtly. "Dear, Harper Timithial ha'Dicovys."

Harper extended himself, swaying slightly, kissing the woman's hand in a fashion out of style for more than nine hundred centuries. "My pleasure," he said cheerfully, noting how this offended Borct. "I'm told I have you to thank for my nomination." He did not release the hand.

She smiled happily at him. "Well, I had never heard of you originally. But when my Borictalim mentioned your exploits, I just felt . . . and when I heard you'd been made an Ironwearer but were still actually *Septless*, it—it just had to be done. We're terribly proud." She squeezed back.

Borictalim, Harper thought gleefully. *Darling little Borctie. I won't forget that name.* "Well, thank you. I've heard so much that's good about you, too."

A Teepblind on Borct, none on his wife. He had met a couple of the daughters he had been threatened with, but the promised orgy had not begun yet. He smiled hopefully at the woman and massaged her hand gently, concealing recognition that she knew nothing of his history. "If there's any way I could show you my, uh, gratitude . . ." He kissed the woman's hand again, the wrist, then just above the wrist. "Later on in the *season*, perhaps?"

Borictalim reddened. "I'm very sorry, dear, but we mustn't detain Timithial. He has many other people to meet, and—he—will—be—leaving—shortly. Won't you, Timithial?"

Thinks I'm drunk, Harper noted. He grinned widely, privately contrasting Borct's age and disposition with that of the tra'Dicovys, whom rumor said he wished to supplant. "Hard to say. It depends on circumstances." He smiled again at Borct's wife. "So pleasant to have met you. And next time—"

Borct hurried her away with her hand still stretched out for another kiss. Harper chuckled and went back to looking for conquests.

"Enjoying yourself?" The voice was familiar, touched with less good humor than usual.

"Working on it." Harper refilled his wineglass without turning. "Lot of people to talk to, it seems, not much to talk about. What's new with you, Tolp? Thought this was just a Dicovys brawl. Want a drink?"

"This one will do." Tolp got between Harper and the bowl and plucked Harper's glass from a willing hand. He was still thickset, but his paunch had diminished greatly during the past fraction of a year. He was dressed drably, in casual slacks and shirts without the garish colors of the other men present, and Harper remembered that his Sept had held its convocation a tenday earlier. "You look disappointed."

The redhead grimaced. "Expected more single women," he said finally. *More single women, and fewer unsophisticated little coquettes too damned conscious of their value to the single men running around in this provincial court. Damn it, there used to be a country extending over the whole continent which got along fine without a caste system.*

"I am an American." It still sounded good.

"Hm?" Tolp looked about casually, showing disinterest. "You said?"

"Never mind. Gate crashing, aren't you?"

The Algheran considered the words, then gave the idiom meaning. "Yes."

"Thought you were . . . away." That was circumspect enough.

"Wasn't gone for long. You know." Tolp threw his head back and swallowed deeply. "Trill didn't make it. You don't see him again, you'll know why." He followed with a sip, shook his head, then dumped the drink deliberately on the ground and left the glass on the table for others to use. "You Dicovys! This is cheap stuff, Timt. If it had been Ruijac . . . Look, I'm parked just outside. Suppose I take you off for something better. Think you can keep your balance for that? Here, swallow these just in case. Come along."

He had Harper out the gateway and onto his levcraft long before suspicion dawned.

"Returning your bouncing boy," Tolp said caustically. "He's feeling a bit uncomfortable. Here, find a place for this." Hands fiddled with straps around Harper's waist and lifted away the weight that had slapped at his leg.

"I see." Humor fought kindness in Sweln ha'Nyjuc's voice. Humor won. "I think we'll leave the 'blind on. I've sensitive daughters. Cyomit! I think you should spend the night elsewhere."

"Is he all *right*?" Her voice was shrill.

Harper shuddered. "Pipe down, kid. I'm a bit hung, that's all." Fear of uncertain consequences kept his eyes shut. Was the world spinning on one axis or two? The band on his head, usually unnoticed, had become an instrument of torture. His stomach twisted, threatening rebellion.

"Just a figure of speech, I imagine, dear," Sweln explained. "Tolp, can you drop her off at Nyjuc House? Onnul and I should be able to get him to bed."

"Don't need go bed," Harper explained with careful dignity. "What's need is, is hair of *dog*. Do you have *dog*? Little animal," he gestured. "Goes *arf, arf*! Chases low-flying levcraft and—and civil servants?" He gulped behind a closed mouth, rocked on his feet, tried to stop.

"No problem," Tolp said, callously disregarding the question. "As soon as she's ready to go. I think Timt's got about two hundred seconds before he falls over." In response to some nonverbal clue, he added, "Borct seemed to think serious action was needed when he called me or I would have used a smaller dose. Hi, Onnul."

"I have the bed turned down," a cool feminine voice interrupted. "Dad, if you can take one side—"

Shrinking wasn't enough of a refuge. Harper let himself pass out.

* * *

Blackness. An unfamiliar bed. Breezes featherdancing on his legs. A hand resting on his head.

Harper reached stealthily for—

Not in 'Nam. No knife. No one to kill.

"Feeling better?"

Sweln ha'Nyjuc. Nighttime. His own bed. Windows were open.

He considered existence carefully. No headache, no fuzzy tongue. His Teepblind had been removed. "Yes. But I'm thirsty."

"You've been sweating. I'll get you some water."

Left alone, he raised one eyebrow, then both. Blinds were flapping softly over the windows, so he stretched to turn a wall switch, which brought dim lights on. Third watch and a tenth, the wall clock told him. Which meant . . . it didn't matter.

Nighttime, anyhow. Fortunately the nights were warm now; they'd simply dropped all his clothes on the desk and put him on the bed nude. He grimaced, then told himself that modesty probably was wasted on telepaths. Probably.

The Fifth Era was totally free of mosquitoes. Maybe that was a consolation.

When Sweln returned, Harper was sitting up. "Sorry about all this. I didn't mean to—" He shook his hands uselessly. "I'm really sorry."

The telepath chuckled. "Onnul will forgive you."

Harper sipped water and kept his mouth shut.

Sweln chuckled again and held something out. "Look at this carefully, at the lettering. It's Common, not Speech; just remember the pattern."

Red capsule, yellow characters. "All right." Harper handed the pill back. "What about it?"

"It helps metabolize alcohol. Taken before a drinking bout, it prevents drunkenness. Taken after, it intensifies intoxication, then produces soberness quickly. The effects are often unpleasant, so a sleeping potion is sometimes added. You were given two of them."

"I think I'll kill Tolp."

Sweln snapped his fingers. "He did what seemed best. An Ironwearer is expected to act as an Ironwearer."

Harper frowned. "I'll think about it. Right now, I need a shower." He gave the older man a wan smile. "I'll try not to rust."

"Do so." Sweln stepped back to let him rise. "And perhaps you will find time to reflect that our pharmacology was created without reference to the famous Plates of the Fourth Era."

Harper put ideas together. "I'm being rebuked?"

"If you feel it's required, yes. Go shower."

To his surprise, the older man had not yet gone to bed when he returned from bathing but was reading a medical text in the summer living room.

Sweln was sitting on a favorite chair dragged in from the back living room, but Harper sank without selectivity into one of the cube chairs, pulling boots over his feet as the chair molded itself to him. He had put on ordinary clothing—slacks, white pullover, green overshirt—that did not fit as comfortably as his uniforms but seemed more appropriate for home life.

"So you feel I need scolding?" he asked good-humoredly. The inner windows had been taken down that day but waited for removal to storage under the house. He would get to that task the next day. "I'm a bad boy?"

Sweln rubbed his wrist, considering an answer. "Perhaps. Wait." He left the front room and returned with a red-covered book Harper had brought from the past. "You've said this was a science text of your day."

Harper smiled. The book, its binding splotched by melting snow and dirt, was an anthology of English literature. "Close enough."

"Did you invent all your science personally, or did you receive it from people who came before you?"

Harper frowned. "Received it, but—"

"As we have. And hoped to add to it, as we do. And intended to transfer it to later generations. As we will."

"Hmmm. My thoughts have been rude."

"Very. As an Ironwearer, much is expected of you. Required."

An Ironwearer is expected to act as an Ironwearer. Harper thought about words he had heard more than once. "What happens if—"

"The title is a formality," Sweln explained. "Any officer can be called an Ironwearer these days." He picked up Harper's presentation sword from the floor and pulled the milky blade partially from the lacquered scabbard.

"Look closely and you will see a line within the crystal. That is iron wire. So—it began as a military title, after all. Yes, for one dressed in armor as in your mind. Still, if one becomes unworthy—" He nodded grimly and tapped a knee with Harper's book. "If the Teeps say a man is not an Ironwearer, he ceases to be treated as an Ironwearer."

Harper thought about that while Sweln eyed him approvingly. "We don't have the formal procedures you imagine, Tim'thy. They are not necessary. What we have . . . An Ironwearer becomes such by saying he is an Ironwearer and acting as such. Honor is not power. Why must you confuse them?"

Harper grimaced with painful humor and decided against an explanation of First Era politics. "Are my thoughts disqualifying me?" *My actions?*

"They are impolite, but that is another matter, and you have kept them away from the faculty members, fortunately. But we who are privileged to view them—"

"Or forced to put up with me?" The redhead smiled. "Life would have been simpler if you'd been out of town when I arrived here, wouldn't it have been?" *I would have missed a friend.*

"If not me, it would have been another, Tim'thy. With the same results." Sweln put the book on a side table carefully, protectively. "I have no cause to complain."

But you didn't stay up late to feed me compliments, Harper thought. And when the older man shook his head in agreement, he asked the question that had to be asked. "Does—do your daughters have cause for complaint?"

Sweln made a meaningless, time-delaying gesture, then snapped his fingers. "Onnul had been buying equipment for a farming team until you came along. It was not an occupation she would have chosen—in other circumstances. But Alghera must do without its apprentice archaeologists for the present. And Cyomit will someday have tales to tell about the famous Ironwearer Harper Timithial ha'Dicovys. You need not worry about your impact on their lives.

"Moreover, I am often gone for long periods, and I can't believe my older daughter is happy without a man to order about or that my youngster does not need attention from a parent. Parenting is not an unnatural role for you, Tim'thy."

Harper could find nothing to say. He nodded stupidly.

"However, it is parenting I must talk to you about now." Sweln's face hardened. "We may speak freely. Onnul is asleep and will not wake up." He frowned grimly, and Harper understood that Onnul's slumber was enforced by her father.

"Several year tenths ago, you frequented a brothel with Tolipim and one of the Hujsuons."

Harper held a hand up to forestall other words, but Sweln did not stop. "This is a different culture, Timt. You are not at home in it, and much must still be explained to you. We are, as a rule, monogamous in this era. One marriage, perhaps one prior unimportant love affair. We have not—the lustiness—you seem to find normal. It is not something we need to be congratulated for or should be pitied for; it is simply part of our life. Which is why—"

"I understand," Harper said thickly. Something had to be said.

"Do you?" Sweln smiled ironically. "I doubt it. Do you also understand that there are accidents, diseases—other events—that leave people without partners, without the possibility of finding other hearth-mates because of our culture? Without livelihood?

"And our society changes. Rapidly from our viewpoint, perhaps even from yours. Not everyone adapts easily. For those with difficulties, prostitution can be a career. And when season-taken, even a blessing." He smiled again, more genuinely. "You've not quite committed the sins you wish to blame yourself for, Ironwearer."

"I—I'll remember." Harper bit his lip, wondering where the discussion was headed. How was Onnul involved?

"So. Onnul." Sweln echoed his thoughts. "We spoke, however, of a local brothel. A Teep prostitute."

Memories rose in Harper's mind. He fought off a guilty smirk, got to his feet, and went to a window. Sweln's image stared at him, crisscrossed by thin lines of metal inside the glass. Beyond the reflection a three-quarter moon gave form to black trees and shrubs, and the silhouettes of houses. Stars bobbed above the river, running lights from merchant ships waiting for dock space. *Peaceful trade despite the war. Are our economies that integrated, or is the Alliance just rubbing our noses in our weaknesses? Or is starving us into surrender against their honor?* "Yes?"

"She became pregnant. She was season-taken when—yes, I see you remember. It meant nothing to you?" Sweln's image leaned backward into his chair, brought up eyebrows.

Harper shook his head, then nodded to conform to local customs.

"Once a year, our women become eager for sexual activity, without great selectivity. Shock, illness, or emotional conflict may also provoke the condition, but it is basically hormonal. It accompanies ovulation, of course. The rest of the time—"

Harper turned from the contemplation of foreign constellations to put memories together. "They are not interested."

"They are not interested. Yes. I gather that in your time—"

Harper sighed sadly. "It was very different. Sometimes." Candor struck. "It *could* be different."

Onnul's father pursed his lips, avoiding comment. "You were with a season-taken woman, and—I'm sorry if it disheartens you."

The redhead chuckled grimly. "Not the famous old Harper technique, eh? My ego may survive. But the girl—she's pregnant. What about her? Does she need—"

"She miscarried." Sweln's voice was flat.

Silence ruled now. Harper stared at the man, then moved across the floor to sit in a chair close by Sweln. So he would not discover the Algheran version of child support, half his mind told him with forced humor. But over that was something close to regret. "Guess it happens."

"Infrequently." Sweln rubbed his wrists and sighed at a private memory. "At any rate, the story came back to me. Not one about you, only that the fetus had been autopsied and found . . . strange. Wrong genetically."

Strange. "How?" Harper insisted. "Three eyes? Tentacles?"

"Normal enough in appearance," Sweln said slowly, staring at him. "But—what do you know of human reproduction?"

Harper did not have the words in Speech till they were given to him, but he had a layman's understanding. Each body cell contained the instructions needed to build an entire body, in the form of genes. The genes were contained somehow in the chromosomes, which were found in the nucleus of the cell. The chromosomes came in pairs. Periodically the pairs would split apart, and the cell would divide into two new cells. Chemically, the genes were a form of acid arranged in a two-stranded twisted form, like the banisters on a spiral staircase. When the cell divided, the banister strands were ripped apart, and each rebuilt a companion strand from the material in the cell nucleus. Reproduction involved combining a sperm from the male with half the normal chromosome set and an egg from a female containing their complements to form a complete cell. He explained that to Sweln haltingly, feeling foolish embarrassment.

"Close enough," Sweln said finally. "You can imagine our surprise at discovering an embryo whose cells contained forty-nine chromsomes."

"A monster," Harper agreed, feeling ill. "Three too many." *Mine?*

Sweln sighed gently. "Three too few, Tim'thy."

Harper stared in horror while Sweln continued. "The woman was normal. So we wondered about the father. She remembered several possibilities, one of them a very large man with a Teepblind and red hair. A man with a limp from a recent wound and an accent. And while it meant nothing to my colleagues, to me . . . I feared. With cause, it seems."

"We had forty-six," Harper said from an abyss. "Forty-six, Sweln."

"We have fifty-two. You are not human, Timithial ha'Dicovys."

"But—forty-six."

"If you prefer, *we* are not human. We are from different species, and—I cannot guess what connection there is between yours and ours. Your warmer body temperature, faster reaction times, the difficulty you had accepting transplanted nerves—those things that puzzled us are now explained."

The pity so plain on his face already wore an alien cast.

Harper clutched at straws. "You're Teeps. What about—"

"The Normals? We and they are the same, two races of the same species. I'm sorry, Tim'thy. You can never have children by our women—never. I'm sorry."

Onnul! "Is there anything—" He swallowed and could not continue.

Sweln sighed from far away, from ninety thousand years away. "It may not be wise to raise your hopes, but a miracle could be possible. Someday. The Plates that have upset you so contain a discussion. It makes very little sense so far, but apparently during the Fourth Era methods were found for adding and removing chromosomes. They were necessary for reasons we do not yet understand, and—if this war does not continue indefinitely, Tim'thy, we may resume the progress we had been making. Two centuries from now, or three centuries. Can you be so patient? And—" Sweln's eyes moved toward the room where Onnul slept. When he snapped his fingers, it made no sound at all.

Harper swallowed painfully. "I don't have three centuries, Sweln. In my time, I might have had another fifty years. I—" A mind other than his own watched him as he rose, a will he did not recognize directed his movements.

Sweln said meaningless things, made meaningless promises. Harper noticed none of them as he fitted on his Teepblind, remembered none of them during the long night he spent wandering the deserted alien city.

He did not cry. He did not cry. He did not cry.

Chapter Nine

"*Ironwearer Timithial ha'Dicovys?" The voice had a formal note.*

"More or less, son." Harper yawned lengthily, rubbed his back against the fallen tree trunk, then yawned again. Some sleep was better than no sleep, and nothing in the voice threatened immediate action. Perhaps he could get more sleep. He certainly didn't need to raise his head or open his eyes. Cap shooter sounds rang in the distance, childish popping noises. *Cowboys and Indians.*

Lawn mower engine racket came from farther down the slope, then sputtered to a stop. The sounds of lawn mower hitting rock followed, then the engine restarted. *Dead cowboys, splattered Indians.*

"Ironwearer ha'Dicovys?"

Not going away. Oh, well. Harper shook his head, opened his eyes after another yawn, and listened more attentively to the gun shots. They weren't going away, either.

An inch-wide slot had been cut into the trunk nearby. He rolled over to it and lifted an eye. What might have been raindrops hammered the ground a hundred yards away—if raindrops whined as they fell, if showers lasted for only a fraction of a second and made the ground smoke.

Treetops quivered on a green hillside several miles away. The distance would not allow him to make out details, but he knew what waited there and anticipated a better knowledge within the day. Five days ago, this slope had been forested also.

It still smelled like a forest.

"Ironwearer?" It was beginning to sound like a complaint.

Other men lay about him, some silent, some making strained sounds in their sleep. Splintered tree trunks and branches were scattered on the ground in all directions. The narrow leaves were curling, already becoming rimmed with brown. More leaves carpeted the ground, along with splinters, black-skinned twigs, and slabs of grub-riddled bark. Like frozen snakes sticking fang-like snouts into the air, tendrils protruded from muddy root holes. Nearby, a thin man pounded his fist on the ground, unfolded it, stared at the fingers, raised the hand slowly, made a fist, pounded it on the ground. Another veteran drank from a cup of stew, not caring that the tremor in his hand caused greasy slime to slop onto his chin, down his grass- and mud-stained uniform. No one was talking.

Harper looked at the unscuffed dark boots and the green pants with only small spatters of drying mud on them. He longed for pants like that, lusted for pants like that.

Rear echelon or a replacement. Which?

Harper tilted his head back, pushed up the visor of his padded baseball cap, and looked without pleasure at a thickset graying man in a uniform that had no rank insignia. A pistol rode in a closed holster; the man carried no other weapons. *Staff.*

"Get down or you're a dead man." *Ask me if I care.*

The old man face grimaced. Blubbery lips pouted.

A hollow *thunkkk!* came then. The tree trunk rocked minutely toward Harper and fell back reluctantly. Sawdust scraps of bark sprayed a man's height upward.

The old man's palsied hands put pressure on the trunk as he let himself drop to his knees. He made a clown's face.

Ankle injury, Harper diagnosed. "You bring the maps I wanted?"

"No. You haven't said who you are yet." The voice was definitely that of a young man, matching neither face nor body.

"You're looking for me." Harper slapped rank insignia on his upper arm. "Where are my maps?"

"I don't know anything about them." The man shifted his weight from one knee to another. "Troop Master ha'Ruijac sent a message for you."

"This is a Dicovys unit. We aren't taking orders from—"

"A message, not an order," the man repeated. "May I rest?" he asked plaintively.

"See the message." Harper held a hand out. *Bet I'm not his ideal of an Ironwearer.* The thought pleased him. "Yeah, sure. Sit." Another treetop waved in the distance, then fell into a pinhead-sized clearing. The popping sounds intensified. Another rock clashed against lawn mower blades; another shell was fired toward the Chelmmysians.

A LongPusher took ninety of the short Algheran seconds to recharge, more in a defensive zone. Men in the Ruijac battalion would be running forward, hauling stubby artillery weapons through the forest, carrying ammunition and supplies up by hand, cursing enemy and friendly shots indiscriminately, at times falling. *Their turn now. And what they can do, we won't have to.*

Harper snapped open the envelope, barely noticing as the old man, carefully placing his weight on stubs of branches, accomplished the difficult feat of putting his hips onto the ground.

The note read: "PUT YOUR BUTTOCKS THROUGH THE TRANSMISSION." The First Era idiom had been translated into Speech because the imagery had amused someone. Harper needed no signature to realize his error.

"Wrong Ruijac," he said sourly, thinking of Tolp's self-bestowed promotions. "Go back and send a message to this one—"

"He's at Division, Ironwearer." The messenger arched his back, grimacing either with pain or at the havoc that had been a forest.

Oh hell, an argument. Harper frowned and snapped the paper in his hand. A date was under the signature. City year 893, day 72.

This was day 56.

Harper cursed, denied the pain in his left knee as he placed weight on it, and clipped his rifle to a shoulder strap. Pretending that fatigue was not a weight that crippled motion, he scrunched on hands and knees through forest debris.

A snoring man with his head pillowed on leaves flinched on a second soft blow, woke on a fourth. "Huh? Food?"

"Rise and shine, Ensign. You're in charge till I get back."

"Huh?"

"I gotta go to Division. You're in charge." Harper turned away and squinted at the landscape to freeze day 56 in his mind. The ensign muttered to himself, a reference to Cimon that might have been a curse or Algheran politeness.

Harper crawled away without parting words for anyone.

"So this is the forest you were guarding?" Harper felt vibration from the body behind him: laughter. "Not doing a very good job, Timt."

"Maybe." The rifle tugged at his shoulder heavily, persistently. He stared downward past the lift plate to a clearing littered with ramshackle plastic buildings and ill-stacked boxes. Men in green and black uniforms walked beneath, not bothering to look upward. Their bodies, the boxes, the buildings, and the clearing shrank rapidly. Trees diminished to vegetable size. Here and there a giant's hand had reached, grabbed, and thrown broccoli sprouts and strands of noodles about. The mixture had been spiced with bodies and portions of bodies. *This is the forest primeval.*

Rebellion surged in him, a swell on a sea of anger. "So where's your pile of dead eagles, Tolp?"

"Rotted away by now. Those that weren't buried." Silence followed till the levcraft floated a thousand feet above the ground. "If you want to jump, do it now. I'll make better time getting back."

"Sentimental, aren't we?"

"Yes or no." Tolipim ha'Ruijac sounded more weary than annoyed.

I'm thinking, I'm thinking. Harper sighed. "I'm not jumping. Bastard."

"Save it for the Battle Masters. It took a signature from them to get you ordered out, not anything I did."

While Harper thought about that, the levcycle rotated smoothly to face away from the sun. Summer grain was visible in the distance, pale gold from a world with no connection to the green and brown of the forests.

Tolp sighed as the grain fields slipped toward them. "Some were eagles. Men who flew with such grace, even died so well that . . . The war killed them all, on both sides."

Harper's hostility began to abate. "But not you?"

"Not me. If I had stayed." Tolp grunted. "Why didn't you come back when I sent you the first message?"

"I was doing something useful here," Harper lied. "That Project you and Sict have running. Nothing works. All the little games played, all the big ones—when I couldn't do anything with a Cimon-lost tank, I could see the effort was a waste. So I reported and—"

"Killed a couple of Chelmmies. A couple. Maybe. Wheee."

"That bother you?"

"Killed a *bunch* of Chelmmies with that tank, you sure did. That change got in the history books, Timt."

"And what else changed?"

Tolp snapped his fingers. "They won a battle, but it took a battalion instead of a company. They *paid*."

"They still won." Harper repeated the words. "History doesn't want to be changed, Tolp."

The Algheran made a spitting sound. "Lift up the front of the seat pad, push the button on the right."

Harper obeyed awkwardly and was not surprised when the sun swung past his shoulder to plunge over the horizon. After-images warred with darkness. A long banked ember of curiosity glowed for a moment. "What day is it, really?"

"Seventy-two, going on third watch when I left. Nobody's gotten farther uptime." Tolp paused. "About the Eagle Slayers. Sict ordered me out two years ago."

Sunrise came as a rainbow flash upon the horizon. Tolp's gloved hands twisted the hand throttles. "I had some skill at this when the war began, and learned more, but my reflexes were already getting slow."

The horizon dropped suddenly. Centrifugal force pressed Harper into his seat as the levcraft's nose pointed upward. A skyline appeared where it should not have been. The air was filled with earth, which exploded upward, slipped past the levcraft, then fell into proper place. The horizon was where it belonged, and there had been no crash.

Tolp laughed curtly. "Tricks aren't enough. Experience isn't."

Nighttime came, and Harper could see a trio of houses at an intersection of gleaming lines that were roads. The moon leaped between clouds. "People I had once flown cover for were protecting me."

Daylight and the earth rotated as if on a turnstile. "Some of them died doing that."

Night. Day. Another night.

"You got killed day 57."

Harper heard the words and gave them meaning one by one. "And did I rise up to Cimon and have my soul weighed properly?"

"A LongPusher shoved you into a tree and ripped off a leg and half your belly," Tolp said evenly. "When they got to you, you didn't have the strength to moan, and nobody understood what you had been screaming before, anyhow. The story that came back to Borct was that you were trying to make Cimon's cross when they shoved the knife through your neck and that you smiled while they did it. Might be true. Me, I doubt you liked any of it."

Harper shrugged. "Sounds quick enough. I've heard worse ways."

"Die in bed if you can. Ask your pal Sweln which he'd prefer."

"We can't all be shot by outraged husbands at the age of—" Harper stopped, the jest ash in his mouth.

A silver gleam that was a canal flowed with sunset red, then vanished into night. "Onnul was upset."

Bitterness that must not be aimed at—loss that could not be blamed on—sadness that would not be felt by— "She'll survive. That's a pretty cheap shot, Tolp."

Tolp chuckled without humor. "No one's calling me an Ironwearer. I can try anything that works." The alternation of day and night had stopped. A sliver of moon scythed the heavens, giving less illumination than the gauzy, ragged Milky Way. The earth was a jigsaw pattern of grays and blacks.

"You going to tell me the whole Cimon-taken city turned out at my funeral?" Harper asked. "You think that'll work, too?"

"We don't have time now for funerals." Tolp turned his wrists steadily, increasing the power that flowed through the engine. "Or do you really care anything about the city you were dying for back there?"

"What's that supposed to mean?"

Tolp did not answer.

The earth dropped away, and soon the air was cold.

From a mile away, a man's body is only a speck. It is not possible for unaided eyes to make out a face, boots, rifle, or—easily—the color of his clothing. ChelmForceDrop had red uniforms, Harper had heard.

The dawn sky seemed to be raining blood.

"Punch the button," Tolp ordered.

Do they yell "Geronimo" when they jump? Harper stared with fascination at the wriggling drops of red falling ever so slowly from aircraft-carrier-sized floating platforms. Dragonfly and midge shapes darted erratically through the blood dew, skimmed over the platforms. Wind roar yells came at him: a pipe organ drone, scattered pops and hisses and crackles as if from a malfunctioning radio.

Another part of his mind replayed what Tolp had told him. An early death was not inevitable.

"Punch the button!"

A platform wavered, rocked violently, then spilled a red-glittering shower toward the ground. The organ note warbled, growing shriller, louder, obliterating thin gnat-voice screams. The platform stood on edge for an endless brief moment while crimson pooled in one corner and drained.

"Timt! We're a target! Punch the button!"

He obeyed mechanically, unthinkingly. A watch slipped by.

Borct had been angry when he found Harper missing, angrier when he discovered the subject of his last conversation with Sweln ha'Nyjuc. Angrier yet after Harper died. Borct had let Sweln know that.

Sweln, who had already been reviewing Harper's medical records, used this as an excuse to consult with his colleagues. Algheran medicine was better than that of the First Era, they decided. They gave Sweln's hypothetical patient another century with current knowledge; that would probably let them learn enough to keep him going another fifty years, which meant more time to . . .

They made no promises, Sweln had been careful to tell Borct, but . . . Children were even a possibility; it would surely be easier to alter a handful of chromosomes in sperm cells than to transform genetically an entire living body.

A waffle-iron form lay across the city wall, broken into

thirds by impact. The underside of the ChelmForce troop carrier.

The sky was clear. The cornflower and violet petals scattered without pattern below had been Algheran aircraft hours before.

Ha'Ruijac, did you ever hear tell of parachutes?

Only for the Falltroop, boy. Never wore them in the Eagle Slayers.

Red larva shapes wriggled across the hillsides, explored streets, fastened upon building sides, paid insect homage to black marble domes. In the distance a tea-tray shape settled slowly on tan and brown farmlands. Fleas were leaping from it, enjoying the late morning sun.

"How many were there?" He heard a child's pain in that voice and only then recognized it as his own.

"Fifty thousand. Sixty. They dumped another load that size in the afternoon. There are surface ships coming from—from all over now." Tolp's voice was distant, hollow.

So this is what it means to war against a whole world, a dispassionate voice told him. *Seven years of holding the Alliance at bay, and all along they were getting ready to throw this Sunday punch, and we never knew, we never knew.*

"How did they keep it secret? Didn't our Teeps—" He stopped, feeling foolish. *Politics. Government.* No Algheran telepath would have dared tell the authorities what the Alliance had planned. The Algherans would have refused to listen to him and perhaps even would have punished him for violating their sacred Compacts.

The Final War had ended with the ultimate irony.

"What's left?" His voice was dull.

"Sept house troops. Men on leave or sick. Students, faculty. Women and children. Land Watch is trying to get out to the north."

Scraps.

"What's *left*!" The anger came without intention. He felt sorry about it but not sorry enough to apologize. Without waiting, he jabbed a finger at the button.

Bloody grubs carpeted the carcass that had been a city. Crab louse shapes crawled about hair follicle towers, promenaded obscenely across open sores that had been parks, and oozed corpse-gorged from homes and dormitories. Flames rose from the Gathering Hall of the Muster, red and yellow curtains billowing upward from the windows amid black velvet smoke. Heated air made the scene below quiver.

A desiccated insect body lay on the roof of Resolution Stronghold, unmoving as red warrior ants danced in the courtyard. Finally two red forms appeared on the roof, bent over the body, pushed it off, then wiggled semaphore antennae at those rejoicing below.

Dark maggots retreated before the warrior swarm, pouring at the pace of black molasses across the bridge to the north, and fell under the crimson tide. Algheran soldiers.

"Have to surrender the city." *Why don't you see that?* Tolp's voice asked. "Talks are set up for the morning."

Harper pushed the button again.

Half of Nyjuc House had been flattened. Dusk showed a pair of glistening leech shapes that blundered back and forth through the wreckage, crushing innocent welcoming mites. In a nearby alley, red wasp forms lowered themselves one by one on a writhing termite sacrifice.

The Gathering Hall was a blackened hollow stump, and Resolution Stronghold was a gravel-pelted child's sand castle melting before ocean waves. The bridge over the Ice Daughter had been yanked apart like so much warm taffy and left to droop in the water. Toy boats pressed against the miniature docks and beached on the strip of park grounds along the river. More were approaching from the estuary.

White things leaked from the boats, wandered at will through the crimson-clad ChelmForce paratroopers, leukocytes to tame the frenzied red corpuscles that thronged the arteries of Alghera. ChelmForceOccupation.

"All over. All over." Harper spoke numbly, simply stating a fact.

Borct had told the Teep physicians that a patient existed who had Sweln's hypothetical genetic deficiency. Sept Dicovys had wanted a cure for the problem, and would have paid to the point of bankruptcy to finance the development of a cure.

Harper's finger stabbed down viciously.

Nothing changed. This nightmare was the Present.

End of the line.

We were set up for this, he realized coldly. All the deaths, the courage spent, the pride exhausted, the public costs, and the private pains of the past seven years had bought nothing. The High Command of ChelmForce had deliberately bled Alghera of its wealth, its strength, its youth. Now it was reaping an executioner's harvest, and revolt would never be possible.

Some were eagles. The war killed them all, on both sides. I am an Ironwearer of Alghera. Nothing else matters.

He turned his head backward, half admiring the clean straight crystal line of his rifle barrel against the purple twilight sky. "Set me down anywhere you want, Tolp, any time convenient. I'll kill as many as I can get."

A pudgy hand patted his shoulder awkwardly. "My friend, there's a better way to fight them."

Part 3: A Knight in Rusted Armor

Timithial ha'Dicovys—47,923 L.C.

Chapter Ten

"*Once upon a time, because all good stories begin 'once* upon a time,' there was a man named Tim Harper. He was born in Anno Domini 1945, which means 'in the year of the Lord,' probably dropped dead in 1970, using the same rather dead calendar, and was last seen gallivanting about in the year 47,923 by the Long Count, or maybe 90,000 on what he was used to, having gone AWOL for three thousand years in an invisible flying saucer—well, an invisible flying van—accompanied by Niculponoc Onnul Nyjuc, who was the most beautiful girl in the one world. Several worlds.

"What else? Oh, yes, the flying saucer happened to be a time machine. And the girl was a mind reader.

"A *knight* in rusted armor. I must be bombed out of my mind," Tim Harper concluded. "But then, I am with a lady of intoxicating beauty."

Onnul laughed. "And how does your story end?"

"Ah, without a resolution. It's a very *modern* story."

Iowa, he thought fondly, not for the first time. *Cornflowers and honeysuckle and tall fields of wheat. A hell of a thing to be thinking of, but she does have a husky, Midwestern type of soprano, and how can I find more time to spend with her?*

"And you almost manage to sound worried about it." Her gown rustled as she turned to face him and reached to stroke the back of his hand where it rested on the controls. "Poor, intoxicated Timt."

"That's right, love, give me sympathy. Just think how miserable I'll be when I wake up," Harper said. The van's tiny cockpit was dark, illuminated only by the colored numerals on the consoles, but his eyes had adjusted to that. He shook his head theatrically and smiled at the red-haired man in the green uniform dimly visible in the forward window of the levcraft. "An orphan all alone in a cruel world—sorry."

He bent over the instrument panel, hiding from Onnul's reaction.

The flight of the refugees from Alghera's fall had been hasty, poorly organized, and uncomfortable. Sweln ha'Nyjuc's heart had failed during the exodus, and the damage could not be undone.

Onnul and Cyomit were orphans now as much as Harper, just as alone.

But he had had four years to accept Sweln's death. Those pent up in the Station—the tiny community established in the abandoned First Era nuclear waste repository—had had less than six months.

47,922 and a fraction, he read from the central display. The last year of peace, seven years before the Chelmmysians conquered Alghera.

It would be a conquest without victory.

Short miles away and three thousand years in the past, the refugees waited and labored for their city's liberation. The government-in-exile founded by Borct ha'Dicovys continued in the Station; the hidden warriors organized by Tolp ha'Ruijac still fought to divert the course of history. Inside the Project, the hope of independence remained alive.

Seven years, he told himself. He could reach the Present in two of the long Algheran minutes and once more watch ChelmForce assault the peaceful city before him, once more share the impotence of the younger Harper who had watched the city's conquest from Tolp's levcyle. He could do what he had desired to do four years ago and kill Chelmmysians.

He would have no effect.

History could be watched with impunity, the Present changed only with difficulty.

And the future could not be reached. At the limit of time, the Present advanced slowly, one second at a time. A time traveler could race through the past, moving forward or backward, but he could not go beyond the Present, any more than a boatman could sail upon a dusty arroyo before a flood arrived. The time travelers were sailors upon the seas of what had been and could go only where the currents of history had flowed.

Who ever guessed it would be so Cimon-taken hard to change things?

We can't go on this way, he thought half rebelliously. *The people back in the Station can pretend they'll get their country back any minute, but we Agents are all getting old running around uptime. We've still got some hope, but it isn't the faith we once knew.*

But it was time to prepare for landing. Another year to go, his instruments told him, another couple of minutes. A thousand man-heights of altitude to lose, covering ground at fifty miles an hour by eyeball estimate. He manuevered controls, bringing the tear-shaped vehicle's angle of attack down and reducing power to the engines, ashamed of his self-pity and grateful for the activity.

"There, there." Onnul patted his hand encouragingly. "We can't hold you responsible for what you say while intoxicated." She pulled his hand from the controls and held his palm to her cheek. "Darling liar."

Harper ran his fingers along her jaw and let her soft blond hair brush over his hand, feeling happier. *My girl. My very own chorus girl.*

Her dress, a thick material, was partially electric blue, partially aquamarine, depending on the lighting. It was sleeveless with a high collar and tight-fitting; to please him, she had left the lower seam unsealed, and her calf could be seen now as she curled up beside him on the cockpit bench. "I never lie," he said mock sternly.

Onnul laughed throatily. "You exaggerate shamelessly. Admit it!"

"Never!" he declared. "It's Cimon's own problem, you know, having a Teep for a girl friend. What's the point of pitching a compliment at someone who won't appreciate it? You are very pretty, everyone agrees to that, and to me you are the most beautiful girl in the world. How's that?"

Perhaps she smiled. "Better." But her voice was pensive. She turned away to look at the moon-washed countryside below. "It looks so peaceful down there, all those little farms with people sleeping."

"Yeah." Harper gave his attention back to the controls, slowing the rate of their passage through time, then glanced back at Onnul, admiring the long lines of her back and legs as she peered out the window, feeling a lump of pride in his throat. *So young. So important that she stay happy.*

"You've got me curious now," he said. "Just how do Teeps pay friendly compliments to each other? I'd like to say the right things, after all."

She pushed herself away from the window and moved under his outstretched arm to smile at him. "You do mostly. And when you're wearing that thing so much—" She patted at his head, where his Teepblind normally rested. "I've learned to settle for that."

Harper bent to kiss her, broke for air, and kissed her again. *Sharon*, he found himself thinking. *Just no loss at all.* "You still haven't answered my question."

Onnul leaned against his shoulder, brushed the long hair sideways from her face. Her recognized the symptoms; he was about to get a long answer. The vehicle was approaching a coastline now and he moved the controls gently, banking slightly to turn northward and slowing the levcraft further. They were in no hurry; his Onnul could say all she wanted, and the world could wait.

She saw the thought. "Being patient for once? Now that's a compliment, Timt. Usually you seem so very rushed and running-ragged—you aren't often this relaxed."

"You've corrupted me, love," he said lightly. "Carry on with the job—tell me about complimenting you properly."

Those were his words. The thoughts that lay behind them were memories of the years that had passed for him since Alghera fell, of battles that killed men and accomplished nothing, of tedium and time spent in close quarters. *Ironwearer*, he remembered grimly. *The Project can stand it if I get away and relax for a while.*

Onnul said nothing but rubbed her head against his shoulder until he returned to the present. Then her words had a serious sound. "You almost know how to compliment people, Timt. You have the right thoughts, but you aren't willing to say them. You want to hide from their reactions, and it makes you flippant or exaggerating. Think about us seriously for a moment—don't say anything, just do it for yourself."

"You mean I can't say I got a schoolboy crush on my first-grade teacher?"

"Timt! See what I mean?"

She was in earnest, Harper saw, and he tried to comply. *Darling wonderful girl, so kind and understanding, who means all there is in the world to me. Whom I cannot live without. Who somehow "fits" with me as no one else ever has.* "Is that it?"

Onnul shook her head. "You're being flowery, and trying to be flowery, which is even worse. No, be honest. Pretend you're not thinking at me but explaining things to someone who disapproves of us. Like Cyomit."

Like one of the Hujsuons? Or the less extreme Algheran bigots? Harper wondered cynically. *No matter.*

She was a very pretty girl, he recognized dispassionately, with looks that were more than the simple cuteness of her small sister. She was good company: intelligent, well educated, kind-hearted, good-humored, understanding, not a bubblehead or a clothes horse, and all those were virtues. She had faults, such as daydreaming, but at twenty-four she was young even by First Era standards, and Alghera was not a place where people grew up rapidly.

Resilient, though. The time traveling agents had been spared the tedium of dormitory construction and maintenance work after the Exodus, but he was sure the relocation had not been pleasant. She hadn't been one of those who had sunk into despair, hadn't been one of the suicides that still occurred now and then.

Still, she was only a girl. Being a telepath was a strike against her. Whatever happened to her eventually, who could say?

And he— Tim Harper was nothing special, he admitted. He might be lucky enough to live through the war and see all the biology Plates translated. But even if he could be made over genetically to be like everyone else, just being another ex-soldier wasn't apt to do that much for him.

But somehow we fit. With me looking after her, she is more than just her; with her, I am more than just me. Being part of her life is the most important thing that will ever happen to me.

Harper exhaled slowly. "I guess I'm in love with you, Onnul."

"Not putting me on a pedestal?" she asked lightly. "Even though I am so virtuous and have absolutely no faults, no matter what nonsense you think?"

"No pedestal," Harper agreed wanly. *I want you desperately! Cimon and Nicole! Such pleasure—I can taste it!*

Onnul looked at him warily. "Come back to earth, big boy."

She squirmed away from him momentarily, then leaned back to recline on the bench with her head on his lap. Her hand reached up to stroke his cheek, then slapped him lightly. "Ironwearer! I can sense somehow you don't want to put me on a pedestal."

Harper stretched sideways to pat an exposed knee, then grinned slyly. "A big, big bed. Not by yourself. There's an honest feeling for you. Don't worry, little girl: Virtue can be cured, and you'll enjoy the treatment."

She grinned back. "I bet you First Era men were all the same."

"Comes from associating with First Era women," Harper said blandly. He paused, briefly overcome by a wistful memory of Sharon.

Onnul's face was unreadable. "Poor Timt," she said with light irony. "Such a chance you missed after Dad died. You were so warm and cuddly and tender to me, so pure and self-restrained, so honorable and regretful! One touch that night and I would have wrapped myself around you and torn you apart. But you were so intent on being a virtuous, softhearted Ironwearer who wouldn't take unfair advantage. So frustrated and funny! What will you do next year?"

Harper distracted himself with an unnecessary survey of his instruments. "Regret for me, but not for yourself? Not flattering, love."

"Honesty, remember? Sex is very seldom that important for us."

Different species. "Cultural conditioning," Harper said brusquely.

Onnul was gentle. "Our life spans, dear. We don't need a lot of sex. We're not under the pressure to reproduce that your people were. It's not just our culture that's different; it's our biology."

"So stay a virgin," Harper muttered. There was no sense in continuing an old argument. *Ninety thousand years to choose from, and I have to land up with Victorians.* "I'll woo you with metaphysical poets next time. When I'm *Donne*, you'll *Marvell*."

She smiled at humor noticed but not shared, then rubbed his nose deliberately. "Be honest, Timt."

"I am—" He fumbled for appropriate words. "Season-took. Horny!"

"And any day now you'll begin to menstruate, I suppose?" Her tones were half amused, half sarcastic. "Another surprising First Era trait? Be honest. You want me to reject you."

"So I'm a hypocrite. Is it such a big deal?" He did feel that young women should be virgins, he admitted privately. But that was his own cultural conditioning, and if he was guilty of a double standard, surely he had not sinned consciously. The fault was emotional, not intellectual.

Onnul stroked his cheek. "Please understand, dear," she whispered.

"I understand I'm *horny*," he muttered. "I understand we've got every Teep in the Project as a chaperone. And—why do I bother, Onnul? Why do you bother, for that matter?"

She kept stroking. "The Plates, Timt. They give you a chance."

Depression hit him. "That's a long shot, you know," he said sadly. "If the Hujsuon kids had come back . . ."

The Plates were records found in small time capsules throughout the world. Usually they were located near ancient stelae, solid columns of granite standing free where time and man had not combined to topple them. The decoration, on the handful of columns not denuded by looters over the millennia, was metal, almost miraculously uncorroded.

The records were printed ones, plastic sheets wrapped inside quartz cylinders. Exposed to air, they unfolded and became rigid. Several had shattered when their discoverers had tried to bend them.

The sheets began with an illustrated syllabary, then a child's primer for illiterates that guided the reader into a language structured much like present-day Common. Beginning with simple technology—Boy Scout methods for starting fires and hunting game—they became increasingly complex, discussing engineering, weather forecasting, and applied science at a level beyond barbarian sophistication. Large parts made little sense even now or seemed to contradict earlier material. Several sheets had been covered with blueprints for an elaborate instrument too complex for construction with current technology. The remaining fifty pages appeared blank.

The Plates also contained the historical accounts that had become the Fifth Era Bible.

Myth made the Plates the legacy of the Fourth Era.

Chelmmysian scholars were the current authorities on the Plates. The worldwide distribution of time capsules, in their view, was evidence of a precursor world empire. Neither technical means nor content analysis had enabled them to date the Plates, but from patterns of wear, they had concluded that the stelae had been erected fifty thousand years in the past and provided a pictographic record for a turbulent section of Third Era history undescribed in the Plates. Since the stelae provided no representations of the legendary tiMantha lu Duois, considerable controversy had been provoked.

Some experts had speculated that the Plates were a transcription in a human language of the knowledge of the tiMantha lu Duois, preserved as a memorial to the Friends of Man. In that case, it was possible that the Plates would never make complete sense.

This had not stopped the effort to translate them. Nor had the war. The Plates contained too many oblique references to processes and devices that could become weapons. The defeated Algheran time travelers had sought a shortcut: They sent two men into the past in hopes that the Fourth Era civilization could be contacted.

When it was realized they would not return, two more were sent.

They did not come back either.

Time travel had dangers.

Onnul touched a finger to his lips. "It's not your fault, Timt, dear. No one thought there would be problems. Perhaps there's some simple reason they haven't returned yet. Maybe they forgot the time they were to return to or couldn't locate the cavern."

Harper shook his head. "No, all the time shuttles have homing devices. They aren't back yet, they aren't ever coming back.

"Maybe." He hissed slightly, exhaling while he thought, then shook his head. "I can think of a couple possible dangers, just related to time travel, except I came through that part of history all right. So it was probably some other problem. Hmmm. The levcraft! You know how they work."

Onnul nodded quickly. "Sorry, Timt."

"Basically, they ride on the earth's magnetic field, which doesn't change that much from day to day or century to century. But there was speculation in my time that the field might reverse direction every ten or twenty thousand years. If it did . . ."

Onnul failed to comment, so he drew the conclusion for her. "If it reverses, the strength you measure has to pass through zero. When that happens—no lift! If the field is weak for a long enough time, and you are high enough up or moving fast enough—and all the guys who went back were speedhogs, now I think about it. I'll bet they crashed. So."

"Can you—"

"Can't do anything." Harper frowned. "Still just an idea, and even if it's true, they're gone. Maybe go back sitting on the ground, or with something other than a levcraft to fly around in, and—I can suggest it to Borct when we get back, but—" He grinned wryly. "It was a Hujsuon idea to begin with, and I never saw much evidence that Borct was eager to help that Sept become famous. Still . . ."

A chime sounded at that moment, ending the discussion. He was flying by instruments now, his movement through time fast enough to have blue-shifted visible light sufficiently that it could not be seen but not fast enough to make the radio waves visible. Onnul sat up wordlessly and let Harper concentrate on the controls in order to bring the van to a soft landing.

"See what I mean about getting back? These things." He punched buttons that placed numbers in the small display screen, then checked the gauges once more before flipping on the interior lights. "Idiot-proof. If you have to, just push this lever and the ship will get you home."

He pointed, then reached into a door compartment for a Teepblind. He waited to feel the vampire valves puncture his temple and the band contract, then pushed the release that opened the side doors of the levcraft.

Frowning unhappily, Onnul put on a Teepblind of her own, then jumped out of the vehicle before he did. Sweln ha'Nyjuc had been able to keep his thoughts hidden from the strongest telepaths with his own mind shield, but his daughter could not; the precaution was necessary for her but never comfortable.

Darkness was around them, broken only by the lights from the shuttle disk, and a force field barrier kept them near the vehicle. Harper held Onnul by the waist, then took a giant step forward as the barrier collapsed. For a fraction of a second the van was visible to outsiders. Then the barrier was reestablished.

Onnul broke free to whirl about. "It's gone!" she exclaimed. "It really is gone."

Harper chuckled, then took a dozen paces back and forth through empty space. "Yeah. Told you it would. But it'll be back every thousandth of a day till its controls are shut off. Come here. Take a fix on those trees and that path so you can find this spot roughly, then look over the ground. The barrier pulls up a bit of grass when the van lifts, and if you know what to look for, you can find a circle of bare ground." He bent to demonstrate. "Right here. If you can't see it, you can usually get it by touch. Stand on the edge and jump through when it appears."

Onnul knelt and moved her hand about until her fingers were earth-daubed as well. "We must look pretty silly," she said then, wiping her hand clean on the dry grass.

Harper was untroubled. "It's twilight, and this is a public place. The worst that can happen is that twenty thousand courting couples are staring at us. Act naturally and they won't suspect a thing." He smiled then, and held out a hand. "Come on. You need protective camouflage."

A short time passed. Onnul moved her head back for breath and smiled. "Camouflage? Is that what I need protecting from?" She made purring sounds.

He smiled. "It's protecting you from the foggy, foggy dew."

The twilight had deepened to a purple cast. A sprinkling of stars was visible, but no moon. They stood on the grass of the River Park. Behind them was the river, the broad, slow, flowing, cold waters, glacier-spawned and estuary-bound, even now touched by the tang of salt and the swell of the tides. The faint cries of a leadsman could be heard, the distance-muffled sounds of water falling into the wake of a heavy levcraft, the gentle lapping of waves along the muddy beach. Men had named it the Ice Daughter when the city was younger; in Harper's era it had been called the Charles River.

Before them was the city—Fohima Alghera. In blue and white and gold, its lights were appearing.

Years had passed since Onnul had seen a city dressed in the nighttime finery of lighting, and it was for this that Harper had brought her across thirty centuries: To behold her native city arrayed in the glory it had once worn. He held himself back now, unwilling to speak, so that she might look without distraction.

They were not the only watchers, for the park was well frequented; his jest about the number of courting couples had not been without foundation. But single people were present as well, many more than he would have anticipated, and he heard little conversation.

Teeps, he suddenly realized. Alghera's telepaths filled the park tonight, perhaps most of the seven hundred who lived within the city walls. Normals might guess at the future; the Teeps would already know that the negotiations had broken down. Understanding better than the Normals what the morning might bring, they had come for a last look at the peacetime beauty of the city that was their home.

Harper shook his head and began to look at the sight, turning clockwise without haste.

Blue lights, white, and gold. It was a far cry from the riotous neon display of a twentieth-century metropolis seen at close hand or from the sprawling, gem-bedazzling living thing that such a city became when viewed from high in the night sky. Alghera was simply too small for that; although it was the biggest city in this era, its forty-five thousand inhabitants would not fill a suburb of his time.

Perhaps because of this, there was not the competition in lighting that was customary in the First Era. An Algheran restaurant owner seeking to advertise his presence, for example, was instead likely to display freshly cooked food in his window or to replace a kitchen wall with glass so that passersby could watch the choreography of his chefs.

The technology differed, and that had an impact. Most outdoor lights were elongated versions of the standard ceiling panels, doped with chemicals to produce the appropriate colors, each equipped with its own battery. As the battery discharged, the intensity of the light dropped, and the color changed, azure sliding into lime-green before blackness, gold into an orange-brown shade. Periodically a light vanished for some short period, and it was easy to imagine some cursing proprietor or annoyed householder installing a bulky new battery in its wall receptacle—mishaps caused by battery failures were a standard subject for Algheran humor.

Typically, Algheran lights served as markers, Harper noticed. In the daytime, the homes spread over the terraces in front of the city appeared commonplace enough; they might not even have attracted interest if placed in the subdivisions of his time. As in his day, a householder kept a light by the front door and lights streamed through the unblinded windows. What differed was the placement of colored panels at each corner and on the apex of the roof, as if Christmas were continually in store. On taller buildings, glowing strips ran down the sides as well, lining the silhouettes with light.

This was a response to technology also—it kept low-flying levcraft from smashing into solid, inhabited objects. By some quirk of Algheran logic, low-flying levcraft could crash into other obstacles without hindrance, so the hills and empty buildings were dark. As a form of compromise, the streets and the pathways in the parks were provided with lights that flickered on and off and changed color at irregular intervals.

Little of this was completely sensible, as even the Alghérans about him would cheerfully have admitted, but they would have explained that there was no prospect of change. Thinking about it, Harper had once decided the Algherans as individuals had simply enjoyed participating in culturewide eccentricity. He had been unable to confirm that, however, as their language lacked a term for eccentricity.

It doesn't matter now, he remembered. *The lights made the City a target. After tonight, the blackout begins. And it never lifts.*

Onnul nudged him. "You're daydreaming."

"Thinking of lofty, spiritual matters," he replied airily.

"It's too soon to be eating, Timt. How much more time do we have?"

"Till we eat?"

"Till the announcement, silly."

"I was afraid that was what you meant." The Algherans made no use of portable timepieces, so Harper glanced around for one of the ubiquitous motorized sundials and found one beneath a nearby tree. "A bit over a half tenth—fractional six. Let's look at the exotic trees."

She was agreeable, although this was not new to her. The Algherans had managed to preserve most of the amenities of a high culture during the war, among them tiny botanical gardens. One of these was not far from the site of the vanished time shuttle. Harper let Onnul lead the way, trying not to follow her too obviously; their clothing let them blend with the crowd, but a mixed Teep-Normal couple would have provoked interest that had to be avoided. Fortunately, this section of the park was little frequented.

"You're smiling," Onnul noticed, leaning across a fence rail with him.

He was, Harper noticed. He put a foot out, stirring the thin yellow leaves that had fallen from a forlorn peach tree. "Thinking of the first time you brought me here. Remember how you kept tugging at me, and I couldn't figure out what I was supposed to be looking at? And the guard running over when I picked an apple—I wanted to give it to you, you know—what did you tell him, by the way?"

"That you were a foreign barbarian," she admitted. "Weren't you?"

"Oh, I still am. And I still snitch apples from unguarded exotic trees. And peaches, when they grow. And pears, and cherries, and oranges, and apricots. Also walnuts, if I've got something to crack them with. Too bad you couldn't get banana trees and coconut palms to live in this climate."

"Is our climate that different?"

"Maybe not that much." Harper thought about it. "Colder and damper, I'd say. Hard to say—you people have jiggled my insides around and done some stuff to my skin. So I don't notice that too much anymore. You do like indoor temperatures a lot lower than I do. Outdoors . . . hmmm. Three or four degrees centigrade worth of difference now, I'd say, in the summertime. Your winter's not much worse from what we had inland, actually—I gather warm ocean currents swing westward then. No, I think the main thing is that one of the ice ages killed *all* the vegetation. When it warmed up, pine and spruce and hemlock took root first, and it takes a while for the stuff from temperate climates to move north again."

A five-year-old memory came back to him. "Also it takes people, to clear the land and plant. I've seen it happen, in fact.

I lived on stolen apples from near this place for—must have been thirty thousand years. When I came through time to get here."

She pushed at his arm playfully. "Foreign barbarian. Maybe if you hadn't done that, apples would still be growing here."

"I doubt it," Harper said dryly. "Hard to change history, remember? And I can remember the taste of those apples now. If I changed things, I did you all a favor."

"For which we seized you and threw you into jail—I can see you're thinking that."

"Into durance most thoroughly vile," Harper agreed solemnly, "where I was guarded by cruel and hideous wretches. Fortunately the straw was changed once a year, whether or not it was needed, the mold on the bread probably kept me from coming down with all sorts of diseases that I might have gotten from drinking the water, and some of the *cockroaches* wiped their feet." He smiled again, this time at her.

Her forehead wrinkled. "What's a 'cawk roosh'?"

"If you don't know his name, you don't want an introduction. A pest. A little fellow in dark clothing. To know him is somehow not to love him."

Onnul sniffed. "It sounds like someone I'd have met at an Institute faculty party."

Harper put on an expression of pain. "You might have met *me* at a faculty party," he pointed out. "Without the war, and the Project, I probably would have wound up at the Institute. I wanted to be a scientist once upon a time, you know."

"Do you now?" Her expression was serious.

"Huh?" He was genuinely surprised.

"Do you now?" she repeated. "What do you want out of life, Timt? Besides me. You never say. But you don't owe us anything, certainly not your whole life. You don't *have* to be an Agent. You don't *have* to fight in this war. You could have told them no. Or you could have gotten into a time machine and gone away from us anytime during the last five years."

"Good thing I didn't."

"You're evading the issue," she said angrily. "You know it."

He sighed. "Yeah."

"You wanted to be a scientist, you say. But you're not—you're a soldier, and that's all. There are a *lot* of soldiers, Timt."

"I'm an Ironwearer," Harper said. He grinned. "Maybe that's why they changed the straw for me."

"A glorified soldier."

"An Ironwearer," he repeated. "If you want to call it soldiering, go ahead, but I happen to be a good soldier. I know that. I've got a lot of experience at that trade, here and in the First Era. I've got a little bit of experience with science, too, in my era—even if you people don't think it means all that much—and frankly, love, it takes dedication I don't have. I don't think I'd make much of a scientist."

Harper exhaled loudly at the peach trees and stared at his forearms, trying without success to find the words that would explain things to Onnul.

Yeah, I gave something up, he admitted. *She's right about that*. But had he given up something he really wanted, or had that been just a substitute itself?

He couldn't answer that.

"You can't have everything in life you want," he said finally. "You can't do everything. You can't be everything. Not with my life span, anyhow, and it probably holds for you people. You get to a point, and some of the things you used to want just aren't as important anymore. So you let them slide and hope what's left to you is worth something."

Funny. He'd never really grasped that before.

So maybe you're growing up, chum. How depressing!

Just getting old, he answered himself. *I must be pushing thirty-one now.*

Could he explain his insight to Onnul, who was young and not grown up? Intellectually, perhaps, but— *In her gut? No way.*

He grimaced lopsidedly. *Much more fun being a little kid.*

On top of which, I really am a good soldier.

"I know that," Onnul said patiently. "But you have an opportunity for choice, whether or not you use it. Is this what you *want*?"

Harper stared at her. Didn't she of all people understand? He moved to put an arm around her, using the other to stroke her clasped hands while she looked at the ground, refusing to meet his gaze. "Where am I needed more than here? What am I needed for here?"

"But what do you want, Timt?"

He shrugged carefully. "I don't think it's possible to go off and find someplace better. There aren't any wonderful undiscovered paradises, and you probably find the same number of problems and opportunities wherever you go. I had to stop someplace, and Alghera has been as good a place as any."

The explanation was unsatisfactory, he sensed. He should have ignored the question and offered reassurance instead. "You're here. You're what I want."

But she wasn't here, he realized unhappily. He could hold her closely, and feel her warm flesh pressed against his, and sniff the spicy fragrance of her hair and body, and listen to her husky voice—but Onnul was a million miles away.

We're falling apart.

Five years of fighting for Alghera had altered him inevitably, made him a different man from the one she had understood. She had wanted to be a cultural historian, he remembered, an archaeologist studying the traces left by the nomads who had preceded the Fifth Era. She wasn't doing that now; she was being nurse, and teacher, and secretary, and kitchen helper—all the dull menial jobs the Project's Teeps were stuck with. Six months of that had made her a different woman.

The future he had pictured with her would not happen.

Had it ever been possible? he wondered. Surviving the war, being made a Fifth Era human—those were long shots with such odds that no sensible woman would care to bet on them, and Onnul was a woman who always managed to be sensible.

No, she was a woman who would turn a man down, claiming she did so in spite of her love because she was sensible, then fall head over heels for some idiot and not mind at all that her choice was not sensible.

She had not fallen head over heels for him.

She would not. The time he had spent with her, the night she had spent with him after Sweln died, the banter about being season-taken—it meant nothing.

"Shall I take you up to the Present, love?" he asked quietly. "I can't desert, but there's no reason to hold you captive. I can get your sister back to you. You both should do all right in the Alliance."

"But what if things change?" she asked in a small voice. "What if the Project is successful?"

"Then I'll never see you again." He paused, letting that sink in, accepting the pain. "It won't change anything for you. Or so the theory goes. It's just that you'll be in a place that can't be reached by a time machine from the Project. Do you want me to do that?"

She nodded her head. "No. I can't do that. I can't leave you, Tim'thy." She turned and put her arms around him, squeezing; her head rested on his shoulder. "I can't leave you," she repeated brokenly. "I don't want to be left all alone."

Harper stroked her back sadly. "Neither do I, love."

A voice sounded in the dark. "Citizens of Alghera and residents. The Warder will soon speak."

"It's beginning," he whispered to Onnul. "We should get back to the open ground."

She let him lead her away. The park was almost empty now. He found a vacant bench from which they could see the city, and he glanced at her with concern. Onnul picked at her dress fretfully, not shedding the tears that evidently lay close. He could think of nothing to cheer her up, nothing that would improve his own mood.

Automatically, he oriented himself and visualized a path back to the time shuttle. He'd show Onnul this bit of her history and then take her back to the Project, he decided glumly. They could have a vacation from each other. They had both earned it.

The voice sounded again, repeating its message. He finally placed it: a speaker in the base of a lamppost. There were speakers in all the lampposts, in fact. That should have produced a rather blurry, stretched-out sound, but the voice had been distorted before transmission to make it seem correct as heard. *A cute trick*, he admitted. *Someone clever invented that*.

Stars vanished from half the sky, leaving nothing to be seen to the west but blackness. The empty space filled with images of a long desk, shelves of neatly filed books, a dark carpet—an office. Throughout the city, lights dimmed.

Twenty miles high? Harper had time to wonder. *Thirty? Two-dimensional, so it isn't holography. I wish I knew how they did it*. A ghost within him remembered drive-in movies. He reached to squeeze Onnul's hand and felt rewarded by a faint smile.

A man in a green coverall walked across the office to stand before the desk. Harper could not guess his age, but he read on the familiar face signs of stress long endured, before he turned his attention to the clothing insignia. The broken sword and spindle, in gold; the small embroidered mace, head upright;

the plow and dam emblems; a grounded pike: believing priest, true Master of a Sept, alumnus of the Institute, former soldier—the Warder of Alghera.

"Citizens and residents." The tenor voice was calm, clear-toned—an orator's voice. Harper wondered briefly how many persons were hearing this speech and how many were hearing this voice for the first time.

"Citizens and residents," the Warder said. "I inform you now that negotiations between this nation of Alghera and the Chelmmysian Alliance came to an end early this evening without satisfactory conclusion. We shall be at war by daybreak."

He paused and rubbed his hand restlessly along the edge of the desk. The movement was not from nervousness, Harper realized; the Warder was deliberately allowing his audience time to react. But silence ruled in the park, as it must elsewhere in the city, for the Warder nodded.

"I call upon the Muster to convene within the next day. By the powers bequeathed to me, I order the Ironwearers and soldiers of Alghera to their posts. I tell the Land Watch to stand in readiness, the Forest Guard to assume positions of defense, the Eagle Slayers to equip for combat, the Sea Hold to take battle stations, and the Falltroop to gather in its armories. I place the administrative workers of the nation on double watch for the duration of this emergency, and I double the tax assessments. I request that the Septs release their housetroops to the commands of the Battle Masters. Finally, I request that the believing priests extinguish the fires of Cimon in the shrines and illuminate the Lady Nicole."

A smile twitched momentarily on the corner of his mouth. "I will have additional orders and requests tomorrow, of course. But there is not much more to be said tonight. I might tell you I regret the breakdown in negotiations that has brought us to conflict—that is true, and unexceptionable. I must also say now that I regard that breakdown as inevitable: Without seeking to assign blame, I note that neither side chose to compromise to any noticeable extent the principles and beliefs each carried into those negotiations, and that fact alone preordained that the one earth be turned for some while to an abattoir."

"For some while," he repeated. "We cannot hope to win this war, and it would be dishonorable to pretend otherwise. Still, we are a people with a martial reputation, with much warfare recorded in our history, and more recently than in most states of the Alliance. We are fighting for our liberty and on behalf of principles honored even throughout the Alliance—and we may fairly claim that if the Lord Cimon and the Lady Nicole give assistance to men, it will be we They remember and not the Alliance.

"So, we may defend ourselves with greater or lesser degree of success. If the greater, the Alliance may wish to return to negotiations. I assure all my listeners that this will be possible, that Alghera's position will not grow intransigent during the period left of my Wardenship. If the lesser—"

He paused again to show that ironic half smile. "No doubt negotiations will also be possible. Citizens and residents, I bid you a good night. Cimon guard you, Nicole guide you." He walked from the room.

For a few seconds the image of the vacant room remained. Then the sky flickered, and another, larger room appeared, bare-walled in comparison to the first, though shelves of books were also to be seen. Dawn light was coming through an open window; Harper noticed a red-touched cloud. *Seven or eight hours*, he remembered. *This is live, too.*

Before the window was a small desk, ornately carved and littered with papers. The dark-haired man sitting behind it was signing papers hurriedly, pulling them from one stack to scribble his signature before pushing them to the corner. As they watched, a sheet fell over the edge and fluttered down by others on the rose-carpeted floor. Had Harper not known the reason for this haste, he would have been amused.

A whisper sounded from the lamppost speakers. It was in a dialect Harper did not recognize; the accounts he had read had translated it as "Sir, it's time." The man looked up at that, gazing at his watchers as if he saw each of them, not yet speaking.

Tired, Harper noticed. Legend had it that Talling had spent this night reviewing battle plans. Perhaps that was true, and not just Chelmmysian propaganda. He'd believe now that the man had had no sleep.

"So young," Onnul said. She had moved beside him during the Warder's speech. Harper had not noticed her then, and he raised her hand to his lips to acknowledge her presence.

"Late thirties," he explained. "His job's for a young man, by law. Every country had someone under twenty-five on its delegation, so they would have someone who qualifies if the speakership was declared vacant." Onnul might know the tradition, but he wasn't sure.

Yet another voice could be heard. This time the language was Common, slightly slurred by fatigue or accent; Harper classified it as an underpowered baritone.

"Good morning. To all who dwell on the one earth, may Lord Cimon guard you, may Lady Nicole guide you. I am Talling m'na Ree, SpeakerFirst of the Assembly of Mankind."

Priest token on his collar, too, Harper noticed. *I should have remembered that*.

"You have heard the words of Vardin Tollipim tra'Dicovys, the Warder of Alghera. I can add little useful to them; I can but confirm them. With the sunrise at Fohima Alghera comes war."

He tossed his head up, pushed back hair. "People of Alghera, an inevitable war, you were told. I cannot confirm that. The conference record is public, and I believe fair observers will endorse the willingness of the Alliance to be conciliatory. Very conciliatory. And we will also continue to be willing to negotiate with our Algheran brothers."

His voice grew louder, the accent more noticeable. "However, I will not repeat a promise made by the tra'Dicovys that our demands will not harden during the rest of the war. They most certainly will harden—*that* I may promise. The cost in lives and wealth that war entails can be justified no other way. People of Alghera, you must remember this: Each day you choose to continue fighting is one you will *inevitably* regret.

"People of the Alliance, you are committed to a war, which you can and must win. Can—for the Algherans are far outnumbered and have only a small fraction of our wealth. Must—for the Algherans fight in no honorable cause, and with their defeat the vision of Hemmendur will be realized. Only then will the Fifth Era truly begin."

The baritone grew softer, as if Talling were pleading personally for some favor. "Soldiers of ChelmForce, for the first time in many years the Alliance has need of your skills. Battle against the Algherans with your full might, for conflict is the anvil on which the future of humanity is shaped, and we must bring both skill and strength to that forge.

"Do not, I ask you, fight with wanton hatred or cruelty—brothers should not know hatred or cruelty from one another. But fight with skill and bravery and determination—nothing else will serve so well to speed the conclusion of the war or to add more luster to your bright honor.

"To all of you, honor those who die in your service on either side of the conflict; sing them a good death." He nodded slowly. "So I am done speaking, and after a bit of ritual, the one world will be at war. May you make its outcome justify its cost. May the Lord Cimon ever guard you, may the Lady Nicole always guide you."

He stood then and nodded once more. A soldier walked into the picture, his russet uniform bare of ornament except for golden shoulder patches. Several seconds passed before Harper realized that the newcomer was the High Commander of ChelmForce. He held his breath, knowing what must come.

The soldier bent and picked papers off the floor, then laid them neatly on Talling's desk. "Sir," he said simply.

Talling smiled. It was obvious that he knew and liked the other man. The accounts had said nothing of that. A third of the way around the world, Tim Harper watched two friends meet and closed his eyes to ward off nausea.

There was a sound of cracking wood. That was Talling's staff of office being broken, he knew. That was part of the ritual. The Alliance was now without a SpeakerFirst of the Assembly. A new one would be elected when the war ended, when the High Command of ChelmForce allowed a civilian-headed government again.

If Talling could go through this, Harper could. He opened his eyes.

The last part of the ritual was blessedly quick. Harper watched unflinchingly while Talling walked across his office to the soldiers who had been waiting for him, while they tied his hands behind him and fastened the scarf about his neck, even while Talling's body jerked spasmodically on the floor of his deserted office, smearing the rose carpet with fecal material and the bloody froth from his nostrils.

Chapter Eleven

The song began soon after, faintly, so he could not be sure at first whether it came from voices within the city or from the speakers in the lampposts.

> The morning rains wipe clean the plains,
> And canvas creaks as stretched anew . . .

The dirge, a lament for a fallen warrior, predated the birth of the city. It was normally reserved for times of war, and Harper marveled at its recall by so many and at the Algherans' willingness to pay spontaneous tribute to a foe.

He had sung the song himself, he remembered; the last time had been two days before at a private gathering of the Project's remaining Agents. But now he remained silent, unwilling to identify with the mourners.

> The oxen low beyond the river,
> The drovers near, tall grass a-quiver . . .

The volume swelled as other people in the park joined in, Onnul among them. She sang hesitantly at first, breaking off momentarily as if to see if he objected, then more evenly at his gesture of permission.

It was not a song to be sung loudly. But it was well known, as were the laments that followed it, and throughout the city—over all the domain of Alghera—the people sang, kept in unison by the lead of the telepaths. The air itself seemed to surge about Harper, the one world ringing the death song of Talling m'na Ree.

Harper stirred at last and stood beside Onnul. "We should be going."

Even three thousand feet above the ground, bits of song could be heard, snatches borne on the warm wind like so many scraps of paper to flutter in and out the open windows of the levcraft. Harper adjusted controls till the vehicle hovered to the east of the city; he did not trouble to keep it invisible.

Barges drifting downriver, towing cargo-laden rafts and silver-touched ripples. A small crowd gathered below the narrow entrances of the Old Temple, men and women made antlike by the bulk of the giant cube. A stream of workers entering the suddenly lighted dockyards. Young men wandering aimlessly through the streets, singly or in groups. The firefly lines that were long columns of levtrucks ferrying men and materiel into the Western Forest.

Some were eagles. The war killed them all, on both sides.

Together he and Onnul looked down on the last night before the war.

The singing would last the entire night as people over all the one world bade good-bye to Talling m'na Ree and a century of peace. It would end only as the troops began to move.

And they would move, Harper knew. Talling's death had ensured that. He had staked much—intentionally, according to the Teeps—on bringing the Algherans into the Alliance and accomplishing Hemmendur's dream. Now the grim price that tradition exacted for failure was seen as martyrdom even by his foes.

A soft pine-scented breeze pushed into the cabin, then retreated. Thin, flat-bottomed clouds moved to conceal the lower portion of the silvered moon. Clothing whispered, rubbed over the bench by Onnul's restless movements. Perhaps she was listening. Harper closed his eyes and quoted:

> "For I dipped into the future, far as human eye could see,
> Saw the Vision of the world, and all the wonder that would be;
> Saw the heavens fill with commerce, argosies of magic sails,
> Pilots of the purple twilight, dropping down with costly bales;
> Heard the heavens fill with shouting, and there rained a ghastly dew
> From the nations' airy navies grappling in the central blue;
> Far along the world-wide whisper of the south wind rushing warm,
> With the standards of the peoples plunging through the thunder-storm;
> Till the war drum throbbed no longer, and the battle flags were furled
> In the Parliament of man, the Federation of the world.
> There the common sense of most shall hold a fretful realm in awe,
> And the kindly earth shall slumber, lapped in universal law."

Not the smallest part of the irony was the ease with which the English terms could be translated into Speech.

"A First Era poet named Tennyson," he answered to Onnul's questioning look. "It seemed appropriate. Oh, well." His hands moved to the controls. "We're headed that way. I might as well show you the office."

"Nothing very subtle about any of this," he commented a short time later. "On the other hand, if it looks confusing, it is." His hand tapped at the instrument panel, drawing Onnul's attention to the clocks. "Not time traveling now, just moving at the normal rate. Our force shield is up, so they can't see us—good thing, since ChelmForceLand artillery is pretty sharp. A bit gloomy because of the way the shield works; it's midday out there, actually, not evening. Anyhow, welcome to the First Battle of the Western Forests." He snorted. "My little home away from home. Everyone was a bit eager and inexperienced then, so it lacks some of the technical interest of the last battles there."

His voice changed, becoming slightly harsher and more rapid. "We've hopped over the first few year tenths. What happened then was nothing special—the first Alliance troops to hit us came out of Loprit, just a straight jab at the city. They didn't expect to make it; that was to keep us pinned down while more of ChelmForce arrived, and maybe to grab off some land. We hit back with a pincher attack and bagged some prisoners—not a whole lot, but we did well enough that the Project hasn't tried to alter any of that history.

"Meanwhile, more of ChelmForce did arrive. Which led to what's going on now. What we called a steamroller in my era—a very heavy assault designed to knock over your opponent and make him play dead. Hard to stop. We did eventually, but the cost was pretty high, and the Project has been trying for most of the past year to pare that back. Our basic tactic now is to make sure the Battle Masters get accurate intelligence accounts of enemy numbers and locations and leave the strategy up to them. Of course, enemy dispositions change as ours do, so we have to keep adjusting."

"But the Agents fight, too." That was a statement, Harper noticed. Was it just his imagination, or had Onnul's voice become huskier?

He shrugged mentally. She wouldn't be the first woman to be sexually excited by violent death. It wasn't his bag, but it was common enough to be classified as a character trait rather than a flaw.

"Agents fight, too," he agreed. "In fact, there are a few down there right now. If it looks like a couple of men will make a difference someplace, we stick 'em in. That doesn't happen as often as some of the guys like to pretend, though; mostly we operate a bit back of the front line and tell the people we report to that we came from the front."

Onnul frowned. "The front line—where is it? I mean . . ." Her hand waved hopelessly at the jumble below.

Harper smiled. "Our side of the front line is right down there." He leaned forward, pointing to insect men on lunar hillsides. "Him—him—him. This used to be forest, and the fighting was at closer quarters. Then Chelmforce brought in LongPushers and knocked many of the trees over. So they pushed us out of it, but the destruction slowed their own advance. Then the Eagle Slayers dropped incendiaries once the wood had time to dry out, and we got back in while the Alliance was fighting the fires. Look and you'll see burnt tree trunks all over the place."

"They are so far apart," Onnul mused.

"Less of a target. Any major concentration is asking to be hit by air or armor. Also, take a hundred thousand men and put them around the border, and they are far apart." Harper did mental calculations. "Ten man-heights apart. Remember you've got training, and support, and people in hospitals, and so on, and that number doubles. So you don't use a cordon defense, but even so, you don't have a lot of men on line.

"What happens mostly, they send a force through a gap, we block them, try to surround them. If it's a big unit, it's a good target for us and the Alliance takes a lot of casualties, so normally it's a small unit that pulls back as fast as it can. Or they sacrifice a small unit with the idea of creating a gap somewhere else and exploiting that. Lot of fun and games, that way. Yeah."

He altered controls. "ChelmForce is on the other side of the hills. They've got a recon patrol headed for the pass over there, next to the one the road goes over, and we missed it originally. This time we put in a squad of Agents to bushwhack 'em."

Terrain moved under the levcraft, straw-colored grass covering a rolling landscape, black-scarred over wide areas by fire. The thinly scattered lines of Algheran soldiers dwindled behind, then vanished as Harper brought the vehicle closer to the ground, flying above the vacated brown-shining road. A small stream could be seen, its waters chocolate-laden with mud. A black-limbed bush, without leaves. Sun glare from the roadbed.

Harper noticed a metallic odor. *Check the air cleaners when I get back*, he decided. *This vehicle isn't really designed to be airtight. Something like a real First Era jet fighter now—*

Then they were over the narrow pass. Harper abandoned his daydreams and lowered the front of the levcraft to simplify describing the scene for Onnul. "That rise over where the front part of the hill has been chewed off—our guys are down at the bottom of it. Camouflaged so you can't see them. They moved in at night to avoid—those."

He pointed westward, exposing a line of Chelmmysian levtanks on a distant slope, black-glittering, with rounded shapes, like fattened leeches. "Just watching," he explained. "ChelmForce doesn't have enough armor to risk right now. In my time—you people are missing a whole lot of fun."

His hand moved again, his gestures seemingly producing soldiers from his fingertips as their rust-brown uniforms became visible against the bare earth. "It's quiet down there," he commented. "The infiltrators are Teeps, so they aren't speaking. They don't know what's ahead of them, because our front-line troops wear 'blinds, so they're not making much noise coming up the hill, even though the dirt is loose—you can see them freeze if they start any ground moving. No animals are left in the area; not much even in the way of insects. There's just a bit of breeze, enough to make you want a jacket but no more. About a hundredth part of a day, they cross our trip line, and Cimon's fate falls on 'em."

"You were there." It was not a question. Harper did not answer.

For a few moments more they watched the soldiers of ChelmForceLand trudge up the hillside. Harper's jaw clenched, remembering hillsides he had climbed in the wars of two eras.

"What is that odor?" Onnul's nose wrinkled. "Like acid."

Harper sniffed. She had caught the same odd smell he had noticed and then forgotten. "Dunno. Something spilled?" He sneezed. "Did you bring anything on board?" White smoke drifted from behind the cockpit area. The levcraft lurched downward. "Cimon!"

"What—" Onnul saw his face and was quiet.

The outside sky was suddenly brighter, and the brownish earth below was now tinged with red. Almost imperceptibly, the ground moved toward them, the hillsides seeming to inflate. On the ground, the tiny soldiers moved jerkily, facing toward the falling levcraft.

"Buckle in." Ignoring Onnul's presence, Harper swiped his hands over the console to activate the sensors. "Deep shit," he muttered.

Five out of six battery packs were empty, his inventory told him. The protective force field about them was gone; they were no longer invisible. He did not have enough power to fly the vehicle, to move it through time. "Really deep shit."

He slapped at controls, diverting current to the horizontal motor rings, cutting the drain from the interior lights and the ineffectual force shield, then from the instrumentation itself. It would not suffice—even without visual clues, his senses told him that the levcraft continued to fall.

"Bend forward," he barked. "Head on your knees, girl. Brace yourself. We're going to crash."

But ChelmForce artillery hit them first.

A weight pressed down firmly on his chest. He could not see what it was—his eyes would not open. His left arm rested behind him on a cushion.

That must be the seat bench, he recognized. He must be lying at its base. Yes, he could feel his back pressing against it. His shoulders felt swollen, though he noticed no pain. *Like being clubbed by a padded bat. I must have hit the deck hard. Tomorrow I'm going to be black and blue.*

Every inch of his left arm ached, but the pain was greatest somewhere under the biceps, which seemed to be on fire when he shrugged his shoulders. His fingers would not move. *Broken. That's always the arm I have problems with.*

He sniffed, wincing at the movement of air through his nose. One nostril might have been stuffed with cotton; probably clotted blood, he realized. *Must have broken my nose, too.* That was hardly important. At least the acrid odor he had noticed before the crash was absent; either he was smelling nothing at all or the levcraft had aired out.

Take inventory, buster, an unsentimental army sergeant ordered. *Enough time wasted.*

He obeyed. *Legs bent, but the toes wiggle. Two arms, one broken. A head. Breathing is okay, but something's sitting on me. I'm not missing anything. Onnul. I'm missing Onnul.*

He managed to croak her name out.

There was no response.

He lifted the right arm cautiously, discovered it could be moved toward the wreckage on his chest, and pushed feebly. He moaned as flame seared along his side.

The pain ebbed slowly. *Broken ribs*, he realized when he could think coherently again. *Probably a scalp wound. Great shape you're in, buddy.*

He needed to see. Cautiously, he inched his right hand upward, past the obstruction—the instrument console?—on his chest, squeezing tight his unseeing eyes to avoid whimpering as pain hammered at him. Finally his fingers rested over his forehead. His Teepblind was still in place, he found.

Torn. That was what he noticed next. A flap of skin had been yanked halfway from under his scalp. Now moisture was under his fingers. Tacky, sticky, warm—that would be blood. His hand crept downward, past the hair-covered fold that was an eyebrow.

Be gentle. There was grit sprinkled on his face. *Don't want to get glass into an eye.* A finger went to the side of his nose. He winced, even though the touch was soft. The nose was definitely broken.

But he had more serious worries. He pulled the finger outward delicately to wipe clean the blood that would be matting on his eyelid. It touched nothing.

I'm holding it too high. He pressed downward minutely, again without making contact.

Don't move! the sergeant barked. *Get that pulse down.*

He caught himself before panic arrived, and then checked the other side with equal caution. Skin moved loosely; then his fingertip scraped on exposed bone. A heated knife of pain lanced through his skull. He had no eyes.

Sanity returned eventually.

Blind. So I'm blind. It can be fixed. They can make new ones grow in. All I have to do is get us back.

He accomplished the first step; somewhere in the time he would never remember, he'd gotten out from beneath the weight on his chest. But he had paid a price for that. Blood or plasma was seeping from his forehead; he could feel it dripping over his cheek. A soreness in his belly was at least a bruise, possibly a serious wound. His ribs seemed continuously on fire, and he knew they had been damaged further when he had escaped from beneath the console. Luckily he had not punctured any organs.

Lady Nicole, if you're for real, thanks for waving your cloak over me. Can you keep it there a bit longer? Please?

What he had done might not matter. The loss of blood was already weakening him, causing him to fight against nausea. He sensed from the soreness of his throat that he was breathing more rapidly. Where he wasn't feeling aflame, his skin was cool, moist—clammy. *Shock. I'm in shock*, he thought dispassionately.

He was close to death.

The helpful sergeant had nothing to say.

Waiting was death, he knew. Onnul must be unconscious behind her mind shield, and his Teepblind was still functioning; no telepath probing the wreckage from a distance would know that life remained in it. He could not hope for help from the Agents waiting to ambush the Chelmmies. They could not act without giving away their own position. Besides, they had no way to know who lay in the fallen levcraft; perhaps they had not even noticed it. He would have to save himself.

The body was a tool to be used, not something to be preserved for its own sake. Breathing in deeply, Harper concentrated on calming himself while he purged weight and sensation from his limbs and told himself that his consciousness stood unsleeping in a black-walled room that could not be forced.

When he had finished, he began to search for Onnul.

He found her finally at the side of the cabin, pinned between the uprooted bench and the top of the control console. How she lay his clumsy hands could not tell him; only when she moaned at his touch was he able to locate her head. Time was crucial—he made himself be brutal and shook her to awareness.

"Timt," she whispered weakly.

"How you doing, kid?" He tried to make that cheerful. Then, knowing that it would cause her pain, he raised her hands and laid them palm downward below the sternum, making them rest over slime-covered bone. *Not going to be airtight*, he realized sadly. *But I can't do more without vision. God in Heaven, if You exist, Cimon and Nicole, help me now.*

He tried to smile in case she could see him, and pretended not to hear the gurgling sounds from her chest.

She whispered something that he could not catch, and he lowered his head to hear it repeated. It sounded like "I'm not."

"We'll get out of here," he made himself say. "Don't worry."

"I'm not," Onnul repeated. "Save yourself, Timt." She coughed, and air burbled inside her chest. "I'll die."

"I'll get help back," he told her. Get to the Agents before nightfall, and back to the Station, and back with a doctor—

"I die," she whispered. "I die."

Then her voice strengthened. "Go away! Leave me! Let me be!"

"I'll get help," he promised.

"No!" Her voice was shrill. "You can't do anything. Don't." And then the words poured out of her. "Go away. I don't want you. I don't love you. I never have! I never will, and you don't owe me anything. Go away, Timt! I don't want you, I don't want you, I don't want you!" Liquid splattered from her mouth; wheezing sounded from her chest.

Harper was rigid. She couldn't mean that—she must be in

delirium. "It doesn't matter," he forced himself to say. "It'll be all right."

He was answered by a gurgle, which stopped abruptly. Hands clawed at his arm, then dropped. The wheeze ended. A single choking, protesting sound came from her, and then there was silence. When he held his hand to her mouth, it met froth and not warm air.

He moved his hands past her, blindly groping for the exit, slicing his fingers on shards of broken plastic. "I'll come back for you. Hold on a bit, love. Everything will be all right."

Then somehow he was outside the levcraft, on bare dirt, staggering upward and across the hill slope in a direction that might lead to the Algheran Agents. "Everything will be all right, love. Everything will be all right."

He was still muttering reassurances when he tripped and crashed full length onto the ground.

44,937 L.C.

CHAPTER TWELVE

"You're doing all right, Timt," someone told him.

Of course he was. Why shouldn't he be all right? Harper yawned widely and stretched out his arms, not troubling yet to open his eyes. He was waking up now, he sensed. The mattress under him was too soft to be his own.

Not worried about it. Not in 'Nam.

His eyes opened.

He was back at the Station. A yellow glowing ceiling, wall-mounted cabinets, and medicinal odors told him he was in the infirmary.

It seemed natural to be there. It seemed natural to see Borct conferring in the doorway with an elderly Teep. It seemed natural to have a blond-haired Teep woman standing by him, even though he realized that his calmness was artificial, coming through the hands she pressed gently against his brow.

What injuries would have put him into the infirmary? *Broken bones, cuts, internal damages, shock,* he catalogued, remembering. *Eyes. So they did fix me up with new eyes.* He had expected that; five years of exposure to Algheran medicine had made its miracles seem commonplace.

Had they left anything out? He flexed his toes and fingers to assure himself. *All present and accounted for. I must be ready to go. Good—I've got things to do.*

The triangular door had closed. Borct and the male Teep—the doctor?—were outside the room now. "How long have I been out?" he asked the woman. His mouth seemed cotton-stuffed; a second effort got the words out.

"Two year tenths," she told him. "You're doing all right."

Harper's new eyes blinked. That seemed a very long time to be in a hospital. Evidently he had been banged up more than he had realized.

"Yes," the nurse agreed. "Of course, the injuries alone were not responsible. We do not understand why, but the crust that formed on your wounds was most unusual, and you were overtaken by fever a long while. It was necessary to replace your blood several times."

Infection, Harper recognized. He remained silent, however. It made little sense to explain germs to someone engineered to have natural immunities to most diseases; the Algheran treatment had been successful, and he had no cause for complaint.

He had other concerns now. It was time to rescue Onnul. He moved his head, shaking the woman's hands away, and sat up on the bed. "I want my clothes. And I require the Project Master. Please tell the tra'Dicovys I wish to speak to him."

"No." Borct was adamant. "It cannot be done. It is not even worth doing." He stretched a hand toward a small pile of papers on the corner of his desk. "Forget the idea."

"But she's part of the Project," Harper objected. "We can't just leave her to die! Look, I've figured it out. We go uptime in a bigger vehicle with a cot in it. As soon as the earlier me gets out of the van, a medic and I come out of the field and get to Onnul. We'll have Teepblinds and move fast, and no one will notice us. We put the shuttle on automatic and let it come back a hundred seconds later, and we move Onnul into it and bring her back here for real treatment. It'll work—I know it will."

"No," Borct said again. He took a scribe from a writing block and began making notes on the margins of a document.

"Why not?"

The Project Master scribbled a signature before answering. "She's not there. Will you accept that for a reason?"

"Not there?" Harper shook his head. "How?" He leaned forward on his cube chair. Was Onnul safe? Had she been rescued by ChelmForce?

"The ambush we had planted didn't work," Borct explained grimly. "We moved in a larger force while you were in the infirmary, and that one succeeded. History has changed, Timithial."

"Well, for—change it back, Borct!"

"Absolutely not."

"But Onnul will die! How can you allow that?"

"Easily," Borct growled. "She should not have been uptime. You should not have been uptime with her. You should have known better, Timithial. We can't allow that kind of risk." Anger showed on his thin face. "Fool!"

"Yeah, I know," Harper admitted. "I broke the rules. But now—"

"But now nothing! You Cimon-taken young idiot! Do you realize by how narrow a margin you are alive?"

"Yeah. The nurse told—" Harper started.

"I don't mean that!" Borct snarled. "This Teep doxy of yours—shut up, Timithial! No one noticed her missing until you mentioned her. Now it's all over the Station, and I'm hearing about it from the tra'Hujsuon every quarter of a watch. If the Agents who brought you back had said anything, if we had known she was gone and linked her disappearance to you in any way whatsoever, do you think the Council would have allowed you to recover? Cimon and Nicole, no! You'd be dead, Timithial. You should be dead!"

"Well, I'm not."

"I've noticed," Borct said sarcastically. "Behave yourself, Septling, and perhaps others will notice it also."

It was Harper's turn to growl. "Don't make threats you can't fulfill."

Borct shoved papers aside and picked up more. "You threaten yourself. The Council will not sanction reversing an operation that has been successful—not for a Teep, not for a Teep lover. Press this matter, Timithial, and I assure you that you will nevermore be an Agent. You may not even be allowed to remain part of Sept Dicovys."

"Then I'll go to Ruijac. I bet they'd take me."

"Ruijac is very little these days. And even they would take you only if you had a hearth-mate. Till then, you'd be Septless—a Blankshield. A low Blankshield, Timithial." Borct snapped his fingers. "And Blanklings have no rights here that I do not give them. Settle for the status you have already—it's keeping you alive."

And what is the worth of that? "And Onnul?"

"Is gone." Contempt rang clangorously in the Project Master's voice. "Find another sick-in-the-head Teep if you must play such asinine games. But stay out of trouble and don't disgrace us further."

Harper fought to keep his voice level. "And just how much did that 'successful operation' accomplish? How much extra time did it give the city?"

"The official surrender was delayed by one minute." Borct's voice was flat. "Which is enough to notice."

"And for that you'd let someone die?"

"A Teep, Timithial. She was a Teep! You have lived with us long enough to be aware of what that means. Whatever you may want, whatever even I may think, there are those on the Council who will never look beyond that fact."

Borct turned his eyes away from Harper's glare only after time had made it clear that he could continue the contest of wills. "I have work to do, and there is no point to be served by further discussion. I regret the woman's death. Leave me now, Timithial."

Harper pivoted wordlessly and departed. In the corridor, he paused just long enough to don a Teepblind.

His own time shuttle was now wreckage on an inaccessible hillside, but he was familiar with the workings of other craft. When he reached the hangar, he moved among the vehicles, trying the controls of those he could enter, until he found one with fully charged batteries. Without any display of emotion, he punched in the commands that would take the vehicle downtime, fed power to the levmotor, and moved it off the floor.

Klaxons blared behind him; lights dimmed throughout the Station.

Harper pressed the switch that would return him to the First Era.

Part 4: A Guardian Demon

Kylene Waterfall chi'Edgart—A.D. 5000

CHAPTER THIRTEEN

She came up the hill like a sudden breeze and laughed as she set the fallen leaves aflutter. At the crest, she slowed and stood in the stirrups to watch for her pursuers. Only two were behind her now, and though she knew she continued to gain on them, she wished to see them with her eyes.

Far away, tiny insect-seeming men on horseback were creeping across a rolling landscape. A glow of satisfaction showed in her almond-shaped green eyes; a smile accentuated her high freckled cheekbones. She smoothed back long raven hair with a slim hand and turned the roan away from the winding path.

The hill was badly eroded on this side, and she braced leather-clad knees against the saddle's leg guards as the horse plunged downslope, its hooves sinking deeply into slick brown earth. The trail curved away from her, then came back to a small bridge over a gully. On the far side it veered to the left to avoid an outreaching arm of forest and vanished around the side of another hill. In the distance floated the white tops of mountains.

For an instant she considered hiding among the trees, but they were widely spaced with bare branches offering little concealment, and the ground was soft from the morning's rain; if she turned aside, she would leave a clear track.

The sun was six handbreadths over the horizon, and the sky was clearing; the long chase would go on for the rest of the day, while she continued to build her lead. This was pleasant country, with rich soil and ample water; soon she would come to a village. Where there was a village, there would be a crossroad, and if her followers had not abandoned the trail before that, they would lose her then.

She laughed once more, thinking of the renewed anger they would feel, and reined in at the base of the hill.

The bridge was a makeshift thing of weather-grayed planks lashed to a log frame. She could ride across in a few heartbeats. But gaps wider than her two fists showed between the boards; if the horse made a misstep, it could be lamed.

She dismounted and, holding the reins firmly, walked backward, feeling her way cautiously across the bridge. In the gaps at her feet she could see muddy water swirling. The horse snorted.

She stepped back onto ground and stumbled, falling against a man's shoulder.

He was reaching for her. She leaped away from his encircling arm and tried to free the knife at her side. This man was not one of those following her, but he had tried to stop her. He was in her way. And she had not sensed his presence.

The reins were still in her hand; she tugged to pull the horse between the man and herself, hoping to remount and escape, willing to ride the stranger down if necessary. But she was facing in the wrong direction, and the man was quicker. He seemed to fly under the neck of the horse and kicked at her with both feet, then rolled away and sprang up catlike as she sprawled on the ground.

The horse whinnied and reared, yanking the reins from her grip, then pranced skittishly beside her, its hooves hammering the ground by her head. Before she could react, the man grabbed her by an arm and a leg and tossed her to the side of the trail, then turned to seize the animal's bridle.

"Easy now, boy," he crooned. "Easy. Take it easy." White lumps appeared in the hand he held under the roan's muzzle. "Have some sugar. Easy. That's a good boy."

The horse chomped greedily at the lumps while the man rubbed its neck and forehead, wiping sweat away with his hand.

"Hard-ridden, weren't you?" He stepped back and slapped at the animal's hindquarters. "Sorry, boy."

The roan screamed—there was no other word for it—and reared, pawing frantically at the air. Then it was gone, galloping away, its ears pointed back.

The man tossed a glittering object into the swollen creek, then spun around at the sound of a human scream.

She had run at the man shouting, she remembered. The knife in her hand had been poised for the stroke that would spill guts into the mud. For an instant, she had thought she would succeed. For an instant only, and then earth and sky had cartwheeled about her.

Now she lay on the ground again. Her poncho was folded under her neck. Her back and the forearm of her knife hand were strangely numb, as if struck by an enormous padded club. She seemed to look down on herself from a great distance.

"My horse—oh, my lovely horse. My horse!" she sobbed.

She had been free and independent as few others. Ahead of her, there had been adventures to be undergone, wonders to be known, love to be taken and bestowed, long years of joy and content among her own people, her own family.

And within a dozen heartbeats, all but her own life had been taken from her. Before the sun moved two more handbreadths, she might lose that as well.

She lay amid leaves and mud on a wilderness trail, waiting for her hunters to arrive, and she wept for a chestnut stallion. She was fifteen years old.

"Kylene," a voice said. "Kylene Waterfall chi'Edgart! Be still! I'm sorry about your horse, but I had no choice. Are you all right?"

"He was so lovely," she moaned. Then hands like leather gauntlets fell upon her shoulders and shook her briefly. Her eyes opened.

The man was *huge*. Poised awkwardly as he was, with one knee on the ground, his height could not be truly gauged, but she was sure he stood a full head above any other man in the world. More than that, he had to have the weight of a giant as well. Not that he was fat or ill built, but he was as massive as any two ordinary men.

Clan Bear for him, she thought crazily. *Red Bear*. But what bear would be clean-jawed, with a scarred forehead and light gray eyes? And would a bear dress in green and black or wear a long cloth cap over its red-brown hair?

But if this was a man, where was the rest of him? She heard only one voice when he spoke, and when he gripped her shoulders, she sensed nothing but a vague feeling of concern from him. Now, as he released her, she faced only the moving portrait of a man. No wonder he had surprised her so!

"Kylene— damn it all! Listen to me! In a couple of minutes the guys after you are going to come over that hill and ask if we've seen someone zip by on a horse. Do what I tell you or I'll have to give you up to them. Understand me?"

The deep baritone voice spoke rapidly, as if the big man was familiar with trade speech, but some of his words were stressed wrongly, and the verbs did not always end as they should. Parts of the speech were nonsensical—what was a 'minute,' or a 'guy'? But she grasped the meaning.

And there was something else, more important than the strange language. She sat up eagerly. "You know me! Do you see that in my mind? Why do I not see into yours?"

"Cimon, no!" the man said quickly. He traced an X in the air with a forefinger. "I'm no *Teep*!"

He smiled quirkily. "We've met before. I've spent most of your last year chasing after you, but you don't remember the occasions."

Father! "Were you sent to bring me back home?"

He shook his head slowly, misreading her excitement. "*Kid*, once you've left, you never get home again, however much you want it. Don't argue; we don't have time for it."

When the men on horseback appeared on the hillcrest, two luckless fishermen were sitting on the bank a short-bow shot downstream from the bridge. The larger man glanced up briefly to watch them as they cantered downslope; the smaller one concentrated on rebaiting his hook.

Across the bridge, the younger rider wheeled and shouted. When that drew no response, he whistled shrilly. "Hey, bondsmen! Come here!"

The big fisherman laid his pole aside and stood up slowly, facing the rider as if to display his green and black clothing. Without a word, he stepped around a small fire, then pulled a blanket-wrapped implement from a camouflaged tent.

Light and sound were a kaleidoscope within Kylene's mind.

She focused, freezing the view and stilling the noise, then released. Now she saw through two sets of eyes, heard with two sets of ears.

The young man's thoughts were her thoughts. *By the Ancients, he is one big man . . . never did see that tent . . . the sword he straps on is huge . . . large enough for both my hands . . . a funny way of dressing—wonder what valuables he keeps in that belt pouch he has his hand on . . . angry-looking . . . Pa is here now; he can do the speaking.*

"Mind your tongue, sonny. You guys lost or something?" Too far away to be heard directly, the words of the fisher cum swordsman echoed through the ears of the young rider into Kylene's mind. The giant's voice was flat, and he had called the riders "guys" again; it must be a terrible insult in his native language.

And what had the redhead called himself? His name had sounded like "Tayem." *Tayem*, followed by a nonsense word he had translated for her as "minstrel."

Perhaps the elder horseman sensed the insult, for he looked up from the path and spoke abruptly. "When the sun was four to six fingers higher, a person on horse rode over this trail. Did that rider say anything to you? What condition was the animal in?"

"Saw a horse; sixteen, maybe eighteen hands high. Stallion or gelding, a sorrel, I think. That it?" Tayem's deep voice sounded bored.

"Yes. Go on."

"Youngster on him. Stopped here and tightened the cinch. Then he rode off. Full gallop, not a slow pace. Horse seemed to take it all right, not tuckered out, and the boy seemed okay on him—not kicking or spurring hard. Didn't say anything, though. Got the impression he was a mite rushed."

"What did the rider look like? Describe his clothing. This is important."

"Friend of yours? Not a friend of yours? Well, let me think. Young, I said. Maybe not, but I got that impression. Feather merchant, you know? Black hair, fairly long—too long, really. Sort of girlish. I can't stand hair that way. We don't let our young men run around looking like that in the Central Territories, I can tell you, and just why you people out here—"

"The rider!"

"All right, already! Straight nose, thin face, and no beard

on him. No hair on his face, I mean—the bottom part of the face—sometimes you see that on people, maybe not so much out here. Oh, well. Bare arms, and maybe he was a tad sunburned. Clothes were buckskin, smooth side out. Something like a blanket over his head; there was a hole in the middle his head stuck through. It hung down just about far enough to sit on. It was black mostly, white or yellow border. Maybe it had a flower on the front of it; hard to tell, some decoration anyhow. Little fellow, about five four, and skinny." Tayem slapped at his chest. "About up to here on me, maybe nose high for you."

The description was good, better than the faint recollections the riders retained of her from the preceding night. Kylene stared intently into the muddy water and resisted the temptation to pull Tayem's too-warm jacket over her face.

The long hair was hidden now, wrapped under a shapeless hat he had deemed appropriate for a fisherman. What still showed was no longer black. "Close your eyes," Tayem had said cheerfully. "This may sting a bit, but blondes have more fun. Heads up now, and hold your nose."

She had sneezed anyhow, blowing white powder over the tent floor. "Why do you not just let me conceal myself here?"

"Two people look a lot more innocent when you know you're looking for one. And suppose they noticed the tent and asked for a look-see?"

"Then you could slay them." She had seen the sword.

Tayem had frowned at her. "Let's say I gave up murder for Lent. Oh, never mind that—just assume I swore an oath not to kill anyone without provocation if I can avoid it. Say it's part of my religion."

"What sort of religion would ask such a strange oath of you?"

Another frown. "Let's pretend mine does. Now, pull these pants over what you've got on. Then this jacket—here, I'll zip it for you."

He had had to roll up the breeches as well so that she could walk in them. He had laughed at her then, not unkindly, calling her his chubby little nephew, his favorite relative. "A sight to make glad eyes sore," he had said.

She had blushed.

"Great help," the elder rider was saying now. "We will have to return the service someday. Edgart, give chase, and I shall catch up to you shortly."

That was not right! Edgart Waterfall chi'Allin was a stoop-shouldered man, graying with age, with a passion for digging up the artifacts left by the Ancients in the Great Smoking Valley. The Recorder of Treaties for the Valley Tribes was a busy and important man but never too busy to kiss a skinned knee for a motherless daughter or too important to listen gravely to a small girl's schoolyard gossip. *Father! It cannot be fair for another to share your name!*

"Sure, Pa," said Edgart.

Tayem waited for the boy to move out of earshot. "I've been wondering, y'know? That fellow on that stallion. Do you suppose—"

"A girl," the other man said curtly. "It was."

"Well. Well, well. I'll be damned. Y'know, thought there was maybe something funny—"

"She stole the best horse in my string during the night, and the best saddle of another merchant. Do you find that amusing, stranger?"

"Oh, no. No. Of course not. But a girl! Holy—how'd she do it? Didn't you keep a guard on your horses?"

"She took it from the stable of the inn we were at last night." The trader bit the words off venomously.

Tayem whistled loudly.

"She has been outlawed now, of course. But that does not return my horse to me. And back on that trail, three hands ago, I left another horse—dead—and a son with a broken leg. When I find that girl, I will break her neck."

"Can't blame you," Tayem said. "You posting a reward?"

"A reward! I told you—she broke Traveler's Peace! You barbar—" The tirade broke off as Tayem laid a hand casually over his sword hilt.

"Maybe we do things different in the Central Territories," Tayem suggested. He leered at the trader. "But maybe me and little Roger ought to traipse along awhile with you. When you find her, you planning anything, uh, interesting? Before the, uh, final festivities?"

"This is a civilized land," the trader said coldly. "I shall hang her, and that will be all. You look like a soldier to me—"

"I am."

"Then I will assume that your ideas of justice are those of a soldier rather than of the folk of your Central Territory. Good day to you, stranger."

Whatever Tayem might have found to say in response, Kylene missed. Something was jerking on her line.

"Good fish," Tayem said. "And the cook isn't bad-looking, either, even with all those freckles back. More of this, and I may start make disgustingly honorable propositions."

Kylene smiled while continuing to comb his wretched powder from her hair with her fingers. She guessed from his tone that he was attempting to be humorous, and it seemed to keep him in a good mood. "Tayem, could you get me back my horse?"

The big redhead pushed a log farther into the flames with a booted foot. "It's 'Tim,' not 'Tay Him.' Keep trying, and maybe someday you'll get it right. But I said no business during supper." He picked up a fluted pot steaming amid the coals. "More coffee?"

"Yes, Tayem." She wiped her fingers on her breeches, then held the shiny mug out eagerly. "Coffee" was a black fluid with an oily, acrid taste. Tayem had said it was the most valuable substance in the world, particularly in the morning. She found it indescribably vile.

But Tayem let her put "sugar" in it. That was a grainy white powder, coarser than flour, with a taste like crystallized honey but even more so. Tayem would not let her eat sugar by itself.

"Drink it black," the man urged. "It'll put hair on your chest and make a real man of you—Roger."

She clenched her jaw and added another spoonful of sugar to her mug. Even without seeing into his mind, she knew that he was grinning inwardly. But the offense must be ignored. "Tayem—Ta'm—could you, please, get my horse back?"

"Kylene, that horse is a *county* off by now. Or he's run himself to death on the dose of *adrenaline* I gave him. Forget it."

More strange words. "But why?"

"You're here, and the horse isn't. So the people following you ain't. And that wasn't your horse, anyhow, was it?"

"No," she said quietly. "I—I took the horse."

"You stole it. From an inn, breaking some kind of truce."

"The Traveler's Peace," she said dully. "Yes."

What was wrong with her? She should not be admitting such things. *The trader told you lies!* she wanted to shout. *They wanted to take my horse from me!*

But she could not.

She knocked over her coffee, rushing to the big man's side and kneeling to hold his palm against her cheek with both hands. "Tayem. Tayem, please." Other words would not come.

He was not angry, she found. Tayem would not betray her. He was not taking her back to her village. She was still safe.

A giant's hand patted her head absently, then rubbed her shoulder. The hand was strangely warm, and she noticed a faint musky odor coming from the man's body. "It's okay, girl," she heard him say. "You were in a hurry and got yourself in some hot water. We'll bail you out. I haven't been chasing you to do you grief, after all." The baritone voice was calm, slow, soothing. He had spoken to the horse in that manner, she remembered, feeling quick resentment.

But she remained silent, and after a while Tayem spoke again. "Just perhaps, you maybe are a bit upset about something else. If it's any consolation, you telepaths usually make pretty rotten liars anyhow. Must be—Kylene, is there some reason for all this hand holding?"

I can tell lies, she thought. *I can! I can!* She was suddenly conscious of the flames at her side. Somewhere nearby, crickets chirped.

"I cannot see into your mind," she admitted in a monotone. "Except for a small part when I touch you."

The man recoiled, leaping away instantly, wrenching his hand from her grasp. He slapped at his belt, then held his arm awkwardly crooked so his hand pointed directly at her. He swallowed grimly. Finally he spoke. "Stand your distance after this, girl. You shouldn't be able to read *anything*."

Open-mouthed, Kylene held a hand to her stung cheek. Tayem had hurt her! And he was afraid of her—of her! But he had known all along that she could see into minds, had even made jokes about that.

A screen! she realized abruptly. There was a way the normal people could keep their minds from being seen. He was doing it. Which meant that he knew mindseers or expected to find that. And that meant—

"What are you staring at, girl?"

"Tayem, among the mountains—does a city stand there? Where—where—I was not just imagining it, was I?"

"You came this far and you didn't know?" the man said wonderingly. He touched his hand to his side again and relaxed.

"A city where everyone is a telepath. Yes. Kh'taal Minzaer." The last phrase was whispered. "Yes. Or what will someday become *that*. It's real, it really is."

He seemed to choke, swallowed, then shook his head before continuing. "But now it's just a small town, Kylene. Don't be surprised if—when you get there."

"I *am* going there," she said, suddenly proud. "Tayem, tell me about it."

The man shook his head. "I just caught glimpses, and I'll never see it up close. I'm not one of the Skyborne, kid, so it's not really a place for people like me."

His voice was very strange, and she told him so.

"Yeah," Tayem said flatly. He stared into the night sky before continuing.

> Full black and silver, the City leaped
> From mountains' fastness, solitude keeping.
> Ringed round with rime 'mid magicked nights
> Its crystalled towers were moonlit heights.
> Kh'taal Minzaer in the darkness weeping
> As unspoken majesty unbid it reaped . . .

His voice trailed off. "That's all we remember."

"Kh'taal Minzaer," she repeated slowly, stumbling over the long name to make it sound like "Cat tail, men say her."

Tayem said the name again. "Someday. Be a long time before it gets called that actually, I expect. To tell the truth, for all we know the name was made up during the Third or Fourth Era—never mind that."

"You said it was ordinary. Then why should there be a poem—"

"To teach you not to take poetry too seriously. Next question?"

She hesitated but decided at last that it must be asked. "Tayem—Ta'm Minstrel—why can I not tell to you—"

"Things that are less than completely accurate? You mean, it's not your better nature showing up? Why, Kylene!"

That did not seem to demand an answer, for which she was grateful. "Here, girl." Tayem came close at last to hold before her a vial of grainy white powder, which he then pitched onto the flames.

"Told you it was a bad idea to indulge a sweet tooth." He

gazed intently into the fire, then turned to her with an outstretched hand. "I think, Kylene Waterfall chi'Edgart of Clan Otter, the time has come to discuss some business."

"No!" Kylene shouted. "No! No! No!"

"All right," Tayem said unexpectedly. "Have it your way. I'll go off and change into a pumpkin or something."

She was suspicious. "Do you mean that?"

A silhouette standing before the dying fire, Tayem nodded slowly. "I'm just as tired of this argument as you are—more tired, in fact—and I didn't expect much to come of it anyhow." He chuckled. "I've been squashed."

It had been a very strange argument, Kylene thought. Tayem's "business" had been terribly anticlimactic when it came. And yet, at times she had felt herself transported into an old myth, where Tayem was a demon with whom she had to bargain. But no creature in tribal legends had ever said, "I'm going to offer you a job—work. You probably won't take it, but I'm going to offer it anyhow."

And she had not.

"It isn't all that attractive," the man had admitted. "It's dull work by and large. No one around but strangers who have strange customs you'll have to abide by. Most of them are normal people, though there are some telepaths. The telepaths and the normals don't get along well, Kylene."

He would not explain that. The story was long, he said. There was excuse on both sides for real hatred; it would eventually make sense to her but even if it did not, she would have to put up with it. "Remember this, too: Never—never, *ever*—tell any of the Normals you wanted to get to Kh'taal Minzaer. If you can, don't even let the Teeps know."

The "job" would be for all time; it would never be possible for her to return. *That* had sounded like something out of legend.

"That would be horrible!" she had cried. "No!"

"It is," he had said flatly. "But—the work may be interesting. You'll get a decent education. Living conditions would be better. There would be other telepaths to meet, more than you'd be likely to meet here. And the work itself has—meaning, let's say, value, importance. You'll get a chance to make history."

He had smiled briefly, mysteriously. "Really would. Yes or no?"

"No!"

She had been reluctant at first to refuse a half demon so bluntly. But as time passed and the big redhead began to repeat himself, her feelings had changed from caution to embarrassment and then to anger.

"Why do you do this to me?" she had finally shrieked.

Tayem had looked appropriately sheepish. "Arguing with fate, aren't I? But I made a promise once that I would do this and let you get a chance to choose what your fate will be. Someday you may run out of chances, kid. Maybe it'll be important to you then to remember you did have some choice once."

He sighed then. "Hell. Guess that doesn't make much sense yet."

It had made no sense at all. "Are you threatening me?" she asked.

"Yes."

After a long pause, he added to that. "Keep a person alive and you become responsible for them, whether they live or die after that."

"We have already spoken of that." Her tones had been icy.

It was his fixed belief, she had discovered, that without his interference, the roan would have thrown her while she descended the next hill. "And then you'd break your fool neck."

He had explained this to her quite calmly. He had been equally serene when he claimed to have saved her life on three previous occasions during the year she had been on Pilgrimage. When she touched his hand, he radiated sincerity.

"Which just proves to you I'm nuts," he had admitted wryly.

She had moved away unobtrusively. "You have very strong beliefs, Tayem."

"And since I'm gone off the deep end, everything I say is suspect, and a sensible girl wouldn't buy a word of it. I understand."

She had moved a little farther. "You may have other strong beliefs that people could doubt." Oh, why had she gobbled up that Ancient-infested "sugar"?

And Tayem had laughed! This routine was familiar to him, he pointed out. She should remember that his delusions included memories of prior conversations with her. She was even *squirming* the same way.

"Look, Kylene. I know they're rare, but I'm not after every Teep on the one earth. Just you—never mind why. And I didn't want every Tom, Dick, and Harry told about me, so you were made to forget."

How had he known her name? She had told him. How had he managed to find her? She had given him the route she planned to follow at their last meeting. How had he discovered the dangers he claimed she faced?

"I have my methods, Waterfall."

"Are you an Ancient?" she asked suddenly, half seriously.

"What are Ancients?" He had obviously never heard the term.

"The people of long ago who ruled this land. They had magical powers, but one day they vanished. 'And we were left behind, with the earth,'" she quoted.

That was long ago, she told him again. She did not know how long, and neither did anyone else. No, no one knew more about the Ancients.

"I'll have to take a pass on your question, then. Next one, please."

"Are you my guardian spirit?"

"No. People *like* guardian angels. They even *respect* them. They don't get into arguments with them and call them old men."

She had used her sweetest possible tones. "But if you have supernatural powers and you are not an angel, you must be—"

"Old enough not to play word games with silly little girls!"

Now he told her she had won.

"What are you going to do to me?" she asked nervously.

"Eat this." The man handed her a sugar cube. "Remember, I might be dangerous, so you've got to do it."

She swallowed the cube. He might be dangerous. She had to do it.

Tayem stopped pacing then and sat beside her on the grass. He leaned forward, seeming to ignore her, and tossed pebbles onto the dying fire. "Do you people have an oath to swear or some formula to show they are telling the truth? Some way one normal person can convince another he means well or is honest?"

"No."

"Nothing? You said your father recorded treaties. What are they based on?"

"If a tribe broke a treaty, all the others would fight it."

Tayem sighed. "Familiar-sounding. I won't ask if it works. Do you have anything like *legal contracts*—sort of treaties between people?"

"No, of course not."

"No wonder you're running away from home. Your people don't need telepaths. They've already figured out everything important."

Tayem could not see into her mind. "I left on pilgrimage," she said tartly. "Everyone does. Whether I go back or when is for me to decide."

"And will you?"

"I—Father told me not to, and—well, I can't."

She bit her lower lip after that admission, afraid. But he did not ask about the gold ingot she had gotten from the town treasury or the weapons she had found at the practice area.

Her tension died. If anyone still pursued her, it was not this man. She would have seen that much when touching him. She was still safe.

"Would you go back if you could, kid?" he asked gently.

"No." She surprised herself by answering quickly. "No. I think I always knew that, even before. But—my father would be dead now."

Tayem began to say something, then ceased. A burning log popped; sparks rose into the air.

"I never admitted it," she said in a tiny voice. "Even to myself."

"Probably staying away is the right idea. When I—how many of your people get as far as you have?"

"None. They all stay in the valleys."

"Oh. Tell me about it."

He appeared interested, and speaking kept the unknown future at bay. "You must leave and stay away for a passage of the moon, or more. But it is possible to live in a tent at a place where you cannot see the buildings of the village. That is done by some, by those who wish to wed within the tribe but cannot until both have been on pilgrimage." A thought struck. "Is that a 'treaty between people'?"

He looked away. "Sort of. Anything else like that?"

"No. Should there be?"

He took his time answering. "Yeah. We didn't have such things where I come from either, to tell the truth, but when you have them, you get used to them." He thrust a hand into a pants pocket. "Here, girl, give me your hand."

She obeyed awkwardly, and he slid something over her thumb.

Kylene held her hand before the firelight. The object was a ring, dark bronze-colored, with some tiny animal carved onto a flat rectangular face. It looked worthless.

"What is this?" she asked. "An amulet? What powers does it carry?"

Tayem snorted. "It's called a Brass Rat, and it does absolutely nothing. Think of it as something that makes you part of Clan Beaver, if you like."

"I have a clan already. What else does this mean?"

Tayem held out his hand. "If you don't want it, give it back. I can't wear it around where I'm going, but it means something to me."

"Why?"

"I really think that's just my business," the man said quietly. "Will you keep it, or do you want to give it back?"

Kylene clenched her fingers around her thumb. "What is it that you wish this ring to mean for me? What will you require of me?"

"Oh!" Tayem sounded relieved. "No passes, Kylene, if that's your worry. I'm not out to rob any cradles. I didn't realize rings meant anything at all here; they don't have any significance where I'm going."

Passes? Cradles? What significance had rings ever had? Kylene shrugged mentally. He had said he came from a place with strange customs.

"Thank you for your gift, Tayem Minstrel," she said carefully. "But—"

He waved a hand. "Keep it to remember me by. I feel some obligation to you, and—we seem to have some things in common. So I'll treat you like a *Septling*—within some limits, your friends are mine, your enemies are mine. And *vice versa*, though that doesn't matter so much. If you ever need help or advice, ask me for it or send a message. Okay?"

"Will you guide me to Cat-tay el—that place?"

"Kh'taal Minzaer." He sighed. "That's one of the limits. No."

Kylene rubbed her fingers over the ring. It was quite heavy; there might be some gold in it. Perhaps it could be sold for another horse to replace the one the man had taken from her.

It would not do to remain silent too long. What had he been saying? Oh, yes. "Are you an enemy of—of theirs?"

"Aren't you sleepy yet?" Tayem asked. "You *are* sleepy."

She *was* sleepy. Tayem half carried, half pushed her into the tent and drew a blanket over her. Smooth, white, and flimsy, it fitted snugly about her as might a shroud. It was surprisingly warm.

"Watch my finger," the man ordered. "When I snap my fingers, you will close your eyes and forget the events of this day. One. Two—"

"Tayem Minstrel," she asked weakly. "Will I see you again?"

"Yes. But when it happens, you are not going to be pleased." He snapped his fingers. "Three."

Blackness lapped over her. Far, far away a soft baritone voice was saying. "You stole a horse the night before this, from an inn. It was a chestnut stallion, and—"

Kylene woke before the sun had climbed two hands over the horizon. Rough wool scratched at her cheek. Water was trickling somewhere behind her, and larks sang at the edge of the wood. High above, thin wisps of cloud drifted slowly to the west. Fallen leaves were piled around her, musty-smelling, half covering the blankets in which she had wrapped herself.

Her back was sore, and there was a gritty feeling under her eyelids. Worse than that was the terrible bitter aftertaste on her tongue. She sat up groggily and stretched uncomfortably, shaking the damp leaves away as her legs kicked. It was going to be a miserable day.

Yesterday had begun so well, she remembered. She had stolen a horse from an inn the night before, a chestnut stallion, and harness—wait! Yes, she still had it! The gold coin she had found in the saddlebags still lay beside her in the blankets. And the ring she had found in her room at the inn was still on her thumb. Something had been saved from her disaster.

She had built a good lead on the trader and his sons, she recalled again, lost it during the rain, but then regained some of it. Then she had thought to give the stallion a rest. She had had nothing with which to groom the animal but the blankets she had taken from her room and worn during the night, but they would do. And when she pulled them from the bags, she had seen something gleaming in the bottom. It was gold—a coin fully as heavy as her ring, enough to support a family for over a year.

Unthinking, she had dropped the reins. And, as if waiting for the opportunity, the stallion had neighed loudly and bolted.

She had run after it, of course, but that had been futile. The horse had run down the trail like an arrow in flight, never even looking back at her. And she had been forced to hide in the tall grass at the edge of the woods, covering herself with leaves and remaining motionless until the traders passed.

Once more she was grateful she was not like ordinary people. Trapped beneath the rain-wetted leaves, unable to see through the eyes of horsemen, any ordinary person would surely have made some fatal, self-betraying move.

But suppose she had not hidden herself? Before she had crept down the winding stairway to the courtyard at the inn, she had had the wit to cut and dye her hair. Would that not have been sufficient disguise?

Probably not, she decided. Hiding had been instinctive but justified. The traders might remember her clothing, but not her appearance. And if they remembered neither but found the horse nearby, she would have been suspect simply for being the only girl in the area.

The thought returned not long afterward, while she picked her way down a rock-strewn hillside. If it had been dangerous to be recognized as a girl, she might well have disguised herself as a man.

She kicked at pebbles and watched them slide to rest. "Roger," she said experimentally. It was unusual, but that did seem like a name a man might have. "Roger. Roger." It did not sound quite right—her voice was not deep enough.

So Roger would be not a man but a boy. "Little Roger," she said to herself gruffly. "The older boy of my second sister. Yes, Roger does not talk much. Just between you and me, Kylene, Roger is—well, a little slow."

And what cause would Roger have for skulking through the

wilderness? Ha! "Roger felt himself inadequately prepared for the cultural roles of parent and provider that venerable, but perhaps superannuated, custom might otherwise have decreed for him."

Roger had not been willing to Do the Honorable Thing.

In fact—"Shortly after this unfortunate and trying experience, Roger was given the opportunity to reconsider his decision, though in a different context, and again felt himself inadequately—"

Oh, the cad!

"I suggested to my sister that the talents and interests of her son clearly lay in fields—"

"—in fields, in haystacks, in cheap inns—"

"Don't interrupt, Kylene. In fields less frequented by staider, more conventional personalities and that a tour of duty in the service of someone else's country might open many new opportunities to him."

"Yes!"

"I'll ignore that. Roger himself, I am pleased to say, concurred with this assessment and nobly swore to forsake his childhood haunts."

"Freed of his adolescent stresses and strains," she told herself gravely, "Roger is becoming in every way, every day, a finer, wiser, happier, and more mature individual. He is particularly happy because he has been spared a strain that might have abruptly altered his physical, if not moral, stature."

Kylene laughed and tossed her shiny gold coin into the cloudless sky. It was going to be a wonderful day.

Chapter Fourteen

To the right or to the left? Kylene tossed a battered coin into the air, then prodded her pony forward to where it lay in the snow. A vagrant wind blew snow from the edge of an embankment, throwing it into her face. She wiped it away with the back of a numbed hand, feeling cold metal running along her cheek. Beads of frost glinted in her hair, and her breath was white before her.

Tails. She pulled her arms farther into the too-long sleeves of her overcoat. White clenched knuckles rubbed the coarse fabric through the frayed lining. An ice-wrapped twig slapped at her from the side of the trail. She would take the road to the left, to the high ground.

With that decided, she looked at the sky again. Gray-bottomed clouds were gathering, pillow-stacked above her, too far to reach, but close. For a moment she hesitated, biting at the corner of her lip. She had to find shelter before the storm broke, and even then she faced a miserable night.

She left the coin behind. A carved piece of road stuff from the paths left by the Ancients, it was not worth the trouble of dismounting.

Outside of towns, currency was of little value in the mountain territories. The last village of ordinary people was three days behind her now; the last small, fenced-in homestead, a day and a night back. She did not need money anymore.

She could have spent the winter safely, she remembered. People treated one another well in this land. In a town, snow-trapped strangers would not be cast out but given employment and lodging until spring arrived. And she had come far on the pony, so neither it nor she was in danger of recognition.

But being pent up again by ordinary people and pretending to be one of them for four moon passages would be unbearable. It was so hard to stop, even for a short time, now that she was deep in the mountains. Others awaited her.

The townsfolk had warned her that no one could travel safely over these mountains—the "Rockies," in their language—this late in the year. The homesteaders had offered no such advice, having never known of her passage. *They might have things to say by now*, she thought. Had they counted their hens in the last day?

No matter. She was not going to cross the entire range. Nor was she going to retrace her steps. The next town she came to, somewhere soon, to the north and east, would be her stopping point.

The moon had come to fullness twice since the morning she had awoken buried under leaves with a gold coin beside her, and now she often heard a spectral hubbub of voices, the distant "sound" of telepathic conversation, growing no louder but more distinct day by day. Strangely, the voices sometimes used nonsense words, as if in foreign languages.

"I am coming," she had called. "Am I heard? Do you await me?"

No one had answered, and she realized finally that no one would. Evidently neither telepaths nor ordinary people could carry on simultaneous conversations, or else in that silent Babel her own thoughts were unnoticed. Perhaps she could not be understood yet. Perhaps there were guides to meet approaching telepaths, and she would have to come to them first or learn to throw out some mental shout.

That was just as well, she had decided in the end. She was not eager to attract attention to herself yet.

The journey had grown rougher as its end neared, with each day leaving her more exhausted and seemingly more than a day older. Her clothing disintegrated into rags, and the difference in color between the ashen hair the world was supposed to see and the raven roots beneath had become embarrassingly clear. She had solved that problem by hacking off the lighter hair and wearing a scarf; it was a solution, but it was ugly. She was becoming haglike. Reality concealed her better than the disguise she had donned.

She had lost weight, too, becoming gaunt and hollow-cheeked as well as stoop-shouldered. Not that she had arrived at starvation, but she had the look of one who had never eaten a holiday feast. Perhaps that was from the steady diet of trail meat she had consumed on her journey. Perhaps it was the way she ate, gnawing tiny pieces away from the rock-hard blocks of meat and waiting for each salty bite to soften on her tongue until it could be chewed. Salt and fat and saliva dripping from her lips, the ache within her gums, the unceasing sliding of her legs in their leather breeches as the pony swayed beneath her—after a while, these seemed a part of eating, no more to be separated from it than chewing or swallowing.

Oats and wheat had grown wild in this region for millennia. Even within the mountains, until the snows began, the pony ate better than she.

She was comforted at night, even as she lay asleep beside the trail, by the silent rumble of conversation that told her she was not alone in the world. But at day, the comfort turned to annoyance, and she decided at last to suppress the unanswerable distant voices, listening only to take bearings.

The voices had become very clear of late. Six days of travel lay before her, she had estimated at the last town. Perhaps a few more if a storm slowed her.

But snow was coming down gently before the sun moved a handbreadth.

That first fall was no more than fist deep, so she continued. But another came the following night, twice as deep, while she nibbled pieces of half-roasted chicken. Now the gray clouds were massing again.

The speaking minds ahead of her knew of the coming storm also, she sensed. Knew of it but did not worry; waited for it within thick stone walls made warm by fragrant, roaring fires; ate their more-than-ample dinners and pulled plump comforters to the chins of sleeping children.

Stop it! she told herself. Locate a resting place for the night.

Get through the storm. Ride on tomorrow. *Do not blindly pass what you must find.*

Most of the works of the Ancients had departed with them or disappeared in the intervening years, but the Ancients had left proof of their existence in the nearly indestructible network of paved roads that crisscrossed the land. Weather and neglect had done damage to the pathways in this region, or perhaps there were simply too few travelers to keep rock and soil from spilling over the roads. But the earth had not fully reclaimed its own; arrow-straight, a wide treeless strip lay before her, its edges marked out by gray-green stands of fire and spruce.

Somewhere she would find a place where the Ancients had hewed out a portion of the mountainside to maintain that straight line or to reduce the grade their own beasts had climbed. Such a cutting, perhaps eroded to leave a ledge above, would give the pony and herself protection on at least two sides.

If she was lucky, there would be enough daylight left to drag some fallen branches about them, to be banked with dirt and snow and thus keep away the wind. Perhaps she could find dry wood to make a fire.

Gutted and frozen, another chicken was packed into her saddlebags. When the fire had softened the ground, she could make up mud to cover the bird, then rest it in the flames until her patience fled. The mud would harden quickly; feathers and skin would be peeled off with the baked earth; hot fat would flow over her fingers, and steaming flesh would lie scaldingly on her tongue.

She would try to uncover some grass for the pony.

If she was not so lucky, the pony would receive a few double handfuls of grain; she would again eat cold trail meat.

And if she found no shelter? She would find it or keep going. And if—she would not think about such things. Nonetheless, she was aware that if the need were great, the blood of the pony would nourish her, the gutted carcass of the pony would keep her warm for a night.

And without the pony? A snowbank, she remembered.

Almost a year before, three passages of the moon into her pilgrimage and still in Sierra territory, she had been surprised by a storm. And without a pony to ride or heavy garments to keep the snow from her, she had survived.

The details of that night were no longer clear. But she

remembered waking on the floor of a tamped-down cavity inside a high drift of snow. She had been very tired, as if sleepless, but she had felt confidence in herself despite the seeming exhaustion. And she had been warm, as warm as if she were lying in bed at home and dreaming.

She had had the wit to know the illusion of warmth for the danger it was. And though it had been hard to leave the comfort of her snowy bed, she had clambered out of the drift to build a fire and had forced herself then to run slowly around it until her fingers and toes tingled cruelly. Her breath had left her mouth as steam, and the cold had stung her ears as might hard slaps.

After a while, it had all seemed like play during a winter holiday.

It had not been such fun at first, she admitted now; she had moved about like one under compulsion, somehow knowing exactly what to do to preserve her life, as if following directions. But she had survived—and she could do it again.

A strange dream had come to her that night, she remembered also. There had been a man in it, an impossibly big man with gray eyes and red-brown hair, who wore green and black clothing, who kept the snow and darkness away with some kind of portable fire that made no flame. A man whose mind she could not see into, a man who fed her unusual foods and then spent the night in argument with her. But what the argument had been, she could no longer recall. It had only been a dream.

Now she could remember such dreams from other occasions. They all had something in common, she thought. Something in addition to the big man—they meant that she had spent a restless night. She would be dreaming of him tonight, she admitted wryly.

And why not? She was old enough to dream of men. But why did the giant never appear to her in comfortable inns or in peaceful sunlit glens but only in scenes of fear and squalor? Why did he never take her into his arms, never sit her upon his lap and caress her, never move to unbutton her garments, never listen to her hopes? Much was permitted in dreams, and he was attractive.

But there was no such man, of course. The long arguments were the way she chose to remember the restless nights, or else they were home-recalling echoes of long-ago disputes with her father. The man was large because children viewed parents as giant figures who guarded them from perils and other giants. The protection he offered was a mental transmutation of the peaceful childhood she had known or the sanctuary to which she would yet come.

Sanctuary? Dream words came back to her memory: ". . . exciting at times but usually very dull . . . dangerous work, with importance, let's call it . . . a chance to make history . . ." The man had been promising not safety but a war.

There had been wars once, she had been taught. But they were activities for men. What work might a young woman find during a war?

White mists were about her. The air was chill and very thin. The few trees on the hillside were short and stunted, little more than pine-needled bushes. Small clumps of yellow grass poked above the snow.

The pony flinched and snorted nervously. Behind her something howled.

Kylene whimpered and stumbled on. She could no longer run, but she could limp across the mountain crest. The air was too thin for even that motion, and her sides ached as though beaten; her feet were cold and wet from stepping through the ice over a snow-hidden stream; her hands were bruised and made red by falls. Tree limbs had lashed her face. But those were minor complaints.

Each time her right foot touched the ground, fire lanced through the heel and pulsed up through her ankle. She could no longer run.

But eventually, she knew, she would run. Run and ignore the pain. Run until she had not breath to go another step. Run and try to run until she fell upon the snow and could only crawl. There was no refuge other than running. No trees about her were large enough to climb. She had found neither cave nor building to hide within. And no one who would assist her was within range of her mind. She was alone. *Alone*. She could only hope to outrun the wolves.

As if to confirm her thoughts, the howling began anew. The wolves had found her spoor again.

The wolves—she had thought them dogs initially, when she had looked back after that first call to the pack and had seen the gray-black forms gathering. Dogs. Dogs—which would mean nearby people or at least a deserted house to give her shelter for the night. She had been pleased to see the wolves.

The pony had known better. It had run away with her, refusing to obey her shouted commands and frantic tugging at the reins. The gray dog forms had followed, their numbers increasing, not trying to outrun her but content to let the pony tire itself out.

Perhaps they pursued as they did to herd their prey; a short distance down the trail, another wolf had darted from the brush and leaped toward the pony's neck.

Unable to retreat, the pony had kicked at its attacker, but the wolf had dodged the blow and bitten at the extended leg. The pony had squealed and bucked, trying to throw away the weight on its back and escape.

Kylene's left foot was jerked from the stirrup. She tried to save her seat by dropping the reins and falling onto the pony's neck, but she could not bend over far enough or fast enough. The pony kicked both feet to the rear, arching its back and thrusting her into the air. She fell down and along its side, her fingers raking at the withers and pushing uselessly against its foreleg.

Her right foot had remained in its stirrup. It twisted as the pony pranced over her, and something in her ankle gave way with a popping sound as the frenzied animal dragged her across the trail. At last the frozen straps separated from the stirrup bar, and she was left sprawling in the underbrush.

When she recovered her senses, it was too late for the pony. Torn flesh and broken tendons protruded from long wounds, and blood spurted onto the snow-covered ground. The pony stood on three legs, holding a foreleg curled in the air, unable to run. During its struggles the rest of the pack had caught up to it. Its sides heaved, and it gasped noisily. The pack formed a ring.

In the end, the pony lay on the ground, wide-eyed, alive but offering no resistance.

The wolves bit at its throat and shook it with bloody jaws, as if trying to break the pony into pieces. They yapped and snarled at one another and tore still-quivering flesh away from the kill. Steaming trails of red flowed down the side of the pony, and goblets of blood seemed to have been tossed over the white landscape. The pony sighed loudly and jerked just once, then fouled itself.

Fire pulsed through her ankle when she tried to move. Kylene closed her eyes, half hoping that what she could not see would not notice her. She waited.

Time passed. Kylene felt a nudge at her waist. It stopped when she held her breath. She heard panting. Hot moist air swept over her neck. A gray and black form stood by her, peering into her eyes. Its tongue stretched out, long and pink, wet with dripping saliva. It seemed to laugh at her, to say it would not be fooled by a small girl's playacting. Then the wolf padded away from her and snarled until a position reopened for it along the gory flank of the dead pony.

Kylene slowly rose to her feet, biting her lip to mask pain. She walked into the brush cautiously, trying to make no sound, trying to ignore her ankle.

Even close up, it had looked very much like a dog.

Exhausted now, she sank to her knees at the side of the path. Her breath came heavily. Pebbles were hard against her legs, and powderlike snow cascaded over her boots and leggings. White and pockmarked, a boulder rested against the mountainside. A gust of wind swirled snow about her. The path disappeared into mists. Snow drifts billowed downward, then vanished abruptly into a cloud.

She ran a finger along her knife blade, then stabbed it into the ground before her, hearing it clink against a pebble. Her eyes were closed. Light and sound danced within her mind; flames surrounded her, fiery and capricious.

It was good to run in the pack, good to have a place in it. It was good to feel her strength and to know she could make others submit. It was good to breath the clean cold air into her lungs and exhale whitely, good to feel the snow crunching beneath her pads. And it was good to have known a full belly again, to know the pups would feed, to have the salty aftertaste of blood on her tongue, to see fresh rabbit tracks, to snarl when another wolf nudged her. But this was the cold white time, and there could never be enough to eat while it lasted . . .

Kylene blew unsteadily on her hands and rocked back and forth as she waited. The mountains seemed strangely quiet now after she had been in the world of the wolves. But there were colors to be seen again. Absentmindedly she faced into the wind and sniffed the breeze. Nothing.

Should she remove the overcoat? It kept the wind and snow

from her, but it would also hamper her movements. However, its bulk offered some protection, and if she was able to make an escape, she might need it. She would keep it on.

Ancients, it was cold! But at least her ankle no longer hurt so much. She put a hand down and squeezed the stiff leather, wincing as pain throbbed within the foot. Her ankle felt balloonlike, swollen tightly against the inside of the boot. The bones seemed to float in it, their ends grating together as she shifted her weight.

Was it a simple sprain, or had she torn a ligament when the pony threw her? It did not matter much, she decided; in neither case would she be able to fight on her feet. Which was a pity; she wore sturdy riding boots now with thick strong heels. If only she could kick. What would happen to her boots? Would the wolves eat them as they had swallowed the hide of the pony?

And what price would they pay for the boots? She held out the knife firmly as gray blurs rushed through the mists. They came baying.

The howling stopped abruptly. Barely twice her body length away, a ghost shape appeared. White and motionless, it stood awkwardly balanced on two legs, its muzzle close to the ground and its ears perked toward her. Fur was fluffed up to ring its narrow head. Bunched behind it were other wraiths, as pale and silent and still as their leader. One looked at her with a lolling tongue and a tooth-baring laugh frozen on its snout. It was not a bit like a dog.

The mists had blown away, and the wolves were marbled statues against a pale rose-tinted sky. The ground around her was still white, snow-blanketed, but an armslength away, orange and scarlet soil threw light and sparkles into the air. Boulders and pebbles were green fires now, shimmering flames billowing in a wind she did not feel. The shrubs and trees on the mountain slope were black, bare of snow, yellow-outlined. She saw no shadows.

"Wait another day," a deep baritone voice said from beside her. "Then you'll see him with all four paws off the ground."

She jerked sideways, her knife slashing through the air.

"Cimon! Easy with the pigsticker, girl."

"You! But I dreamed of you!"

The giant quirked a red-brown eyebrow. "You aren't old enough."

"Did you do this?" Her arm swept the horizon. "All this—" Then she gasped as pain raced from toe to knee.

The man knelt beside her, heedless of the snow that wet his green pant legs and black cape. "What's wrong, Kylene?"

"My ankle." She panted momentarily. "A sprain. Should not have sat on it."

Tayem Minstrel frowned. "This didn't—I didn't foresee this. Damn!" He seemed strangely indecisive. "When did this happen?"

He sighed when she told him. "Nothing much to be done, then. Sorry I didn't get to you earlier, but this is the only place you ever came through wide enough for me to land on."

She looked at him with puzzlement, and he hooked a thumb over his shouder. "My ship. It generates the *stoptime*, the field we're in now."

Kylene stared, openmouthed. What Tayem pointed to was a giant ax head the length of ten men and half that width. More than twice Tayem's height at one end, the huge object tapered down at the other to a rounded edge as thick as an arm. The small end overhung the mountainside.

"There is no water for a ship," she protested weakly. "Ancients—"

The ax head hovered at waist height, the small ramp attached to its vertical side not quite reaching to the ground. Above the ramp gaped a rectangular opening, black against the silvery surface. Red hieroglyphs by the doorway seemed to float in the air over reflected snow.

"No, Kylene. The moderns." Suddenly Tayem was once more the man of whom she had dreamt. He pulled a flat triangular object from a pouch on his belt and did things to it with his fingers. It seemed hard and shiny, like a rock.

"Where is your sword?" she asked. "The wolves—why do you not wear it?"

"In the ship," Tayem said casually. He smiled. "Hate to disappoint you, but I'm a *piss-poor* swordsman. That was window dressing, just part of the costume."

She gasped. "But you—the horse traders!"

Tayem shrugged. "They saw a big man with *steel* and decided to back off. What else were they likely to do, hmmm?"

Kylene looked at him with dismay. She had trusted him to

defend her! And he had been without skill at arms. No wonder he had said that he would kill no one, that he would surrender her to the traders to avoid that. The—the *guy*!

Tayem smiled happily. "It's all right. I wasn't in any danger." He held his stone over her ankle, pointing the small end of it a handbreadth to one side, and pushed her calf roughly into the ground.

"I can't do much for your ankle here, Kylene, but at least I can stop the pain. Look away for a moment and think pleasant thoughts."

She bit down on her lip and stared at the leader of the wolf pack. The animal still held two white paws over the crimsoned earth.

She heard a faint buzz, as if a gnat flew about her. Almost at once a shock ran up her leg, but before she could react the sensation was gone and Tayem's hand had kept her from moving. Her foot, her ankle, and the lower portion of her leg were heavy and numb as if frostbitten. When she looked back, Tayem was tucking his stone into its pouch.

Her toes would not move, she found, but she had enough strength left to drag her leg along the ground. Perhaps she would be able to stand now—the leg looked all right. In a few heartbeats she would try.

She kneaded unfeeling muscles, then pointed to the man's side. "Is that for medicine?" she wondered aloud. *Are you a priest of your strange religion?*

"Heap big medicine." Tayem smiled ironically and said unpronounceable words. "Which translates roughly as 'neuro-shocker,' if you want to be formal. But 'gun' will do."

She shook her head.

"A *weapon*," Tayem explained. "You don't have that word either? A tool for killing—you can understand that."

She frowned. "What do you do with it?"

"Kill."

"Oh! Then you will slay the wolves after all!"

"I could," the big man said slowly. "But I won't."

"You—*what?*" She could not have heard him correctly.

Tayem shook his head. She saw pity in his eyes. "I won't. End of the line, Kylene. No more help like that."

No help? But he had said— "Tayem? Are you going to— to let me—" She could not say it. A fist lay in her gullet, and she could not breathe even though her mouth was open. "Did you come just—just to watch me?" She finished speaking in a whisper.

He hesitated, and her head dropped. Something terrible was happening, she knew. Something terrible, and she would be made unhappy by it. She could concentrate on nothing more—something would soon make her unhappy.

"You don't have to die if you don't want to," Tayem said softly. "But I can't—"

"Not die?" Her head rose again. "What do you mean? Of course I do not want to die! I want to go to my city, to—to—the name you gave it."

The man sighed. "Kh'taal Minzaer. You *can't* go there, Kylene. You never did get there, and I can't—I don't dare change that."

"Change? I do not understand, Tayem Minstrel. Will you let your mind be seen?"

"Nope. Too much personal stuff." Tayem walked a short distance away, blocking her view of the ice-sculpted shapes that were wolves and staring into the rose-misted distance. His breeches seemed untouched by the snow, she noticed absently. Did he feel the cold through them?

"Hard to find words," he mused. "Listen to me, Kylene. If you want to live, you have to go away with me. Take my word for it, just like a normal person would. I can't do what you want."

"But I am *not* 'normal,'" she said angrily.

"Tough. I am," he said flatly. "The rest of the world is, most of it."

"I am *not* the rest of the world! I do not *want* to be like you, and I *will* not be! *I want to go to my city!*" She crossed her arms defiantly, her knife pressed firmly against her shoulder.

Something glinted redly on her thumb—the heavy, useless ring she had never remembered to trade. *His*. She tore it off and threw it at the man. "Go away! If you will not help me, go away! *Leave me alone!*"

Thunder clapped, making the world ring.

A lightning bolt shot through the air, painfully bright and rainbow-hued, a long flame lancing past the nearest wolf and beyond, to strike the throat of another. Horribly, it did not stop there but pushed through, emerging instantly from the back of the animal's neck to shoot arrowlike past the edge of the mountain. Somewhere over the valley it dwindled into nothingness. When she blinked, a black afterimage was burned into her eyes.

"Migod!" Tayem shouted. "Was that a signal?" He grabbed her shoulders and shook harshly. "Kylene! *What have you done?*"

"Nothing," she said immediately. She felt the fear from the man then, hot and scalding, pouring from his hands onto her skin. "You—the ring you gave me. I—I threw it." Very, very slowly, the nearest wolf was falling sideways, its stiffened legs folding at an impossible angle. Did those behind it also stir? "Did I break your spell?"

"My spell," he said weakly. "My spell. Cimon and Nicole." He looked sick. "Cimon." He released her, but the fear still lay where his hands had been.

What was wrong with him? Had that worthless ring been so dear to him? Why had he given her something so dangerous? And to whom was he talking, with the name so much like her own?

"I am sorry," she said sullenly. She picked up her knife again, inspecting the handle closely to avoid facing the man. "But they are just wolves, Tayem."

"Sorry?" he said incredulously. "Sorry won't do, Kylene. Yeah, you broke a spell all right. God! Is this happening all over again?"

"Is *what* happening?"

"You may have to die here, *really*. That's what. Oh, I can go back and get the ring away from you, and save that version of you. But that won't do *you* any good, little girl. *Shit!*"

"But they are just wolves, Tayem. Just wolves."

"I know," the big man said softly. "But they were going to live. And you were not. You were supposed to die, Kylene. That's what happened. You never got to your city, and I can't do anything at all to change that. I can take you with me—that's all that can save you. But that doesn't do anything for this wolf pack, and if they have any other impact on history, I may not have anything to take you to. We'd both be exiles."

Only part of that made any sense, but that part . . . She was cold from more than kneeling in the snow. The big man moved away as she stared at him. Just armslengths from her, the lead wolf was still falling to the ground. Perhaps it was the flickering green light from the rocks, but the farther wolves seemed to be moving apart. Tayem was also silent now, unmoving, massive, and somehow as awesome as the toppling beasts outside once had been.

"Would you let me be killed?" she whispered, and tried not to understand the emotions on his face. "Please, Tayem. Please."

But he would not hear her.

The heavy overcoat pressed stiffly against her, cold and far too great a burden for her to stand under. Something stiff and frozen was within her as well. Her breaths were tiny, almost without exhalation. Her eyes would not focus. She closed them and rocked from side to side, holding the knife upright in both hands at half an armslength. The world was hushed.

"I was of the valleys. I was of Clan Otter." Her lips moved, but no sound came forth. "I was Edgart's, I was Samtha's trueborn daughter." What line next?

A giant's hand fell upon her shoulder, and she broke off to look up at the man. He was smiling, and she sensed that he had made a decision. But for all that, a bleakness radiated from him.

"We'll give it a try," he said. "If things change too much, I can still park you somewhere better than this and come back. You're going to live, Kylene."

"Then I can go to my city!"

"I'm sorry, Kylene. You can't go there. I thought that was clear."

Her heart sank again. "Why can I not go? Why do you prevent me?"

Tayem sighed. "You sure are persistent, little girl." He pushed snow from a nearby boulder and sat on it, looking at her quietly. Dressed in green and black as he was, with bright red-brown hair, he seemed suddenly a part of that strangely colored outside world, the world of the wolves.

He bent to run his fingers through the snow, then straightened with a pebble in his hand. He held it out as if for her inspection, then tossed it overhead. "Remember this?"

Thunder crashed. Lightning rose through the sky, rainbow-hued.

"Because of what I did to your ring?"

"Cimon take the ring!" Tayem growled. "It's replaceable, although you ought to get a hiding for that. No."

He swung an arm through the air, unconsciously repeating the gesture she had made earlier. "All this—we call it a stoptime field. Inside this things happen two million times faster than they do outside. You're seeing by gamma rays now—from *Potassium-40*, if that makes any sense. The ring you threw, that pebble—" A thumb pointed at the blue-white ball still climbing through the pink sky, then the man snapped his fingers. "With the velocity they have out there, they melt like *that*. If they didn't, that ring would go round the world in two, maybe three seconds. More than escape velocity, so it won't."

She blinked. None of this made sense.

". . . counterpart of something called runtime," Tayem was saying. Then he noticed her face. "Kylene, do you understand a word I'm saying?"

"No, Tayem Minstrel," she said unhappily. "No one would understand you."

"Would it mean anything to you if I said I came from the *future*?" He seemed to be picking his words carefully; she waited for him to continue. "Well?"

His question seemed to be important, but he could not have been speaking correctly. *"Fute chure?"* she asked timidly, trying to pronounce the word as he had.

He sighed. "Maybe you have another word for it. Tomorrow, the day after tomorrow, next year. And so on. That's the future. What do you call them?"

She shook her head with puzzlement. "Tomorrow. The day after tomorrow. Next year. Why call them anything but that? Why do you need another word?"

Tayem seemed upset for some reason. He would not look at her.

"It's an *abstract noun*, I know, but the concept ought to be common enough. Are you real sure you don't have such a word, Kylene?"

Was he trying to make fun of her? "Yes, I am real sure," she said crossly. "I do not use a word like your 'fute chure.' Neither does anyone else. *We do not need it!* And no one has ever heard of your 'bracked nowen' either!"

"You have now." He sounded angry also.

"I do *not* care." Oh, Ancients! How long would this go on? Suddenly she was crying. "I want to go to my city. Please, Tayem, let me go!"

Tayem called on his gods again. "I am going to get you the hell out of this rathole," she heard him say bitterly. Then he was pushing a Tayem-sized handkerchief over her face, careless of the knife she still held loosely. "Don't cry, Kylene. Please don't cry. I'm sorry. I didn't mean to hurt your feelings."

She sniffed cautiously. "Then I can go to my city?"

"No, damn it!" He had been kneeling before. Now he stood abruptly, his clothing strangely untouched by the snow, uncreased.

"We're running out of time, Kylene. I can't keep this field up forever. How does your ankle feel? Has the stun worn off?"

"I do not feel it," she said. "But my knees are sore, and my legs are cold." At least he was talking about sensible things again. She held his handkerchief in the hand opposite the knife and smiled at him. Perhaps in a while he would change his mind about the city.

Tayem would not smile back. Instead he clasped his hands to her waist and hoisted her into the air like a great doll, to face first the slowly falling wolves and then his shiny, misnamed ship.

"Pick one of them," he ordered. "*Now.* Sorry, girl, it would take me just too damned long to give you the information you need to make a rational choice. You don't have the background. But I told you once you might run out of choices someday, and now you have." He stood her in the snow and stepped back several paces.

"If you stay here, you will die." He patted the stone thing in his belt pouch. "Don't worry about the wolves. I wouldn't ask that of anyone. I'll send you up to Cimon on my own and give you burial."

Was he serious? She stared into the giant's unblinking eyes, then was unable to meet his gaze. He looked so serious! Serious and something more than that. Oh, it was so necessary! Why could she not see into his mind?

". . . can go with me," he was saying. "And fight in my war. And live and die in the world I take you to. Which will it be, Kylene?"

"If I go with you, will I like it there?"

"No. Probably not, anyhow."

"Will you be there?"

"From time to time. For short periods." He raised an eyebrow.

"Will I be able to see you there?"

"If you wish to." The eyebrow subsided.

"Will I be happy there?"

"I don't know what makes happiness, Kylene. Ultimately—I hope."

She took her time trying to word a last question. "What would you expect me to do, if you had been able to explain what you wanted to explain?" There, that touched on his thoughts, she was certain.

Tayem's mouth quirked. It was not quite a smile. "Stall. Delay. Like you're doing now. No more leading questions, Kylene."

She bit her lip and looked once more at the wolves, then at Tayem's ship. Then back at Tayem. He was not holding his *gun*, but she was holding a knife, half covered by his handkerchief. She could not run, but she could turn quickly, and the knife would fly quickly. She knew how to kill the wolves now, and Tayem had implied his spell would soon end.

"What have you decided, Kylene?"

She turned her back on him. "I have trouble thinking. Give me a dozen heartbeats and I will be able to tell you something."

She wiped her hand on the handkerchief and stuffed it in her sleeve, then took the knife back into her right hand. The throw would have to be good. Fortunately, he was close. The knife was not meant for throwing but she had practiced well, and the man was neither as small nor as wary as a squirrel.

. . . nine, ten, eleven, twelve, she counted silently. "I have decided," she called out, stepping back and spinning on her heel as it touched the ground. Her arms pinwheeled, the left flailing down and past her side as the right rose through the air and snapped toward the earth. Metal flashed.

She was off balance, but she remembered not to catch herself on her clumsy right foot with its fragile ankle. Instead, she let her knee buckle and sprawled on the ground, even though that left her unable to watch the flight of her knife.

What of Tayem now? He had looked so surprised, so disappointed!

He had meant well, she had time to realize. She would try to get his body into his ship and protect it from the wolves as he had offered to protect her.

Thunder crashed. She knew that sound! That light—blue-white flame lancing into the green mountain! Her face turned sideways.

Tayem stood over her, his *gun* pointing down. There were no cuts on him that she could see, but a dark stain was growing on the underside of the cloth over his left forearm. Blood dripped past the cuff and onto the snow. It was red; it might have been anyone's.

"Persistent, aren't you?" he said, tight-lipped.

There was nothing left to be said. She waited.

Agony flashed through her. She could sense her body jerking. Then darkness fell.

When she awoke, strangers took her away.

Part 5: Fight Another Day

Timithial ha'Dicovys—44,938 L.C.

CHAPTER FIFTEEN

In the Present a city was burning.

Its golden streets now red-stained by flame and blood, its proud towers felled by distant artillery, its residents crushed beneath rubble and the inexorably advancing armor of their enemies, Fohima Alghera was being razed by the forces of the Chelmmysian Alliance.

This was in early summer of the city's 893rd year, or 47,930 by the Long Count—around A.D. 92,000 on a calendar remembered by only one man—and a world had just been won.

A frozen image of the scene hung on a wall lined with silver mesh, fifty feet beneath the ground, some twenty centuries before the city would be founded.

The viewscreen faced the open end of a broad, U-shaped table. Close to the ground, dark brown and shiny, the table was surrounded by waist-high black cubes. A small dais was built into a front corner of the room. The ceiling glowed whitely behind its mesh, casting cobweb-line shadows across the furniture. The air was chill and dry.

Some thirty men were present. None seemed older than a century, though the impression of early middle age was not always correct; the majority were much younger. One was a man in his early thirties with red-brown hair and gray eyes set in a deeply tanned face. Dressed in forest green, with a short black cape wrapped about his bulky shoulders, he was both the tallest and the heaviest person present. A jagged scar crossed the hairline on his left temple.

Eventually all the men were seated, the black cubes distorting softly under their weight to flow into the semblance of armchairs. A portion of the wall drew back on both sides to form a ceiling-high triangle. A young woman entered. Pale, blond, wearing a knee-length green gown, she stepped noiselessly past the table to a cube at the back of the room. Arms folded, she waited impassively. Her forehead bore a jade-green plaque. The men ignored her.

A slight, graying man dropped papers at the front of the table and stepped to the dais, then bowed his head briefly. Tired in appearance, he wore a buttonless black coverall. Golden insignia gleamed on his collar: the broken sword and spindle of the believing priest, the inverted mace of the acting Sept Master.

"Cimon guard us. Nicole guide us." His tones were nasal. Voices echoed him raggedly.

"I am Birlin Borictar tra'Dicovys, and Project Master," he stated formally. "Would another challenge my authority?"

His words translated that way. Literally, he claimed high military rank and the right to exercise paternal control over those present, then asked if Ironwearers or High Blankshields desiring his position wished a duel between champions. This was ritual; there were no Blanklings present, High or Low, and Borct's right to command was ultimately backed not alone by his Septlings and his standing in the Institute but by the Muster and the Warder of the Realm. So there was no reply.

"I am very pleased to see so many of our young men today," he said. "I do not believe we have come together like this since the earliest days of the Project. We have not yet been successful—obviously not—but virtually all of our personnel have survived, and we have managed to extend the lifetime of our city a fraction of a day tenth. This may seem a small reward for the labors of the last two years, but it does show we are learning to function in this strange new dimension of conflict. We are meeting to consider additional efforts and new tactics, however, so I shall now surrender your attentions to the young man who is one of their originators, Tolipim ha'Ruijac. Tolp?"

"Thank you, Project Master." Tolp was a paunchy brunet with a quirky smile, which he used often. He spoke rapidly.

"The last year and a half, I've been working with Siccentur tra'Ruijac on what we rather grandiosely term Mission Planning. There is some doubt as to whether a pair of physical scientists, no matter how justly famous, should be doing this or whether we should have palmed off the job on some professional historians. Of course, we don't have any of the species around, so the question is somewhat, ah, academic. And it turns out as well that events are affected by factors that historians have never conceived of."

He paused while chuckles ran through his audience. "So it becomes possible to doubt their interpretations of other factors, leaving us to our own resources. And of course, if the historians had been able to make useful predictions, there would have been no need for this Project.

"I realize that to you Agents we nonhistorians may not seem very effectual either. However, we are improving. Beyond that, I note that none of us at the inception of the Project had had experience with time travel. No one had ever had, with the exception of Timithiallin ha'Dicovys-then-Cuhyon. And regretfully, his initial field work was limited—and poorly documented."

The laughter from the young men was loud but not unkind, and many of their elders wore broad smiles. The big redhead ignored them, staring at the speaker and drumming his fingers impatiently on the table top.

"His discoverer or creator, Vlyntinm Herrilmin tra'Cuhyon, was a famous experimentalist," Tolp continued, "but Herem was also unfortunately apt to rush into theoretical battles only half armored. So the papers left after his, er, untimely demise were of little use. Before his own death, Timt ha'Cuhyon prepared a manuscript detailing his conjectures, but with all respect to our young friend, his intermingling of First Era superstition and alchemy was also not of value." He paused as if waiting for a protest, but none came.

"Our experience was nonexistent," he summarized. "However, our aims were correspondingly modest. We had outgrown whatever crusading impulses our ancestors might have given themselves up to; we were certainly not so quixotic as to hope to free member states of the Alliance—for to be honest, the Chelmmysian bondage was never particularly harsh, and we had no desire to see it replaced by potentially heavier yokes, even on those who willingly wear yokes.

"We did deplore the handling of the Teep issue within the Alliance, but this seemed a subject for negotiation. Warfare makes such memories vanish from our minds, but it was once widely accepted, despite what younger folk are often told, that Alghera would bow to Alliance demands on this point, perhaps by creating special government posts for the Teeps, perhaps by allowing them representatives in the Muster. Of course, that was not the concession the Alliance sought from us.

"I mention this since it is sometimes suggested—I name no one—that we mount a more radical effort. We might, for example, slay Hemmendur as a child."

Tolp frowned. "We have been given a weapon of great power, but not omnipotence. Even were there no Hemmendur, his Solution might have been evolved by another, likely by someone lacking his vision and decency.

"You must also recall that did the Chelmmysians settle for less than hegemony, each member state—and each unresisting citizen—of the Alliance would be in violation of the Second Compact. That would commit us to a war such as has never been seen. The practicality and morality of this must be doubted."

He broke off to look beyond his audience. No one interrupted.

"What we sought to preserve was our independence, that alone. We would accept subordination to Chelmmys, but we would not become subjects. We felt then, and now, that the completed structure of the Alliance would immediately begin to rot and be transformed through the centuries to tyranny—one even harder to overthrow than that of Kh'taal Minzaer. The Fifth Era is yet young; we had no wish to condemn it to a third Eternal War.

"Of course, the peoples of the Alliance would not accept such a description of their empire," he added dryly. "Nor would their rulers, who are permitted by Hemmendur's Solution to make no exceptions."

His hand gestured at the portrait of the burning city. "So, this: the outcome of a war between one small state and all the rest of the one world. But here we continue to defend our city and try to avert that fate. Let us win enough battles, and the

Chelmmysians must give up. We can then return to the prewar situation and reopen negotiations.

"But we must win more than a handful of time for our city. We have not done that. Such small changes as we are able to make are frequently canceled out by unpredicted events, as if there is an 'inertia' to history that resists long-term alterations. To give an example, if we strengthen Algheran forces on one front, they will be weakened on others; a lost battle there may be converted to victory, but elsewhere we suffer greater loss of life and territory than was previously the case. This cancels out the gains made by our interference.

"The most likely explanation is that our efforts simply have not affected the overall strength of the Chelmmysians, so their strategy and timing remain unchanged. It has also been suggested, however, that the inertia I referred to is a real effect. This fits some of our observations; it also goes along with some of Timt's more bizarre speculations.

"Sict and I have discussed this at length without arriving at firm conclusions. I hope someday to find time—ha!—to prepare some experiments to shed light on our difficulties; once we are back at the Institute, I will arrange a small seminar on time travel theory—I invite you all to enroll. No applause, please; just pay your large fees to the department secretary. And now I turn this session over to our first guest lecturer, Aryntyl Siccentur tra'Ruijac."

He bowed theatrically to polite laughter and sat next to the big redhead. "That's over," he said quietly. "I hope you didn't feel unfairly treated, Timt."

Tim Harper shrugged. "Remind me someday to read my book."

Tolp snapped his fingers. "A waste of time, my friend. It was very dull. I'm told your lectures were much more interesting."

Harper smiled faintly. "But since history has been amended to leave me out of it, *I* missed out on both of those. So I'm envious in a way. Besides, who cares how dull the book was? Did it have my name in big letters on the front cover? That's what matters."

The Algheran nodded. "Never got published, Timt. Sorry, but you weren't much of a writer. It was just a notebook. Sict has a copy if you really are curious."

"Hmmm." Harper pursed his lips. "Yeah, I would like to see it."

"Tolp has oversimplified. He often does," said the man now at the dais. He was of medium build and blond; large bones made him appear gaunt, while heavily lined cheeks hinted at his age. Several of those present wore the insignia of a Sept Master; Sict alone did so without inverting the golden mace.

"Are there questions before I proceed?" he asked. "From anyone?"

A hand shot up immediately, with a question following before the tra'Ruijac could react. "Are these problems explained adequately by the Moving Window theory?"

A side issue, Harper noted. *Who? I used to know everyone.*

"Lerlt ha'Hujsuon," Tolp whispered helpfully. "That Sept is still raising grief for us, especially the last three seasons."

A year locally—was it a coincidence that the period began at roughly the time Onnul had been killed? But he had been uptime two years since returning to this strangely altered Project and had avoided most of its politics. Harper only grunted.

The tra'Ruijac nodded. "The tra'Dicovys' bidirectional continuum hypothesis. Yes, our observations are also compatible with it."

The questioner was not through. "Despite the logical flaws of the hypothesis?"

"See what I mean?" Tolp whispered.

Harper nodded absently. Borct had theorized that time flows in two directions but that time travel is possible in only one of them. A time traveler was like a man who could walk only east or west while riding in a boat going north. If he changed history, he could see the effects of that change; he could not see the effects of changes that he had not yet made or that he had undone. His "view" of time was through a "window" that traveled along with him.

There was much the theory did not explain, Harper realized, but it would be interesting to see what arguments were brought against it. He listened attentively.

"Such as what, Lerlt?" the tra'Ruijac asked in a bored voice.

"This is day 93," the other began. "We have a future ahead of us—"

"I certainly hope so," Tolp said, sotto voce.

Lerlt ha'Hujsuon, a thin brunet with a petulant expression, cast a glare that Tolp blandly ignored, then repeated his remark.

"We have a future ahead of us, which I'll label F-93. A season ahead we will have a future I'll label F-200. Suppose I travel from then to now, day 200 to day 93; which future will I see?"

"That which you saw at day 200," Sict said calmly.

"But I'm at day 93. I'm surrounded by people at day 93 who see the future as being F-93—"

"You don't understand the theory. *That's* what we see here in day 93," Sict snapped. "Multidimensional time, remember? What you see now is a particular future, say F-x at day 93, *not* F-93. If history is changed in some fashion so that you see a different future later, say F-y at day 200, and come back, you return to day 93 sub y rather than 93 sub x. The people around you will see the very same future you saw at day 200—and make no changes in it. Do you understand that?"

"But we *do* change things between day 93 and day 200!"

"We do; they don't." The tra'Ruijac was curt. "We are not the same people. You do not return to us—you return to our doppelgangers."

"But if I persuade them to change history?"

"Then change history. From F-y to, say, F-z. You can go uptime then to F-z at day 200 if you want. But you will *not* return to any date having F-x as a future. You've lived through that change in the one world; you cannot take it back."

The moving finger writes, Harper remembered in the middle of his own ruminations. Then he returned to serious thought.

If history was changed by no one, the universe simply did not need multidimensional time. That was a philosophical objection to Borct's theory, but it was the most valid one in his mind. It was not logical to assume that the universe had been set up to facilitate manipulation by time travelers, and the fact that time travel existed did not prove that reality was going to cooperate with them.

But it took more status than he had to argue with an acting Sept Master and a faculty member of the Institute for the Study of Land Reclamation Issues.

"Sict," a voice called. "If I may."

It was the Project Master. Fatigue showed on his face; one hand on the table slid papers back and forth. "Young man, I suspect you wish to create paradoxes. You would be wasting your time and effort; that is what the tra'Ruijac is trying to explain to you. The future—each future—stems from a history in which *no* changes were made. Any changes you make will only produce a future that seems natural and inevitable to all but yourself.

"Precisely why some futures are more natural and inevitable than others—that is the inertia that Tolp referred to, or the cause for that inertia. We do not understand this well, to be honest. The possible explanations supplement the existing theory, however; they do not contradict it. Is that clear?"

Lerlt hedged. "I'd like to think about it."

"Do so." Borct was curt.

Tolp was less kind. "Oh, cloak-covered Lerlt," he murmured loudly. "Another brand-new experience."

Harper winced. "Trying to provoke a fight?" he growled softly.

Tolp smiled. "It's safe," he whispered back. "The Council is split, Timt. We can still agree on some things, but there is no peace between the factions anymore. We're on one side—the Ruijacs and you Dicovys. And the Hujsuons are on the other. It's changed since you went on your last mission."

Harper grimaced. "Vrect and me—that hasn't changed, I gather. All right. Just remember who'll have to implement your clever ideas out in the field."

Tolp smiled at him ironically.

A second questioner was on his feet now, a blond Agent whose face Harper found familiar. *Bann.*

"Another of them," Tolp answered. His face wore a sneer.

Harper waved a hand irritably. Tolp had made him miss the question.

Fortunately the tra'Ruijac repeated it. "Why speak of futures rather than of one future? Because there are an infinite number of futures. Of course, we see only one at any particular time and can travel through only that one."

The blond man frowned. "If I leave this date and travel to another, an interim date, during that period *some* decisions will have been made, and *some* events will occur that change the future, even if only in small ways. Won't I get to different futures if I start at different dates?"

Sict snapped his fingers. "Only if you live through them. Time travel is uninfluenced by the exterior continuum. Think of it as you would any other journey; breaking the trip into stages doesn't change your destination."

Bann looked troubled. "But I'm an Agent. I get to my

destination, as you term it. *I change things*. That destination is *gone*. What do I come back to?"

Glancing around the room, Harper noticed other unhappy-seeming Agents. *They're catching on,* he thought.

Sict had probably made the same observation, but he waited for another question from Bann.

"Master, do we Agents return to the Project we leave?"

"Succinct," the tra'Ruijac commented. "No."

"But—" Bann stopped, obviously at a loss.

This was Sict's show, Harper decided. Borct's theory was several years old; there was no excuse for the ignorance being demonstrated here, and he felt a little impatient with his fellow Agents.

"You don't change very much," Sict pointed out. "That's what we started to talk about today. You don't change things abruptly—as you've all learned from experience. You make small changes that you hope will become significant *after* you have returned to the Project. To a different Project, formed by your efforts, whose natural future you helped create."

Catch-22, Harper thought ironically. *The "natural" future is one in which we Agents have no effect. So we're always coming back to a Project filled with people complaining that we're accomplishing nothing*.

The situation was not quite that bad. In some fashion the future was able to shape the past; Harper sometimes speculated that causality functioned as a two-way street with unequal flows of traffic. Perhaps there were not an infinite number of virtually indistinguishable timelines but some limited number of discrete universes. *Or just some sloppiness in the way things happen—some kind of uncertainty principle*.

No matter; intuition was not at odds with reality, and it made sense to go on thinking of one future, one timeline. People in the Station could see things improving. A couple of minutes here and there, nothing big—"naturally."

The Project had once been more ambitious. His memory receded to its pre-Exodus days, bringing back . . .

. . . blood mists all about . . . yellow-outlined tree silhouettes but honest green grass scudding under the levcycle . . . a lump in his throat for fear that he was going to lose his balance on Tolp's hoked-up motorcycle and he needed more practice but it was a little late . . . the first ChelmForce armored vehicle, looking like an eighty-foot slug, floating a foot off the ground

. . . the plating seeming blue-white hot and donning goggles against the glare . . . aiming at the drive train, throwing his handful of pebbles . . . the crew cabin pinwheeling leisurely through tree branches till the stubborn pines brought it down . . . the mangled forearm and portions of viscera the levcycle drifted over . . . the demon's harvest of shattered men and vehicles he had once reaped in scant seconds . . . long years ago . . .

All for nothing.

His actions had not affected the fate of Alghera. When he returned to the city, history still recorded the tank column debouching from the Western Forests, practically untouched. Other agents, sent to repeat his task, had returned with the same negative result.

History protected itself from sudden changes.

Only by aping normality could time travelers modify events. Anomalies and anachronisms had to be avoided. *Seven years of being an Ironwearer and I'm stuck at acting PFC*, Harper thought cynically. *Promotion came faster in 'Nam.*

Hands had shot up. Sict ignored them. "We encourage you to return to a time close to the one you left. That makes it possible for you to come back to a Project very similar to the one you left—so close you probably will never notice a difference. But a different Project nonetheless."

One hand remained, waving impatiently.

"I don't read your Sept's field language," Sict said dryly. "Nor am I a Teep. But I presume you wonder why you do not meet yourselves when you return."

The hand went down. Sict smiled briefly and continued. "Paradoxes are not possible, or at least are uncommon. A million Agents go to the future, from a million Projects, and return to a million Projects: one per Agent without need for doubling up. Of course, a million is too small a number."

He smiled again. "Don't worry, young men. The continuum appears to be natural from your viewpoint as well. You leave one Project and return to one where you fit in; effectively, there is just the one. Are there any more questions?"

There were no more questions. The tra'Ruijac cleared his throat and began anew. "As we have discussed, history shows a reluctance to be molded as we wish. Tolp and Borct have spoken of this in terms of one physical concept: inertia. I now suggest another: leverage.

"We have been working close to the Present, restricting

ourselves to the seven years of the war. Whatever ripples we have set up on the stream of time may be limited by the small expanse of duration open to them. Perhaps we could operate at significantly earlier dates and let our ripples spread out a bit."

"Incompatible concepts," someone interjected. "Inertia implies convergence to me. If you have a stream of history, or whatever, and it *wants* to flow in some particular channel, you've Cimon's own chance of diverting it easily into another riverbed. Over a long period, any changes we make are going to be damped out."

"I agree," Sict said. "We must be very selective about the changes we introduce. They must seem 'natural': unsurprising events that nonetheless have large consequences. And we must expect that convergence will push the situation toward the status quo. In other words, we might give ourselves a large advantage early in city history for the sake of a smaller but still significant advantage at the Present. I have an example."

Men leaned forward throughout the room. There was complete silence.

Harper was suddenly conscious of the chill. His left shoulder twitched. Good rhetoric, he recognized. Sict's knowledge of time travel was all wet, but he had not won his Mastership without learning some politics.

And what was the great plan the brass were planning now for the poor blood infantry?

"Let us consider the year 312," Sict said quietly, "47,349 by the Long Count. Alghera had as Warder then one of the ablest generals of the Fifth Era."

"Mlart," someone breathed. "Mlart!"

Sict nodded. "Voridon Mlaratin tra'Nornst. The Unifier. Mlart the Great."

The slowly spoken words hit his audience like hammer blows.

Tim Harper alone was immune to the spell. *What in the hell?* he wondered. Even the girl at the back of the room seemed to have stopped breathing, and he saw tears on the faces of the men around him. Why?

A memory of his own past returned then. And a set of initials.

But JFK had been a contemporary. Mlart had been dead four centuries before any of these people were born. Was Algheran history so littered with nonentities that an exception stood out like the truly great of the First Era? Harper shifted uncomfortably, feeling the chair remold itself beneath him.

Perhaps he was being unfair. His world had a population of four billion people. This one had what? Forty million? Fifty? And F'a Alghera had been—would be—a major metropolis, because forty-five thousand persons lived in it.

And two percent of those fifty million could read minds, and that constituted a "problem." Harper turned sideways, looking through the corner of his eye at the woman in the back of the room. She ignored him.

The redhead shrugged. Mlart. What did he remember about Mlart? He had read some Algheran history once; he closed his eyes, trying to remember. Almost-forgotten facts returned.

The only major city in this section of the continent for some years, Alghera had exercised an economic rather than political hegemony over the region Harper persisted in thinking of as New England. That hold weakened as migration brought new residents from the lands made uninhabitable by the advancing glaciers, and party squabbles among the Septs produced a series of ineffectual Warders. Rival urban centers grew up, taking advantage of Algheran impotence to annex territory previously dominated by the city. This gave rise to a series of border wars in which Alghera fared disastrously: "the Tempest." Finally the bickering nobility in the Muster submerged their differences to offer military command to the only undefeated general in the city—Mlaratin ha'Nornst.

Nornst was a small Sept without power in the Muster. Mlart refused the commission until his demands were met: A true army was to be formed from the housetroops of the Septs; its soldiers were to swear fealty to the City and take orders only from the Warder. Mlart was to be Warder as well as Battle Master, serving in those posts for two years rather than at the pleasure of the Muster.

War seemed imminent. Reluctantly, the factions accepted his terms.

Mlart acted at once, leading the housetroops of Nornst through the Western Forests to make spoiling attacks against unprepared Lopritian outposts. His forces were suppressing local bandits, he announced, and he called for the Lopritians to assist in policing the border region.

Meanwhile, his supporters had elected Mlart the Master of

Nornst; his authority over his own troops could not be removed by a vacillating Muster, and housetroops of Dicovys and Cuhyon were en route to the border. Caught off balance by events, the Lopritians accepted the face-saving offer and signed the treaty Mlart had composed, a carefully worded document pledging eternal peace between the two states, to be renewed at three-year intervals.

Using the breathing space he had won, Mlart forged the units of his new army into a single entity, drilling and barracking together men of different Septs, assigning senior commands to his supporters, and enlisting Septless mercenaries—the Blankshields—with the promise of future citizenship.

A year later, Mlart informed the surprised Muster that Lopritian forces were violating the border peace by offering sanctuary to brigands again and that the Swordtroop of the Realm was moving to protect the safety and peace of Algheran citizens. The First War of Consolidation had begun.

That war lasted two years and expanded Alghera's territory by forty percent. A now subservient Muster reelected Mlart to a third term as Warder.

During the period of peace that followed, Mlart remolded the state as he had earlier shaped the army. The Muster was enlarged to allow representation for the Blankshields and the residents of the New Territories. The powers of self-taxation within the Septs were restricted, curbing their independence, while state taxation was doubled, then redoubled to end the Warder's dependence on voluntary contributions. Systematically, responsibility and authority were stripped from the Septs and transferred to the enlarged Office of the Warder.

Punitive taxes were levied "for the duration of the Realm" on non-owner-occupied farmland to end a nasty species of serfdom beginning to take root in the newly conquered lands; criticized in the Muster for this, Mlart forced through legislation extending to the entire realm the same protection from bondage.

In three years, he survived as many assassination attempts and suppressed two coups. His election to a fourth term as Warder was without a dissenting vote in the Muster—perhaps the turbulent crowds surrounding the Gathering Hall had something to do with that. Mlart was not present to witness the scene.

The Swordtroop was marching southward at the time.

Sict was still speaking. "The Unifier was slain at the climax of the Third War of Consolidation. Late in the siege of Fohima Loprit, the defenders made a nighttime sally; Mlart was not in armor and received wounds from which he perished the following evening. Shortly after this, the siege was abandoned.

"Now we can keep him alive," he closed flatly. "Are there volunteers?"

There were. Harper drummed his fingers monotonously on the table top and watched impassively as a dozen men marched from the room. Soon, two millennia hence, they would join Mlart's army, then maneuver their way to the general's defense during the fighting at Loprit; the survivors would return.

Most did survive. Only rarely did an agent fail to return from a mission. *Surprising,* Harper thought, *considering the risks we run.*

Was that another flaw in the theory? Possibly. Very probably.

Probably? *Probability.* The Algherans were weak on probability. They had never made the leap from computing gambling odds to routine statistics, let alone something as sophisticated as Bose-Einstein or Poisson statistics. *No quantum theory, no quantum statistics.*

But that was not necessarily so. Boltzmann and Gibbs had established the equivalence of thermodynamics and statistical mechanics long before the quantum nature of the atom was known. All it took was the notion of phase space.

The Algherans didn't have that notion. It wasn't even an idea Fifth Era mathematicians would play with.

Too much time spent trying to read those Plates, Harper thought. *The scientists in this culture are glorified linguists. Real theoretical physicists would blow these people off the map. The Fourth Era types who inscribed those records didn't do us any favors.*

Except for the biology Plates, he acknowledged wryly. *I'd really like all them to get translated.*

He was too harsh. The problem was not a lack of competence. The Algherans simply looked at the world differently than did the First Era scientists. They used different techniques to investigate it and different concepts to explain it.

Their way worked, he admitted. The Algheran picture of the universe was as complete as the one he had been used to. In some ways it was superior: conceptually simpler, just as practical as the science of his day—though it was infuriating to hear electricity called "ghost fluid," with the explanation that something that could not be weighed on a bathroom scale obviously had no mass.

No semiconductors here, no computers, no field theory—but holography, television, electrical circuits, and room temperature superconductors. No quantum theory, no astrophysics, no astronautics—but celestial mechanics, catalyst chemistry, materials, and levitation. They were weak on genetics, strong on medicine.

Give them that credit, guy. They gave you back the use of your arm.

I won't forget it. But they took stuff away from me, too.

Harper clinched his lips firmly and swallowed, then turned his thoughts back to probability. *Suppose time branches continually . . .*

Tolp was trying to speak; Harper waved a hand to silence him.

No. Notions paraded through his mind, too many and too disorganized for evaluation. Borct's explanations were not good enough, he was certain, but he did not have grounds for rejecting them.

He needed more theories, he decided. A priori philosophizing had to play second fiddle to experience, but a theory that was derived only from experience was worthless.

He frowned unconsciously, dissuading Tolp from another conversational gambit. Men were beginning to leave the room, he noted absently; he should do the same.

Distance-muffled, a Klaxon sounded. The light dimmed momentarily throughout the Station. The Agents were gone.

The girl at the back of the room rose silently and slipped through the triangular doorway. Harper watched through the corner of his eye and rose to follow.

A hand on his wrist stopped him. "Are you unwilling to assist in this effort, Timithial?"

Harper was polite. "To what end, Magister?"

"Do you disapprove, Shieldling?"

"I might. The rationale for this was not explained to me. Or to any of us."

The Project Master frowned. "Mlart was a great man."

"Yes, but so was Abe Lincoln. Shall I return and save him from John Wilkes Booth?"

Several questions showed on Borct's pinched face, but he did not ask them, and Harper remained silent.

"Very well, Septling," the older man said at last. "You know that the proximate cause of the conflict between the Alliance and ourselves is a dispute over the metal farming in the southern coastal region."

New York City, Harper translated. *After the ice ran over it twice*. "That area is beyond our borders."

"Our current borders only." Sict had joined the conversation; others listened in. "It was within them during Mlart's day, and our claim to it actually predates him. It was lost after his death; no one knew the territory was valuable, so it was left undefended during the civil wars of the Regents. Perhaps this time we will be able to hold onto it and remove a cause for friction."

Harper shrugged. "We could also try abandoning the claim. Never mind—don't you think somehow the Alliance will find a pretext for starting a fight?"

Sict copied the gesture. "Yes."

"So we'll go to war again, anyhow," Harper said evenly. "But with additional assets, isn't that it? More metal, of course, but not enough to make a difference against the rest of the one world. Some more land to defend. And what else? People. But that southern area is still mostly wilderness. If it were Loprit now—ah! What happens to Loprit, do you suppose, Sict?"

"It's impossible to predict." The tra'Ruijac affected unconcern.

"Impossible to predict," Harper repeated dryly. "Stop feeding me crap, Sict, or I'll ask the Teeps what you're up to. General knowledge isn't politics."

"Timt!" Tolp protested.

Sict ran skeletal fingers through his hair and looked toward the mesh-lined ceiling. "It's all right, Tolipim. Timt, Loprit falls to Mlart, of course. After that, we do not know. It might disappear as an independent state. Mlart is certainly apt to incorporate portions of it into Alghera. Our languages are similar; it should not be difficult to assimilate the Lopritians."

"Long live Greater Alghera," Harper said dryly. "Just Loprit, Sict, or will Mlart keep going? You don't have to answer—it's pretty clear from your face." He stopped to look around the group. "Everyone seems to like the idea, I see. Especially the tra'Hujsuon, now that you've bought his program. Just my idle curiosity, but whatever happened to restoring the status quo?"

"We've tried that, Timt." Tolp looked up, his face at the level of Harper's shoulder, the look of amusement gone completely for once. "We have tried that for two years, *and it has not worked.*"

"Two years?" Harper said softly. "I've been at it for seven."

No one would return his gaze. "I know it hasn't worked," he admitted. "I know we have to try something else. Nicole's tits, people! I've been through the Western Forest Campaign four times now, and I'm as Cimon-taken tired of it as you. But at least I've learned not to jump without inspecting the territory."

Borct bit the corner of his mouth at the blasphemies but said nothing.

Sict reached a hand toward the redhead's shoulder. "Timt, we certainly appreciate your—"

Harper knocked the arm aside. "You sure as blazes ought to. And now, if you near-immortals will let me through, I want to get some sleep. Send for me when the men get back."

He left the room alone.

CHAPTER SIXTEEN

A hand was shaking his shoulder. Harper felt stealthily for a knife, but his fingers encountered only folds of cloth. Someone was speaking near him. His fingers scrabbled frantically, uselessly. Then he was awake.

Dark. Cold. But he knew this bunk.

Not in 'Nam.

His shoulder was shaken again. "The Agents have returned," a soprano voice told him. "The Council will meet shortly."

Harper arched his back and stretched while yawning widely, then shook his head. How long had he been asleep?

"A watch," the voice said. "Two day tenths."

Almost five hours. Harper sat up quickly, pushing the bedding off his still-clad body. "Light," he ordered. "Medium intensity."

A yellow-glowing ceiling lit the room, and now he could see that he was resting on a padded white shell that protruded from a mirror-shiny, red-brown wall. Bare of furniture, the room was roughly ten feet long and six feet wide. Standing, he would be able to put his palms against the ceiling.

Not a room with much character, he decided. But dormitory

housing beat nothing, and the Algherans had done wonders with the long-abandoned nuclear waste repository. He was moderately amused by the recollection that the Project had housed itself inside a relic of the First Era.

Another distant memory returned. Harper smiled frostily.

"Ironwearer," the voice asked, "what is a *pee-oh-dub-you*?"

"Just a person," he said absently. "Like you or me." He swung his legs over the side of the shelf and looked to his right. He had not recognized the voice at first, but a name came back to him now. And another: *Onnul*.

"Hello, Cyomit," he said steadily. "You've grown some, haven't you? How are you?"

"I'm fine, but I haven't grown. And I *don't* have a sister."

Harper swallowed. "Yeah. I won't argue."

Cyomit was still a small girl, barely over five feet tall, with brown hair and an elfin face. She was still cute rather than pretty, he decided—a bit thin, but her figure was good, even in too-large white coveralls. Sixteen now? No, seventeen, or had that changed also? In a few years men would be fighting over her.

"I really doubt that," she said, sounding both alarmed and amused.

"If honor and decency and all that is proper prevail among the men of Alghera, they certainly will," he assured her.

Cyomit seemed doubtful. "Well, they haven't yet."

Harper smiled. She had not met enough young male Algherans. But there were few of those continually in the Station. Perhaps that was why Onnul—

"There *isn't* any Onnul," Cyomit said angrily. "There never was. Stop thinking about her!"

Harper stared past her, looking at the glint of light from an irregularity on the wall. *There was an Onnul*, he remembered as waves of guilt and anguish poured over him. *There was. I killed her. I didn't save her. I ran away, and when I returned, even memories of her were gone—from everyone but me. Onnul!*

"Stop it!" Cyomit screamed. "You're hurting yourself deliberately—and you're making all of us in the Station feel it."

"Sorry," Harper squeezed out. "I'll get over it."

Cyomit looked at him sharply, then walked past him and put her fingers against a small black rectangle set into the wall. A storage bin underneath swung open on hidden hinges. The yellow light gleamed from something lying inside.

"Careful, the sword is sharp," Harper warned.

Cyomit shut the bin so that it seemed once more part of the wall, then extended a hand with silver mesh resting on the palm.

"Wear your 'blind," Onnul's sister commanded. "The tra'Nyjuc asks you, please."

"All right." Harper rocked the Teepblind over his scalp until enough hair had penetrated the screen to conceal the mesh. As body heat warmed it, the plastic rim contracted along his temples, forcing the vampire needles through skin to his skull. For an instant he was conscious of the prickling, then he ignored it.

He stood and pushed the bed shelf back into the wall. The floor was cold; after retucking loose clothing, he took fleece-lined boots from another storage cabinet and slipped them on. Cyomit was barefoot, he noticed wryly. *Kids!*

Donning the 'blind had had a calming effect, he noticed. He had needed some routine activity to distract him. And Onnul was long gone now, part of his past. Like—he groped for the alien name—like Sharon.

His face was permanently depilated, so he had no need to shave. The 'blind kept his hair in place, and the world would survive if he failed to shower. *What is really essential is a decent breakfast. Scrambled eggs, ham, orange juice, a Danish, three cups of black coffee . . . not going to get them here.*

He stretched absently and traced a finger across Cyomit's forehead, rubbing it gently over her plaque. *Unhappy little girl.* He did not ask if the 'blind was functioning; that would have been a breach of etiquette. "Ready to go, kid?"

Cyomit jerked her head away. "Don't touch me!"

"Because of Onnul?"

"You're a Normal," Cyomit said, as if that explained everything. Her voice had risen half an octave, and she spoke with angry precision. "I have a life of my own. I do *not* want it disrupted by strangers."

She was here, Harper reflected. Her life had been disrupted already, and her fate would be determined by the actions of strangers. "Sure," he said.

He dilated the door and left without another word. Cyomit stared after him, frozen-faced, then scurried down the hallway behind him. Harper slowed his pace, allowing her to keep up easily, but he did not look back. The ceiling lights in his room flickered and winked off. The triangular doorway closed.

Harper halted by the shrine near the entrance to the Council room. Cyomit had a question, he could tell. Smiling, he waited for her to ask it.

The shrine was a solid slab of ebony glued to the rock wall of the corridor. A tube mounted below cast a harsh blue light over the surface of the wood, making the depressions of the sculpture look like clouds over a satin sea. Faces hung before him, more than twice life size: a man's, hatchet-thin with short hair and determined lips; a woman's, oval with flowing hair, seeming both young and matronly; a pair of fur-covered gargoyles, wide-eyed and bear-snouted, with friendly humorous smiles. The eyes of all of them focused on him.

Onnul had been a believer, not him. But for an instant, Harper was conscious of Powers who watched his actions and wished him well—who loved him. *Superstition,* he thought angrily. *Paganism. I'm not going to fall for it.*

He turned suddenly without tracing in the air the customary reverence of sword and scythe. Then his anger abated.

No sense taking it out on a timid little girl. He forced a smile. "If you wonder, you are much like the Niculponoc Cyomit Nyjuc I knew back when—before things got changed. Of course, I wasn't paying much attention to Onnul's kid sister, and I don't know how long it's been for you, but you're a bit bigger, a bit more grown-up now. You used to be very quiet and solemn when I was around, I remember, and you didn't approve of us; that doesn't seem to have changed. Your voice is different, a little higher. But my memory may be wrong. Okay?"

Cyomit gave him an tentative smile. "Okay."

So she's going to let me live. It's a change. Harper was half pleased, half amused. "Different topic. Kylene Waterfall?"

"Otterfill Kylinn R'sihuc," Cyomit corrected, stumbling over the name herself. "She isn't happy, and she doesn't fit in. She's *dumb*!"

"Oh?"

"She can barely read or write! In any language, not just ours."

"Well, it takes time to learn," the man explained patiently. "I was still learning stuff even after—well, for a long while. And she comes from a culture that didn't stress that kind of knowledge, particularly for girls. She is smart, and she'll learn eventually. How long has she been here?"

"More than two seasons, almost a year. But she doesn't *want* to learn, so she won't. She's lazy. Not just at reading; there are things she should be doing with her mind that she won't learn. She *hates* it here. And no one likes her!"

"Sorry to hear that," Harper said slowly. "But I guess I'm not real surprised. Is there anything I can do? Like talk to the tra'R'sihuc or whatever?"

"You should have left her where she belonged. And maybe an Onnul would have been here for you. Why couldn't you leave things alone, Ironwearer ha'Ruppir?"

"Duty," he said bleakly. "Duty and obligation. I had no choice."

Cyomit nodded disagreement. "Not for one of the Skyborne. And you knew she was—she had to be. If the Normals find out what you did, they'll kill her and you both."

Harper said nothing. Cyomit bit her lip and ran down the corridor.

After a long pause he entered the Council room. The meeting had not begun yet.

They'll kill her. He took a seat at the table and stared toward the front of the room, not noticing as the black plastic softened and reformed under his weight. *No one likes her. They'll kill her.*

The image on the viewscreen now showed a brown paved road that passed by dark-colored low buildings on a green hillside. A notched parapet ran parallel to the road, and silver-tinged storm clouds hung overhead. *They'll kill her.*

"Are you all right?" Tolp asked. Concern showed on his chubby face as he sat next to Harper. "Do you wish the room to be made warmer?"

Harper started. "Just preoccupied. The temperature is all right." He smiled. "I've had enough time and rebuilding to be used to it."

"Well, you looked—never mind. I think we are ready to begin. Everyone made it back, I see."

They'll kill her. "Everyone always does."

A man wearing green coveralls stood up at the back of the room. A green rectangle was on his forehead; golden insignia were pinned to his collar. "The drone is in runtime," he reported. "The eye is now at City Year 240."

Borct nodded from the front of the table and pointed to a thin, balding man who had been talking in whispers with several of the returned agents. "Vrect tra'Hujsuon, none here know more of our city's history than you. Will you comment on the changes we see and what they may signify?"

"Polite today, aren't we?" Harper muttered.

"Politics," Tolp whispered back. "You know."

They'll kill her. The hell they will. "Yeah."

The man stared blankly at the Project Master, then blinked. "If you so wish, tra'Dicovys." His voice was slow, incongruously deep, still marked by the burr of the eastern delta despite his centuries in the capital. Vrect stepped to the dais and fished through his coverall pockets for an instructor's light pen, then waved it so a white arrow danced over the brown roadbed.

"Move it," he muttered.

The view began to turn, pivoting about an offscreen point as the camera drone flew about the hill. The road tilted to the left and moved downward. More hills became visible, then a gleam of water: a broad river flowing from the northwest that fanned out to empty into a tongue-shaped bay.

Not the Charles, Harper reminded himself. *The Ice Daughter these days*.

Together the bay and the river resembled the snout of a rhinoceros. Did this world still have rhinos? And elephants and giraffes? It was strange that he had not wondered about that before. No words for those animals existed in his Algheran vocabulary; he would have to ask one of the telepaths.

"Fohima Alghera in 240," the man on the dais said. "Not yet a F'a, of course; just a little town with pretensions."

Harper glanced at the screen. A handful of buildings, few of which were larger than a house, were visible at the base of one hill.

"City Year 250," the man in back said.

Between the village and the bay, grain fields bobbed up and down, green, yellow, white, then green again. The fields became flat strips on level terraces with rock wall boundaries. Perhaps the village buildings edged nearer the river.

"No changes yet. Most of the urban growth is off the screen, south of the hills over here." The white arrow moved jerkily. "Not suburbs as yet, but other small towns that we later absorbed.

Population is rising faster than the housing stock; don't be misled by what you see. Alghera is getting big."

"Pay attention, students," Tolp called out. "Quiz at the end of the period."

There was laughter at that; Vrect tra'Hujsuon's jaw tensed.

"City Year 275," the green-dressed man reported.

Harper tapped his friend's arm. "Why do that?" he whispered.

"A matter of image," Tolp whispered back.

"Yours or his?" Harper asked sourly, but Tolp only smiled.

"City Year 300."

Metaled roads flowed like quicksilver through the village, then cascaded over the terraces down to the bay. Lines of stubby trees swept over hillsides. The village was larger now, almost city-sized. Barracks and drill fields suddenly covered grain and grass. Harper glimpsed a bridge just above the river delta before it spun from the screen.

"Officially Fohima Alghera now," the tra'Hujsuon said. The light pen threw an arrow onto the gray walls of a massive building. "Regent's Keep—Castle of the Unifier, I should say. This building on the right is where Mlart actually lived, the one presented to him by the Muster. Much smaller than the castle.

"City growth has speeded up, not for the better. Esthetically, anyhow. These fields of ironberry trees provided some metal for army use, but most of the crop was exported. It *paid* for the army."

"City Year 350."

Buildings tumbled out of the city down to the bay. Roads looped over hillsides like thrown pieces of string. The delta at the river mouth eroded away.

"City Year 400."

"This is all different. These may be arsenals and other military buildings—very utilitarian architecture. Note that the docks have been shifted closer to the Ice Daughter. These might be grain storage facilities. For imports, of course. I'd guess that fluvial commerce has become more important than seaborne, which was never the case for us. A larger population than before may lie to the north. Mlart may have turned his attention to colonization at the end of his reign; it would be in keeping."

"Wouldn't he still be alive at this point?" someone asked.

"Possibly," the tra'Hujsuon said dourly. "But we were a

turbulent people, and Mlart probably realized that when he resigned after the Second War. If he had not been recalled—I doubt that he died of old age, or peacefully."

The arrow moved again. "Much ornamentation on this building. It's about the right size to be a political assembly, if smaller than BrightHonorKeep. We still use the old Gathering Hall for the Muster, but something special could have been built for Mlart's empire."

"City Year 450."

The outward growth of the city had stopped, but it was still changing, becoming lighter, more colorful, less densely packed. The dock region contracted and moved to the east, toward the ocean.

"Age of the Autocrats, I'd say. It's indicated by these villas on the terraces—large, very expensive, quite indefensible. They've come about fifty years late. You'll notice also the river has not been diverted yet."

"City Year 500."

"There it goes." The river had joined the bay from the north; now it flowed southwest, then made a loop encircling much of the city and returned northward to enter the bay from the west. Buildings vanished and were replaced by greenery.

"Now *we* control the use of the river. Ornament coming off the assembly building. Official end of the Empire, I suspect. Too bad. The walled section over here must be Teep Quarter; it's in the right place. In our original history, we talked about building the wall but never got around to it. Teeps were first admitted to the city in 513, so we have convergence on one date."

"City Year 550."

A hilltop had been sliced off, and a large white cube dropped onto it.

"Back view of the old temple. The buildings going up around it are the original home of the Institute. We're getting a great deal of convergence now."

"City Year 600."

Alghera shimmered. Ripples moved across it, leaving a metropolis of gold and white. Roads widened here and there, vanished in other places. Small parks were dotted throughout the city.

"Ambitious public works. You should recognize most of them. Economically and technically feasible because of industrial growth—the Institute paying back the Realm. Very pretty, but notice that the new construction simplified troop movements within the city and served to channel public transportation. So it was a riot-control scheme. Didn't work—the Autocrats got pitched out on their fundaments anyhow."

The arrow pointer jumped. "Watch this tower closely."

"City Year 650."

A tall building in the middle of the Institute was suddenly halved, jaggedly chopped off. The city seemed frozen and motionless, as if in shock. Then it slowly came back to life, its outer edges stretching over previously untouched hills. The stump of tower vanished.

"Our very own Timithial ha'Cuhyon—ha'Dicovys now—has arrived," the tra'Hujsuon said sourly. "That explosion marks the death of Herrilmin ha'Cuhyon. Young ha'Dicovys arrived in 657, so this is a good test for convergence."

"Yay, Timt!" There were other calls, which Harper stolidly ignored.

"City Year 700."

The Institute was blighted in appearance. Buildings thinned out around it, then were replaced by trees and widely spaced houses.

"Call it fashion. Teeps are moving from the Quarter—they were permitted to do that in 712. Note how houses on the other side of the wall look much the same as these, except for being closer together. The better elements are moving away from the city. They went south originally; here the motion is to the west."

"City Year 725."

"See all these little fields to the north of the river? Few houses, so I'd guess at the existence of a gentleman farmer class. It can't have much to do with feeding the city. Notice how large the dock region has become again."

"City Year 750."

Harper stood. "Master tra'Hujsuon, those fields seem to bear the same crop year after year. That does not jibe with the idea of gentleman farmers. I'd say it's a cash crop, for export, which would explain the dock buildup."

Vrect frowned. "It is not possible to decide from here, and I know of no crop valuable enough to justify such extensive cultivation."

Harper was still on his feet. "Something new, then."

"City Year 775," the man in back called.

"Not very likely," the tra'Hujsuon said. "Harn, this is your specialty. Explain the matter to the Ironwearer—simply."

"Timt, our records may not be complete, but we are positive we have every useful plant known to the Fourth Era." The speaker was burly, sandy-haired, and ruddy-faced. His fingers wiggled at chest level as he spoke, and he smiled frequently. "So your cash crop would have to be something really new."

"Genetic manipulation," Harper suggested. "It's possible."

"*We* can't do it," Harn said. "And we're two centuries later on. We're still trying to make sense out of the biology Plates—not to translate them, mind you, that's been done—but to make sense of the translation. We're not even sure we've got a complete set or that they're in correct order. And even if we do, and they are, the techniques and apparatus needed are way beyond us. The relevant engineering Plates make even less sense. Maybe in another century."

"Perhaps they threw the Plates away and started from scratch?"

Harn laughed. "Then they wouldn't be Algherans."

"Your point is made," Harper said dryly, and sat down.

"City Year 800."

"Much construction has gone on," the tra'Hujsuon summarized. "The Institute is being extended into the eastern hills. Here's the new Resolution Stronghold going up. Much evidence of prosperity. Money is going around, more than in our previous history, and not just for the temple and the Academic Septs. Even Teep Quarter looks less seedy."

The Project Master looked up from the sheaf of papers he had been leafing through. "Any guesses as to why, Vrect?"

The tra'Hujsuon snapped his fingers. "Perhaps a better class of Teep. Perhaps part of the general prosperity. Perhaps Teeps are being used in Alghera as they are in the Alliance, and fattening their nests in the same style."

"Is that compatible with general prosperity?" Borct asked blandly.

"I see no reason to believe they are linked." Vrect seemed ill at ease. The tra'Dicovys nodded absently and returned to his papers.

"City Year 825."

The central region of the city was deserted now. Buildings were rising at a frantic pace on its outskirts.

"We are moving away from the established pattern. *We've*

done it!" Men shifted forward throughout the room, trying to be soundless but showing the same excitement.

Harper glanced to his side, noticing that Tolp wore a genuine smile for once rather than his usual amiable grin. For an instant he envied his friend's happiness, then his doubts returned. *Wait and see.*

". . . these massive building programs," the tra'Hujsuon was saying. "No windows, so it is not housing. This isn't like our amphitheater. This mound by the side of the Ice Daughter, at the end of the bridge—what function it serves, I can't even guess."

"City Year 850." One voice had remained calm.

Roads moved away from Alghera in all directions, vanishing over the horizons. There was no new construction visible within the inner city. Older buildings showed dilapidation and disrepair. A second dockyard appeared nearer the ocean, then vanished as the image on the viewscreen spun. Areas of the city were transformed within seconds into wide expanses of grass and shrubbery. More parks?

"The city is being cannibalized," Vrect muttered. He was ignored.

"City Year 875."

The reduction of the city continued. Silence filled the room.

Getting ugly, Harper thought. *This is like shattering a jewel.*

"City Year 890."

A moment later, the viewscreen went black.

"Turn it back," Vrect ordered. "Show 890 again and move up from there."

The man at the back of the room looked preoccupied. He shook his head in agreement, more to himself than to the tra'Hujsuon, closed his eyes, and only after some time opened them. When he spoke, he gave his attention not to the man on the dais but to the Project Master.

"There is nothing left. The drone is gone or malfunctioning. It does not answer our signals."

"Send out another." Borct was on his feet, his voice drowning out whatever words the tra'Hujsuon might be uttering. "I want everyone back here at the end of two watches. Siccentur, Tolipim, Timithial, I want a conference with you."

The Teep was not through. "We did. We lost that one also."

CHAPTER SEVENTEEN

"

. . . barrel burst," someone was remembering as the door widened. "The gun chief was a fat old High Blankshield buying citizenship with the campaign, and when Mlart heard that—"

"Here's Timt," someone else said. "Ask him."

"Let's not ask Tim," Harper responded, "and just say we did. I ate last with the tiMantha lu Duois, and I don't know much more than you."

The man at the head of the nearest table grinned. "So Borct's errand boy doesn't know what's going on. I can believe that, I guess." His finger moved, pointing. "You two Dicovys cubs—food for the Ironwearer. Have a seat, Timt boy."

Harper remained standing, looking around the room. There were several cafeterias in the Station; custom had made this the one where off-duty Agents congregated, and nearly forty of them were seated at benches around the narrow wooden tables. *Just about the full crew.* His eyes moved on.

The conversation in the back was equally lively, he judged from the number of gestures the diners made, though he heard no voices. The lighting was dim, so he saw no forehead plaques, but he recognized the behavior. Telepaths. His entry would have been noticed, but his mind was shielded from them, so he waited to catch the eye of the man at the head of the table, then nodded his respects curtly to show that he did not have to be ignored.

"Don't mind me," he muttered, taking a seat at another table, which was occupied only by a pair of middle-aged men drinking beer. The men hesitated, on the verge of leaving, but went back to their conversation when he showed cold disinterest.

Technicians, he guessed, half listening to the scraps of talk that reached his end of the table, the mechanics who kept the levcraft operational and made life in the Station livable. The conversation was matter-of-fact, even gossipy: a bossy supervisor with family ties to one of the Septs, a not yet competent trainee, the deterioration of the work ethic in the older generation, the arrogance and impatience of the Project's Agents. Trivial matters, the petty concerns of working men, and infinitely comforting at that moment. Harper held his expression frozen when their eyes lit upon him, and drummed his fingers on the table top, pretending his attention was focused on the open doorway to the kitchen area. He listened with gratitude to their calm voices. He almost could envy their casual certainties, their sane lack of passion. Almost.

What is a war, a First Era voice asked him, *but patriotic workers of one country killing patriotic workers of another, benefiting neither?*

War is opposition, he answered within. *A conflict that is capable of producing resolution without compromise.*

There were things civilized men had to oppose without compromise.

There were evils in the world, sins that had to be punished, crimes that had to be stopped. If it required force and violence, so be it.

Pacifism was a half-truth. It was true that ordinary life went on during conflict and afterward, and it was probably true that for most people, in the end it did not matter who won. It was well to remember that, valuable to be exposed to the people who lived unchanging lives in the world he and the other Agents built and rebuilt.

It was also true that war held cruelty and despair, that war corrupted.

None of that meant that wars should not be fought.

Evil was banal, the thinkers of his time had concluded. Petty cruelty, intolerance, insensitivity, irresponsibility, lack of goodwill—there were no devils that afflicted the human race, only ordinary human beings with ordinary vices who let themselves be ordinary.

And what were the opposite qualities? Kindness, goodwill, honesty, foresight, fair dealing, understanding—ordinary values held by ordinary people. Virtue, too, was banal—should be banal.

"Thanks," he muttered, accepting a tray brought to him from the kitchen. A steaming purple mug of broth, a rectangular plate of the same material with a thick circular sandwich. *Tasteless,* he predicted. *Rabbit on potato cake, or giant pigeon, or something tasting that way.*

There was a terrible sameness about Station meals, he had noticed. Of course, the defect might be in his own taste buds. Someday he would have to ask a Teep if flavors were the same regardless of species. Meanwhile . . . *filet mignon wouldn't be attractive now, either.* He waved a hand unhappily, dismissing his younger Septlings, and glowered about the room. When they were reseated, he turned to his own meal.

The food *was* tasteless.

He recalled a bit of doggerel Sweln had taught him: *Once, twice, three times, and four have men built cities. Now at Alghera begins the Fifth Era* . . . Five brief periods of civilization and none of them long enough to extirpate the evil from the human soul. The weaklings who had let the First Era fall had much to answer for.

"Damned commie pinko bastards," he muttered. Which changed nothing but felt marvelously self-consoling.

"Stupid bull dyke bra burners." That felt good also. "Peaceniks. Peanut farmers!"

He should get back to the cabin soon, he realized. Unwind. He was overdue a vacation and some edible food. *Steak, french fries, coffee. Loads of coffee. Ten pounds of steel off my sword for that hideaway, and it was worth every halfpenny nail.*

Though here I can have my potato cake and eat it, too.

He set the mug down and rubbed a finger over the plate, noticing how the tinted plastic distorted the pattern of the wood grain beneath it, how the ceiling lights made a fuzzy, off-center cross phosphoresce on its surface. *Pretty, even if the food is monotonous.*

Some sad day he would exhaust the supply of coffee, he reflected. *Wonder if I should suggest to some bright biochemist that alkaloids can be fun.* No, that would be irresponsible. The Algheran metabolism could cope with caffeine, but coffee was an acquired taste none of the Agents he had experimented on wanted to develop. Which was probably just as well. Some paths of knowledge did not merit exploration, and not all the bad habits of the First Era needed to be introduced to the Fifth.

No, they're capable of inventing their own evils.

The workmen left. There was nothing to distract him from brooding.

". . . then I met this girl," he overheard.

It was not an unreasonable thing to hear in a group of young men, and he turned half his consciousness toward the story. The narrator was the tall blond man seated at the head of the Agents, he noticed, the one who had taken the place Harper normally occupied. He poked at his sandwich and thought about leaving.

". . . watched the house for nearly a season," he heard. "Then she didn't leave for half a tenday. And I knew that was the time."

"Either that or she'd broken a leg," someone threw in.

"If she'd broken a leg, that was also the time. I was im*patient*!"

General laughter followed.

"So I went back to the start of that time and waited till she was alone. Well, there was a little brother, but he didn't count."

"And was she?" he heard.

"Was she *ever*! I went through the door and started pulling clothes off, and she—"

"What about the brother?"

"Shoved him in a closet. Hit him to shut his yap, but—"

"What about her parents? They give problems?"

The man laughed. "We were gone before they could. It was such a dump, I just took her off to the city and a hotel. *Which* we did not leave for five days. You guys got to try a Teep! I mean, *everything* goes when one of the bitches pops, and they know *just* what you're after." He laughed again. "After five days, I was almost worn out."

"Getting hard to get hard, eh, Herm?" That brought snickers.

"But *not* impossible! So, after I took her home, that's when the old folks raised a stink."

"What was their problem?"

"Oh, their little angel had never been with a real man before, and now she was spoiled and all that crap. And I'd roughed her up a bit, *which* she liked, I'll have you know, but *they* didn't see it that way. And little brother was hurt and sore, and stuff like that. I just laughed and told them state business and who were they going to complain to, anyhow—that shut them up. So I came back next year, and they were gone, what do you know?"

"Chase 'em down?"

"Easiest thing in *the* one world! And she was just as good the second time, too. So, all in all, that was one *good* thing about our little trip, wasn't it? How'd you fellows do?"

"Nothing like that," someone said sourly.

"Well, you're stupid! Do it with a *Teep*, fellows. Nothing like a *really* hot Teep! Vrect's *all* wrong when he says we don't need them!"

Harper stood with the care he would have given to standing on ice.

"Well, the Ironwearer! How do *you* like the Teeps, Timt boy?"

Harper looked at the sneering man, memorizing features. *Young, strong, and brainless,* he decided. The blond's face was ruddy, and he was unusually tall and heavy for an Algheran. He had never seen him before. *Thought I still knew everyone, despite the other changes.*

"I'd like your name." It took an effort to keep his voice even.

"Santin Herrilmin ha'*Hujsuon*. How about *that*, Timt boy?"

Harper nodded. "You know me." It was a statement.

The blond snapped his fingers. "Unfortunately."

There were laughs, which died quickly.

Harper waited for words to form in the ha'Hujsuon's mouth, then beat him to speech. "I feel the same way."

This time the laughs were with him. The blond glowered. "Do you know who I am, little Timt boy?"

Harper kicked at the bench. "An asshole. Haul ass, ha'Hujsuon."

"You *don't*, do you? What *do* you mean, Timt boy?" The

man simpered, looked down the table for support. A man stood—one of the Hujsuons.

"Leave," Harper said evenly. "Now. You're a disgrace to your uniform. Don't ever let me hear you talking this way again."

"I'm a dis-*grace* to *my* uniform," the blond said, making cute as his Septling approached. "Did you hear that, Lerlt? The Teep-lover doesn't want to hear about *anyone* else sharing his fun."

A man was at Harper's back now. Two men.

Dicovys. His own Septlings. He waved them off.

He snapped fingers, then pointed at the door. "Get moving, ha'Hujsuon."

"And if I *don't*? What will you do then, Timt boy? Cry on a *Teep*?"

Harper smiled happily. "I'll break your back."

"Herrilmin," Lerlt said, swallowing rapidly. "Not here."

"Well, to please you, Lerlt." The big blond stood, raising blue eyes to meet Harper's. "To please Lerlt. We'll have to talk again, Timt boy." He pushed his buttocks back as he left the room, and farted. Two more Hujsuon Agents wavered, then bolted from the table to follow.

"Running low on Agents, aren't we?" Harper commented. He glanced down the table, curious as to who would meet his eyes. Not many did.

"You going to meet him?" the younger of his Septlings asked.

He shrugged. "I'll wait for a challenge so I can pick weapons."

"What'll they be?" the other one asked.

"If he does?" Harper thought about it. "Filthy words at fifty paces. We'll find out who the real soldier is." Then he dropped the grin. "I will break his back if he talks that way again."

"Timt, he didn't actually, you know—"

Bann ha'Hujsuon. *A onetime friend*. Harper frowned more at the irony than at the man. "I know. He just wanted to upset—" He poked a thumb in the direction of the still silent telepaths.

Bann shook his head. "And, well—you. You have a reputation, not for—I mean, but for treating Teeps as—"

As people, Harper finished sourly. *As citizens*. "Tough."

The word needed supplementing, and he stood a bit longer,

looking for more words without any luck. "It's you people who are changing, not me," he said finally, knowing he would not be believed.

Defeat is not good for children and other Algheran things.

He sighed inwardly and took the seat Herrilmin ha'Hujsuon had left. "Anyone wondering what we do next? I can tell you a little. Stick around, Bann; we need one of the Hujsuons here.

"Something up there is eating our probes. Three so far. Yeah, three. Borct sent another off after the meeting. It was advanced more slowly, so we got the date they vanished but nothing else. It wasn't the Present, by the way; it was about two years this side of it.

"So the next Council meeting is a couple of days off. We have to make some more probes."

There were questions.

"We don't have any more probes," he explained. "We never lost one before, and we never worried about it before. So now we are plumb out."

The job would take a day, he estimated. "From the viewpoint of everyone else, that is. It'll be ten or twenty days for us, and we'll be busy. We can't run up to the near-Present anymore and get five-fingered discounts on stock from the Institute laboratories. The world has changed too much—it isn't clear there's an Institute at all, anymore."

That affected them. He smiled grimly at the shocked expressions and continued. "We'll have to get components manufactured specially for us, little pieces of the whole thing so we don't give any physical principles away or let people guess what we are doing. Some of you will be doing that, anyway. The rest of us will be putting those little pieces together."

The work would be dull, he agreed. But extra hands were needed now, and most Agents came with two of them.

Another question. Harper stalled, reaching back to scratch his neck before answering. "My opinion? We got to kill Mlart, that's what."

There were cries of outrage. He waited them out.

"We got to kill Mlart," he repeated. "Saving him caused too many changes, most of them not good ones. Right now, just believe me. Those of you who go uptime will see what I mean. But you all saw the original probe pictures. Was that the city you grew up in?"

"No." Only one Agent made the admission. The others were still.

"No," he echoed. "But if it looked strange from the air, think how different it is on the ground. Different history, different politics. It isn't home. And when this Project began, that was the idea: keep Alghera just the same but avoid the war. If Mlart stays alive, we have failed."

That brought surly silence.

He nodded slowly. "It always was a gamble, you know. A compromise, with the Project Master and the tra'Ruijac letting the tra'Hujsuon get his way once just to see how things turn out. We all know that, even if no one is saying it openly."

"You're saying it, Timt." That earned someone a laugh.

Harper smiled. "Regardless, we have to build some probes."

"You were there?" someone wondered. One of the Ruijacs.

"Yes and no. I went up to about a century before the end. Then I figured I'd seen enough and came back to report. After that—those are very strange people uptime. I wouldn't want to fall into their hands or any of you to fall into their hands, so the more tin heroes we have to send, the better."

"Why? What would happen?" a Dicovys asked.

Give them time travel and they'll hunt us all down, Harper thought. He hesitated as one of the telepaths stepped beside him.

"The Project Master presents his compliments to the young men," the Teep said gravely. "He wishes them to meet with him in the Council room at their convenience. He is there now."

He glanced curiously at Harper as agents rose and left the room. "The tra'Dicovys does not want this matter discussed openly."

Harper recognized the Teep from the second meeting and noticed the mace on his collar. *The tra'R'sihuc. I have to talk to him about Kylene.* "You found out from him what I saw uptime?"

The other man snapped his fingers. "It's under iron. Your little secrets are still secret. Go to your meeting, Ironwearer. We'll clean up the mess you Agents left."

Harper wished he could.

CHAPTER EIGHTEEN

"I've got this battery pack in solid. Toss me a screwdriver."

"Catch!"

"Got it." Harper reached out to snag the flying tool, then fitted a pie-pan-shaped cover over the battery compartment and pushed needle-tipped "screws" into the plastic. One end of the "screwdriver" fitted over the screwcaps; there was a ratchet mechanism in the knurled handle that he rocked back and forth to drive in the screws. "Hate these screws of yours—they never seem to fit very snugly in this tool."

"Really?" the blond man asked politely. "We're more used to them, perhaps."

Harper sat on his haunches and looked across the bubble, squinting slightly in the harsh actinic light. Beyond the bubble was darkness, though if he looked carefully he could make out the blue-tinged frozen forms of men and machinery. Inside the bubble were two men, himself and a short blond Algheran, boxes of parts, tools, calibration equipment, a floating light, and a dozen time-drive units. It had been a long day, he thought, looking around. *Long couple of weeks.*

How much time had gone by outside the bubble? Perhaps

a halfday, most of that during the intervals when he and Bann left the stoptime work station to rest and eat in their quarters. *Every few minutes we get back from a hard day and switch on the stoptime field and go to sleep—that room of mine is beginning to stink, and I'll bet his is no better. Good thing we don't have to contend with roommates like the Teeps.*

He had seen Kylene in the halls a few times, but she had pretended not to recognize him. That was just as well, he realized. *We ought to get together sometime, though. Maybe when this mess is wrapped up, we can get her straightened out.*

But at the moment— *Screwdrivers. We were talking about screwdrivers.* "I know," he said reflectively. "Funny thing, it didn't take me long to pick up your language and most of your customs. Of course, I got help from the Teeps. But things like screws and nuts and bolts are harder to get used to."

"You will someday."

Harper shook his head. "I don't know, Bann. I've been running around up here for seven years now—" He broke off and sighed. "Must be thirty-three now, maybe thirty-four. Getting old doing this."

"Old? At thirty-four?"

"Yeah." Harper spoke evenly. "I'll be good for another fifty, sixty years, but nothing like the three or four centuries you people get."

Bann looked startled, so the big man gave him a short-lived smile. "Wrong kind of biology. Seems I didn't come with a full set of little things in my cells. For my time, I was perfectly normal. Here—" He shrugged.

"Throwback," the blond man said carefully. "So that's why—sorry, Timt."

Harper shrugged again. "I've heard the term."

"The tra'Hujsuon—I—Cimon!"

Harper waved a hand. "Well, it's no secret, so you don't have to look so guilty. Seven years, remember? I've gotten used to things."

"Is there something that can be done?"

"Maybe someday." The redhead shook his head abruptly, then grinned. "Some possible things. Used to figure I had some kind of vested interest in getting this war won so people like you could get back to translating all those biological Plates." Not anymore though.

Bann looked at him speculatively, then turned away to screw down the cover before him. "All right. This does my part of things, so we're through. I'd like to thank you—vested interest or not—for helping me with these assemblies, Timt. It would have taken a lot longer if I had had to do them all by myself."

Harper fought to keep his voice even. "I was curious. I'd done maintenance work on these gizmos, but I'd never seen one put together from scratch. Maybe someday the knowledge will be useful." *Onnul.*

"In the field, you mean?" Bann slapped at the top of the unit beside him. "Not very likely. Not much ever goes wrong with them. Lovely things!"

Stay calm. "I had one explode on me. I was three hundred man-heights up, and it took out all my power. I came visible in front of some Alliance guns and got riddled. And crashed."

"Not possible." Bann was definite. "You must have done something wrong."

Onnul. "I was being very careful."

Bann nodded. "It just can't happen."

That leaves sabotage. "It did."

"That was a year ago, wasn't it?" the ha'Hujsuon agent asked suddenly. "Station time. I was on a mission, but I heard something about it when I got back. You crashed near a group of Agents and walked away from it without injury. Nicole really had you under her cloak!"

"Something like that," Harper agreed, thinking of the body left in the wreckage. "Something like that. Isn't time travel wonderful?"

Don't be bitter, chum. You had to work your way back in somewhere.

I still want to know who killed me.

Bann stared at him speculatively. "Some ways. But if you think you've seen enough now to build a drive unit by yourself, I hope you never fall into the hands of the Alliance."

"We've had the same conditioning. Kill or suicide, so no one gets information out of us. I'm told it works very well."

Bann hesitated at the bleakness in the big man's voice. "It's necessary, isn't it?"

"Probably." Harper changed the subject. "Question for you: How often do you recall losing an Agent?"

"Hmmm. Not lately. We lost some at the start of the Project, before we left Alghera. You wouldn't know about that, but Tolp ha'Ruijac could tell you what that was like."

"All right. Any others?"

"We lost two from my Sept just about the time we picked you up. They tried to go back to the Fourth Era and never returned."

Harper grunted, remembering his angry flight back to the First Era. "It's insane there for a while. Not surprising if they hit trouble. I was damned lucky to get back when I tried it."

The earth had undergone a reversal of its magnetic field twenty thousand years earlier. During the transition period, the missing men almost certainly would have lost power in their levcraft and crashed, but he was not eager to explain that to the Algherans. *Let them go on thinking it's just a war, and I've got a bolthole*. "Any others?"

Bann snapped his fingers without concern. "One or two, but mostly we've all been under the cloak. Maybe—if it's hard for us to change the future, it's also hard for the future to change us."

"Worth thinking about," Harper said. *If a time traveler dies in the future, where does the cause lie? When?*

Bann broke up his speculations. "So, could you build one of these?"

Harper snorted. "I hope I never have to find out." He began to speak more rapidly. "Maybe I could. The design makes some kind of sense, and I wouldn't have to copy it exactly. I could rig up something and fine-tune it till it was working, I think. I wonder—do you suppose you could build one of these with very small circuits, fingernail-sized or smaller?"

"Why?"

Harper shrugged. "Curiosity. What could you do with a time machine as a component in electrical devices? Think of the switching speeds."

Bann nodded curtly. "What we have works fine. Even if we don't know why or how."

"I could make a guess if you're interested."

"Sure. I'm a science student, after all."

That was a very rough translation. The Institute for the Study of Land Reclamation Issues was not exactly a university, and its faculty members were not really college professors, despite Harper's persistent beliefs that they should be. A profit-making organization owned by several Septs, it was partially controlled by, and partially controlled, the Algheran government. Bann had described himself as one learning technical knowledge that would qualify him to give orders to working engineers.

The redhead grinned maliciously. "Okay. This electron gun—the doohickus you call a 'ghost fluid pump'—"

He traced the circuitry through the casing with the screwdriver as he spoke, pausing from time to time to remember English words for the concepts he was using and translate them into terms the Algheran would understand. *This is fun,* he found himself thinking. *I haven't talked real physics to anyone for years.*

"Neutron decay involves the weak interaction," he concluded. "So parity isn't conserved. Charge remains the same, so by the TCP invariance theorem, time reversal has to go. In other words, there is some preferred direction for things to happen in, locally. So some small region of space is very apt to move one direction in time, and some larger surrounding region is at least a little more likely to move in the same direction. In fact, now that I think about it, that might be enough to explain just why the arrow of time points as it does—why the entire universe moves through time in the same direction. Hmmm . . .

"Anyhow, you've got massive violations of parity here—billions of these neutron-antineutron pairs are being created every millionth of a day tenth—so in practice, a fairly large region of space is being kicked through time at a faster than normal clip."

He dropped to a deadpan. "Simple, isn't it?"

"No." Bann looked at him with glazed eyes. "I didn't understand a word. Did you make it all up as you went along?"

Harper stared at the man, juggling the screwdriver in his hand without speaking until the other man looked away. "I was quite serious," he said then. "I really was. Perhaps it was over your head, but that doesn't make it a joke. In my time enough people would have understood me to populate a dozen Algheras. There was a man named Dalton—basically he showed us that the world was not made up of perfectly continuous quantities, and after that our physical science went off in very different directions than yours, and we worked on it very hard with a lot of people. Tolp likes to call it all superstition, but it really wasn't. As you say, what we had worked."

He sighed. "I hate to draw morals. Still, the First Era was

not the same as the Fifth, but that doesn't mean it was filled with idiots swinging from tree branches. Don't make fun of something of which you're ignorant. Okay?"

Bann nodded slowly.

"End of moral pointing." Harper smiled again. "It would take a while to give you the background you need to understand my explanation, years to teach you enough First Era physics to really work with it. But if you ever get curious, you can look through the library files. Once upon a time, I'm told, I taught some classes on the subject and wrote a few books. The Project, at least, should still have them."

"Is it true you taught the tra'Dicovys?"

"*I* didn't teach Borct a single thing. Some other guy with my name and some of the same history, but not me. In this history, I'm the guy you people yanked out of a collapsing building and brought back here. The guy you kidnapped."

Bann was not apologetic. "It seemed a good idea. It still does."

Convinced him, Harper thought. *Well, it was true for the guy in the crash.* "I won't argue. Anyhow, Borct says he took one class from me. He was going to take another, but I dropped dead of old age and he never got the chance. I suppose students always tell their professors nice things like that. I was off in a corner somewhere, I'm told, so it was probably a fluke that he ever heard of me."

"Interesting. Things would be different for us if he hadn't."

"I don't know about that," Harper said. "My experience has been that history always manages to stay on track."

Without waiting for an answer, he stood to capture the floating lamp, then manipulated switches on a box at his feet. The outer world brightened, taking on color. The frozen shapes of men moved once more.

CHAPTER NINETEEN

"*Where have you been lately?" Tolp asked, handing over* a portfolio. "I've been carrying these since yesterday."

"In stoptime," Harper answered as he slipped into his chair. "Don't worry. Pictures aren't contagious." Across the table, Bann ha'Hujsuon's eyes met his, then glided past as if the contact embarrassed him. To his left was the blond man Harper had expelled from the cafeteria.

Harper raised an eyebrow but said nothing and looked over the Council room. The Teep at the back this time was a stocky brunette woman in a red coverall. *Teenager,* he estimated. *Something innately gawky about young telepaths, no matter how solemn and mature they try to be.*

The girl fidgeted suddenly, light glinting from her forehead plaque, and her hand plucked nervously at the black stuff of the cube chair underneath her. *Reading my mind,* Harper thought with amusement. *You are really young, girl.* He stared at her. *Leave us. You won't like the picture show.* He continued to stare until she obeyed.

"Wish this thing would start," Tolp muttered. "I hate waiting."

Some things don't change. Harper looked at him, then jerked his eyes back to the viewscreen lest they betray affection. "Yeah."

The camera drone was suspended high above a frozen ocean. Perhaps it was dusk, for the overcast sky was dark and the motionless wave that ran diagonally across the screen was indistinct.

Something was wrong with the Council room, he noted absently. Just what was different now? The distribution of men, he decided; two distinct groups were apparent on opposite sides of the table, with fewer gaps between individuals than normal. More were on Bann's side than his. Did it mean anything?

Borct entered the room, ending his speculations. As usual, the Project Master carried a bundle of paperwork, which he dropped on the table before stepping to the dais.

"Cimon, guard us. Nicole, guide us." The nasal tones seemed rushed, as though he were out of breath. "I am Birlin Borictar tra'Dicovys, and Project Master. Would another challenge my authority?"

There was a stir on the other side of the table as men cast short-lived sideways looks at one another. However, no voice was raised, and after a brief hesitation Borct spoke in a more determined tone.

"We are here to investigate the failure of our probes of two days ago. I have some good news: The first of our new probes is at the Present. The view shown on the screen is from City Year 893, day 75. So the barrier at the end of time is precisely where it should be. We did expect that, but checking it seemed sensible."

"Did you expect it?" Tolp whispered.

Harper shrugged and waved Tolp to silence.

"We also have some very bad news, which I understand is beginning to circulate through the Station. Timithial ha'Dicovys has begun an investigation of the new future, and I have asked him to report to us."

My cue. Harper stood and opened the portfolio.

"You did not take these photos yourself, Ironwearer?" someone asked.

"No," Harper agreed flatly. "They come from several historical accounts that Borct now has available in his office. Frankly, it seemed like a good part of time to stay away from."

There was a pause while the Council members stared again at the charred bodies tumbling from the incinerators, the endless lines of hospital beds, close-ups of dying children and vacant-eyed survivors. He heard whispers but ignored them, trying to appear impassive.

"How fast did it kill them?" an Agent asked. Fascination sat on his face, along with a touch of fear.

"The incubation period ran from four to twenty days," Harper said mechanically, "depending on the victim's general health. Some people were infected without becoming ill at all, but they probably helped spread it. After symptoms appeared, death followed in one day or ten. Several different strains of the disease were used, so generalizing is difficult. Full recovery might take a year tenth, maybe two."

"No, I mean—" Embarrassment registered on the Agent's face.

"Numbers? Ten million in three years, about two-thirds of them in the Alliance. There were cures available the last year, so the total didn't have to be that high—but things were pretty disorganized since the Alliance had depended so much on the Teeps."

Someone needed that part explained. Harper sighed inwardly but complied. "The illness lodged in the brain, and Teeps and Normals were affected differently. About one Normal in five who got sick cashed in his chips, but for Teeps the figure was three in five. Which is why when the epidemics finally ended, only nine million Normals were dead, as opposed to a half a million of the much smaller Teep population.

"But to add to the fun, about one Normal in five who was hit survived but was brain-damaged, so you had one moron for each corpse. For the Teeps, just about everyone sick who didn't die became a moron, without telepathy. So the Alliance, which once had six or seven hundred thousand healthy telepaths, suddenly had only eighty thousand.

"Frankly, it's a miracle they won that war. The books sort of suggest they kept going only because it was their only hope of getting their hands on the antidotes."

No, he had not picked up samples on his return from the future.

The antidotes had not been completely effective, and the Janhular—the Fifth Era Australians—had lost a tenth of their own population, "not counting those sort of punctured along the way by ChelmForce."

How had it worked? "Well, the microbes won, and I was always told I should root for the little guy." Anything that killed a quarter of the human race had to be regarded as outstanding in some technical sense. On the other hand—but maybe the Janhular liked being in the Alliance now that nearly two centuries had gone by.

Yes, the Alliance had won. But it had changed; with sixty percent of all the Teeps in the world dead and most of the rest mentally retarded, Hemmendur's Solution had become Hemmendur's Dream and was disregarded. The Alliance continued, but now it sought to rule the world just for the sake of ruling the world.

"Of course, now the argument is that the world isn't safe from germ warfare unless there's only one government. And since Chelmmys has the most experience at running such a thing . . ." Harper grinned ironically.

Things were pretty much on track, he told them. The Alliance had been slowed up for a while, but the final plague had reduced population and strength in all nations, so, relatively, things had not changed as much as might have been expected. By City Year 800, the political maps looked about the same as they had in the original version of history.

How had the plagues *really* worked? Harper hesitated, looking for an appropriate answer, then settled on truth.

"The Janhular wanted to use strains of equine encephalitis that were transmitted by contact to make sure the disease would spread. That was easy enough; the problem was to get the disease established in the first place, without any natural carriers. So they got the idea of using *Escherichia coli* as their vector; it's a bacteria most people have in their intestines already, so the risk of rejection was low.

"The next problem was getting the disease into the bacteria, since what causes encephalitis is a eukaryotic virus consisting of a single RNA strand, and the bacteria is a prokaryote. What they did is, they slammed together a pair of viruses and some other stuff to make a retrovirus. Then they used a plasmid to slip this into the cell, so it wound up in the bacteria's DNA. Now they got really clever, because they had also added genes that deactivated the retrovirus, so the bacteria still seemed to be *E. coli* from the body's viewpoint. So if you could get someone to swallow some of the bacteria, it'd wind up in his gut, breed like hell—and make lots of copies of the retrovirus.

"So far, so good. Now things get even better.

"The retrovirus is still not doing anything, but *E. coli* comes in different flavors, and the Janhular selected ones that can cause diarrhea. Of course, practically no one got sick because the body created antibodies to fight the infection. But when the *E. coli* bacteria mobilized to fight the antibodies, *they switched off the genes deactivating the retrovirus*. So the next time the bacteria divided, the retrovirus was released. Except the production of the protein that held the two RNA strands together had been stopped also, and the pure encephalitis virus was being released. In gobs. And it took no time at all after that to wind up in the brain.

"Even better, people had different susceptibilities to the *E. coli* in the first place, so someone might react in a few days, or it might take a year—you couldn't predict. Pure time bomb. It could pop up anywhere, so even after the Alliance knew what they were up against, it was too late to do anything. Of course, that's how it spread to places not in the Alliance.

"Brilliant, though, wasn't it? And they pulled that off *four times* before the Chelmmysians were able to stop them. Just think what would have happened if they had used a really dangerous virus."

Of course, the explanation did not satisfy everyone. Finally, defensively, Harper gave up on meeting objections. "Look, I just answered a question, I'm not going to teach a course. Now, it's like this: The biology the Janhular used is based on the Plates. I was told once that Alghera might have that kind of technology in City Year 1200 or so; these people simply got it by City Year 700. If you really want to understand it all, go uptime and ask them. Me, I think it's a little risky. But I'll listen if anyone wants to argue."

He paused, then shrugged at the silence. "Any other questions?"

"How did they feel about it, our contemporaries, that is?" That was one of the faculty members, a man old enough to have been a participant in the Janhular war.

Harper raised an eyebrow. "In what way?"

"I mean, were they bothered by it in retrospect, or proud, or what?"

"They didn't throw festivals, if that's what you mean."

Harper snarled till the laughs stopped, then continued. "It happened. That was their attitude. It just happened. Like one of the Eternal Wars.

"I got an impression of envy in some of the younger Algheran people, in fact. They seem to regard the Janhular as people who were particularly determined and tough, and they want an opportunity to show they could be equally tough. That may explain the numbers of wars they had since then. Also, I think most of them felt they survived by personal merit rather than by being under Nicole's cloak. Many of them lost family in the plagues; I think it made them a little harder, a little more callous in some sense. They seemed more ambitious. Those are subjective opinions; if I'd gone up to the Present, I might have found different attitudes; I figured I'd seen enough by then, though."

How did he mean that he had seen enough?

Harper frowned. Wasn't the result obvious? He waved a hand toward the photos to make his point. "Cancel this—"

"Thank you, Timithial. Sit down now." That was the Project Master. Harper hesitated but nodded grimly at last and then took his seat by Tolp.

Borct returned to the dais slowly, then looked over the Council with an expression of unease. "It would be proper to decide to undo the change we agreed to yesterday," he began. "Who would . . ."

Silence followed. People exchanged glances, but no one rose.

Harper stood impatiently. "Let's undo it."

"No!" The protest came from a faculty member. "Not this fast."

"Why not?" Harper waved at the photos again. "You really want to be a part of that?"

"Timt!" Borct said sternly. "Watch your temper."

Harper shook his head with exasperation and settled in his seat, then turned to the objecting faculty member. "Harn, do you have another suggestion?"

"No." The man's face suggested he was being mistreated. "But it's too early to let Mlart be killed. This—" He waved a hand toward the photographs. "It's distasteful. We have to change it. But the Janhular did it, not Mlart. There has to be something else we can try."

"Yes, something else."

"More study."

"Rash to just kill."

Harper lost track of the voices. He turned to Tolp with thunder forming inside.

Tolp snapped his fingers without humor. "Mlart is popular, Timt."

Harper pointed a thumb at the photos. Words seemed unnecessary.

"I know," Tolp said through the hubbub. "But—all right." He stood, then rapped on the table till attention turned to him.

"Project Master, tra'Ruijac, others. I understand the reluctance people feel toward Timt's idea. But it is our most obvious course and the simplest. Certainly, it was a tragedy for the Realm when Mlart died and one that we are capable of undoing. But in nine hundred years there have been many tragedies, and we cannot undo all of them. Our real concern is with the war, something that has lasted for seven years of our history. Seven years, and Cimon knows we have had problems making changes in it. If Mlart is left alive, we are going to have to make changes in five hundred eighty years. That is not practical."

"Why?" someone asked.

"Because the world that has emerged is so very different from the one we know," Tolp explained carefully. "Something like our Alghera may still be opposed to something like the Alliance, but they aren't the ones we are used to. The issues are different; the people are different. As we have seen, the technology is different. We would like a Present that makes us feel at home, and this world is probably not it. Suggesting changes to make it that way is something we are not yet prepared to do."

"You need more time?" one of the Agents asked. "Time is cheap." He snapped fingers to dismiss the issue.

Others agreed. ". . . only his word about it," one voice said. Which meant little till Harper heard ". . . can trust Timt. Ask a Teep if—"

"What Teeps?" someone said sarcastically.

He heard laughter.

Harper started to stand but was forestalled by Borct.

"The killings Timt described will not be part of our history," he said crisply. "No true Algheran would suggest it."

Sict broke the silence with a cough. "We could continue

this discussion later," he suggested. "Why don't we postpone an argument until we view what our probes show us?"

The tra'Dicovys shook his head. "I think you're right. Is everyone agreed? Yes. Timt, would you get our Teep back?"

The girl in the hallway was kneeling at the icon, weeping.

"It won't happen." He laid his hands on her shoulders and shook gently. "It. Won't. Happen. I promise you."

Cimon met his gaze calmly, Nicole with serenity. The tiMantha lu Duois shook with laughter.

"Ready to go back now? There's nothing to worry about."

The icon was really only a carved piece of dark wood.

". . . beginning at City Year 889," Borct was saying as Harper returned to his seat. "We will move forward slowly to 890, day 342."

The picture on the viewscreen had changed. The waters under the probe was dark blue; the waves had become smaller and more frequent. The image blinked as the probe alternated between day and night.

Soon a gray-brown landmass drifted into sight at the right of the picture. The tableau was still for an instant, then the probe was rising and continuing to move to the right. At the top of the image, low-lying clouds rested near the ocean's surface in thick formations.

Europe, Harper remembered. *Always wanted to—*

"Ten thousand man-heights above the surface," the brunette Teep reported. "City Year 888, day 1." If there was a stutter in that speech, a trace of hysteria, it soon vanished. Harper recognized the timbre of the tra'R'sihuc's voice.

A mountain crest was directly beneath the probe now. It changed directions abruptly and moved along the ridge for a while; then it veered diagonally down and to the right, flying parallel to a long line of mountains. At intervals, small lakes could be seen. The land itself was covered with green and gold rectangles, even on the lower slopes of the mountains, and broad lines crisscrossed the surface—fields and roads. When snow covered the earth, villages and small cities could be seen at the major intersections, clumps of tiny brown and black squares resting on white, which disappeared when spring brought green back to the land.

"Year 889. Day 1."

The probe halted, then the peaks on the screen rose and glided sideways as the probe ran along the back of the mountain chain. Ocean was again visible at the top left corner of the screen; then it was hidden.

"Descending to five thousand man-heights," the girl announced.

The mountains swelled to fill the screen, becoming forest and ravine and snow patch. The image crawled upward. The earth was dappled by clouds. Rain was falling at the left of the screen.

Harper found he was moving his fingers rhythmically, keeping pace with the alternating days and nights. He shook his head and closed his eyes, fighting the hypnosis, willing his fingers to be still.

When he opened his eyes again, the probe had descended from the mountains and was gliding over a broad expanse of low, rolling hills. This had been sea bottom in his time, he remembered. Italy proper had been left behind them. The line of hills ahead had been the coast of Sicily.

"Year 890. Day 1."

The probe swooped over a high rampart and overflew seemingly endless fields of grayish earth—mud flats that reached thirty miles to the south and almost as far to the north. This had been dry ground at the height of the last ice age, a ridge that stretched across the Mediterranean Sea to link the Italian boot and Tunisia. Now it was escaping from the water again as the ice caps grew, but when the high tide came in, waves still poured over the land from north and south, moving at a faster pace than a man might run.

According to archaeologists, the plain had existed since the Third Era, more than sixty thousand years—the longest-lasting and most substantial alteration of the surface of the earth ever made by man.

"Year 890. Day 25."

The probe dropped toward the ground again, skimming over a narrow V of green water, then was surrounded by hills once more. It turned and flew along a white paved road, running parallel to what was now the seacoast and bordered on the other side by brown stubbled fields. A city suddenly came into view, white-walled, its low buildings widely spaced and clinging to hilly ground and beaches rather than flat ground. Within the walls, the roads were salmon-colored.

Syracuse, Harper thought. Men had built cities on this land even before the First Era. The one that lay here now was named Chelmmys.

"Day 50," called the telepath.

"The outer wall looks the same as ever," Sict said conversationally. Unnoticed by Harper, he had replaced Borct at the dais. The interior also does not seem to have been altered from what we are familiar with. I am inclined to regard that as good news."

"Day 75."

The probe flew parallel to the walls, then turned in a clockwise direction at perhaps two thousand feet of altitude. For an instant, Harper remembered planes circling a First Era airport; then he was back in an underground room, and the viewscreen showed a rock-studded beach.

"Chelmmys never had much of a dock region," Sict said. "At this stage of its history, there is none at all. The population has been kept small and is supported by agriculture from the rest of the peninsula. Imports are brought in by levtruck along the coast highway."

As if to counterpoint his words, the probe swung west, then north again so farmland was made visible at the top of the viewscreen. A narrow irrigation canal passed beneath, seemingly bone-dry.

"Day 100."

"Are there signs of any unusual activity, either military or otherwise?" The tra'Dicovys, who was sitting near the front of the table, had looked up from his paperwork to ask the question.

"The city seems to be at peace," Sict answered dryly. "Given the date, Project Master, that is unusual."

"Day 125."

"This may be an answer to your question, Borct. These barnlike structures house the administrative offices of ChelmForce." Sict's arm swiped at the screen to poke it with a bony forefinger. "There should be some temporary buildings behind them to give extra room during the current war—but there aren't any. They've got fields instead."

"Trees," Borct said distantly.

"Hmmmm . . . yes," Sict said. "The ground has been left as it is for some time. Fifty years, perhaps. So the buildings weren't simply removed; they never were there."

"Day 150," the girl at the back called.

The drone was now over a flat-roofed circular building. More than a hundred man-heights in diameter and ten stories tall, it was ringed by a thin moat and a broad concrete plaza. Bare of decoration, built of varicolored stone slabs, without windows, the building was carefully isolated from other buildings lest they be dwarfed by it. "BrightHonorKeep," the tra'Ruijac said simply. The home of the Assembly of Mankind. Even Harper had recognized it instantly.

"Day 175."

"We're at a residential section now," Sict continued. "Clean and modern but not ostentatious. Residence in the city is restricted to ensure that it remains free of slums. Common workers live across the straits or elsewhere on the peninsula. There aren't any slums there either, by the way—wages in Chelmmys are set very high, and the authorities oust nonjobholders."

"Day 200."

"National buildings along these streets. I'd call them embassies, but the term is too grandiose. They house envoys to the Assembly. Staff people there negotiate trade agreements and cultural exchanges and the like on a bilateral basis or with the Alliance as a whole. Quite a lot of these buildings—if Chelmmys hadn't come along, a number of very small nations would have been absorbed by their larger neighbors over the past few centuries."

"Day 225."

"Fall is coming on. Notice the tree leaves changing color. There are not many trees in Chelmmys, and most of the ones that are here were imported or gifts from Alliance members. Keeping them alive in the arid climate requires a major effort, and a special branch of the city government was set up to tend them."

"Day 250."

"We're at another residential section now. Apartment buildings mostly, resting on the hillsides and set back so the tenants can use one another's roofs as yards. Many of them grow flowers, so this can be extremely colorful during the summer. The Chelmmysians call this New Town, though it is actually one of the older portions of their city. There should be some military buildings near the top of the screen, but I don't see them. Maybe Chelmmys really is at peace."

"Day 275."

Except for a small stand of firs, the scattered trees were bare-limbed now, and the city seemed unpopulated, abandoned. For a few seconds the red paved roads were covered by white.

"Snow comes infrequently and doesn't last for long," Sict explained. "But it can get bitterly cold when the wind blows from the east. And in summer it gets stiflingly hot. The Chelmmysians say they picked the best place in the world to run an empire from—because no one in his right mind would ever try to capture their capital."

"Day 300."

"This clump of buildings holds the government of Chelmmys—the state itself rather than the Alliance. Not much to see, partially because very little that is not concerned with running the Alliance goes on within the state, partially because the government is dispersed throughout the peninsula. The Chelmmysians hold themselves up as an example in that, but only a few states have copied the pattern." Sict frowned momentarily. "Of course, we aren't sure about that in this history. We'll slow the probe now."

"Day 310," the telepath responded.

"ChelmForce headquarters at the top of the screen again. We've gone full circle. Still no sign of unusual—or even of usual—activity. Frankly, I cannot explain it. It looks like peace."

"Day 320."

"BrightHonorKeep on the right. Something is on the Outer Promenade. Freeze the image, please. Bring us lower."

"Day 326. Third day tenth," the girl said. "The probe is at two man-heights." The man's voice still spoke from a woman's throat, still was impersonal, but its tone was crisper than before. *Echoing the senior operator,* Harper guessed. "We've switched into stoptime."

The circular plaza was crowded. As the probe floated over the concourse, frozen men and women reminded Harper of long rows of statues. *Or an enchanted castle, waiting for a prince to break a magic spell.*

"Most of them from Chelmmys," an Agent remarked. "Never saw so many blonds at one time in all my life."

"But at this time of day everyone should be at work," Sict noted.

"Holiday?" someone suggested.

"No," Sict said in a worried voice. "That doesn't look like a holiday crowd, and this is not the place for one in any event."

One of the frozen forms seemed to be addressing the others, Harper noticed. A stout man, arm outstretched and mouth open, wearing a black tunic and trousers. More space than usual appeared between this figure and the rest of the crowd, and a ragged circle of statue-people looked inward at him.

"Political demonstration," he said confidently.

"A what?" Sict demanded.

"Demonstration," Harper repeated. "A protest meeting."

His explanation still made no sense, he could see. He sighed and tried again. "It's a way people who are too polite and refined to riot tell their government they feel like rioting. It usually means they don't like something the government has done, and they want the government to stop doing whatever it is in a big hurry. It usually means they don't have a lot of actual power, by the way."

The tra'Ruijac was obviously still puzzled. "But if they do not have power, why—what is the point of this, then?"

Harper sighed again.

"Sict!" Borct called urgently. "Lower-right corner. A soldier."

"That can't be," Sict said immediately. Then he looked and did a double take. "Cimon and Nicole! You're right! But they have never—"

He stopped. The probe was still moving, and more soldiers could be seen: tall, lean men in the russet battle dress of ChelmForceLand stationed in pairs before every entrance into BrightHonorKeep. Each was armed with a neuroshocker in an unbuttoned holster, and tiny unsheathed knives had been fastened at one side of their brown combat helmets.

Killing Right insignia—on men facing civilians! Harper heard a whistle of surprise. He looked about, noticing shocked expressions on the faces around him, then turned his eyes back to the screen.

The soldiers were standing at attention with their hands clasped at belt level. They looked bored, Harper decided at last, unconcerned by the crowd. They were more likely to use their metal-bound Wands of Persuasion than their lethal weapons if they were ordered into action.

National Guard. "What's the problem?" he said casually.

"Troops are not permitted on the Promenades," Tolp answered in a whisper. "*Never*. They are not permitted to speak to Assembly delegates unless requested to by the full Assembly of Mankind, and they are not permitted to prevent citizen access to the delegates. But that seems to be what they are doing."

"So?" Harper was puzzled. "Why shouldn't that change?"

"It goes back to Hemmendur. The first Hemmendur. It was one of his commandments; he made his successors swear to it, and they did the same."

"Oh," Harper said softly. "Another little change."

"Maybe." Tolp looked sick.

Sict had reached some decision. "Let's go on," he called out.

"Day 330," the Teep responded.

The Outer Promenade was deserted again. The Algherans watched in silence as the probe floated over the city of their enemy.

"Day 340."

Motion was visible throughout the city again. "I think we are watching an exodus," the tra'Ruijac said in a strained voice. "The dark appearance of this side of the coast road suggests lines of traffic, while the other side looks bare. There—that building is on fire! And it has been left unattended."

"Day 342."

The screen went black.

"We've lost contact," the girl telepath announced.

"So they got it, too," a deep voice said. Verrect tra'Hujsuon wore a look of grim satisfaction. "Chelms and Teeps both, and they can share hearths in hell. A clean sweep!"

There was an appalled silence, broken only after a long moment by the Project Master, who stood and hammered a fist on the table.

"That's quite enough, Vrect," he snapped. He turned to face the girl in the red coveralls, the only man present willing to do so other than Tim Harper.

"What has been spoken cannot be fully retracted," he said formally. "But I implore your understanding and forgetfulness during these difficult times. If careless words are taken by you as insult, the fault has been made mine by the circumstances. Please accept my apologies as Project Master and my personal regrets as Acting Master of Sept Dicovys."

The girl stood, her face flushed so that the green plaque on her forehead showed like a suppurating wound. "No insult was noticed," she said in a small voice.

Then her voice changed, becoming rougher and crisper,

masculine again. "We've some standards also, tra'Dicovys. We would ourselves be most distressed if the brats of some newly created Sept, little more than a generation away from blankshieldry and brigandage, were to seek hearths in Nyjuc or R'sihuc. No offense taken, Project Master, none given."

The message delivered, she sat down. Confusion showed on her face.

Tolp chuckled on Harper's left. "Nicely said," he explained when he noticed the puzzled looks of the younger man. "The Hujsuons are *two* generations away from blankshieldry now—though Vrect can remember it well enough—and the brigandage is unproven but probably there if you look far enough back. So the tra'Nyjuc obviously wasn't referring to them. But we all know it anyhow." He chuckled again.

Vrect tra'Hujsuon clearly understood the reference—his angrily flushed face made that clear. Bann ha'Hujsuon was breathing heavily as well, and that was something Harper had never seen before. He started to shake his head to commiserate but stopped without catching Bann's eye when he noticed the glare he got for this from the irate Herrilmin.

Upstarts, Harper thought. *Social climbers*. He could see how that accusation would sting an Algheran. *Big deal*.

"We will return now to the surveillance of Fohima Alghera," the Project Master was saying. "Let us begin the sweep, please."

"Beginning the sweep," the telepath said, echoing his words in soprano tones. "The next probe is at day 342, shortly before dawn. We are bringing it up to the Present at a fifty to one time ratio." A quaver remained in her voice, Harper noticed, but she was getting it under control. Good.

Little was to be seen on the viewscreen. Then the faint outlines of buildings could be distinguished, high among them the giant cubical shape of the Old Temple. The blackened figures grew sharper; details became visible. A red disk moved over the eastern forests, brightening to yellow as it rose. Sunrise.

The forests were green and cool-looking, with tall trees neatly arrayed and little visible underbrush. There should be deer and otters within it, and beavers and bears . . . *and picnickers*, Harper thought. *All peacefully coexisting somehow*. It had always seemed the place for that sort of thing. *Onnul!*

Then the probe was over the southern ramparts. Far in the distance more forests could be seen, no more than a dark line on the horizon. Grassland reached from the lip of the fortified road out to the forests, a wide pasture for the great domesticated rabbits and the occasional cattle herd. The grass was tall, improbably green, dew-soaked. Perhaps rain had fallen during the night.

"Two tenths of the day are gone," the telepath called. "We are slowing to a twenty to one ratio. Now at two hundred man-heights."

As she spoke, the probe cleared the wooded tops of the low hills to the west of F'a Alghera and swept through a long arc toward the Ice Daughter. A barge passed beneath, its cargo lashed under dark tarpaulins. Harper glimpsed a red-garbed steersman at the stern; then the barge was gone, and the thick white line that was water falling in its wake swept over the viewscreen.

A strip of parklike beach along the river reminded Harper of the Esplanade he had once known. Then the probe moved over farmland. Crops were being harvested, and the great reaping machines seemed to race up and down the long fields, leaving brown stubble behind. *Watertown,* Harper thought. No, even before they diverted it, the Ice Daughter had run south of the Charles's course.

Brighton and Alston. The big bay coming up—and Cambridge.

And what was his reaction to that? *Nothing,* he decided. Nothing.

"Anyone recognize that crop?" Borct asked softly.

No one answered, either from reluctance to speak or from ignorance.

Harper frowned. Most of the Algheran crops were variants of plants common in his day, extensively reengineered to increase their yield or to shorten the necessary growing season and eliminate the need for nitrous fertilizers. This might be a further mutated wheat, but having raised the suggestion once, he would not bother to do so again.

"Three tenths of the day are gone," the telepath reported. "We are turning the probe so that the city may be viewed."

Harper turned to Borct. "Magister, a suggestion: We seem to be dealing with a local phenomenon. Since we do not know the range, I suggest the probe be pulled back as far as possible while still giving us a clear image."

Borct made no answer, but the image on the viewscreen dwindled.

"We are fixed at five thousand man-heights from the city center; we are at one thousand man-heights above the ground. We are proceeding at a ratio of ten to one. Four tenths of the day are gone," the telepath announced.

And there was Fohima Alghera. Something swelled in Harper's chest.

Across the bottom of the viewscreen was the Ice Daughter, made to look turbulent by the probe's motion through time so that tiny boats bobbed frantically in the boisterous waves. Beyond this were long, broad terraces, their lines obscured by flowering trees and houses so that the whole appeared to slope evenly and gently toward the green hills beyond.

The hills upon which Alghera rested—the low hills, softly molded by the passage of ice and time, green- and purple-garbed by the continent-spanning forests of postglacial North America, then smoothed again and sculpted by the even more insistent hand of man.

"Home," someone whispered. Others made shushing sounds.

The city was dominated by the massive white cube that was the Old Temple, resting on its own separate hilltop at the center of the screen. Off to the right, where lines of hills had come together to form an oblique angle, an amphitheater had been carved into the earth and slopes. By First Era standards, it was small, holding no more than half the forty thousand residents of Alghera, but here it seemed huge, saved from monstrosity only by the simplicity of its design. Parks surrounded it, stretching back to the terraces.

It was a lovely city. It was almost familiar.

Between the amphitheater and the temple, at the bottom of the screen, was a bridge. The brown paved road that ran across it split into three wide avenues on the Algheran side of the river, and those streets ran straight into the city. To the east of the intersection was a gray concrete mound, shaped like a haystack and perhaps ten man-heights tall. A long stream of people were entering it; none could be seen coming out.

In the distance were similar mounds, smaller but with the same shape. There were orderly lines of people in front of them as well.

"One to one," Borct ordered. His eyes did not stray from the screen.

"One to one," the telepath agreed. "Forty-seven hundredths of a day are past." Perhaps someone in the room was listening to her.

An evacuation, Harper thought. People going into refuge, each trying to save whatever his arms could carry, whether it was a child holding a single doll or an adult staggering under the weight of some treasured family heirloom. Do they have time and space to save everyone?

He understood already that the city itself would soon die.

But when he glanced around the table, though he saw curiosity and some tension mixed with other feelings on the faces of men who stole looks at the girl Teep, there was none of the terror and recognition of loss he had expected.

He was from the twentieth century of the First Era, he remembered anew. That made him wiser in many ways than those gathered here. And he pitied these Algherans now, even as he envied the moments of ignorance that were left to them.

He waited among them and said nothing.

The end came without warning. One instant the viewscreen showed the citizens of Alghera crowding into the haystack buildings; in the next, nothing was to be seen but a tiny red-brown dot, painfully bright, which swelled almost at once to the size of an orange on the screen, then winked out. A burned spot was on Harper's retinas; he saw dark splotched afterimages wherever he looked.

"Don't watch!" he shouted. "It will blind you!"

But the advice was unnecessary. The viewscreen was black.

Borct started to speak, but the telepath stood to cut him off. "We have lost a lens on the probe rather than the probe itself," she explained. "It appears to have been overloaded. We will reduce the fraction of the light penetrating the force field and rotate the probe to view the city through another lens."

"Pull it back," Harper told her harshly. "Move back another five thousand man-heights, maybe ten thousand. You don't know what you are dealing with."

"Do you know, Timt?" Borct asked in a carefully controlled voice.

"Yeah. The city's gone." Harper would say nothing more.

Men around the table looked at him strangely. Many of them were blinking or had tears streaming down their cheeks. He made himself ignore them.

"Ten thousand man-heights from the city center," the girl called out. Her voice was shaky, and she paused to gnaw at her lower lip. "We have lost a second lens and are further increasing the opacity of the force field."

Even at the increased distance, the fireball was huge. Nothing else showed on the viewscreen but the red-brown form, sitting before them like a partially inflated beach ball pressed down on unseen obstructions that were the Algheran hills. Then, within a dozen heartbeats, the color faded through pink-tan to a gleaming white, streaked in places with brown and black splotches. Harper stood, pushing the heavy cube chair aside with a foot.

The fireball began to rise then, at race car speed but seemingly slowly because of its distance from the probe. As it ascended, it expanded into a true sphere perched on a thick white column.

Perhaps a hundredth of a day passed before the cloud reached its maximum altitude and the probe had to be moved back twice more to reveal the full height of the mushroom. The fireball puffed outward to form a ragged, bloated disk.

"Out of the troposphere," Harper said distantly, speaking more to himself than to those about him. "The center of that top part is twenty thousand man-heights above the ground. It's a big, hot cloud of gas, too dense to rise any farther, so the disk will spread out till it's sixty or seventy thousand man-heights across before it starts to dissipate.

"All the white stuff you see is steam basically—from the river, or from water in the air, or whatever. The brown stuff that looks like scum—that's rock, dirt, pieces of buildings. What doesn't melt gets knocked apart by the shock wave or by flying debris. No pieces of people, if anyone wonders—they're mostly water, after all, and that fireball has an absolute temperature forty or fifty thousand times that of boiling water, so it vaporizes bodies.

"That column underneath—expansion of the fireball creates a vacuum that sucks up air and everything not nailed down. They go up, and eventually they begin falling down again—the heavier stuff, anyhow. Some stuff really gets pulverized and won't fall out of the air for days or even years.

"The fallout is poisonous, by the way. Even if you don't notice it. Your hair drops out; you get sick to your stomach; the red corpuscles in your blood die; you get sores that won't heal. Get enough exposure, and you die anywhere from a few hours to a month later. That's a great little toy you're looking at."

He broke off suddenly. "Nothing more to see at the top. It'll be another day tenth before it starts to disperse. Run down to the base."

The telepath did not respond, but no one else was speaking now. The image on the viewscreen drifted upward, changed, then was gray-shaded. For a moment Harper thought another lens had been lost. Then he realized his error.

"Restore the original viewing conditions," he ordered. "It will be very bright but bearable."

Soon he was once more looking into hell.

"The firestorm," he explained aloud. "All that heat, all that incoming air, everything smashed up into tinder—you get a fire. It is big enough by itself to consume enough oxygen to reduce air pressure, so it sucks in additional air from outside to keep itself going. It will last for a good part of a day or until there is absolutely nothing left that can be burned."

He turned back to the telepath. "You see what I'm looking for. Find it."

She nodded soundlessly. As the probe moved toward the firestorm, flames swelled till detail was lost and the screen seemed no more than a portal into an incinerator. Then a gap appeared in the curtain of fire. The probe passed through.

"There is a hole here," Harper continued. "Nothing left to burn at this spot, because this is the crater the bomb left. Looks about a thousand man-heights across, maybe more. Perhaps a hundred man-heights deep at most—enough to get down to bedrock; even the rock and dirt here were turned to vapor."

He looked over the room slowly before speaking again, deliberately pausing to get the attention of his audience.

"Take a good look, people," he said softly. "A Cimon-taken good look. This hole in the ground—the heat from the bomb did that. The shock and the blast from the thing—they weren't needed. You can guess what they were like. And you can see what they all did to F'a Alghera."

The probe spun about, panning the flames and destruction beyond the crater. Harper waited, letting the camera tell the story for him.

"Chelmmys probably looks just the same right now. And F'a Loprit. And a dozen or so other places. Maybe some of you will take that for consolation. Or maybe you can take some pleasure from seeing weapons used that weren't even thought of during the Eternal Wars. All the rest of you—" He stopped.

"That's F'a Alghera," he said at last. "See what we did to her."

The long silence that followed was broken by the Project Master. "You seem very certain, Timithial. I think you should provide us with an explanation."

Harper nodded and went to the dais. But he paused before he began to speak. He no longer saw the men in the room as individuals. They were a blur of faces, a crowd. He looked among them until he found Bann ha'Hujsuon and made himself focus on that face, half hoping that if he could persuade one Algheran, the rest of his audience would be won over.

"There were things like that in my time," he said then. "We called them hydrogen bombs or, sometimes, *thermonuclear* weapons, and they were probably the single most destructive weapon ever devised in any era. All the damage we've seen was done by one of them—just one, probably weighing less than three man-weights. A medium-sized one. It killed everyone in the city who failed to get into a shelter—and probably all of those who did, actually. It certainly was powerful enough to destroy the probes we sent earlier, even though they were within force fields.

"I suspect there has been what our military theoreticians called a spasm war. One day tenth—and the Fifth Era is over. Too many people dead, too much destruction to carry on. Maybe ten thousand years after the Present, ambitious people will begin setting up a Sixth Era. Maybe."

He sighed. "How the bomb worked—I won't try to explain it to you. A way was found to convert a very small piece of matter—less than the weight of my hand—into energy. A lot of energy. Beyond that—it's not important, and perhaps I wrote something once to explain it. What is important is that these were built and tested in the First Era and that they have been redeveloped here."

He changed his focus. "Sict, Tolp, you two have been twitting me all during this Project about First Era alchemy and superstition. Look at that viewscreen and see just what our alchemy could do."

His voice became grim. "It took us better than three hundred years to get from Galileo to that bomb, and there was a straight line of development between them. We worked considerably harder on the sciences than you people, absolutely and even relatively, but—three hundred years. And even so, it took thousands of our very best technical people to build the first hydrogen bombs.

"Alghera and Chelmmys were not on that line of development.

"But here they must be. You realize that did not happen in the last day tenth. You cannot create a hydrogen bomb by chance. It takes a major effort consciously aimed at building those weapons. You don't need one new theory—you need dozens even to begin guessing that such a thing is possible.

"So the sciences developed over the last few centuries in this version of history are going to be very unfamiliar to you people. I could probably understand some of them, but you all have different patterns of thought, different intellectual heritages, different ways of looking at the world.

"The city we saw on the viewscreen—it looked like Alghera. The people living in it probably called it Alghera. But it wasn't—not the Alghera you knew anyhow, not the Alghera you wanted to save."

"So what do you suggest?" Siccentur tra'Ruijac wondered.

Harper stared at him. "Bring back our Alghera. What else?"

Sict shook his head. "And how would you accomplish that?"

Harper snapped his fingers. "Kill Mlart. Let him die as he did originally. Undo what was done to save him."

"No!" the voice of the tra'Hujsuon thundered. "A thousand times no!"

Harper snapped his fingers again. "Him or Alghera, tra'Hujsuon. Take your choice. Remember what I said: It takes centuries to build those weapons. Whatever happened to change Alghera was not recent; it probably began soon after Mlart was saved. I don't know what the connection was, but I don't believe it was a coincidence. Do you?"

"I'm not going to permit the killing of Mlart," Vrect snapped. "This is the only significant change we have ever established. Maybe it is not perfect—but we have done that. Everything else we've heard are your guesses. Maybe there is something we can work with here. I'm not going to throw off Nicole's cloak just because of the idiotic notions of a stupid, foreign, Teep-loving freak!" The last words came in a shriek.

Borct stood abruptly, rage showing redly in his own face.

"Timithial is an Ironwearer of Sept Dicovys," he said slowly and dangerously.

"He shouldn't be!" Vrect screamed.

"Verrect!" Siccentur tra'Ruijac exclaimed. "This is uncalled for. And unseemly. Timithial is—"

"Shut up!" Vrect snarled.

Harper looked toward Bann ha'Hujsuon, but the younger man refused to meet his eyes. Bann's words suddenly came to mind: *Borct is going to have some problems*. Was this the scene that Bann had hinted at? Probably. The showdown was coming early.

He turned to the tra'Dicovys. "Magister, this is pretext. The tra'Hujsuon is seeking *now* to oust you as Project Master, to carry out his own plans for Alghera—for this Project."

Vrect's face told him that he had guessed correctly. Bann now wore a look of acute embarrassment. Harper viewed the assembled Hujsuons with cynical amusement, then looked to the back of the room. The girl telepath was displaying a mixture of interest and stark terror; she was obviously communicating everything she saw to the other Teeps. Harper blinked, suddenly overwhelmed by the recognition that Normal politics provided spectator sports for the apolitical Teeps, then turned his attention back to the front of the room.

"Is that it, Vrect?" Borct asked, smiling to display his teeth. "I am still the Project Master. I asked earlier if anyone wished to challenge me for the post, and you said nothing. Change your mind perhaps? That's the prerogative of small children—not the Acting Master of a well-established Sept."

Vrect was stung and showed it. *Losing points*, Harper observed. Soon Borct would call for a vote of confidence; this playacting by the two men was obviously intended to sway the undecided. At the moment, Borct held the edge.

"Yes, I've changed my mind," the tra'Hujsuon said venomously. "I'm tired of seeing that Teep-lover of yours in this Council and of hearing from my young men about his stupid antics. I'm tired of his cowardly, inane ideas. I'm tired of seeing him humored at your expense, because of your lack of proper control over him. You are not fit to be a Project Master, and I do challenge you!" His voice had again risen to a screech.

Mad dog, Harper thought. Vrect would have to be destroyed someday, and Harper had excellent reasons for wishing to take charge of that himself. Meanwhile, he waited impassively at the dais.

Borct must have been thinking similar thoughts. Distaste showed in his voice. "I can see considerable discussion ahead in the Inter-Sept Council, tra'Hujsuon. You intrude upon Dicovys internal affairs."

Vrect was contemptuous. "So be it."

"So be it," Borct agreed. "Count your votes yet, tra'Hujsuon?"

Vrect nodded curtly. "Enough and more. You're through, tra'Dicovys."

Borct shook his head thoughtfully. "I believe you, actually. The Teep just took a count and signaled me you're telling the truth."

"Then you'll step down?" Vrect smiled nastily. "Good. I'll see what I can do afterward to safeguard your future reputation, when we recover Alghera."

"Oh, no," Borct replied, bringing the other man's smile to an end. "I'm just not going to listen to a vote. That's all."

"But you have to!" Vrect looked comically dismayed.

My cue again. It's a busy day. Harper took a step toward the quarreling Sept Masters.

"No," Borct explained patiently. "Remember the formula: Ironwearers or High Blankshields may contend for the post by sponsoring a champion to fight my champion. Or by fighting themselves. The only person here that really applies to is Timithial, you know. But I'll generously grant you the same privilege."

"It is not done," Vrect protested.

"It is being done," Borct said grimly. "It's a very old tradition—and thus law. Voting is one of those newfangled notions we Project Masters sometimes allow. It serves as a guide to us—it means nothing else by itself. The only real way to impose your will on a Project Master is to take his post from him. And if I say that will take a duel—it will take a duel."

There was shocked silence in the Council room. Borct finally broke it. "Who is your champion, tra'Hujsuon? I'll give you no more than a minute to produce him." His voice was stern, triumphant. Harper smiled covertly.

But Verrect tra'Hujsuon laughed! He laughed till he sensed that every eye in the chamber was focused on him. Then he suddenly cut himself off.

"Tra'Dicovys, you've been foolish." He sneered. "You are predictable, and it is going to cost you. Nicole's cloak is off you now!" He wheeled about and pointed to the tall blond man sitting beside Bann. "Him. Santin Herrilmin ha'Hujsuon. He is to be champion for me."

Herrilmin ha'Hujsuon shook his head in agreement. He seemed pleased rather than dismayed by the attention he was getting now.

Confident, Harper thought, remembering. *Thinks he's good*.

"You know who my champion will be," Borct was saying.

Harper bent his head to the Project Master, then turned and faced the audience impassively. He shook his head.

Now he was committed to a duel.

CHAPTER TWENTY

Siccentur tra'Ruijac rose from chalking a square on the hangar floor and slapped at the nonexistent dust on the legs of his coveralls. "This is of at least the minimum dimensions, Project Master," he reported. "Would either of the Champions wish it measured?"

The length of a man's body and an arm was the formula, and this was easily a twelve-foot square. Harper nodded his head. Across the width of the hangar, Herrilmin ha'Hujsuon made the same gesture. His motions were smooth and unhurried, without a touch of jerkiness to reveal underlying nervousness.

Still thinks he's hot stuff, Harper analyzed. *Cocky or what?*

Something like déjà vu struck as he looked around the hangar, its familiarity stripped away suddenly so that for a moment he saw the loading dock as he first had seen it, millennia before.

It would be terribly ironic, he thought, if the last First Era man died in the last First Era relic.

Then, as if a bubble had been pricked, he was again in the hangar he had known for the last seven years.

"Ironwearer ha'Dicovys has first choice of blade," Sict said gravely.

Harper had been briefed by Tolp. He dropped off the platform to the pavement, then walked past the edge of the square to the Project Master. Two paces away from the man, he halted to make a narrow bow. Borct in return took one step toward him. Strapped over each hip was a sword. Harper chose one at random—the right—and pointed the tip to the four corners of the hangar before returning to his starting point. Herrilmin spurned the steps as well and repeated the ritual.

Ought to feel more concern, Harper thought. *There is really going to be a duel, and I'm really going to be in it. I've never done this before, and I ought to be scared. But I'm not. Borct seems to be thinking more about this than I am.*

Pressing my luck. Thinking breeds worries. I can't afford that.

But he persisted in analyzing his reactions nonetheless. He had always felt tension while on patrol or before combat; why not now?

It feels as if I'm not really here, he decided at last. *I'm standing back and watching little puppets go through the motions. That's a ha'Hujsuon puppet that just took a sword from a Borct puppet. The Tolp puppet is laying a hand on the shoulder of the Tim Harper puppet, and soon the puppets will walk toward each other and wave their tiny swords, and I'll still be watching.*

The hand on his shoulder was clammy, and it was being tightened rhythmically. "For the sake of Cimon, Tolp," he muttered. "Don't worry. I'm bigger than him. I weigh more. I'm stronger. I've probably got more speed and endurance. I don't care how good he thinks he will be."

The hand did not stop pumping. "Herrilmin is very good," Tolp whispered. "Two years ago, at the citywide games, he won first place in this style of competition. One of his opponents died."

"I see," Harper said thoughtfully. He glanced down at the length of his weapon and waved it minutely.

A whipsword had roughly a thirty-inch falchion-style blade, much like an overgrown bowie knife, with a curved, sharp edge and a heavy, straight back. The blade was broadest near its point and then tapered over the width of a man's hand to a flexible extension. The "whip" was half the length of the edge and about an eighth of an inch in diameter, with a roughened surface, as on a coarse file. Properly used . . . *Yeah. That could kill.*

Harper nodded suddenly. "Herrilmin wasn't with us at the start of the Project, was he, Tolp?" He kept his tones casual.

Tolp sounded shaken. "I don't know. I have vague recollections of his face, but his name was never mentioned before this in the Council."

"I'm sure he was a student," Harper said. "Vrect wouldn't screw up anything that could be checked. Still—remember him from any classes?"

"I don't know, Timt. I don't know what he was studying."

"You're a big help, Tolp. You know you are."

"I'm sorry, Timt."

"I'll just bet you are. Vrect pulled a fast one, didn't he?"

"He's a Sept Master, Timt. You can't accuse him of—"

"I just did," Harper growled. "He's an Acting Sept Master. Boy, is he! An old Blankling, and he buffaloed all of you—all of us."

"Timt, I—I'm sorry."

"Gee, thanks," Harper whispered sarcastically. "It's just idle curiosity, of course, but what will you do if he kills me?"

"I don't know," Tolp admitted.

"Bright today, aren't you?" Harper exhaled loudly. "Oh-hhh, Tolp!"

"I'm sorry, Timt."

"Send back your own crew and bump off Herrilmin when he pops up the first time," Harper suggested finally. "Better, Vrect, but for sure Herrilmin—you really don't want him around."

"We can't," Tolp protested. "If we start fighting among ourselves and manipulating our own history, we're lost. We won't be sure how true an idea of our city we'd be holding. And how could we restore it then?"

"Maybe you can't." Harper bit the words off.

Tolp pushed him toward the Project Master. "They're watching us. You've got to get your Teepblind."

The Harper puppet walked stiffly around the square again to the Borct puppet and knelt to let the Project Master fit the cap of silver mesh over his hair. This was part of the ritual as well, he remembered, an integral part. An unprepared telepath suddenly deprived of the ability to read minds could be easily vanquished by any Normal swordsman of average competence. Algherans had used duels in the past to detect telepaths. And to execute them.

He shook his head, returning to awareness of his body as he felt the mesh settle against his skull. The plastic headband was cool against his temples, then warmed as it contracted. The vampire needles pricked his skin, but the pain lasted only for an instant. Years ago these had been unpleasant sensations, he remembered, and they might have destroyed his concentration; now he was accustomed to them.

Every Teepblind felt a bit different. This was not the one he wore normally, but the fit was similar, and he would adjust more quickly than most people since much of his life was now spent under metal. It might even give him an advantage.

No. Herrilmin was making the same motions. A champion swordsman, he would be accustomed to fighting under metal.

"Are the Champions ready?" Borct asked.

Herrilmin nodded.

"No," Harper said flatly.

He was suddenly conscious of quiet. He let it continue, using the opportunity to look around the dueling area.

There had never been a duel during the Project or any other event with a comparable attendance. The Agents had created space in the hangar for this one by moving a dozen time shuttles several day tenths into the future, returning to the present moment in one of them.

Two vehicles had been left in their original position. Harper's silvered ax head lurked in one corner, hovering just over the concrete, huge and ominous, as if waiting to attack. The tear-shaped transparent bubble near the center of the hangar, where the small booth once had been, was probably the one used by Herrilmin ha'Hujsuon.

The remaining vehicles had been crowded to one side. Sitting on them, standing in front of them, waiting in the spaces left by the departed shuttles, surrounding the duelists and the fighting square, were the people of the Project. Others, with green-tabbed foreheads, stood on the dock, staring down at him.

The last free citizens of Alghera.

The last citizens of Alghera, period, Harper thought, remembering the bomb that had fallen on the city. *Cimon! They look like refugees. They are refugees.*

Some three hundred people were there, with roughly equal numbers of men and women. None were old as this culture measured age, only a few were children, and there were no infants. Perhaps one person in four wore a green forehead plaque.

It's the light that does it, he thought. *Only Agents ever get above the ground into the sun, so everyone else is pale. And they dress so drably, as if bright clothing were reserved for the Agents.*

No, there was more than that to cause the impression. They acted like refugees—silent, passive, cowed. *Natural, I suppose. Agents get to do things. Borct and his crew decide what we do. Everyone else is family or works to keep us fed and equipped and amused. Conscripts, all of them, waiting for us to give them back their homeland.*

Poor bastards.

"You have a protest, Ironwearer?" Borct asked. Harper could see no sign that the man recognized him. *Here goes nothing. Trite as it is.*

"You term me Ironwearer," Harper said loudly and haughtily so that his voice was heard throughout the hangar. "As a Champion, I request the privilege of fighting with my own weapon. As an Ironwearer, I claim that as a right."

Borct stared at him, blank-faced. Harper held his breath.

A challenge between champions: Individuals were in conflict here, not masses of interchangeable men using interchangeable arms. The dueling ritual was old enough and primitive enough. It had to be older than the stylized weapons he and Herrilmin were holding. The choice must be Borct's, but in a primitive culture one did not separate a man from his sword.

Borct continued to stare, unspeaking. An elderly man with a green forehead plaque stepped through the crowd. Gold insignia could be seen on his collar. Harper's heart began to sink.

The tra'Nyjuc, he thought sickly. *So I'm going to look like an idiot. Or a coward. And maybe there will go being an Ironwearer—at last. Well, I can call it First Era tradition and save some face. If anyone will believe me.*

Except the Teeps will give me away. Cimon!

"What are you planning to use, *Ironwearer*? Your 'Cease?" That was from a deep voice tinged with acid. Verrect tra'Hujsuon had pushed through the crowd to stand by Borct's shoulder.

The Project Master twitched suddenly as if seeing something filthy.

Play it out. Harper half smiled, baring his teeth. "My 'Cease? No, I don't need that today. But every officer of the Realm has a personal sword or two. I have one I am fond of, and I am more accustomed to its feel."

Indecision showed on Vrect's face. The officer's sword that he assumed Harper referred to was a real enough weapon—a crystal blade with an embedded metal wire, every bit as sharp and deadly as the cavalry sabers men had swung in the centuries before Harper's birth, though its major purpose was the symbolic one of inspiring honorable conduct. It could kill and maim, however, and if Harper was used to it—but it was a hand length shorter than the main blade of the whipsword.

"It is permissible, Project Master," Sict said gravely. He, too, had moved to join the group. He looked at Harper questioningly, then to the elderly Teep. "If the Champion insists."

The tra'Nyjuc would not volunteer an opinion, Harper understood now, and the opportunity for Vrect to raise an objection was passing. He would not have to raise his 'blind and submit his intentions to the telepath's scrutiny. *Home free*, he thought with gratitude.

"The Champion does insist," he said softly. *You betcha boots I do!* Another thought came to him, and he made his voice casual as he turned to Vrect. "Or would the tra'Hujsuon prefer to forfeit the challenge?"

Vrect sneered at him. "Use your toy and die. I had intended to have Herrilmin leave you alive if you begged sufficiently. But I won't interfere with your suicide."

"Project Master?" Harper inquired. "By your leave, Magister."

"Permission is granted, Ironwearer," Borct said woodenly. "Timt—"

"Thank you." Harper turned away and looked through the crowd till he saw the face he wanted; then he lifted his Teepblind. *Cyomit. Look there. Hurry.* For a moment, his eyes met those of the Teep Sept Master. There was no expression on the other man's face. Harper nodded imperceptibly, then lowered the Teepblind.

"My weapon will arrive shortly," he told Borct. "Why not perform the invocation while we wait?" *Then it will be too late for anyone to bitch.*

Borct nodded, his eyes closed. "Silence," he called out. He spread his arms, palms up, and raised his face to gaze at the ceiling of the hangar. "Silence!" he shouted. *"Silence!"*

". . . ence . . . ence . . . ence . . ." the echoes of that shout rang above the crowd.

Borct prayed.

"Lord Cimon. My Lady Nicole. It is not often that we who serve your memory ask for your intervention in mortal affairs. But so I do now—I and all those gathered here before you.

"It is not for our sake alone that we implore your aid. Nor is it for those friends and kin, though they be numbered in thousands, that we left behind us in our flight from Alghera. Nor is our prayer alone for great Alghera itself. But rather for all men do we beg your aid, your guidance, and the compassion that is yours. For those of Alghera and of Chelmmys; for Normal and for Teep—for the present moment and for all time to come.

"We do not presume to offer direction or even to declare our wants. We vow to accept the decision you will effect, and swear as well neither to rejoice nor to know regret when contemplating the outcome—for we realize our vision is dimmed by mortality and our understanding clouded by our passions.

"Our lives are not preordained, we are taught. We become what we will for ourselves, and thus we are given a second chance. This is the one world; these our lives are the only existences we will ever know, and what we choose to make of them is our own choice, our own responsibility. Thus we have been taught; thus we teach. In setting aside for this moment that freedom, we do acknowledge that even this is our choice and our responsibility.

"And now, Lord Cimon and Lady Nicole, behold these Champions, Ironwearer Timithial of Sept Dicovys and Herrilmin of Sept Hujsuon, who stand beneath your gaze and will themselves to accept what fate you shall decree for them in the service of causes they hold high. Even as did you, Lord Cimon and Lady Nicole.

"We beg your aid. But if you will do naught else, know still that we do honor you. And in the spirit of that honor, honor yourselves these two men. Bless them with grace and dignity; let neither die meanly.

"This I ask of you: I, Birlin Borictar tra'Dicovys, your priest and servant. Lord Cimon, Lady Nicole—*hear my prayer!*"

". . . ayer . . . ayer . . . ayer . . ." the echoes rang. Then other sounds could be heard: muted conversations resuming, shuffling feet, coughs, crowd noises.

Harper shook his head. The priestly side of Borct was easy to forget until one saw the priest in action. The Project Master had begun the invocation in his normal guise: a decent enough man, perhaps better suited to responsibility than to authority. He had ended it as one expecting deities to heed his words. Even his voice had altered.

Now he seemed to shrink, becoming once more the Project Master, and mortal.

Harper shook his head again. Cimon, Nicole, the tiMantha lu Duois—he still thought of this as a nut cult. But Borct's tones had been religious. This was a religion.

The religion.

It had few fixed tenets, and those were mostly ethical. Men might regard Cimon and Nicole as real beings or not, as conscience or fashion dictated. They could accept the literal truth of the martyrdom or view it as allegory. They could believe in saints, an afterlife, and other deities as they chose. Borct himself, though a believing priest, did not expect that mortals could aspire to any sort of afterlife. What no one could do was believe something else.

For there was no other religion, even among the Teeps. There was barely even the memory of other religions. When Harper had tried once to explain the different beliefs of his era, only the telepaths had realized that he was not jesting.

Harper had been a lapsed Catholic for half his life, smug in what he termed his cynical agnosticism. That had not changed; if anything, his skepticism had increased. But the Cimon cult disturbed him greatly. It was pagan, and deep within him that seemed incompatible with true religious feeling. That he was analytical enough to probe himself and uncover the reasons for his objections was no consolation—his feelings would not change. Ultimately he would have to come to terms with them, he realized. But that day had not yet arrived.

The crowd on the dock seemed to pulsate like a living thing, which was torn apart as people moved to open a gap. A small girl came down the steps slowly and walked toward him. She was brown-haired and elfin-faced, and she used two hands to carry a sword that was nearly as long as she was tall. A green plaque reflected light from her forehead.

"I found it," she said nervously. "Here it is, Ironwearer ha'Ruppir."

Harper smiled. "Thank you, Cyomit." He raised the long First Era sword with one hand, lifting and twisting it to make light glint along the blade, and displayed the edges to the crowd. "Excellent," he pronounced. The ten pounds of steel ground from the sword had made it very sharp.

Cyomit looked about cautiously, as if unable to believe the existence of so many non-Telepaths. Then, panic-stricken, she darted away up the stairs and into a doorway behind the crowd.

Harper did not notice. He was smiling at the expression on Vrect ha'Hujsuon's face. "I came to Alghera as an Ironwearer," he growled. "Project Master and Master tra'Ruijac, I am now ready."

Harper stepped warily, crouching slightly, keeping his sword arm close to his side. Herrilmin advanced with equal caution, holding his blade out straight.

Not presenting his side to me, Harper noticed. It made sense. The whipsword was designed for slashing rather than thrusting. He wriggled his wrist, making his own sword dance, and watched how the tip of the other man's blade moved in unison with it, even while Herrilmin kept his eyes focused on Harper's face.

The bugger may actually be good, Harper admitted. *Probably is*.

How was he doing himself? He noted the whispering sounds as he scuffed his feet over the concrete floor of the hangar, the tension in his biceps and shoulder as the sword dragged at his arm, the soreness along the right side of his back. *Fair enough*.

Did it matter how good Herrilmin might be? Skill was not apt to be a factor here. Or time. Using a whipsword himself, he might have managed to outlast the other man. But with the sword he carried, he would not have the endurance or speed needed for such a contest.

Forty pounds originally, he remembered. Even shaved down to thirty pounds, roughly a fifth of the Algheran man-weight, it was a preposterous weight for a sword. He could not last long in this fight.

Herrilmin was still coming. He was moving less heedfully now, evidently intending to advance until Harper was forced out of the square into defeat. One foot was in the air—

Harper lunged as if fencing, using his sword as an extension of his arm, stepping off his back foot and leaning sideways to increase his reach. His front foot stamped loudly onto the concrete. Herrilmin danced to the side, narrowly avoiding the point, then stretched to swing at Harper's head. The sting on the whipsword lagged behind the blow and then made a *pffft* sound as it cleaved the air.

But Harper was not under it. When his lunge swept past Herrilmin, he followed, half stepping and half falling to the center of the square. With one knee on the ground, he swung his sword in a roundhouse blow at the man's unprotected side.

Herrilmin's hasty parry made metal ring. The noise or the shock seemed to surprise him, and his pause gave Harper the opportunity to regain his feet.

The two men faced each other warily, moving clockwise about the center of the square, their sword tips almost in contact. Neither man was sweating yet, but they breathed loudly. Harper was already conscious of an acrid odor.

"Hiah-yaa!" He stamped into a lunge once more, then stepped back from it instantly. The spine of Herrilmin's sword whistled by his face.

"Missed me," he taunted. Herrilmin ignored it.

Harper feinted to the left, curious to see how the other man would react. The Algheran moved in unison with him, his blade slapping against the big sword, then darting toward the taller man's chest. Harper rocked backward, pulling his sword arm across his body to deflect the blow, and dropped into a lunge while Herrilmin was off balance.

Herrilmin spun out of the way, letting his momentum carry him to the side, then took a position more than a man-height from Harper, deliberately mimicking the redhead's stance.

Not going to close, Harper realized. *He'll try to outlast me*.

That strategy might work; already his shoulder and arm muscles were protesting the strain on them, trembling, making the tip of his sword wave about. How long had this lasted? *Three or four minutes*, he guessed. *Perhaps less. Got to get that bugger to move*.

Herrilmin smiled leisurely, as if reading those thoughts. He made no attempt to attack but merely wiggled his sword in time with Harper's movements, bobbing it upward now and then to make it clatter dully against the redhead's.

Playacting, Harper thought angrily as metal clanked against metal. *He could be taking me apart despite this toad sticker if he had the nerve. Either he's playing it safe or he wants me to look like an idiot when he does move.*

Clank . . . Clank . . . Harper forced his hand to be steady while letting his arm wave minutely. *Got to stay vigilant.* Herrilmin watched him attentively, his face serious, swinging his blade in a small arc that made the sting dance against one side of Harper's blade, then the other. He was looking for an opportunity now, Harper could see, not guarding against an attack.

In his place, I'd tell the other guy to quit. Be disgraced if that's the penalty—but stay alive. Herrilmin won't do that.

Clank . . . Clank . . . There was moisture on his arm, Harper noticed. Under his arms, across his chest, over his forehead—sweat. *Better that than blood.* Amusement struck him. *And I don't have anything running down my legs.*

The acrid odor he and Herrilmin seemed to radiate was stronger. For an instant, he again watched a tiny Harper puppet in his mind's eye. It stood woodenly before a dancing Herrilmin puppet while a soundless puppet crowd waited all around them. Some of the puppets had faces—Borct, Tolp, Bann, the Nyjuc Sept Master. An infinitesimal Cyomit had crept forward to the first row and watched frozen-faced, unaware for the moment that she stood among Normals rather than Teeps. And beside the ax head that was his time shuttle—was that Kylene?

Them—not me. This fight is for them.

They don't understand I'm going to win.

The puppet images vanished. Herrilmin was left. Herrilmin, and the clattering, chattering, light-splattering swords, the gray-white concrete beneath his feet, the sweat along his trembling arm.

Herrilmin. And after Herrilmin? *Someone.*

There would always be someone, he realized finally. Not because Vrect or Borct would set up such conflicts but because he was always fighting in one way or another against particular Algherans or Algheran culture itself.

I don't fit in. I'll never fit in.

Clank . . . Clank . . . Harper responded like an automaton to Herrilmin's motions, neither expecting an attack nor preparing one of his own. He noticed his antagonist's presence and returned to his thoughts.

Did he want to fit into Alghera?

No, he decided suddenly. *They cost me Onnul. The way*

they did it can never be right, and if I can find a way to change things, I will.

Duty and privilege overlapped. *This is the one world,* he remembered. *This my life is the only existence I will ever know, and what I choose to make of it is my own choice, my own responsibility.* Legend had put those words in Cimon's mouth.

But first he would have to deal with Herrilmin. Harper forced a smile. *It must be time to establish a moral ascendancy.*

The blond Algheran had fallen into a pattern, rocking his torso at the waist in time with the swing of his sword arm. At regular intervals he flicked his wrist to extend the sting.

Now! Harper broke his own rhythm abruptly, slammed his sword at the juncture of blade and sting on Herrilmin's weapon, and jerked outward with a shout.

Almost got it there. If he had been closer . . .

But that was not the idea. Bothering Herrilmin had been his goal, and in that Harper thought he had succeeded.

The Algheran recovered quickly, sweeping his sword about a broad arc to return and clash noisily against Harper's weapon. But he stepped back rather than follow through with an attack. For an instant, he had appeared surprised.

The bugger is still breathing easily, Harper noticed. *Maybe stage two will get to him.* He stepped backward, letting his sword droop. Herrilmin moved along with him, not pressing but keeping the same distance.

Cold air down here. Harper was suddenly conscious of the chill.

"This is a two-handed sword, Herrilmin," he made himself say evenly. He gripped the long hilt as he might a baseball bat. "Ready for it?"

Then he was moving forward in giant strides, advancing steadily, swinging the blade from side to side in a flat figure-eight pattern. He did not attempt to guide it but let the momentum of the sword tug him in its wake. "The sword is after you, Herrilmin," he growled. "It wants you."

It was too bad the Algherans were not superstitious, he reasoned coldly. But some of them believed that *he* was. That might be enough. *Upset the bugger. Make him think he's up against a savage.* He smiled broadly, purposely showing his teeth. "It wants you, Herrilmin. It wants to drink your blood."

Herrilmin retreated slowly, taking several steps to each of Harper's lurching strides. He used his weapon now to measure his distance from Harper, not to provoke. Wariness showed on his face.

Still intending to wear me out, Harper decided. *Well, he won't.*

Feet stamping on concrete . . . ice-tinged air rushing through his throat . . . clothing slithering along his limbs . . . sweat glistening on his forearms . . . the blond hair and florid face of the Algheran jerking up and down as the other man gave way . . . *Migod! I'm alive! I enjoy this!*

Another thought came along with that, almost simultaneously. *Cyomit—Kylene—good thing the 'blind keeps the kids out of my head.*

Stage three. Time to disappoint Herrilmin.

Harper sprang backward, leaving the Algheran poised along one side of the fighting square. The two champions faced each other, glowering across its width.

Harper spat noisily, deliberately, and lowered his sword so its tip dug into the concrete floor. He smiled, loosening his fingers from the hilt and flexing them rapidly, then shook imaginary kinks from his arms. "I think I'm going to rest a bit, Herrilmin. You don't mind, do you?" *Calculated risk time. Place your bets, sports fans.*

The blond man watched cautiously, his sword arm extended, the sting on the weapon drooping. *Expecting a trick,* Harper analyzed.

There isn't one, of course. Let me explain that to him.

"This is an awfully heavy sword," he said conversationally. "So I can use a breather from time to time. I'm not going to let it tire me out—not going to let it do your work for you." He raised the weapon and poked it in the direction of the Algheran's chest. "Understand me?"

Herrilmin leapt toward him, slashing downward.

But the move had been telegraphed. Harper skipped to the right and watched calmly as the other man awkwardly prevented himself from overstepping the borders.

"Too far away, Herrilmin," he commented. "You have to be closer for that to work. And you're slowing up." He lowered his sword. "Time for more rest."

Herrilmin advanced again. Harper moved once more.

Thirty pounds. Gad! he thought. He called out, "Still resting, but I'm going to get tired of that soon, Herrilmin. You're dead then, you know?"

Herrilmin grunted an epithet and sprang.

This time Harper did not move aside.

The whipsword was falling upon him in slow motion. Herrilmin's hate-filled face, despairing, gargoyle-grimacing with effort, was behind it. The man was off balance, toppling toward Harper.

Committed now, both of us, Harper had time to think. He stepped sideways, toward Herrilmin and into the falling blade, tugging upward on his toothpick-weighted sword, half pushing and half pulling it through the molasses air. A hot, heavy weight pressed the side of his arm below the shoulder, pushed down into the triceps. Something lashed his back, bursting knifelike through skin to cleave at deltoid muscle.

Okay, he hit me, Harper thought calmly. *I've lost that arm.*

The fingers of his right hand would not release from his sword hilt. He accepted that, hoping they would still serve to hold the weapon even though they would no longer propel his blow. His throat was raw.

I'm screaming, he realized with surprise, feeling impact more than pain as Herrilmin's blade smashed into his forearm, hammering bone to fragments, then twisted in the deep wound, driving splinters into contorted flesh, yanking the arm from its socket. *Later this will hurt.*

But that would be later. Now he had all the time he needed and no more, and Herrilmin would never be able to get in a second blow. His own blade drifted toward the Algheran's side, dimpled clothing, and pushed a V-shaped crease before it at the bottom of Herrilmin's rib cage.

Stop it now! he suddenly willed to himself, and tried to lock his arms to restrain his swing. *Or I'll cut him in half. There's no need for that.*

Herrilmin's tunic sprang outward, burying the middle of Harper's sword under red-soaked cloth. The red expanded, the tunic splattered by growing rosebuds and sudden crimson blooms. The Algheran's mouth opened, wide, silent. His body arched to one side, away from Harper. His sword hilt slipped through lax fingers. His eyes were open. Harper heard nothing when he fell onto the floor.

Flame-hot liquid flowed down Harper's back and along the length of his right arm. Acid poured beneath his skin, searing muscles like so much raw meat hurled into fire. His teeth gnashed so hard that he felt his jaw must break, and his head was pulled back so the muscles and cords of his neck stood out like ropes. The world was gray, blurred, and now black-rimmed. It stank.

The sword slid from his unfeeling hands, clattering under his feet as he staggered toward Herrilmin's body.

The blond Algheran was on his side, doubled up in almost fetal fashion, one arm stretched over the border of the square, his top knee arm-cushioned within a handbreadth of his sweat-washed forehead. Froth drooled between his twitching lips, red-tinged; mucus dripped from bloody nostrils. He soiled himself.

"Save him," Harper whispered.

No one moved.

Harper half fell to his knees and pushed futilely against Herrilmin's chest. Red flowed under the Algheran's belly and stained the concrete about Harper, soaking into his pants legs. Drops of the same color splattered around him, trickled from his sleeve, and ran off his fingers.

Harper grunted, then seized Herrilmin's bent knee with the crook of his left arm. Half lying on the other man, he forced his knees to pull him backward, trying not to scream as his damaged right arm jammed into the rough concrete.

"Give me help, you mothers!" he shouted. Uselessly. Soundlessly.

Smeared chalk was under his hands. It meant something—he had forgotten what. He tugged again and once more to pull himself and Herrilmin completely past the chalk line, then pushed the Algheran's outstretched arms down and over his red-painted torso to make hands cup the bones that protruded from his side. Dimly, he remembered doing this for another person. Then the memory was gone.

"He's out," Harper gasped thickly. "You can keep him alive."

He stumbled to his feet and turned his head slowly, trying to make out faces on the silhouettes about him. "He lost. *Out!* Save him."

Hands tugged at him. He ignored them and forced himself to stay on his feet, to stagger away from them, away from Herrilmin's body.

An empty space now . . . chalk under his feet again . . . then behind him. It was important that he had found this space, important that he be here for some reason. There was something he had to put off until he got here. Something important . . . he had not done . . . till now . . . but he didn't . . . remember . . .

Sharon! Onnul! Kylene! Harper fell facedown into oblivion.

CHAPTER TWENTY-ONE

"*Now wake,*" *a voice from far away ordered.*

Then he was awake, lying on his belly with his eyes tightly shut.

Not 'Nam, he remembered. A fight—the duel. He was in the infirmary. His eyes opened, but he was unable to move his head, so he remained blindfolded by the cloth underneath him.

"Do not stir," the voice ordered. "Stop trying, Timithial, and we will give you back control of your motor nerves. But at the moment I am gluing up your back, and if you are not willing to remain motionless, I will have Puan keep you that way." The voice was familiar, although Harper could not place it.

His Teepblind had been removed, he sensed, so he answered by thought. *Keep the nerve block on. I'd probably move some.* He closed his eyes again and reopened them, testing the limits of his volition. *Who else is here?*

"Puan Nyjuc. You. Myself—Santinur tra'R'sihuc. Just we three."

The nerve block kept Harper from jumping. *Why you?*

There was no immediate answer. "Why not?" the telepath

said finally. "R'sihuc cannot afford an idle Sept Master. I was a doctor at the Institute when the Project began, and when it ends, I expect I will be again."

Medicine was a standard occupation for Teeps; Harper relaxed mentally. He felt no pain, but he could sense the hands moving over his back, aligning the severed muscles and blood vessels. Shouldn't the nerve blockage keep him from noticing that as well as pain?

"Your body does the alignment," the tra'R'sihuc commented. "I give it directions, monitor its progress, and pour on sealant. Were you not aware that all surgeons are Teeps? No, I see. Well, they are."

After a time, he spoke again. "Part training and part talent; not all Teeps possess either of them." He chuckled comfortably. "So even after nine hundred of your centuries, Timithial, doctors still live elevated on food animals."

Harper had his voice back. "That's high on the hog," he corrected after a brief moment of thought. When had he spoken English last? Two years? Three?

"Never mind," the Teep said. "I spoke to you of training and talents. I am informed you wished to speak to me. Of training and talents and of Waterfall Kylene of my Sept. I am finished with your back now, so let us speak."

He must have uttered a telepathic command as well, for the redhead was suddenly free to move. He rolled onto his side and looked about.

An infirmary was another thing that had changed little in ninety thousand years. The bench he lay on was a green translucent block rather than a white-sheeted operating table, but its function was clearly the same. Glass-fronted cabinets holding jars of medicine and instruments were in recesses along one wall. A viewing machine rested in a corner under racks of holographic books. The walls were white but were blue-tinged by the ceiling glow. Harper glanced at the doctor—yes, his skin was tanned; ultraviolet was in the lighting.

The woman beside the tra'R'sihuc was also tanned. Both were hazel-eyed and black-haired. *Two hundred for him,* Harper guessed. *Maybe one fifty for her. They look similar somehow.*

"My sister, Niculponoc Puan Nyjuc," the man said. "We are both a bit older than you think, by the way. Teeps last a bit longer than Normals, remember."

"Niculponoc," Harper said flatly. He willed himself to rise but failed. Immobility was being forced on him again. His eyes focused on the thin yellow cast that covered his right arm. *No pain.*

"The nerve blocks deaden the body's response to emotion also," the Teep explained. "Without that feedback, your feelings can be sustained only by conscious choice. So relax and be calm; if Puan should release control as you wish, she will be forced to release your physical pain. You would be in agony then."

"Let me be," Harper growled.

"No. We are in stoptime. Each day tenth of your pain would be felt by Teeps through the Station only for an instant, but increased in intensity proportionally. Left to yourself, you would indulge your senseless sorrow for days—and that could kill."

"I'll wear my 'blind then."

"No. I said your heartache was senseless, and I will not allow it. There is no Onnul; there never has been one; there never will be." The Teep sighed and shook his head. "Accept that, Timithial. I am sorry. All that I myself will ever see of my niece lies in your memories, and I suspect that I would have liked to know her. But none of us ever will. Forget her, ha'Ruppir."

Onnul! "I can't forget."

"You refuse to forget, you mean. Ironwearer, there are those among us with talents other than mine. We can take those memories from you."

Onnul! "No!" Harper gasped, half in tears, half frozen emotionally by the nerve blockage so that the protest was aimed almost as much at his own forced callousness as at the Teep. "No!"

"She is *gone*, Timithial. You will never get her back. Admit it."

"No," Harper repeated. "I'll find a way."

"You are a *fool*, ha'Ruppir! Think of what your hope demands: to reverse not one Council decision but scores, to single-handedly bring back an Alghera doomed to destruction on the off chance that one woman will be reborn. All so the two of you can find bliss in each other's arms," he closed sarcastically.

Had it been possible, Harper would have flushed. "Yes," he whispered.

"Fool!" the Teep snarled. "I know your memories, Timithial! She was lonely—not in love—and she scorned you with her dying breath!"

"She was dying," Harper said shakily. "She wasn't responsible for what she was saying. She didn't want me to mourn."

"Fool! Teep and Normal cannot mix. And you—you with only half a mind and a quarter of a lifetime and with absolutely nothing to offer her after that—she would never have you, ha'Ruppir. Only your oddity and her boredom would have caused her even to playact at it."

"They are my memories," Harper said stubbornly with as much dignity as he could. "Don't insult them and her in my presence."

"You do not know us, ha'Ruppir!" the Teep shouted. "You try so very hard, but you do not know us, you will never understand us, you will never be one of us! You are an alien, and you will never be happy here. Why on the one earth did you ever come back?"

"Because I was a freak there, also," Harper admitted slowly, softly. "I tried. But I couldn't fit in. I'd been gone too long, and everything I had hoped for or ever valued had vanished down a rathole. It wasn't the same country or the same world anymore, and no one noticed but me, no one cared but me."

"You had a time machine," the Teep pointed out in a calmer voice. "You could have changed things, rebuilt the world to your desire."

"And what would that have done to Alghera?"

"No one can say. But you owed us nothing—in your mind. Why not?"

Harper sighed, then closed his eyes and searched for the words that the Teep Sept Master had unknowingly echoed:

> "Ah, Love! could thou and I with Fate conspire
> To grasp this sorry Scheme of Things entire,
> Would not we shatter it to bits—and then
> Re-mould it nearer to the Heart's Desire!"

He had spoken in English. The Teep stared at him uncomprehendingly.

"An answer for you," Harper explained. "Without reason to use it, all the power in the world is meaningless. To change things just for yourself is pointless, and there I would always have been alone.

"Here—my arm. My love. I owed Alghera for them. I had friends here and none there, a cause to fight for here and none there. Besides, the Present is here, not in that dead backwater of time. Those people were content with their world. They could have it—I didn't even want to rebuild it my way. That's why I came back."

The tra'R'Sihuc nodded. "I can understand without agreeing that I would have done the same. But you felt that way, and you came back to Alghera, to the Project. And your Onnul was not here. So all at once you were ready to throw away this world—again. Just as you threw away that one, were you not?"

Yes, Harper admitted silently. "Whatever her feelings, do I not owe her her life back?" he said. *And to find her killers?*

"Lie down," was the only response. "I want to work on that arm."

"I want an answer." But Harper obeyed. He could still feel no sensation in his body, but he shifted his weight into what he assumed was a comfortable position. Then his ability to move and speak was taken from him again.

The tra'R'sihuc took the ends of the plastic cast into his hands, pulling smartly in opposite directions till it split along its length and fell from Harper's arm. "Look away."

Involuntarily, Harper's head moved to the left so he could view only the Teep's arms from the corner of his eye. He heard a bottle being uncorked, then a drawn-out gurgle. An odorless fluid moved over the green plastic of the table, pooled at his side, and began to evaporate. It had been poured over his arm, he presumed. *I want an answer.*

A scraping sound filled his ears instead, and he sensed a vibration along his upper arm. When it stopped, more fluid spilled over the table.

"If you save Onnul, you slay all of us," the telepath said at last. "For how can you reshape events to recreate and rescue her unless you destroy these alternate versions of people you once knew—and whom you know now as us? You may speak now, Timithial."

"You make me sound like a mass murderer," Harper said bitterly.

"You are," the Teep said evenly.

"No more than any other Agent."

"True. But they operate in our future. They have not gone into the past to alter the Project or our existence. You have. Perhaps, as you suspect, the tra'Hujsuon has done this as well, but the effects have been negligible—and the Teeps must treat that with the same discretion given to your adventures."

"Onnul—was she negligible?"

"In this world, yes. The tra'Hujsuon here did not kill there and could not. Perhaps the one in that world did sabotage your vehicle, as you suspect. That would be aimed at *you*, not her or us. *You* are our mass murderer, ha'Ruppir."

"I saved a teenage girl from being eaten by wolves. What would you have done in my shoes, Doctor?"

The Teep moved into sight so Harper could view his thin smile. "Nothing else, sharing your ignorance at the time—Ironwearer. I did not say any of the Teeps blamed you. But you saved one of the Skyborne; you knew that then, and perhaps you should have anticipated great consequences from your actions."

Harper sighed. "What is done is done. I'm told she is not liked."

"So you wished to speak to me. Why? Did you hope to make her popular, a festival queen?"

A brass ring . . . a dying fire between a wood and a gully . . . a sullen, frightened girl-child made faceless by night and the passage of time . . . a jest about the Beaver's clan. "I have an obligation, Sept Master," he said. "I have made promises."

"How nice of you to remember," the telepath said dryly. "A year has passed since you dumped her on us. How frequently did you remember your promises during that time?"

"Often enough," Harper replied. "I heard no complaints, after all."

"You were uptime, fool! Not reachable. Besides, *I* am Master of R'sihuc. Do you think I admit Normals to the private affairs of my Sept? No Teep would. Of course you heard no complaints!"

"I am here. I hear complaints," Harper growled. "What is the problem?"

"A moment." The Teep lapsed into silence, and the scraping sound resumed. More liquid was poured over Harper's arm and spilled onto the pallet. Hands tugged at his shoulder and elbow.

"Give the new bone time to set," the Teep said finally. "Now then—your Kylene. She is one of the Skyborne, basically just another Teep. Very close, anyhow—I do not think Teeps have what you term mutations as commonly as your First Era people did, but enough time may have passed for some changes."

"Is she different?"

"We do not know," the tra'R'sihuc said flatly. "Nor can we find out. She is exceptionally strong—and exceptionally stupid. Do not misunderstand me—there is no fault with her native intelligence. The problem is that she can read minds, and she can put up a block—but that is all."

"Isn't that enough?" Harper asked.

"You can hear," the telepath said. "You can speak; you can whisper; perhaps you can sing. If you met a feral child who could only shout, would you think him complete?"

"No. But I might try to teach him."

"And if he did not want to learn? Or could not? And simply shouted whenever you tried to teach him, so that you could never even be sure he had understood you? That is what your Kylene is like, ha'Ruppir; that is what you gave to us."

Unable to move, Harper could only stare helplessly along the length of the green plastic block. "I don't understand," he said finally. "Is she insane?"

"Organically? No. Psychologically? Probably not, in her proper time and place. Which is Second Era barbarism, ha'Ruppir, and not a Fifth Era civilization. Here she is just as much a freak culturally as you. More so."

The tra'R'sihuc's voice softened. "Timithial, she is one of the Skyborne. Do you not see what that means? Think!"

The Skyborne. Kh'taal Minzaer. *Tell the world what fate holds for those who dream of challenge.*

"She's arrogant," he guessed. "Stiff-necked. Stubborn."

"'Unbroken' is a better word," the Teep said. "This is not a small matter, Ironwearer. She is not simply feeling youthful high spirits. She's wild—and all the rest of us are domesticated animals and tame."

"Are you proud of it?" Harper wondered.

The telepath moved around the table so Harper's eyes could focus on him. "I state a fact. We have been tamed. Two Eternal Wars, two Compacts, four Eras. They have had an effect. For good or for bad—" He broke off and shook his head. "Normal and Teep can coexist now, and I doubt they would otherwise."

Then he smiled frostily. "Besides, ha'Ruppir, did you think

I meant only the Teeps have been domesticated? It applies to the Normals."

Harper thought deliberately of snapping fingers. "Maybe I'm arrogant."

The telepath kept his smile and shook his head up and down.

I'll prove you wrong, Harper thought. The Teep's expression did not change. "All right," the redhead said flatly. "She's wild. What about being a barbarian?"

The telepath sighed. "She is that also. An illiterate from a tribe of mostly illiterates. Fortunately, she understands the concept of writing. She is intelligent. We have taught her a great deal, but it takes constant supervision, because she is a barbarian, with all the barbarian attitudes: no realization that putting off today's pleasure may be beneficial tomorrow, no ethical guidelines other than a desire to avoid punishment, almost no grasp of any abstract principles, certainly no understanding of how people can be motivated by them." He hesitated. "She hates you, by the way."

Harper stared down at the green plastic. "It doesn't matter much."

"Perhaps not. If you are curious, to her you are a kidnapper who sold her into slavery. You pretended to help her for some strange reason, and just before she got to her goal, you betrayed her and stole her from her homeland."

"Does she know why?"

"The full story? No, we have kept it from her. You were probably right in doing the same. So she has developed her own explanation: You were playing with her, making a game out of her life."

Harper reviewed memories. "Maybe she's right," he said bitterly. "I guess it doesn't matter much now. So she doesn't fit in—would you rather have her be dead?" His voice turned sarcastic. "Or shall I just give her a free ride home?"

The telepath moved around the table, where Harper could not view him. "She is a danger to us," he said evenly. "To all Teeps, not just those of Alghera. And perhaps to all Normals. Can you doubt that, you who have done so much in one day to show us how narrowly balanced the human races are on time's scales? You, who have brought us this terrifying child who roams the corridors seeking someone with authority, to threaten them with imagined Second Era vengeance? Yes, Iron-wearer and murderer—take her home."

"You know I can't do that!"

"You went back once. Why not risk it again, arrogant Ironwearer? Flee with her, never return. And if you will not dare that, then kill her. Yes, we would like her dead."

Harper was silent. *I saw this coming,* he admitted to himself.

"Why place this in my hands?" he asked. "Why not kill her yourself if she is such a threat to you?"

"And enrage Harper Timithial ha'Dicovys-once-ha'Cuhyon, Ironwearer, Champion of the Project Master—who is well disposed toward the Teeps? No, Ironwearer ha'Ruppir, you hear no cynicism, for I am not being cynical. Truly, we have no wish to become your enemy."

"Particularly if that made one of Borct," Harper said sarcastically.

"Say, rather, particularly if that made a friend of Vrect." The Teep's tone was cynical now but soon returned to normal. "No. We are ourselves civilized and tamed, remember? We have no heart for slaying children, especially those who are innocent of the harm they may do, especially those of our own race."

"But I do?" Harper gibed.

"You spoke of obligations and responsibilities," the Teep said, "which you have discharged through murder. If the child must be slain, who is more appropriate an executioner than one proclaiming he is equal to life and death responsibilities—and admitting such for her?"

"I've an obligation to defend others. Not to be an executioner and not to hand down judgments."

"And you have slain—and allowed to be slain—billions. Consider that your actions will certainly slay one man—with our prayers behind you. Why is that, Ironwearer?"

Harper shrugged. "Useful consequences."

"So you have foreseen those consequences? Judged them acceptable?"

"You're the mind reader, tra'R'sihuc," Harper said. "Why ask me? Is there something to debate?"

"You *always* see consequences? Except for one time?"

"Except for one time. So tell Borct what I did. Tell him Kylene is one of the Skyborne. Let him decide."

The telepath leered at him. "Be political? *Interfere?* Violate the Second Compact? There are great penalties for Teeps who do that—in Alghera. And I think, as you do, that the tra'Dicovys would not dare believe us. For if the girl is to be disposed of, the same would have to be done for the Agent who brought her to us and endangered the Project—even the very existence of Alghera. And who then would shore up his power? But—what would you do if Borct ordered the child killed, part-time Ironwearer and full-time Defender?"

"I don't know," the man admitted. "I'd hope it would not come to that."

"Because then you would have to accept responsibility."

"Because I gave my word to her. I won't go back on it."

"And will you accept the responsibility when she is executed for some meaningless adolescent rebellion? Will your responsibility suffice to bring her back to life? Do your obligations extend to those who will perish with her, because of her, who will die without ever having heard of Timithial ha'Dicovys and his pledged honor? Will you rebuild the foundations of history to preserve those innocents, Ironwearer? And how many millions will you slay doing that?"

"I gave my word," Harper insisted. "I don't go back on it."

The other let out a snort of laughter. "Ironwearer, I begin to suspect you may be just as arrogant as you would like to think you are." He walked around the table again to stare Harper in the eye.

He smiled unpleasantly. "Think of this, ha'Ruppir: Onnul Nyjuc."

"What!"

"Onnul, ha'Ruppir. Your Onnul."

"She's gone. She has nothing to do with this."

"You are *blind*, ha'Ruppir. You think every change in the Project has come about because of some plot of Vrect's. That is utter nonsense! Who went back in time, past the Second Era, if not you? And who changed history in the Second Era, if not you? *You* changed this Project!"

"No!" Harper shouted.

"Yes! You! Your Onnul is gone here, ha'Ruppir, and that is your responsibility, too—yours and that little brat's!"

"No!"

"Think about it, ha'Ruppir," the telepath growled. "Think!"

Onnul—and Kylene. Love—and hate. Loyalty—and honor. One to live, and one to die. *"I can't decide that!"*

"Think about it, ha'Ruppir."

"No! I can't kill an innocent child!"

"She was dead *already*. She died some ninety thousand years ago, ha'Ruppir. She died *twice*—think about that."

Onnul! No! Harper screamed inside. "No! No more arguments!"

The Teep smiled and said nothing.

CHAPTER TWENTY-TWO

The door dilated, admitting Sict and then Borct. Behind the triangular opening the rock wall of the corridor flamed, crimson and sparkling. The two Algherans moved cautiously as they adjusted to the dimmer light of the infirmary.

"Welcome," Harper said sourly. "I feel just peachy and thanks for not asking."

"You haven't given us time, Timt," Sict pointed out.

Harper raised an eyebrow, then realized that the gesture was wasted; the two men would not notice it. He pushed himself into a sitting position on the green table and swung his arm to point the visitors to a pair of cube chairs. He was being unfair, he recognized; a second of delay outside the infirmary amounted to hours in stoptime.

Borct hesitated before seating himself. "Are you comfortable, Septling?"

"Fair enough," Harper answered. "Still some soreness, and I try not to move fast. But I'm healing, and I'm bored. I've been stuck here for six days now with nothing to do. For you, I gather, it's been a few minutes. What's the rush?"

Borct snapped his fingers. "Politics. We would not like to

send you on a mission in poor health, Timt, but getting this episode out of the way quickly would be an excellent idea. So your Septlings are loading your vehicle now. The Council will accept a fait accompli, but the less the members have to think about it beforehand, the better. I would prefer not to have the topic raised again, and this way we will avoid unnecessary debate."

Harper nodded. "You had this all set up." He waved his arm around the room, then let it stop pointing at the time engine in the corner. "Did you expect the duel to end as it did?"

They did not answer for a moment, then Sict leaned forward. "No! We thought you would win without difficulty. We did not expect *this*."

This time Harper did raise an eyebrow. "No quick trips uptime to see how things turned out?"

"Of course not." Sict appeared shocked.

Harper locked his fingers about his knees and stretched, grimacing as his back muscles moved. "So we're in a rush. Even with the duel?"

"Even with the duel," Borct said. "Especially with the duel."

Harper nodded once. "All right. But I'll have to spend some while uptime recovering. And I may want some help."

"Perhaps." Borct was noncommittal.

There was a pause. Harper waited for the elder Algherans to break the silence. Sict seemed the more uncomfortable, he noticed.

"You ought to tell him," Sict said at last.

"Tell me what?" Harper asked.

"Herrilmin," Sict answered. "He's outside. That's where the doctor went."

Herrilmin was outside? Harper was startled. He had assumed the other Agent was receiving the same care as he. "What shape is he in?"

"Fair," the telepath said, reentering the room from a side door. His eyes focused on Harper, ignoring the other men. "He is getting blood, and once you are out of this room, he will be worked on. It has only been a few hundred seconds, ha'Ruppir; let him revive first and make his choice."

"Choice?" Harper echoed. "What choice?"

"To live or to die," the tra'R'sihuc said calmly. "Life and death are balanced within him; which way they shift is for him to decide."

"What!" Harper snapped out the words. "I wanted him to be saved."

The tra'R'sihuc gestured at Borct. "So did he. But that choice is yet for Herrilmin to make. Whether to rise to Cimon or continue his life on the one earth is his choice. Not yours, Timithial ha'Ruppir, and not mine."

"Is he insane?" Harper snapped. "You're a doctor—are you?"

Hands moved along his side, poking at his rib cage. Harper gasped as pain knifed into him and black-rimmed his vision.

"Hush," the telepath reproved him. "Herrilmin who-was-once-ha'Hujsuon will know greater pain than this, within his mind, where we cannot provide relief."

"Why not?" Harper asked. "You told me—"

"We offered relief," the tra'R'sihuc said. "We did not compel you to accept it. You were allowed free choice. We will offer that peace as well to Herrilmin. Ultimately. Now he must make a choice without our intervention."

"Why?" Harper demanded. "He is alive. He should be happy."

"You forced him from the square—do you not see the meaning of that? No, I see you do not. He must choose now to die as a shielding of Sept Hujsuon or to live as a serf of Dicovys. Which choice would you make in his position?"

"Serf? There haven't been any for centuries! Since—since Mlart."

"You are correct," the telepath said coldly. "And thus the greater disgrace. No man has left the square alive and defeated for centuries, either. Did you think such duels were an everyday occurrence among us?"

"Why not?" Harper was suddenly conscious of Sict and Borct, watching silently from positions along the wall. "Why not? I hear of them every day."

"You hear talk of duels," the telepath said sarcastically. "Those brave noble Agents you associate with, who say, 'I should have challenged him' or 'We almost fought' or 'He was afraid to duel'—how many duels have you *seen*, ha'Ruppir? Tell me. How many?"

"This one," Harper said quietly.

"You do not know us, ha'Ruppir! I told you that. When will you learn?"

"Leave him alone, Teep," Borct said threateningly.

"Address me by my title, tra'Dicovys," the telepath growled back. He turned so that the Project Master could see the insignia on his breast.

"I beg your pardon," Borct said stiffly. "In my concern, I had not realized I spoke to the Master of R'sihuc. but this is Timithial *ha'Dicovys*."

"Yes," the telepath said flatly. He turned back to Harper. "There is a price to be paid for leaving the square. You entered it without that knowledge. Yes, it might have been you, Ironwearer."

Harper swallowed. If he had been the one defeated . . . *yeah, Vrect would have collected his prize, all right. But Borct—* Then he colored at the contempt he had heard in the other's voice.

"The tra'Dicovys has demanded his property from the tra'Hujsuon," the telepath informed him. "The tra'Hujsuon waits now to discuss this with Herrilmin."

Harper glanced back to the Project Master, but neither Borct nor Sict spoke, and both acted as if they had not heard a word.

"Why?" he asked.

"I have no knowledge of that." The tra'R'sihuc, too, seemed to be waiting for a response from the side of the room. "The Project Master is under metal. So I can only speculate, as you do now, that political considerations are involved."

"And politics is a dirty word," Harper said sourly.

"Teeps are not concerned with politics," the telepath said evenly.

"I am," Harper said. "Say something, Magister."

Borct snapped his fingers. "The account is correct." His voice was cold.

"Why? Our Sept needs no slaves. Let him go, Borct. Let him be a Blankling if he has to be outside a Sept."

"No." The Project Master was firm. "You won this duel. It was strangely done, but the fight was honorable, and the blood will be sealed into the floor to mark it. But will you win the next duel? Or the one after that?"

Harper started to speak, but Borct cut him off.

"The tra'R'sihuc was correct. Duels are not common. But we do love to speak of them—and it is not fear or custom that keeps them infrequent occurrences but wartime restraints and constant justice-haggling in inter-Sept councils. Neither condition applies to the Project. Do I err, tra'R'sihuc?"

"No," the telepath admitted.

Borct snapped his fingers again and looked directly once more at Harper. "The Realm can fall very quickly into anarchy. 'Feudalism,' you termed it once. Alghera's social system constantly leaves us hanging over such an abyss."

"Mlart," Harper said suddenly.

"Yes. Mlart." The tra'Dicovys stared unblinkingly at his Septling. "We were sliding backward, and he saved us. I know what you think of him, Timithial. You are wrong. He was not our version of your First Era tyrants. The wars he fought preserved the Realm. He fought two of them—which hardly reveals an implacable lust for conquest—and then he resigned his offices to keep us from becoming dependent on a dictator. He came out of retirement after that only because the Realm was in peril and the Muster asked it of him. He saved us again—and it cost him his life.

"That's why everyone on the Council but you wanted to save him. And why we must act quickly now, lest the Council try some other changes to keep him alive and thus make things even worse for the Present."

Harper stared back at the Master of his Sept. A voice echoed in his mind, a shout: *You don't know us, Harper. You don't know us!*

"Borct!" he cried. "It's been six hundred years!"

"What of it, Timithial? My grandfather fought in Mlart's armies. Sict's father did. What is six hundred years?"

Ten lifetimes. Ten of my lifetimes. But Harper could not say that.

Borct exhaled slowly. "We have strayed from the path of the conversation. Without Herrilmin to do his bidding, Vrect is spent. And he's mine now."

"To do what with?" Harper wondered. *Ten of my lifetimes.*

Borct merely snapped his fingers.

"To be an example, Timt," Siccentur tra'Ruijac explained at last. "To scrub floors or to scrape vegetables. To be conspicuous. When Alghera is recovered, perhaps he will be released, but in the meantime—"

"In the meantime, few people are going to risk losing a duel. I see." Harper lapsed into silence.

The gap in the conversation grew uncomfortable for everyone. Harper kept his lips pursed, determined to make the others speak first. Borct stared at him unblinkingly, obviously with the same intent. Sict glanced around the infirmary restlessly, somehow managing to imply that he had never seen such a room. Meanwhile, Santinur tra'R'sihuc busied himself in a corner, pretending to check the contents of medicine dispensers, transparently hoping to be overlooked.

The tra'Ruijac broke the silence finally. "You mentioned help?"

"Yes." Harper was purposely terse.

Sict squirmed uneasily in his cube chair. "You've heard the Project Master. I doubt that another Agent can be found willing to help you."

"I know that. So . . ." Harper made his voice trail off.

"Then what do you want?" Sict asked.

Harper moved his shoulders about to stretch his muscles, ignoring the pain signals running along his side, deliberately holding off his answer and rebuilding determination.

"A conversation under iron, for starters."

There was silence again. After a long moment, Borct shook his head.

"So I must leave," the tra'R'sihuc said reluctantly. "Very well. Please make no violent motions, Timithial. If you wish me back, I shall be in the next room—simply rap on the door." He moved to the end of the green pallet and looked Harper in the eyes; then he shook his head in resignation and left the room. As the triangular doorway closed, Harper glimpsed a blond man stretched across a second pallet.

"What was that about?" Borct asked with asperity.

"A private matter. Several days ago he offered some advice that had to be rejected."

Harper said no more. Borct leaned back and snapped his fingers. "You sought a private conversation. This room is not metal-lined, but we are in stoptime. Begin."

Harper leaned back, resting weight on his elbows. "Want a Teep."

"A Teep?" Sict was incredulous. "A Teep? For what?"

"Yeap, a Teep. To train as an Agent."

"To take—" The tra'Ruijac broke off his remark, then continued sarcastically. "Just one? Not a dozen?"

Harper smiled grimly. "Just one. I'll take more if you offer."

"Why, Timithial?" Borct said. Sict appeared unable to speak.

Harper tried to shrug. Then remembering that the gesture would not be understood, he snapped his fingers. "Why not?

They're Algherans also; they have an interest in the war—and a particular interest in it now. And as you pointed out, the other Agents won't be much help."

Borct nodded. "That cannot be enough, Ironwearer. We are not allowed to use Teeps."

"Even in a situation where half their race dies? Be serious."

"Half their race will not die. That's one reason you're killing Mlart." Borct hesitated. "If there were no other alternative to extinction, the Compacts might be set aside. But that is not the case. This is, in the end, merely a political matter, and the Second Compact explicitly forbids their employment—as you should know."

Harper moved his head back to gaze at the blue-tinted ceiling lights. "The Second Compact as it is interpreted by Alghera. One version of Alghera, anyhow."

"The version we attempt to restore. No, Timt, forget the idea."

This time Harper did shrug. "Then I will be a good Algheran in all ways possible. Are you prepared for that?"

"Prepared for what?" Sict demanded. "Borct, what is your Septling babbling about now?"

The Project Master sighed. "Ironwearer ha'Dicovys is threatening *not* to arrange the reassassination of Mlart."

Sict stood abruptly. His face showed outrage. "But he has to! He said he would. He fought that duel. He always argued that saving Mlart was a mistake. I don't understand this at all. Explain yourself, Timt. Are you or are you not prepared to restore Alghera? An instant ago, I thought you were."

Harper blew breath between his lips. "I changed my mind. I've had lots of free time to do that—remember?"

"You are trying to extort something from us—that I'll remember," Sict said tartly. "I won't have it. Borct, order him to be reasonable."

Borct leaned to one side in his chair, his expression wry. "I'm sure the Ironwearer thinks he is being quite reasonable, Siccentur. He wishes to establish a precedent, I gather. And if he does not get his way, he will now say he does not want Mlart slain, and virtually all the Council will agree with him."

"But that's nonsense! If Mlart is saved—that illness was monstrous! Those people were insane! Ten times worse than Vrect!"

"I know," Harper said flatly. "That's why I can count on your giving me a Teep."

"But it is forbidden!"

"No, it isn't!" Harper snapped. "No one but Algherans ever interpreted the Compacts so strictly—and you didn't always. Sict, talk to some of the Agents. They'll tell you Mlart used Teeps in his armies, some of them with high rank, even if the history texts don't admit it."

"No!"

"Yes! Look, you want to keep Teeps out of politics? Then why have any in the Project at all? Why use them as soldiers up at the Present? Are you really obeying the Compacts, tra'Ruijac, tra'Dicovys? Or are you keeping slaves in their place? That's what it looks like, doesn't it?"

Harper flipped his legs back onto the pallet and sank onto his back. He breathed heavily, regaining strength for the argument, making the others realize his intent. The Algherans watched wordlessly. Siccentur tra'Ruijac slowly moved back to his chair and sank into the black plastic.

Finally Harper continued. "I don't want Alghera back just the way you remember it, Sict. I want it *changed*. Every person on the Council wants a changed Alghera, and you know it—even you. Or we'd never have gotten into this mess. But some of them, like Vrect, have at least been honest about it."

"I had not expected you to defend the tra'Hujsuon," Borct said tightly.

"I'm not. He's someone whom no Sept would claim at birth. But he has been honest when he makes arguments in Council. Our Alghera ended up at war with the Alliance, and any Alghera we recover that is just the same will also end up in a war, only maybe later—but with the same outcome likely. All those little changes we try to make—if they ever work, it'll be because they add up together to something big. Don't you see that?"

Borct leaned forward. "No. Oh, I recognize the justice of your argument. Don't think it was never considered, Timithial. The Warden and I spoke of just such matters when he established the Project. Certainly we have had our difficulties since then, but neither he nor I ever expected to be successful easily."

Harper raised himself onto an elbow and shook his head sadly. "Magister, I respect you. But I'm using logic against religious faith."

"Not faith, Septling." The tra'Dicovys's voice was equally

sad. "Loyalty. This Project was not set up to save an Alghera; it was set up to save our Alghera. It was a very decent place, for all the flaws you may have detected in it; it was our country, and we are the very last hope for its survival."

Harper stared back, struck with anguish so deep that for an instant he wondered if he was seeing into the other's mind, as if he had become a telepath.

"Magister, I've got loyalties—" He broke off and began anew. "Borct, please! Give me what I want and I will do all I can to give you the Alghera you wish. Let it be different in just one way: Let the Teeps be treated like everyone else."

"We can't do that, Timt," Sict protested. "We can't allow Teeps to act in the government. That was the cause of the war. You know that!"

"And I know that Alghera lost," Harper answered. "Look at the viewscreens, Sict. What shows in them now? Two days ago? Two years? An Alghera that lost a war, that's what—and a world where Teeps are part of the government. Nicole's tits, Sict! Just the other day Tolp was telling the Council that this was a war for independence and that our city had been willing to go along with the Alliance on the Teep issue—you heard that, and you didn't argue."

"But that was years ago, Timt. When we didn't have any choice. Before the war began; and before we remembered about you."

"Before you had time travel," Harper said sourly. "Before you had a secret weapon." He turned sideways stiffly and lowered his feet toward the floor.

"Yes! We don't need to compromise with the Chelmmysians now."

The big man grinned crookedly. "True. You need to compromise with me."

Hearts and minds, Harper. You want to win their hearts and minds, you grab them by the balls—the hearts and minds follow easily.

It was still that way. Perhaps it always would be.

He dropped onto his feet, trying not to show that his side protested against the strain, trying not to lean too obviously against the green pallet. "Give me a Teep, Borct."

"Timt! You ask too much." Sict's mind was unchanged.

Harper shrugged and watched the Project Master.

"All right, Timithial," Borct said suddenly. "What is your

compromise? We cannot let you blackmail us, but perhaps we can arrive at a settlement."

"Borct!" Sict was incredulous. "You can't agree to this!"

Borct snapped his fingers. "I don't know. Let's find out what we might have to agree to. You forget that Timt is one of us. He is an Ironwearer of Sept Dicovys, and he volunteered to join the Project. It's our Alghera he is used to, for all his words about changing it—and he asked for just one change. He knows Alghera. I don't think he wishes to smash it to bits." The Project Master smiled cynically at both his listeners. "And the conversation is under iron."

Harper nodded and gave the man a quirky smile. "Thank you, Magister. A compromise, then. Right now, I want one Teep to take into the field. I will train him. After that, he'll be an Agent and he'll be used as one."

"A way might be found for part of that," the Project Master said slowly. "But an Agent? No. The Council would never stand for it."

Harper forced himself to smile again. "We'll be gone before the Council meets. And there is no reason for it to find out all at once that I've trained a Teep Agent. Tell them I needed some additional medical care—that should satisfy them, particularly if they found out even that after the fact."

"Uhmm . . . go on."

"When I get back—as you said, the Council will accept a fait accompli. The precedent will have been set. When I go out again, I'll take another Teep. And after that, another. People will get used to it. Eventually any Teep operating with me will obviously be doing so as an Agent. And the Council will swallow it. Other Agents will begin to work with Teeps in the field. And it'll grow."

"But the Second Compact? Even if the Council comes to accept this, Timithial, you will be operating in times and places where the Compacts are sacrosanct. Your Teep will be reported by other Teeps to the authorities. What will happen then?"

"I don't think it's a problem," Harper said. "There's a risk, yes—so the Teeps going out will have to be volunteers. But who are the proper authorities, after all, assuming that we don't win the war?"

"The Chelmmysians, of course," Borct answered. He smiled thinly. "In City Year 893. And we know their position on the Compacts."

Sict nodded jerkily. "But where does it all end?"

"I don't know." Harper looked the older man in the eyes. "I don't care much. Maybe it never ends. And maybe it ends when we recover Alghera—an Alghera we can all be happy with."

"But why, Timt?"

Harper continued to stare at the tra'Ruijac. *Because I spent a week lying on that cot,* he wanted to say, *realizing I've given you seven years of my life and have nothing to show for it but a batch of scars, understanding I was getting older and older and I was never going to get one more thing from this world except the satisfaction of being an Ironwearer. Because I realized being an Ironwearer—a real Ironwearer—made up for everything that had happened, but it meant doing more than going through the motions.*

But that couldn't really be said, and he was not sure it was true anyhow, because as he looked at the other men now, they seemed hidden behind a flag. A flag with red and white stripes and stars in the corner, waving against a blue sky, the flag of a nation that had said that all men are created equal and government is the servant of the people rather than the master. The flag he had once been sworn to defend.

Nations need ideals as well as men.

"I remembered where my loyalties should be." He fought against his voice to hold a neutral tone. "Settle for that, Sict."

"A precedent, you said, Ironwearer," Borct said. "Would you accept a compromise and abide by some restrictions?"

"Let me hear them." Standing was becoming a strain; Harper closed his eyes to concentrate on the Project Master.

Borct rose to make his points. "Any Teep you take out must be selected by the Master of his Sept. The Masters have knowledge and discernment that you do not. Moreover, they have the internal order of their Septs to consider, which is also beyond your vision. You can pick no one against his Master's will or in any other way interfere with the affairs of another Sept. That's the first condition."

Harper nodded. "All right."

"Secondly, you understand that this is an experiment. If it is successful, you can experiment again. If it is not, you will take out no other Teeps, and you will not raise the issue again. Is that clear?"

"No more talk about Teep Agents?"

"No more talk about Teep Agents, Teeps in government, Teep rights, or anything else that affects the status of Teeps. Yes or no?"

Harper hesitated, then realized he had no choice. "Yes."

"You understand this will mean an honest appraisal. The Teep is not required to be superhuman but will have to function adequately as an Agent. If need be, Ironwearer, other Teeps will be asked what your real opinions are."

Doesn't trust me, Harper thought. *Oh, hell.* He leaned backward against the pallet, faking nonchalance. "Sure."

"Finally, you are risking yourself and our city. If you are betrayed by the Teep or think his actions will harm you or Alghera, you must kill him at once. And you must strive to complete your mission with or without the Teep."

"That's two conditions," Harper pointed out.

The Project Master waited, saying nothing.

"Yes. And yes."

So he was committed now. Harper snapped his fingers.

Borct hesitated a long moment. "All right, Septling. One Teep."

CHAPTER TWENTY-THREE

T*en Algheran minutes later, three men stood in the deserted* hangar. In the mid-distance, the floor was stained by red-brown splotches that the men carefully avoided noticing.

"We leave you here, Septling," Borct said. "Your craft is loaded and prepared for you. Return soon, is my suggestion, so your absence is not remarked." His voice was low, without echoes.

The shoulders of the big redhead jerked upward for an instant, making his short black cape sway. "Soon enough. Five or ten minutes."

"Well enough. Your companion will be here shortly. And soon the shuttles moved from downtime will arrive—we don't want anyone going back to report seeing you alive and unharmed."

"Yeah." But Timithial seemed strangely reluctant to move. "Magister, the Teep I'm getting—can I be told something about him? What his background is, what sort of skills he has, and so on?"

"I really don't know, Timt," Borct said carefully. "I explained the situation under iron to both Teep Sept Masters. They told me they could find someone suitable—young, vigorous, healthy, with potential—but they seemed to have several possibilities, and I asked for no names, since it was an internal matter. You'll know soon enough."

The redhead made his shoulder motion again. "Okay. Thanks, Magister." He held his hand toward them. "Wish me luck."

Borct hesitated, trying to remember the ritual, then took Timithial's hand in his and waved it gingerly from side to side. "Nicole's cloak, Timt," he murmured.

Sict repeated the gesture but not the words. He was still opposed. "Here," he said gruffly, thrusting a hand-sized holographic book at Harper. "Tolp wanted me to pass this on to you."

"Thanks." Timithial smiled ruefully at them both before looking at the blank cover, then walked away soundlessly. Even at the far side of the hangar, diminished by distance and the dark green and black colors of his uniform, he was outsized.

"We should leave now," Borct said briskly. "Let's get to the control area."

"A moment, Borct," Sict responded. "I want to see this."

Borct snapped his fingers. "From the control area." He turned and led the way toward the back corner of the hangar. From there, a waist-high flight of stairs brought them to the loading dock. A doorway and a short corridor led to the control room. A pair of male Teeps manning the consoles glanced at them incuriously as they entered.

A viewscreen high on the wall above the consoles showed the hangar. Borct gestured at it, and one of the Teeps adjusted controls until the Project Master nodded his satisfaction. He might have been watching Timithial through a window at a distance of three man-heights. Borct jerked his head. "Sict."

The elder Sept Master was staring at a second viewscreen, one focused on a shattered hillscape, barren but for a litter of glassy-surfaced rocks: the Present. He seemed not to hear.

"Sict," Borct called again. The other man turned around. "This is what you wanted to watch."

The first viewscreen showed the form of a young woman walking parallel to the rough wall at the far end of the hangar, straight at Timithial's time shuttle. A bag dangled from both hands before her. She wore a dark brown dress; jade green was on her forehead. Behind her, barely visible at the side of the hangar, was Cyomit Nyjuc, motionless, expressionless.

"Traveling without much kit," Borct murmured.

"He did get his Teep," Sict said.

"Of course," Borct said absently. "I told him he would."

"A girl," Sict wondered. "What if he claims this is not a fair chance?"

Borct snapped his fingers. "He agreed to take what the Teep Sept Masters gave him. He was promised no feats of Cimon."

"You expected this, didn't you?" Sict asked. "You had this in mind when you gave in to him, didn't you?"

Borct ignored him, turning instead to the Teep who had adjusted the first viewscreen. "You people like Timt, don't you?" he asked suddenly.

The Teeps stared as if they had not noticed him until this instant.

"We get along with him," the farther one said at last.

"He means well," the other Teep said. "He tries to be friendly. He thinks he should be defending us. He's an Ironwearer. We give him credit for that."

"Do you agree with him?" the Project Master asked.

The Teeps continued to stare at him. On the viewscreen, the red-haired man put a finger on the side of the silver levcraft. A rectangular hatchway became visible, first as an outline and then as an opening as it hinged about its bottom. It became longer as it slowly descended till a ramp twice the length of a man led down to the hangar floor. A second hatchway slid down to plug the gap.

"Do you agree with him?" Borct asked again.

"About what?" the farther Teep asked.

"About rights for—political matters."

The nearer Teep looked at him coolly. "We're Teeps. We don't talk about politics. We don't think about politics."

Borct nodded with satisfaction. "And when the Ironwearer talks—or just thinks—about politics?"

"Then we change the subject. Let us do so now." The Teep's tones dismissed the issue, and the two controllers looked away from the Project Master.

Borct turned back to Sict. "Have I made a point?"

"Maybe." But the tra'Ruijac sounded unconvinced.

Borct glanced at the viewscreen. Overlong raven-black hair, almond-shaped eyes, slim, freckled, nervous in appearance but her head high—pride to spare, he decided. "Not a very pretty girl, but her looks are striking," he commented. "Headstrong and childish, I was told."

The redhead waited beside the access ramp. His face was impassive, though he looked briefly at the control room as if he knew he was being watched. His hand moved abruptly to shake out his black cape, baring the sword dangling from his waist; his lips were opened briefly, but since sound circuits were not incorporated in the scanners, Borct was unable to guess what was being said.

The viewscreen focused on the girl's face. Her lips were tight, frowning. "Doesn't like him for some reason," Borct commented. "*Good!* The tra'R'sihuc has chosen well."

Timithial attempted to hand the girl up into the levcraft, but she ignored the help and pushed past him to board the vehicle. He leaped to slap at the outer entry plate, opening the hatchway for her, then cast an appraising glance toward the control room. The expression on his face could not be read.

His right hand raised and moved toward the watchers, its fingers clinched awkwardly so only the middle one protruded from his fist. Then he hunched his shoulders again and entered the levcraft. The hatchway moved upward, dwindling in length, and merged with the fuselage until no crack could be seen. The vehicle was featureless once more.

"Did the gesture have a meaning?" Sict wondered.

One of the Teeps smiled. "A First Era blessing upon his friends here. He wishes us all suitable love lives."

Borct snapped his fingers. His hearth-mate spent a year tenth with him at irregular intervals; he found her visits boring and distasteful.

Sict started to speak again, but the operators had also begun to talk, and his voice was drowned out.

The nearer Teep reached above his head for a floating bulb and pulled it close to his lips. His tones altered, becoming crisper, and he spoke in a foreign language. *"Tower to aircraft, do you read me? You are cleared for takeoff. You have a ceiling of thirty feet and visibility is poor. Go when ready."*

Then he dropped back into Speech. "Timithial, Mission 17. The time now is 44,938 by the Long Count, day 96, fractional seven seven five four two . . . mark."

The bulb spoke back in Timithial's baritone. "Nine three eight. Day nine six plus seven seven five four two. *Roger, I'll be seeing you in five minutes. And tell the old farts I'm going to see them choke on their little joke.*"

"What was that all about?" Borct asked.

"Just something Timt likes," the Teep explained. "He said once that that kind of ritual was customary before departure in his era; we memorized some parts of it and feed it to him when he goes out and returns. It makes him feel at home."

"Interesting," Borct said, dismissing the topic. "Sict, you had a comment?"

"I was wondering what Teep left with him."

A hissing could be heard from the entrance to the control room. On the viewscreen, the wedge-shaped levcraft was rising slowly to half a man-height above the concrete. It bobbed and weaved momentarily, partially obscured by billows of dust. Lights dimmed throughout the cavern.

"Just a name to me," Borct admitted. He snapped his fingers. "Waterfall Kylinn R'sihuc."

A Klaxon sounded. The viewscreen showed a vacant hangar.

Here ends Book One of *The Destiny Makers*.
The tale will continue in Book Two,
Morning of Creation, in which Harper and Kylene
prepare for a secret mission that will
determine the fate of Alghera.

About the Author

Mike Shupp is a thirty-nine-year-old aerospace engineer living in Los Angeles. He views himself as following in the footsteps of Frederick II of Prussia: serious artist, friend of philosophers, a public servant determined to annex Silesia.

This is his first novel.